## BURNING KISSES

"Release me," Samantha fussed. "Release me at once."

Troy ignored her struggles and harsh words. Instead he lowered his lips and captured hers fully in a fiery kiss.

Samantha felt a crazy spinning inside her head and slowly twined her arms around his neck, to return with fervor the kiss that she had so hungered for. It was everything and more than she had dreamed of. It was causing a rush of desire spiraling through her so keen that she was becoming lost to all reality.

She no longer wanted to fight him. He was causing wondrous sensations inside her, and she couldn't refuse him anything any longer. She wanted this. She wanted him. . . .

# ROMANCE
From the Civil War to the Wild West

**REBEL PLEASURE**　　　　　　　　　(1672, $3.95)
by Mary Martin

Union agent Jason Woods knew Christina was a brazen flirt, but his dangerous mission had no room for a clinging vixen. Then he caressed every luscious contour of her body and realized he could never go too far with this confederate tigress.

**SAVAGE TORMENT**　　　　　　　　　(1739, $3.95)
by Cassie Edwards

Judith should have been afraid of the red-skinned warrior, but those fears turned to desire as her blue eyes travelled upward to meet his. She had found her destiny—bound by his forbidden kiss.

**FORBIDDEN EMBRACE**　　　　　　　(1639, $3.95)
by Cassie Edwards

She was a Yankee nurse, and he was a Confederate soldier; yet it felt so right to be in each other's arms. Today Wesley would savor Serena's sweetness because tomorrow he had to be gone with only the memory of their FORBIDDEN EMBRACE.

**PASSION'S VIXEN**　　　　　　　　　(1759, $3.95)
by Carol Finch

When Melissa ran away into the mountains, her father paid the handsome woodsman, Zack Beaugener, to find her. Succumbing to her captor's caresses, she prayed he would not betray her love.

**WILDFIRE**　　　　　　　　　　　　(1737, $3.95)
by Carol Finch

If it meant following him all the way across the wilderness, Alexa had to satisfy the sensual agony Keane ignited in her soul. He was a devilish rogue who brought her to WILD-FIRE.

*Available wherever paperbacks are sold, or order direct from the Publisher. Send cover price plus 50¢ per copy for mailing and handling to Zebra Books, Dept. 1872, 475 Park Avenue South, New York, N.Y. 10016. Residents of New York, New Jersey and Pennsylvania must include sales tax. DO NOT SEND CASH.*

# PASSION'S FIRE
## CASSIE EDWARDS

**ZEBRA BOOKS**
**KENSINGTON PUBLISHING CORP.**

ZEBRA BOOKS

are published by

Kensington Publishing Corp.
475 Park Avenue South
New York, NY 10016

First printing: August 1986

Printed in the United States of America

*I wish to dedicate* Passion's Fire *to Bev Stevenson, a dear and special friend, whose acquaintance was first made when I autographed books at her Village Book Shoppe in Effingham, Illinois.*

—Cassie

Could you but guess
How you alone make all my happiness,
How I am more than willing for your sake
To stand alone, give all and nothing take,
Nor chafe to think you bound while I am free,
Quite free, till death, to love you silently,
Could you but guess. . . .

—*Anonymous*

*Chapter One*

A mile long avenue of oaks with their gray beards of Spanish moss hanging from their wide branches led to Johnston Oaks Manor, a magnificent three-storied plantation house. Its pillared facade was rectangular with wide porches, stained glass windows, and a mansard roof. Having been built high on a hill to bring it river breezes, its terraced lawn spread out like a green carpet down to the blue waters of Ashley River, and its upper rooms had a commanding view of Charleston Harbor.

Though dusk had fallen, the shutters at the many windows of Johnston Oaks Manor had not yet been closed by the servants, and lights from kerosene lamps danced golden at most. But the brightest lights emanated from the dining room where a birthday meal was being shared by a party of three.

Bored and with her green eyes moody, Samantha Johnston sat at the very long and dark mahogany dining table sipping her coffee. It was becoming harder and

9

harder for her to sit politely quiet while her father continued to discuss politics with their dinner guest Franklin LaFontaine, a middle-aged widower of French descent and a wealthy plantation owner in his own right.

Not having feelings one way or the other for Franklin LaFontaine, though he was pursuing her now that he was widowed, Samantha felt that her new gown and fresh hairdo had been wasted for the evening, though it *was* her nineteenth birthday.

With her personal maid's assistance, Samantha's auburn hair had been brushed into a lustrous sheen. It had then been shaped to be fairly flat on top with the sides waved and the back of the hair coiled and held up with a slide, with soft curls at her temple and ears and a small portion of her hair left hanging in ringlets at the back.

Most agreed that Samantha was shatteringly pretty, and so it was no surprise to her father when his houseguest couldn't keep from openly appraising her. In her evening gown of pale green satin trimmed with lace and velvet ribbon with its low, tight-fitting bodice, there was quite a display of her creamy white bust, so that even a diamond necklace couldn't detract from her magnificence there.

Samantha had the auburn hair of her Scottish heritage, and her eyes, large and green and always sparkling, showed her personality to be high-spirited, independent, and adventurous.

Sighing, tired of hearing talk of slavery, the outcome of the Republican party's second National Convention, and of Lincoln's having won the election, Samantha placed her coffee cup back in its saucer and tried to focus her thoughts elsewhere, blanking out the words being spoken on either side of her.

Mindlessly, she let her eyes wander around the room, seeing the beautifully frescoed walls, the fourteen-foot high ceiling, and the wallpaper with its medallions of egrets and marsh scenes. Gold-brocaded draperies were drawn back over lace curtains with thick gold cords looped back along the corniced windows. The china closet and exquisitely carved cherry sideboard had been shipped from Seattle, and upon the table an elegant lace tablecloth had been spread, lighted by candles in huge candelabras.

An array of food for which Johnston Oaks Manor was famed had been served in Sevres porcelain china. Platters of cold ham and rich cheeses, fresh pompano with sherry-flavored sauce of lobster, and scallops and shrimp baked in brown paper had been impeccably served with a cold, smoked grouper appetizer, a hearty seafood bisque, and tasty salad.

Wishing the evening were over, though it *was* her birthday celebration, Samantha toyed idly first with her Irish linen napkin, then with the fresh raspberry romanoff which sat half eaten before her. She sank her spoon into her dessert and moved it from one side of the long-stemmed crystal dish to the other. Then she jumped, startled, when her father's booming voice broke through her shield of silence, brusquely speaking her name.

"Sam? Where has your mind taken you?" her father said, raising his voice even more. "We're movin' to the parlor. Surely you don't want to stay alone at the table. It's quite obvious that not even the raspberry romanoff was to your liking."

Fluttering her thick, feathery lashes, Samantha rose

her eyes to meet the challenge of her father's. "What?" she said, clumsily dropping her spoon noisily into the dish. "Did you say something, Father?"

She had grown used to her nickname Sam, having realized long ago that her father had branded her with a boy's name because of his disappointment in not having been given a son at birth. It had seemed that even then he had known that he wouldn't father any more children. How he would have known that in advance had always been a puzzlement to Samantha and a question that would be left unanswered. She could never ask her father such a delicate question as to why she had been an only child, and she no longer had the opportunity to ask her mother.

Grace, her mother, had been dead for ten years. She seemed to have died a broken, unfulfilled woman, *another* thing for Samantha to silently ponder over since her mother had only been forty-two at the time of her death.

But she had always noticed that her mother and father had never shared a bedroom. Had they stayed from each other's beds except for that one time when she had been conceived?

Or was it a hidden truth that the great, powerful plantation owner Craig Johnston wasn't as virile a man as he appeared?

Craig pushed his chair back and rose to his feet, displaying his heftiness and towering six-foot-seven height even as he leaned both hands against the tabletop, to speak down into Samantha's face.

"Damn it, girl," he grumbled. "We have a guest. Act accordingly. Get up. We shall now retire to the parlor. I believe Franklin here has brought you a fine birthday gift. At least act anxious, Sam. Franklin is not only our neighbor but my best friend as well."

He leaned even closer, speaking almost beneath his breath. "And, Sam, he's my choice for you. Remember that."

Feeling color rising into her cheeks, and her eyes growing hot with anger, Samantha glared at her father. "Father, please," she whispered. "Not here. Not *now*. You're embarrassing me. It's best that you continue speaking of politics instead of—of—courtships!"

"I thought our talk of politics was borin' you, Sam," Craig challenged, with a half smile playing on his thick lips.

Samantha gave him back a half smile yet wondered if she and her father would ever stop trying to outsmart the other. "Yes, I was bored," she said tersely. "So doesn't knowing that prove to you just how much I do not wish to speak of marriage, Father?"

She watched his penetrating green eyes take on a darker shade as he set his jaw firmly. Once more she felt the victor as she was wont to do as of late. But she knew it was only because her father had been so preoccupied with his loyalty to the state of South Carolina where they made their residence, and he had been among the leaders who had encouraged that South Carolina pass an Ordinance of Secession which had declared the Union be dissolved as far as that state was concerned.

Clearing his throat nervously, Franklin also rose to his feet, dwarfed by Craig's largeness. "Now just once you two cut out the arguing," he said, chuckling. "We're gathered here to celebrate a birthday. Or did you forget?"

Samantha's gaze moved to her right and up onto Franklin's thin and angular face. She looked back toward her father, then back to Franklin, comparing the two

13

gentlemen. With her father's thick crop of bright red hair and sideburns which came down on his cheeks making cheek-whiskers, and with his rugged facial features displaying red and shaggy eyebrows shading his green eyes, there *was* no comparison to Franklin and his bland facial features, pale gray eyes, and balding head. The only thing common between them was their wealth, *and* their interests in keeping the Southern states separate from the North.

They were even dressed almost identically this evening in expensive dark frock coats, and even darker velvet waistcoats with white shirt ruffles at the chest and satin cravats at their throats.

Samantha focused once more on her father. He was a very rich man. Aside from his slaves, plantation, and household items, he possessed a schooner, two large barges, a sloop, and a number of canoes. It seemed that he could perhaps lose more than he could gain *should* there be a war.

"He's right, Sam," Craig said, going to her chair, to urge her up from it. "All bantering aside for the evening. What do you say?"

Shrugging and smiling softly, Samantha rose from behind the table. "All right, Father," she said. "Whatever you say. It would be nice to go sit by the fire. It seems the shutters haven't been closed to the river breeze early enough this evening. I feel a chill in my bones."

As an arm was offered on each side of her, she walked between her father and Franklin through handsome sliding doors which opened the dining room to a parlor bathed in a pleasant glow from a fire in the fireplace.

The parlor was an elegant setting with a huge and glistening crystal chandelier lighting a room which was a preponderance of ornate plaster scrollwork. The room was filled with silk-covered sofas heaped with velvet pillows, seventeenth century French and ancient Chinese marble-topped tables, and white silk damask-covered chairs.

A Waterford hurricane lamp sat on a grand piano before double windows framed by gold velvet drapes, and the oak floors were as shiny as glass.

At the far end of the room a dramatic red-glazed wall set off a traditional marble fireplace with elaborate detailing, and before the hearth, on a small, oval-braided rug lay Checkers, Samantha's gorgeous, sleeping Collie.

With the many layers of her petticoat rustling beneath her fully gathered gown, Samantha stepped on away from her escorts. Spreading the skirt of her gown and petticoats around her, she settled down on the floor beside Checkers. Smoothing her hand across the dog's back, she absorbed the warmth from his fire-warmed fur into her own flesh.

"Checkers, if I could trade places with you, I would," Samantha whispered into her dog's ear. "I don't look forward to the rest of the evening. How nice it would be to be able to do as one wished most of the time as you do, my sweet pet."

Checker's lazy dark eyes opened and looked up at her. He lifted a paw and scraped her arm with it, wanting her to continue petting him.

Samantha giggled. "My, but *aren't* you spoiled?" she said, leaning down to hug him. "You *are* my best friend, you know."

"Sam, good lord. Behave like a lady and get up from the floor," Craig scolded, offering Franklin a thin cheroot from a silver cigar case. "One would think that

15

an expensive gown such as that would deserve better treatment from its owner."

Lifting a beautifully plucked eyebrow, Samantha eyed her father quizzically. Until only recently he hadn't wanted her to behave so much like a lady. He had enjoyed having her ride beside him on a horse while jointly checking the plantation grounds in her man's breeches and a wide-brimmed straw hat which hid the length of her beautiful hair beneath it.

Ah, the indigo crops that Johnston Oaks had boasted of shipping to Europe before her father's main crop became cotton. Used for making dyes, it had been common knowledge of all planters that the weight of indigo increased by dampening it; thus the profits would rise as well. But Craig Johnston's indigo had always been as dry as indigo could be, making Samantha proud to be the daughter of such an honest, upright man and to have the opportunity to travel on horseback by his side.

But now that she had blossomed into full womanhood, with her dips and curves that couldn't be hidden even beneath a man's clothes, her father had accepted her change and was behaving accordingly. With her seductively full mouth and high, firm breasts, how could he for one minute forget she *was* all female?

But he still stubbornly refused to call her by anything but Sam, even though it had now become an awkward relationship between father and daughter.

"Sam," her father growled. "The floor! Get up from the floor. Chairs were made for sittin'. Not the damn floor."

"Oh, if I must, I must," Samantha fussed, pushing herself up from the floor. She saw the eagerness in Franklin's eyes as he pulled a small wrapped gift from his waistcoat pocket. Not wanting to have to accept anything from him, Samantha wryly began talk of secession again. Though cringing at the thought of hearing it all over again, she knew what to expect, once her father was guided, purposely, into the subject so dear to his heart.

"Horace Greeley, the editor of the *New York Tribune*, openly expressed the opinion that our southern states have a perfect right to form a Union of our own," Samantha said, easing down into a wingback chair as her father and Franklin sat down on a sofa opposite her. "But I disagree," she quickly added. "All this will do is definitely cause a war between the North and South. Father, is your need to be separate from the North so great you would risk Civil War?"

She ignored the rage in her father's eyes and instead smiled to herself when she saw Franklin ease the gift back into his pocket, frowning with annoyance toward her. She had to wonder, though, which had caused Franklin's change of mood: her obvious ploy to switch the subject from herself back to politics, or his dislike of her mixed loyalties to which she had so often openly expressed.

But it mattered not to her how he felt about anything. She had at least for the moment been spared his attentions!

"Sam, you watch your tongue," Craig growled, his face expressing anger and fear. He could understand why she would be drawn into a concern over the trouble between the North and the South since her heart was divided. For ten years now, since her mother's death, she had traveled north to spend her summers with her mother's parents in Springfield, Illinois, to ease their loss over their only child.

At first, when Craig had agreed to let Samantha go to

17

Illinois, it had been planned for only that once. Somehow, it had gotten out of hand, and he had now lost part of her to her grandparents and to the North.

Yes, he understood her feelings, but no one else would. Even *he* didn't understand this attraction of hers to spend summers on a small farm in near poverty, when he had to offer her so much at Johnston Oaks. He had tried many ways to draw her full attention back to him and what he had to offer: a prized pony, a grand piano, beautiful clothes.

No. Nothing had dissuaded her from her yearly summer journey to the North. He had to sometimes wonder if there was a man drawing her there. His mood would grow sour quite quickly when thinking on that possibility. There had been a man earlier in her mother's life—a man who had taken her mother's virginity before even himself—her husband. The wedding night had been enough for him to know that he had married a loose woman, and never had he bedded her again.

A white-gloved houseboy was Craig's reprieve for the moment as the houseboy entered the parlor with a silver tray displaying a crystal decanter of whiskey and two tall-stemmed glasses. He set this down on a table and, after pouring whiskey into the glasses and giving one each to Craig and Franklin, he lighted the gentlemen's cigars and, just as quietly as he had entered, he made his exit.

Samantha understood why the houseboy hadn't offered her the same refreshment as her father and houseguest. "A lady does not abide in spirits," he had told her many times.

But she could remember his having said something else in the past: "A southern gentleman does *not* drink

18

spirits in the presence of a lady."

Samantha drummed the fingers of her right hand on the arm of her chair, thinking: First he treats her like a perfect lady, and then he does not. Where does he draw the line?

"The economic rivalry between the industrial North and the agricultural South has gotten out of hand, Samantha," Franklin said, scowling. "We planters of the South must be left alone by the government so that we can continue to have free trade with Europe in order to freely exchange our indigo, cotton, and tobacco for their manufactured goods. But the manufacturers of the North have insisted that the government put a tax on manufactured goods coming into the country in order that *they* might have control of American markets. And now they've begun their attacks on slavery, the source of southern power. Slavery is absolutely essential to carry on the plantations of the South. If war is needed to protect our rights, then damn it, let there be war!"

"Lincoln is wrong in his assessment of slavery," Craig grumbled. "Slaves were taken away from barbarism in Africa and brought up to a degree of civilization in America. They are looked after in their sickness and old age by kind masters like me and Franklin here and are not as cruelly treated as workmen in the mills and factories of the North."

"Yes," Franklin agreed. "The modern workingman is in a sadder plight than the slave because he has to work for long hours and low wages in factories. In case of sickness or accident he is compelled to starve, and in his old age he is turned out to die or live in a poorhouse because he is no longer valuable to his employer."

19

"The wage system of the North is more cruel to workers than the slave system of the South," Craig interjected.

"Discontented workmen are more dangerous to the country as a whole than peaceful bondsmen," Franklin said, nodding his head.

"And, Sam," Craig said, twirling his glass around between his fingers, "Lincoln continues to harp about the nation as a house divided, half slave and half free and is against the spread of slavery into new lands in the West. Any law that man as president passes against slavery is a danger to our way of life. It's imperative that we now set up our own nation: the Confederate States of America."

Hearing such talk caused shivers of fear to race up and down Samantha's spine. She started to air her feelings but was interrupted when Franklin once more spoke, this time to Craig, leaving Samantha out of the conversation as though she wasn't even there. With a soft pout on her lips, she accepted Checkers as he came and placed his chin on her lap. She combed her fingers through his soft fur, regretfully listening to more talk of the seceded states taking their place among the "free and independent nations of the earth."

"The convention to be held in Montgomery, Alabama, on the fourth will draft a plan of government like the Constitution of the United States which will declare that each of our seceded states is free, sovereign and independent," Craig said, leaning forward, his face anxious.

He emptied his glass of whiskey and set it down on a table. "I look to Jefferson Davis of Mississippi with confidence and affection and will, personally, encourage that he be elected our new nation's president. He is a man of undoubted ability and courage who has long defended the rights of the South. He could be a great leader."

"Alexander Stephens of Georgia would be my choice for vice president," Franklin said, flicking ashes from his cigar into a crystal ashtray he had positioned on his lap.

"If war does come because of what we plan to do, the southern states have certain advantages," Craig boasted, once more relaxing against the back of the sofa. "Our men are now feverishly preparing for war. And in addition to men and supplies, the South has devoted generals like Robert E. Lee, Thomas Jackson, and Joseph Johnston who have been well trained at West Point. They surely will feel bound by allegiance to their native states to place themselves at the service of the Confederacy."

"Ah, yes," Franklin said, getting a faraway look in his faded gray eyes. "In the control of an aristocracy, brave and dashing with such leaders, the southern states will be a foe that will have to be taken seriously."

"Europe will come to the aid of the South," Craig said, ignoring the continued look of distaste on Samantha's face. "Great Britain and France depend on southern cotton for their textile industries. A shortage of cotton will force them to intervene on the southern side."

"Two diplomats have already been dispatched to Europe to persuade Britain and France to take up the southern cause," Franklin said, once more removing the wrapped gift from his pocket. He looked contemplatingly toward Samantha and then down at the gift, yet continued speaking.

"Yes, John Slidell and James Mason have already sailed from Havana, Cuba, on a British ship called the

21

*Trent,*" he said. "By the time we have organized our new nation and have appointed Jefferson Davis president, our diplomats should be receiving a favorable answer to bring back to us."

Finally catching a pause in the conversation, Samantha spoke quickly. "Father, what you plan can most surely interrupt my travels north, to visit grandmama and grandpapa," she said sorrowfully. "If the country is so divided, how am I to—to—even choose?"

His face a mask of rage, Craig jumped to his feet. "Sam, you can say such a thing?" he shouted.

Then he leaned down into her face and spoke shallowly. "You can talk openly in only *my* presence of your divided loyalties," he growled. "But refrain from doing so in front of *guests*. What must Franklin be thinking?"

She met his challenge. "I don't give a darn what he thinks," she hissed. Then she recoiled when she saw the sudden red flush rising into her father's cheeks and his eyes flashing hot and angry back at her.

"You will one day be disobedient one time too many," he snapped. "But as it *is* your birthday, I shall ignore this evening's insolence on your part."

"But I *do* want to travel north again this summer," she softly argued. "I *will* travel north, no matter what!"

Craig sighed heavily, shaking his head slowly back and forth. "I loosened my reins on you too much after your mother's death," he said. "Your spitfire personality is my fault. Now I must accept that you *are* as stubborn as a mule."

He straightened his back, yet still stared down at her. "We shall discuss your travels north later, Sam, after Franklin is gone."

"I *will* go," she said beneath her breath, smiling devilishly up at him.

He swung away from her, pretending not to have heard her reaffirmation of continued disobedience. He forced a laugh as he went to take a colorfully wrapped package from its hiding place, behind a deep-wing chair.

With a red satin bow tied around the package, he took it and handed it to Samantha, giving Franklin a quick glance. "Fathers first on a daughter's birthday," he chuckled, winking at Franklin.

Samantha accepted the gift in her outstretched hands. "Happy birthday, Sam," Craig said, brushing a quick kiss across her cheek. "And may you have many, many more."

"Thank you, Father," Samantha whispered, giving him a kiss before he had the chance to move away from her. Kisses and hugs were rare between them, and Samantha wondered if he had ever felt the need for such affections. She had learned to patiently wait until the summer when she could get this sort of attention from her grandparents. They had always been so free with their love, and she was able to store enough in her heart to last her all winter long, until she was with them again, the next summer.

Lifting the package to her ear, she rattled it, sensing its weight to mean more than a box of fancy stationery. "Hmm," she said. "It's something that seems to shift from side to side in the box as I turn it from one end to the other."

Craig shifted on his feet nervously. "Good Lord, Sam," he said. "Just open it. Why do you always play this guessing game whenever given a gift?"

She lifted a brow toward him. "Because it's much more

23

exciting than just tearing into the package," she said, once more tipping the gift next to her ear. "Don't you see? The waiting enhances the mystery of what's inside."

Clasping his hands severely behind him, Craig glowered down at her. "If you don't hurry and open it, I'll see to it that the mystery is quickly dispelled," he growled. "I'll *tell* you what's inside."

A hurtful expression shadowed Samantha's usually lovely face. "Father, why are you in such a hurry?" she murmured. "Don't you have even at least a few moments to truly share with me on my birthday?"

"I leave for Montgomery tomorrow," he said, his eyes wavering under her close scrutiny. "There's much to be done here before I leave. I've got to see to it that instructions are understood and that cotton seeds are readied for planting in March. If the crop is good, picking time could extend on into December."

"That is, if the war doesn't steal not only our southern men away from us, but also our crops as well," she softly argued.

"The war, if it does become a necessity, will never be fought on southern soil," he argued back.

He unclasped his hands and flung one wildly into the air. "Now, damn it, Sam, open your gift. Franklin has waited long enough to give you his."

"Oh, all right," Samantha sighed, flashing Franklin a harried look, anxious to be done with this and to be away from these two gentlemen's company, even though one was her father. They were too alike, these men who talked of war as though it were a fluffy piece of cotton, to be tossed idly about in the wind.

With determination, she scooted the ribbon from the package, careful not to harm it in any way, with future plans of wearing it in her hair. Then she tore the paper away, opened the box, and gasped when her gaze fell upon the tiny, fancy lady's pistol resting in tissue paper inside the box.

Samantha's eyes shot upward, seeing a playful gleam in her father's eyes. "A pistol?" she said. "For—me?"

She had asked for her personal firearm since she had been taught the art of shooting her father's heavier pistols at the age of twelve. But up to now, he had refused, warning her of the dangers that one false pull of the trigger could shoot a toe clean away in the blink of an eye.

But now? To even give it to her on her special day— her birthday? She was shocked and almost speechless.

"With the talk of war, the need for everyone to own a weapon becomes a necessity," he said thickly. "Even you, Sam. But be careful with it. It isn't something to take casually, this ownership of a dangerous weapon."

"But, Father, you just said that the war would never be fought on southern soil," she tested. "If not, I truly don't need a gun any more now than before."

"If war is ever legally declared, the fighting will be kept from southern soil," he argued. "But until then, small wars are springing up everywhere. There have already been armed conflicts in Kansas. Should it happen here, you must be ready to defend yourself at all times, Sam."

Samantha lifted the pistol and let it rest in the palm of her left hand. "It will be wise to carry it with me on my journey to Springfield," she said.

Then her eyes once more shot up with an idea. "Father, I must leave for Illinois soon or I won't be able to go at all. Once the news reaches Washington about the Confederate States truly being formed into a separate nation, war is inevitable. I must see grandmama and grandpapa before that happens. I can leave tomorrow! As you leave for Montgomery, so shall I leave for Illinois!"

Craig's face darkened with renewed anger. He slammed a doubled fist against the palm of his other hand. "Never!" he roared.

"So that's it," Samantha said, rising slowly to her feet. "This year you thought you had a surefire plan to keep me home. You thought that talk of war would frighten me into staying in Charleston!"

"Any lady in her right mind wouldn't want to travel alone in these troubled times," Craig stormed. "Why must you be so different?"

She stood on tiptoe and spoke smoothly into his face. "I reckon because I'm your daughter," she said dryly.

Flattening her feet back solidly against the floor, Samantha spun around and faced Franklin. "So now I am ready to open your gift, Franklin," she said, placing the pistol on a table. "I pray it's of a more delicate nature. Seems my father still looks to me as part boy since he chose a firearm as my birthday gift over, let's say, a frilly dress?"

Then she gave her father a half smile across her shoulder. "But I forget so quickly," she teased. "It was a lady's pistol, wasn't it, Father? I'm surprised it wasn't a six-shooter, shipped in directly from the wild and woolly West."

She giggled as she directed her attention back away from her father and to Franklin and the small package he was offering her.

"Thank you, Franklin," she said, accepting the package that was smaller than even the palm of her hand. "But you know that this wasn't necessary. Around here,

26

birthdays seem to lose their importance."

She could hear her father's quick intake of breath and now wished that she hadn't said that. But he did continue to rub her wrong, and she felt the need to return the favor, though there was no denying that she wished things could be different between them.

But perhaps anything different would make life even more boring.

Wasting no time with this package, more from eagerness to leave the room than from the need to see the sort of gift given her, Samantha opened the box and gasped. She felt warmth rise to her cheeks having never seen anything so beautiful!

"Why, Franklin, I swear I've never seen anything as lovely," she murmured, lifting the gold-enameled, shell-shaped locket and its gold chain from the box. "Such a different sort of locket."

"It's more than a locket, Samantha," Franklin said anxiously. "Open it. See what's inside."

With a sharp fingernail, she snapped the lid open and once more gasped. "Why, it is so much more than a locket," she said. "It's a watch. And look at the scenes painted in colorful enamels decorating the face and inside cover of the watch. Lovely. Just lovely."

She tried to ignore the heartshape, romantic designs of the paintings, knowing his purpose of choosing this particular gift. Oh, if such a gift could have been given to her by a man she loved! It would be something to wear next to her heart! But there was no special man in her life, and she had to be sure that Franklin would not fool himself into thinking that he was.

Quickly dropping the locket back inside the box and closing its lid, she then went and grabbed her pistol and strolled casually toward the door that led into the hallway. "Thank you both for my gifts, but I best leave you to your further plans," she said smoothly. "I shall see you in the morning, Father, for breakfast. We can say our good-byes then as I leave for Illinois, and you for Montgomery."

Franklin stood aghast at her quick departure.

Her father glowered toward her, his fists doubled to his side. "You shall not," he growled.

"I shall," she said, tilting her chin stubbornly. She swept on away up the stairway that spiraled to the third floor, where a chandelier hung from the cupola. She rushed to her room. She had much to do. She had her trunk to be readied for her journey.

# Chapter Two

Dust clouds rolled up from behind the wheels of the stately black carriage as Samantha watched her father's departure from her upstairs bedroom window. She knew that she should feel victorious since she soon would also be leaving on her journey to Illinois. But strange how her father had backed down so easily, agreeing to let her go to Illinois this early after all. He had even informed her that he would send a wire to her grandparents from the train depot in Charleston, so they could know when to expect her arrival in Springfield. It was as though he welcomed her leave this time, though in Franklin's presence he had spoken strongly against it.

Yet she had to believe it was because of his complete involvement in politics, now placing her secondary in his life. If she were his son, he surely would have been behaving differently toward her. With the talk of war, he would be preparing her for the fight!

But since she was only a daughter—

"Miss Samantha, honey?"

Samantha jumped with a start and let the sheer, lacy

curtain that she had pulled aside flutter from her fingers when she heard Jewel, her personal maid, enter the room and speak her name. Swinging around, Samantha smiled a silent hello to her.

Jewel, short and plump, attired in a plain, starched, calico dress with a white collar at her wrinkled neck and long sleeves tight at her wrists, began walking heavily around the room, gathering up discarded clothes.

"Honey, it's sho not wise of Massa Craig sendin' you on your travels North with such unrest in the country," she said, her round-cheeked, dark face framed by tight ringlets of gray hair.

Samantha was ready to leave, dressed in her floor-length, black velvet princess coat edged with ribbon and decorated with silk embroidery and jet beads. Only wisps of her auburn hair showed around the edges of her matching bonnet. Her fine-lined cheekbones were blooming with color as were her green eyes sparkling, excitement building to extreme proportions inside her.

"It was not Father's idea that I go at this time," she said, smoothing her imported butter-soft leather gloves on, a finger at a time. "It was solely my idea to leave earlier than the month of May."

With a silk chemise draped over her left arm, Jewel clasped and unclasped her stocky fingers. "It just ain't right," she said. "There's talk of war. What if you find it impossible to return home? And, honey, you've neva' missed cotton plantin' time. The fields will be empty without you there, plantin' along with the rest of us as though you were one of us."

Samantha went to Jewel and framed her pleasant face between her hands. "Oh, Jewel, I know," she sighed. "I'll miss being there. But you have to know that in the past I always chose to help with the planting, mainly to busy my days away because my travel time was always so near. But this year I'm leaving earlier. You know how I've always looked forward to going to my grandparents' house. It's like another world, Jewel. I love it."

"But you've said it ain't as grand there as here," Jewel said, puzzled. "How could you be so anxious to leave this behind? Yo' pappy don't let you want for nothin'."

Smiling almost dreamily, Samantha twirled away from Jewel and went to check her appearance before an ornately framed mirror. "It's a feeling of freedom that I have while there," she said. "I feel less inhibited. I enjoy being a part of the simpler way of life."

Yes, she thought. It will be simpler. Her assigned bedroom at her grandparents' house was quite different than in her South Carolina home. She wouldn't find a bedroom decorated in pinks and greens, of satins and chintz, with a solid white, four poster-canopied mahogany bed, a granite washstand and thick carpet so plush her bare toes could curl into its depth.

At home her room was designed especially for her with its soft pink rosebud-bedecked wallpaper coverings on the walls, and sheer, lacy curtains at the windows.

She would miss it, but only barely. Though she had only a simple iron bed and no matching furniture in her grandparents' house, she had the cozy comforters handsewn by her grandmother to crawl beneath. It gave her a peaceful feeling even now, remembering.

"Tsk, tsk," Jewel said, shaking her head. "You sho are a hard one to figure out."

Her dark eyes took on a sudden gleam. "Unless," she said, placing a forefinger wonderingly to her chin, smiling mischievously toward Samantha.

31

Samantha's eyes widened as she caught Jewel's playful smile staring back at her in the mirror. She spun around and faced Jewel squarely, with an eyebrow lifted. "Unless what?" she softly questioned.

"A man?" Jewel giggled. "Honey, is there a young man up North who's caught yo' fancy?"

Samantha threw her head back in a soft laugh. "No. There's no young man," she said.

She lowered her chin, wiping a laughter tear from the corner of an eye. "Not yet anyway, Jewel," she teased.

"If you know what's bes' for you, you'll not let yo' heart be captured by a northern gentleman," Jewel warned, now stripping the bed of its sheets. "Massa' Craig wouldn't stand for that."

She placed a hand to the small of her back and groaned as she bent to scoop up the sheets into her other arm. "And with the talk of war, it's not a good time to be attracted to any man be he from the North or South," she said, giving Samantha a look of concern from across her shoulder. "There'll be casualties, fo' sho, if fightin' breaks out. Who's to say who'll survive and who won't?"

Samantha lifted the skirt of her coat and dress up into her arms and spun around, searching the tabletops for her purse. "Oh, Jewel, this is no time for such talk," she scolded. "I'm leaving soon. I don't want to think of anything but the exciting travel ahead."

Spying her purse on a splay-legged nightstand, she picked it up, its weight reminding her of its added contents. Her birthday. The pistol and some extra bullets had been placed there by her father earlier in the morning with instructions to use the firearm without a second thought if faced with a threat to her life or body.

A pinprick of fear ebbed its way inside Samantha's

32

heart, but she shook herself free of it, not allowing it or anything to spoil her day.

Laying the bedclothes aside on a chair, Jewel went to Samantha and placed a hand on her arm. "Promise me somethin', Samantha," she murmured.

Samantha fluttered her thick lashes nervously as she looked down onto a face shadowed with fear. "Promise?" she said softly. "What, Jewel?"

"That if a war do break out you will hurry right back home while travel is still possible," Jewel said hoarsely. "I don' want to think of you bein' trapped up there, so far from home."

Samantha emitted a nervous laugh. "Yes," she said. "I promise."

Once more she spun away from Jewel. She went to her wardrobe and rifled through the remaining hanging clothes. "I guess I'm taking everything that I need," she said. "I don't need much finery there."

Clutching her purse to her chest she went to a window and stared down at the waiting buggy. "Did you tell Joshua to load my trunk?" she asked, seeing the harnessed chestnut mare stamping a hoof restlessly against the gravel drive.

"My husband sho nuff do what I say," Jewel said, tittering. "Seems bein' Massa' Craig's overseer ain't made his head swell too much that he don' listen to what his woman say."

"Such a devotion is what I hope to find in a man," Samantha said. She went to Jewel and softly embraced her. "I must go now, Jewel. Are you coming down to see me off?"

Jewel placed her thick arms about Samantha and hugged her fondly to her. "No. Partings are too sad," she said, tears brimming her eyes. "I will say my good-byes here. I don' want to see the buggy takin' you away."

"If things remain peaceful in the country, I shall return at the end of summer as I always do," Samantha said, giving Jewel a final squeeze before breaking away from her. She gazed down into Jewel's red-brimmed eyes. "And don't be sad. I'm doing what I want to do."

"You always were a willful chil'," Jewel said, shaking her head. "I guess you'll never change."

"Jewel," Samantha said, laughing softly. "I really must go. I'll write. I promise!"

Without another look backward, Samantha rushed from the room, down the majestic, spiral staircase, and on outside, to stop and stand on the wide porch before boarding the buggy. Checkers meandered over to her and lifted a paw, scraping it against her coat, his dark eyes pleading for attention.

Samantha's gaze lowered, seeing her dog, already missing him. Not worrying about her expensive coat scraping the floor of the porch, she bent to her knees and smoothed her gloved hand over the sheen of his fur. "You sense it, don't you?" she whispered. "You know that I'm leaving."

Checkers whined and hung his head as even his shaggy tail drooped. Samantha softly apologized. "I'm sorry I can't take you with me. But you've many friends who'll take you for your long walks beside the river."

She was referring to the children of the slaves who lived and worked at Johnston Oaks Plantation. She looked toward the unpainted pine shacks which made up the long line of many slave cabins that sat far back, away from the grand Johnston Oaks Manor.

Having the run of the plantation grounds, Samantha

34

was not only familiar with the cotton gin house, the smoke house, the garden walls and walks made out of handmade bricks, she had also become friends with most of her father's bondsmen. She had mixed with them, as though she had also traveled on the same ships with them which had brought them from the African nation of Angola.

But there were still many of their customs that Samantha would never understand, especially the blue paint that they all painted on the windows and doors of their cabins which they claimed prevented evil spirits from entering their houses.

"Ma'am?"

Samantha rose quickly to her feet and looked over her shoulder at Jewel's husband Joshua who was standing beside the buggy, waiting.

"I see you're ready to leave," Samantha said, spying her trunk now fastened to the back of the buggy, ready for the journey into Charleston, and then for her to board a stagecoach for her further journey to Illinois.

Her gaze moved back to Joshua whose lanky height was more pronounced in his tight cotton breeches and shirt, revealing corded muscles at his shoulders and the thighs of his legs. With thick, gray hair, his dark eyes were pits in his long and narrow face, and his nostrils were wide as were his lips. But the most prominent thing about him was the kindness that he radiated when with him. And because of this he had not only been appointed overseer at Johnston Oaks, but was also a trusted friend.

"I tol' Massa Craig that you shouldn't leave," Joshua said, frowning.

"Oh, not you, too," Samantha groaned. She gave Checkers a last, wide stroke to his fur, then determinedly swept the skirt of her coat and dress on down the steps and past Joshua, climbing unassisted into the buggy.

"There!" she exclaimed. "I'm ready to go. Now please do me the courtesy of taking reins in hand and take me to the depot."

Never one to balk at a command, be it from the master or mistress of the house, Joshua gave no more argument to the matter at hand. "Yes'm," he mumbled, climbing onto the front seat of the buggy. "It *is* a nice day for a drive into town."

"It's a nice day for a drive to Illinois," Samantha eagerly corrected, having already breathed in the freshness of the morning air and welcomed the crystal blue of the clear sky. "It's not hot as when I usually travel the month of May. I shall enjoy it even more, Joshua."

"Do you plan to stay the spring and summer months?" Joshua asked from across his shoulder as he flipped the horse's reins. He clucked to the horse as it made a wide circle, then began trotting away from the house on along the avenue.

"If all goes well," Samantha answered, clinging to the seat and turning around to take her one final look at the three-storied mansion. It seemed so peaceful in these cool hours of early morning, the time before all shutters were thrown back to welcome the warm splash of sunshine into the spacious rooms.

Samantha let her gaze move past the house, now taking in its full setting. The Johnston Oaks Plantation consisted of acres upon acres of awesome beauty. Near the house were gardens where tall ailanthus bushes grew, which had been planted to dispel the tempers and torpors of the dreaded malaria fever.

Huge cypress and oak trees shaded the house, and

spring had brought with it banks of camellias, delicious-smelling magnolia blossoms, and azaleas with their riots of colors.

In the swamps which lined the river close to the plantation grounds the maples had turned red with seed, and wading birds such as the pelicans, herons, and egrets had already arrived for their nesting rituals.

The activity around the freshwater ponds had also increased. The cattails were growing stately tall. Alligators basked in the sun, and the grasses of the salt marshes had turned green.

A sudden shiver coursed through Samantha as she realized that this serenity that she had just enjoyed could soon be a thing of the past. Already throughout the state of South Carolina military drills were kept up by all men capable of bearing arms, and the city of Charleston was under military patrol, heavy guns having been mounted on the wharves on Charleston Harbor.

Now focusing her eyes straight ahead, Samantha clutched tightly to her purse which rested on her lap. She didn't want to think of unrest, war. But the weight of the pistol in her purse would always be there, a reminder.

Several nights had been spent comfortably in inns along the way, but now Samantha could finally see the telltale signs that she was drawing closer to Springfield. The stagecoach in which she traveled bumped along a rock-covered road, its interior crowded with passengers.

But Samantha had been lucky, having secured a seat by a window. Her eyes and lips were bright and her bare shoulders were gleaming as she gazed anxiously from the window. Her coat was draped across her lap, which was

37

cooler for her that way in the heat of the bodies crowded close by her. Her low-cut dress revealed her anxiety in the heaving of her bosom, her whiteness there only marred by the gold-encrusted, shell-shaped locket resting against the satin of her flesh.

Without her bonnet, her hair flamed red against the rough unpainted pine boards of the coach's interior. The pins were loosened from her hair so that it could cascade loosely around her shoulders. Another luxury afforded her by the freedom when away from her father's aristocratic, watchful eyes.

Absorbing the landscape stretched out before her, Samantha reveled in this pleasure. She had never seen such flat land. Sometimes it was as though she could see clear to the ends of the earth where meadow met meadow, with only an occasional island of trees growing around farmhouses.

Silos and barns also dotted the land, along with grazing cattle and horses, and spring wheat, waving gracefully in the breeze, appeared to be an ocean of gold.

And then all of this was taken suddenly from sight as the road led through a dense forest where only filtered rays of sun, resembling streams of gold satin, broke through the forest ceiling.

Then once again the stagecoach found its way to blue sky and bright sunlight and traveled alongside miles and miles of cedar fencing where beside it wild flowers grew in beautiful blues, golds, and reds.

Leaning her head slightly from the window to capture more of a breeze on her face, Samantha tensed when she saw the lone figure of a man standing at the side of the road just ahead. She looked more intensely toward him, wondering why any man would be standing alone, in the middle of nowhere.

Her eyes widened. What was this? This man was now waving his arms as the stagecoach approached him. He was trying to flag the stagecoach down, to become another passenger in what was already a sweltering mass of human flesh tightly squeezed together.

Disgruntled, she looked for his travel valise, and was even more puzzled about this stranger when she saw none. She had read about roadside bandits, but at least this man seemed innocent enough of these charges. He was dressed impeccably, and he wore no visible firearms. And without a horse, how could he escape if he did steal from the stagecoach passengers?

No. He seemed innocent enough. Yet, was he? It still seemed strange: his being on foot, alone, far from any other signs of life other than this traveling stagecoach of passengers.

Drawing her head back inside the window, Samantha tensed even more when she felt the stagecoach come to a bumping halt. She purposely listened as the stranger and stagecoach driver exchanged a few words, then she tried to ignore the stranger as he opened the door and crowded himself in among those passengers sitting opposite Samantha.

The stagecoach lurched forward, and the horses picked up speed. Still Samantha tried to refuse to take notice of the stranger's presence but ignoring him was impossible. He was sitting directly in front of her. And not only that! His knees were almost touching hers as were his feet which rested at the froth of her lace petticoats. He exuded a delicious-smelling, expensive man's cologne that pleasured Samantha's nose. She turned her full gaze to him, finding his eyes sweeping over her.

Samantha's heart fluttered, and her body turned to liquid under his close scrutiny, almost feeling branded by the heat of his gaze. And then their eyes met and locked, and Samantha was filled with sensations she never felt before as she was so taken by his absolute handsomeness.

His eyes were the color of the sky, even bluer against his deeply tanned, clean-shaven face. His nose was straight and long and seemed almost sculpted; his lips were sensuously full. The slope of his jaw was square and hard set, and all of this was framed by neatly coiffured midnight black hair worn to the collar of his shirt with neat sideburns grown halfway down his cheeks.

When he smiled ruefully and nodded a silent hello toward Samantha, tapping his right forefinger against his brow as though tipping a hat to her, Samantha shook herself free of his steady stare, embarrassed. She lowered her eyes away from him but not before she once more observed his total appearance.

Hatless, he was impeccably dressed in a dark brown wool frock coat worn over a fancily embroidered satin waistcoat adorned with an abundance of ruffles. A diamond stickpin sparkled from the folds of his maroon cravat, and his fawn-colored breeches fitted him tightly. And he wore knee boots, with only a spot or two of road dust spoiling their highly polished brown leather finish.

Although she had afforded herself only a quick glance, she could tell well enough that beneath his well-fitting clothes he had a fine-boned frame, broad shoulders, and narrow hips. He was the epitome of a man and the first to ever stir her insides. This was all new to her—this attraction to a man—a stranger who had suddenly appeared, as though from nowhere.

Realizing that her cheeks were ablaze with a heated

blush and knowing that he was still looking her way, Samantha shot him a look through her lashes. Her hand went nervously to her locket and began twisting its chain as she felt the scorch of his piercing blue eyes as they lowered and captured the swell of her breasts in the pleated silk, plunging neckline of her dress.

Frustrated, Samantha glanced quickly about her, at the other passengers. She feared that they would notice the blatancy of this man but was relieved when she saw that they were oblivious to everything but themselves and the heat from the pressed bodies against them.

Annoyance flashing in her crisp green eyes, Samantha leaned toward the man. "Sir, will you please direct your eyes elsewhere?" she softly hissed.

His low chuckle and his gaze, which swept from her face, down to her bodice, and up again, made a silent rage tear through Samantha's insides. He had a nerve, the cad!

And then she happened to glance downward and quickly saw the cause of his entertainment. When she had leaned forward, her dress had partially given way beneath the pressure of her breasts, causing them to spill more openly into view where her cleavage lay deep.

"My word," she gasped, her lustrous lips agape with horror.

She straightened her back and quickly covered herself with a hand, and dared not give another look in his direction, fearing these sensations his presence was creating inside her.

"Your name?" he suddenly blurted in a deep, masculine voice which seemed to reach clean to Samantha's soul.

"Sir, I don't usually make it a habit to talk to strangers," she said dryly, stubbornly tilting her chin.

She gave him an icy half glance. "Especially those who obviously are scoundrels."

His eyebrows forked and another chuckle surfaced from between his lips. "Scoundrel?" he said. "Hmm. Interesting."

"Yes. Scoundrel," she reaffirmed, setting her lips in a straight line.

"Even scoundrels have names," he teased. He mocked a half bow at the waist. "Troy Gilbert at your service, ma'am."

"I do not ask for your service," she said icily, casting him another half glance. "But I do ask that you leave me be. I'm anxious to watch Springfield come into view."

"Oh? So your destination is also Springfield?" he asked, drumming the fingers of his right hand nervously on his leg.

"I didn't say that," she angrily snapped, somehow afraid for him to know. Too much about him disturbed her, and most centering about her heart. She couldn't be foolish enough to let her feelings for a stranger cause her to do crazy things. No. She couldn't let him know anything about her. In these times, who could even be trusted?

"No need to say," he said, shrugging. "I soon will see for myself. In a matter of minutes, we shall arrive in Springfield."

"Oh!" she said, then averted her eyes away from him. Leaning her chin in her hand as her elbow rested on an armrest, she watched houses multiply at the side of the road. Her heart was beating erratically, and she had to make herself believe it was due to her anxiety in seeing her grandparents and not Troy Gilbert whose eyes were surely still upon her.

Casting him a quick glance, she was disappointed when she discovered that he was now preoccupied by something besides her. She straightened herself on the seat and looked more squarely at him, catching his deep frown as he studied a half-unfolded piece of paper. Watching even further she saw him slip a gold watch from his waistcoat pocket to study the time. Then her face flushed scarlet when he looked quickly toward her and caught her staring at him. With a jerk of her head, she once more looked out the window, almost swallowed whole now from her thunderous heartbeats.

The stagecoach came to a sudden halt. Samantha lifted her coat up into her arms and clung to her purse, ready for the door to be thrown back. The sooner she could alight the coach, the sooner she would be able to be her old self again. How had she let a man disturb her in such a strange way? And hadn't she succeeded at only making a fool of herself?

The door at her side quickly opened. Samantha started to rise from her seat but was stopped when Troy Gilbert brusquely shoved his way out, ahead of everyone else, without even first offering Samantha a hand as a gentleman was expected to do.

"My word!" Samantha gasped, paling. "I was right to call him—a—scoundrel."

Still stunned, she watched until his hurrying figure got lost from her view. Then fighting the encumbrance of her skirts, she stepped from the coach herself, looking anxiously for her grandparents' buggy. But there was no denying that she hoped, somehow, to see Troy Gilbert again. Though a scoundrel, he was a handsome one!

## Chapter Three

Standing alone with her trunk on the ground beside her, Samantha slipped back into her coat as she waited the arrival of her grandparents. Though the sun was warm on her face, there was a chill in the air as the wind whipped across a barren, flat meadow on her left.

On her right, the outskirts of the city of Springfield stretched out away from the depot which was shared both by train and stagecoach. There was a flurry of activity of people loading and unloading from a train that had just arrived, intermingled with shipping crates being taken from a boxcar of the train.

Stretching her neck, Samantha looked toward the road, looking for her grandparents' horse and buggy. And when she saw it in the distance, her heart swelled with joy.

Breathing excitedly she began to run toward the road, pushing her way through the throng of people. Then her attention was drawn to the side of the brick depot building which she, until now, hadn't been in a position to see.

"Good grief," she whispered, stopping to see what the commotion was all about. She inched her way further into the crowd of people standing in a wide circle, then stopped, stunned, when she saw two men scuffling. Her eyes widened when she found that one of these two men happened to be Troy Gilbert, the man from the stagecoach!

Covering her mouth with a hand she watched as the two men exchanged angry blows, and she let out a soft cry when she saw a trickle of blood surface at the corner of Troy's mouth. Something compelled her to rush forward with thoughts to help him. And as she broke through the circle of cheering onlookers with her purse raised, ready to add her own blows to the fight, in defense of Troy, several other men joined the fight, causing her to stop suddenly.

"Marion Yarborough," Samantha gasped, recognizing one of the men. There was no mistaking this man's unpleasant features with his shifty eyes and everlasting, annoying half smile that was caused by a scar which drew his upper lip into a constant, tight curve upward at the right corner.

A loathing so intense it gave her a sick feeling at the pit of her stomach soared through Samantha when she remembered this man who had tried everything in his power to torment her grandfather into selling his farm and few acres of land which sat adjacent with his. Her grandfather had stubbornly refused to sell, yet Marion Yarborough had seemed to strike fear into her grandparents' hearts for other reasons which had not been disclosed to Samantha. But surely it had only been his ruthlessness that had been the threat. In having such a neighbor, no one would ever know what to expect next.

Samantha's heart skipped a beat when the sky blue of Troy's eyes captured her standing there. For an instant she was held prisoner by his intense stare, then was jarred aware when he broke suddenly free of his assailants and rushed toward her. With mouth open she watched his right hand move in a flash to his waistcoat pocket to take a folded paper from it and, just as quickly, thrust it into her hand as he hurriedly brushed on past her.

Turning on a heel, confused, she watched him disappear around the corner of the depot, then she let her gaze move slowly down, to where her fingers were clasped tightly to the paper that he had given her.

With a racing pulse, she only momentarily looked toward her hand, full of wonder, then opened her purse and dropped the paper inside. For some reason, Troy Gilbert had given her something of importance to keep in trust for him, and she knew that he didn't want the men to notice. Perhaps this paper was even the cause for the fight.

The thought of having something of such a mysterious importance excited, yet frightened Samantha. And how did this Troy Gilbert plan to get it back from her? Why, he didn't even know her name.

Remembering her grandparents, Samantha tried to shake thoughts of Troy from her mind, but she couldn't. She was anxious to unfold the paper and see what it was that was worth fighting over. And it did appear to be the same paper that Troy had become preoccupied with on the last leg of their journey.

Recalling his rude behavior when arriving at the depot, Samantha now wondered why she had felt the need to defend such a rogue who had not been born with manners required of a gentleman!

But then all she had to do was envision him and his handsomeness and the command of his blue eyes, and she knew well enough why she would always be drawn to him.

Rushing on ahead, she found her grandfather searching for her through the crowd. He was not a hard one to see as he towered above everyone else. It had always been said that his physical makeup made him appear to be the father of Craig Johnston instead of his petite daughter Grace. Even their rugged personalities matched.

But it was the property ownership—the wealth factor—that separated these two men. One was rich. One was poor. But Samantha loved them both, sometimes finding it hard to place her true loyalties, though she had always known that a father should take precedence in these particular matters of the heart.

Waving her hand frantically, Samantha began shouting her grandfather's name. "Grandpapa! Over here!" she yelled, shoving her way on toward him.

When she came into his full view her smile broadened as her gaze swept over his familiar attire of bulky coveralls snapped over a faded denim shirt which covered a wide expanse of chest and muscled shoulders.

Though he was not a man who made it his habit to read, his eyes had weakened anyway, and he wore gold-framed spectacles with thick lenses strangely magnifying his fading blue eyes. His hair was short-cropped and was of a salt and pepper texture, still thick, though his age now was nearing a hardy sixty-five.

Fine wrinkles crisscrossed his face, and his lips were a slight shade of purple due to his battles with an ailing heart.

But his smile brightened everything it touched, and Samantha felt a pure pleasure as she flew toward his eager, outstretched arms.

"Oh, Grandpapa," she said, consumed by muscular arms as she worked herself into her grandfather's embrace. "It's been such a long winter. I'm so glad to be here and so soon this year."

Samantha inhaled the familiar fragrance of her grandfather, recognizing the smell of straw, wind, and tobacco. She gave him a final hug, then stepped back away from him, smiling coyly.

"I bet you were surprised to receive the wire from Father of my arrival," she said, laughing softly.

"Surprised ain't the proper word to use," he said in a low growl of a voice, fitting his thumbs to hang over the bib of his coveralls. "I'd have expected more caution from your pa. These are troubled times, Samantha. It ain't safe for a girl your age to be travelin' alone."

Samantha sighed. "*Lady*, Grandpapa," she corrected. "I'm no longer just a girl. I'm a lady."

He touched a finger to his glasses, adjusting them, then gave her a quick once-over. "Yep, maybe you are at that," he chuckled. "And a fine lookin' lady at that. If'n not for your bein' taller and with those green eyes like a cat, I'd say you could pass as your ma's young'un all right."

Color rose to Samantha's cheeks. Her lashes lowered. "Grandpapa, what a thing to say," she said laughing. Then her gaze moved in the direction of the road. "Did Grandmama come with you? I'm so anxious to see her."

"No. She stayed at home," he said, lighting a cigar and tossing a burned match aside. "She's preparin' supper. We'd best get a move on or she'll be harpin' at us even up into next week for bein' late."

His body trembled as a deep laugh rumbled through him, always jolly and enjoying his own jokes. Then he looked over his shoulder. "Where's your travel paraphernalia?"

"Over there." Samantha nodded. She took one of his massive, quite callused hands in hers. "Come on. I'll take you to it."

"Brought your whole wardrobe, eh?" He laughed. "Never know why you bother. All's you ever wear while you're on the farm is jeans. Should'a been a boy, Samantha. Should'a been a boy."

"Yes, guess so." She shrugged. "Perhaps things would have been easier for all concerned had I been."

"Didn't say I was wishin' on you bein' a boy, Samantha," her grandfather corrected. "It was just a play on words. I like the way you are, bein' so pretty and all."

Samantha tensed when she caught a glimpse of Marion Yarborough out of the corner of her eye. He was leaning against the depot in his fancy waistcoat, breeches, and top hat, watching her, as though measuring her for future pickings. He had never been one to pursue her as a man does a woman since he was her grandfather's age, so she had to wonder if he had seen Troy pass her the paper.

"The sonofabitch," her grandfather said beneath his breath, tossing his half-smoked cigar over his right shoulder. "Standin' there as though he owns the place. I hate that bastard. Sure wish he wasn't too old to go to war if the North and South do clash in battle. I'd like to see his fancy breeches get blown clean off'n him."

Samantha's eyebrows rose. "Are you speaking of Marion Yarborough?" she asked, leaning closer to her grandfather.

"No one else riles me so much," he growled. "He ain't

nothin' but trouble, that one. If'n there is a war you can sure as hell 'spect that one to cause more trouble stayin' around here than bein' on a battlefield. I don't trust him. Not an inch."

"Grandpapa, why do you hate him so much?" Samantha asked, once more giving Marion a sour look. "Up to today you've never said much about him to me one way or the other."

"That's because your grandmaw was always present when discussin' the man," he said.

"Why do you hate him, Grandpapa?" she persisted.

He gave her a guarded look. "It's not somethin' to be discussed between us," he said dryly. "One day you'll know. But now ain't the right time, Samantha."

Samantha gave him a silent, quizzical look. Up to now she had always thought her grandfather feared Marion Yarborough. But now she suspected it was feelings that ran much deeper. He hated the man, and hate was stronger than fear. She had always wondered why her grandfather had held onto his property when the money offered him for it by Marion Yarborough had been triple what it was worth. Her grandfather could have sold out at any time and had the money to buy a bigger and better farm somewhere else.

Now Samantha suspected it was more complicated. And this feeling of hate had stemmed from the times when her grandfather and grandmother had treated the topic of Marion Yarborough as taboo.

Yes. For some reason, her grandfather hated Marion Yarborough, and she wondered if she would ever truly know the reasons why.

She tagged along beside her grandfather as he loaded her trunk onto his simple buggy and then proudly sat beside him as he clucked to the gray mare and headed out, away from the city.

Feeling peaceful, Samantha watched the countryside pass beside her. Illinois. She was finally there. Melvin and Dorothy June Ainsworth. She was finally going to be a part of their lives again, if even for a short while. Surely there were no other grandparents on earth like them. Simple, loving folk. That was the best way to describe them, and she would fully absorb this time with them to store in her storage house of memories inside her brain, for eternity.

Her gaze moved to her purse as she remembered the paper and her anxiety to view it. Soon. She would see it soon. In the privacy of her bedroom at her grandparents' house.

"You sure missed a show the other day at the depot," her grandfather said, shouting over his left shoulder, into the wind.

"Show? What sort of show?" Samantha asked, fluffing the skirt of her coat around her ankles. The buggy was now traveling along a dirt road where on either side was edged by rich, fertile, coal black, freshly plowed farmland. The scent rose sharply from the black soil as the wind whipped across the land, causing Samantha's nose to curl.

"Lincoln," her grandfather said, giving her a half glance. "Honest Abe. If you'd arrived a few days earlier in the month you could'a had the opportunity of seein' Lincoln standin', at the rear of a train, sayin' farewell to everyone in Springfield as he was leavin' for Washington, to be inaugurated."

"You saw him, Grandpapa?"

"Sure did. Wouldn't have missed him. He's common

51

folk like me, you know.''

''Yes, I know,'' Samantha murmured, feeling guilty, remembering what her father was planning against Lincoln and the people of the North. But she couldn't let the guilt in her knowledge of this ruin her homecoming to Illinois. It was foolish. In no way was she responsible for her father's actions.

''He spoke some fancy words that day, Samantha,'' her grandfather said, giving the reins a slap against the back of the mare. ''He said somethin' to the effect of havin' lived here in Springfield for a quarter of a century and had passed from a young to an old man. He talked of his children being born and of the one that was buried here.''

''Sad, the loss of his one son,'' Samantha sighed.

''Sad, the loss of any child,'' her grandfather grumbled. ''Though my Grace has been dead for ten long years now, I miss her very much.''

''Malaria. She couldn't hold up against it,'' Samantha said, yet remembered that it was more than the malaria that had killed her mother. She had given up on life way before that.

''If she hadn't been livin' down by them Carolina swamps with your pa, she'd never come down sick with malaria,'' her grandfather growled. ''I sometimes regret that she was in New York the same time your pa was those many years ago. She'd been better off marryin' a farm boy from Illinois than an aristocrat from the South.''

Samantha gave her grandfather a guarded glance. ''You say Mother had been in New York visiting Uncle Terence?'' she quizzed, never before able to draw answers from him as easily as today. She would take full advantage of it, for just around a bend in the road they would arrive at the farmhouse.

Her grandfather cleared his throat nervously and kneaded his chin with his left hand. There was a trace of worry in the light of his eyes. "Yep. She went to visit my brother Terence and his wife for a spell that one year," he said. "She—uh—needed the change, Samantha. Yep, she needed the change."

"But why?" she persisted. "Wasn't she happy on the farm? Before Uncle Terence's and Aunt Phoebe's recent deaths at sea, they lived the life of the affluent. Uncle Terence had been quite successful in his shipping ventures. Did Mother want to experience that sort of life? Is that why she went and stayed the year there?"

"It wasn't a full year," her grandfather said blandly. "Eight months to be more exact."

"But you still haven't explained why, Grandpapa."

He gave her a dark frown. "Damn it, girl," he growled. "I've already said too much." He ran his fingers through his hair. "God, I don't know what got into me. Seems you've acquired a knack at keepin' a person talkin'."

Samantha's eyes lowered. "I'm sorry, Grandpapa," she murmured. "I didn't mean to—"

"Now don't you start apologizin' for somethin' that ain't your fault," he interrupted. He laughed throatily. "It's just that your ol' grandpaw had best be on guard this summer. You've a way about you, Samantha. A winnin' way. The young men in and about Springfield better watch out. You'll send their heads and hearts to spinnin' for sure."

"Grandpapa." Samantha giggled, shaking her hair to fall from her shoulders and down her back.

Then her face lost its smile. "Grandpapa, do you truly believe there will be a civil war because of

53

Lincoln?" she softly tested.

"If there's a war, Lincoln ain't the cause," he said. He gave her a sidelong glance. "It's people like your pa who'll be the cause of a war. Him and his funny ideas can't stand for no good for the country. And haven't you heard the rumors, Samantha?"

"What rumors?" she asked, grabbing hold of the seat as a buggy wheel fell into a pothole in the road.

"Of an assassination plot to stop Lincoln before he can become the sixteenth president of the United States," her grandfather said dryly.

"No," Samantha gasped. But her shock of the news was quickly cast aside when she caught sight of her grandparents' farmhouse ahead. Her heart began to thunder against her ribs, absorbing the setting of the simple white-framed house with tall elm and maple trees completely shading it. On its wide front porch, Samantha saw her grandmother waving to her. And then she saw another figure on the porch.

"Julia?" she whispered. "Julia Ainsworth?"

She turned her eyes to her grandfather. "Why is my cousin Julia there with Grandmama?" she cautiously asked. Julia was one who Samantha could do without, and she certainly didn't need Julia around to spoil her homecoming! Having been the only child of Terence and Phoebe Ainsworth, Julia was spoiled. Samantha had always found this to be very annoying when forced to be in Julia's company for any length of time.

"I guess your grandmaw hasn't taken the time to write you of the latest developments on our farm," her grandfather said dryly.

"What developments, Grandpapa?" she asked, now fearing to hear the answer if it had anything to do with

Julia's being there!

"Since Terence and Phoebe's death, Julia has been left alone in the world."

"But she was to go and live with Uncle Timothy and Aunt Marge in Seattle."

"It didn't work out."

"It—didn't?"

"No. And since it didn't, it was suggested she'd be better off on the farm with your grandma and me."

Samantha's insides splashed cold. "No," she whispered. "She isn't, is she?"

"She's moved in bag and baggage," her grandfather said. "Seems she was a bit wild for your Aunt Marge to handle. Out on our farm she won't get much opportunity to show her wild ways. There ain't no way for her to run wild."

"But to live with you, forever?" Samantha asked shallowly.

"When she turns twenty-five, she can have her inheritance. That's what was wrote in the will. But 'til then, she's at the mercy of those who're kind enough to look after her."

"Why twenty-five, Grandpapa?"

"I guess Timothy didn't like thinkin' on her squanderin' her money at her younger age of twenty." He shrugged. "At twenty-five, she'll probably be married, and her husband can take charge of the dollars and how they're spent. Yep, it was when she turned twenty when he wrote that will."

"I can't believe it," Samantha said softly, already feeling second in her grandparents' heart. She didn't want to be jealous. She didn't.

## Chapter Four

Samantha alighted the buggy, ignoring Julia's presence on the porch. It was Samantha's grandmother who drew her most devoted attention. Her heart pounded in anticipation of being warmly hugged by her grandmother's fleshy, loving arms. At Johnston Oaks that sort of attention was, indeed, lacking!

Picking up speed in her steps, Samantha traveled the stone path to the porch. She lifted the tail of the skirt of her dress and froth of petticoats above her ankles and ran up the steps, almost falling into her grandmother's outstretched arms.

Having to lean over so that her grandmother could fully embrace her from her shorter, stocky height, Samantha returned her grandmother's embrace. "Grandmama, it seems an eternity since I was last here," she said, her nose picking up the clean, fresh smell of her grandmother's starched, plain cotton dress and the pleasant, tantalizing aroma of potatoes frying on the stove in the kitchen. Ah, it was pure heaven to be with Dorothy June and Melvin Ainsworth again!

Yet out of the corner of her eye, Samantha caught the half smile curling cousin Julia's lips upward in a smug, sure smile.

Tiny, to the point of almost being frail, Julia seemed to need to be pampered. And her frail petiteness seemed to enhance her loveliness, though her pale white shoulders were much too thin in her low-cut silk dress which clung to her tiny bosom and extremely thin waist.

But her eyes of golden brown which were shadowed by long, thick lashes, and her high cheekbones rouged with a soft pink color, were the cause of many a man's downfall in New York, as gossip told it. Her hair was swept back in long, gold curls and tied with a green satin bow to match the green of her dress, and minute curls framed her delicate face.

Yes, Samantha scoffed to herself. A face of innocence.

But Samantha knew too well that that innocence was, indeed, faked, as was Samantha's smile that she now returned to her spoiled cousin.

"After we received word from your pa that you'd be arrivin', I've not had a restful moment since," Dorothy June said, easing out of Samantha's arms. She tested Samantha's face by running her hands along each cheek, her blue eyes studying Samantha as though she were searching for signs of battle scars from hardships of the long journey.

"Are you all right?" Dorothy June asked. "There's such unrest in the country. You could've been caught in the crossfire of crazed men who don't know better than to think that war is already declared."

Samantha reached and took her grandmother's hands in hers and squeezed their pudginess affectionately, wincing when feeling the hardened calluses that covered each palm. "I'm fine, Grandmama," she reassured. "Don't you see? I'm fine. Not one hair on my head was disturbed by friend or foe."

Then Samantha's eyes took on a faraway dreaminess as she allowed her mind to wander to Troy Gilbert, and she remembered that he had been her only threat—a threat to her heart.

The weight of Samantha's purse tucked beneath her arm was a reminder that not only a gun was hidden inside the purse, but also the mysterious note. Was there a danger in having it in her possession? Oh, how she itched to see it! But she couldn't. Not until she was fully alone. Later. While alone in her bedroom. Then she could become drawn not only into the mystique of the note and what it disclosed to her, but also to the man whose handsome features could materialize so hauntingly at the mere command of her mind's eye.

"Ha! She confesses to being all right yet she drifts in and out of conversation with the sudden look of a school girl in love," Julia said with a crisp, haughty jerk to her head. "Samantha, my dear cousin, where does your mind take you? Only a man can cause such stars in one's eyes."

Julia's sarcasm snapped Samantha out of her moment of reverie. She swung away from her grandmother and went to Julia, proud that Julia was not as tall as she. Samantha was pleased to be able to look down at Julia while talking to her.

"And, cousin Julia, you would be the one to know about anything that has to do with men, wouldn't you?" Samantha said dryly. "How is it that you could tear yourself away from your many beaux in New York?"

"Are you saying that I will not be as fortunate in Springfield?" Julia challenged. "From what I gather, soon there may even be a lot of men in uniform frequenting the streets of Springfield. Should there be war—"

"Girls, *girls,*" Dorothy June scolded. "Shame be upon you both. Let us not hear any more talk of men or war."

Samantha felt a blush suffuse her cheeks. She glanced over at her grandmother, seeing her soft, kind face which showed the telltale signs of having once been beautiful herself and surely the cause of many a man's heart to flutter. But fresh butter churned each day on the farm, and the love of biscuits and milk gravy for breakfast each morning had not only added weight to her face, but also years. Her hair showed no signs of ever having been anything but gray in its coarseness now as it was circled in a tight bun atop her head. And her attire? Always the same. A plain cotton dress of a faded flower design on a white background, over which was always worn an apron. Her eyes were blue, still crisp in color, possibly even snappish in her youth, clearly proving that Dorothy June had been of a spirited nature.

"I'm sorry, Grandmama," Samantha quickly apologized. "I've just arrived and I've upset you." She wanted to say that it was only because of Julia, but that would sound not only childish, but spiteful. Samantha couldn't let jealousy harm the special relationship already formed with her grandparents. Julia's presence would have to be tolerated. Or was it the other way around? In truth, wasn't Samantha, in a sense, the intruder? Julia now made her fulltime residence there while Samantha was only an occasional visitor.

Melvin stepped up on the porch after having seen to the securing of the horse and buggy. "Well? Have my girls said their hellos?" he said, his eyes twinkling as he looked from one to the other. "What say we go in and have supper? I do smell taters cookin' on the stove, don't I?"

He winked at Dorothy June. "Maybe there's even apple pie for dessert?" He chuckled. "Grandma couldn't resist makin' our Samantha's favorite pie, could she?"

"Apple pie?" Samantha sighed. "Oh, Grandmama, you do know me well, don't you? No one makes apple pie like you. I do love it so." She gave Julia a smug look, enjoying being the center of attention again. Then she felt ashamed, remembering Julia's reason for even being here. It was only because of the loss of her parents. Samantha had to show more heart, at least for the next several weeks while sympathies were in order.

Sweeping her purse from beneath her arm, Samantha went on inside a simple house. The living room was crowded with odds and ends of pieces of overstuffed chairs and homemade tables. Hand-sewn and fancy-embroidered doilies weren't only on the tables beneath kerosene lamps, but also on the arms of the chairs.

A fire burned cozily in a stone fireplace near a sofa with a blanket spread across it to hide its faded shabbiness. The walls were a display of more embroidered work, framed needlecraft of colorful flower arrangements and landscapes of mountains and prairies.

Samantha still clung to her purse, the anxiety to study the note which lay protectively inside it almost taking precedence over any thought of satisfying her hunger. But her grandfather was already headed for the kitchen.

"What's holdin' you girls up?" He chuckled, giving Samantha, then Julia, a look over his shoulder as he paused at the kitchen door. "You can gossip after supper while I'm out seein' to securin' things 'fore night sets in."

Shafts of red blossomed through the sheer curtains at the windows, the first full night at her grandparents' house, a usual time for Samantha to be filled with happiness. Morning would follow night and with it the pleasant warble of the robins and the crowing of the rooster, reminders of just where she was. During the following weeks she would try to feel free, away from the problems in being the mistress of Johnston Oaks Plantation, a title she had acquired upon the death of her mother.

But somehow her freedom had been stifled with the presence of Julia.

"Melvin!" Dorothy June scolded, smoothing her apron down against her dress. "Give Samantha time to get her breath. She only just arrived. I'm sure she has a need to make herself more comfortable before eating."

"Yes," Samantha said anxiously, grasping at this chance to be excused to her room, to read the note. "I would love to change into my jeans."

Julia's eyes rolled. She sighed disgustedly. "Jeans? Haven't you grown out of such nonsense, Samantha? Ladies only wear dresses."

"No one could ever mistake Samantha for bein' anything but a lady," Melvin said and chuckled, now facing them as he leaned against the door frame. "Julia, seems your cousin could be competition should a man try to pursue you here on the farm." His faded blue eyes appraised Samantha, looking her slowly up and down.

Julia thrust her chin haughtily into the air and, brushing on past Melvin, disappeared into the kitchen.

"Seems I got her dander up a mite," Melvin said, idly

scratching his brow.

"Melvin, shame on you," Dorothy June scolded, rushing after Julia. "Do you forget how fragile Julia is? Not only in body but in spirit. Please refrain from teasing. She hasn't yet gotten over her loss. You see to Samantha's comforts. I'll see to Julia's."

Samantha and Melvin were left alone. Melvin went to Samantha and placed a solid arm about her waist and began ushering her out of the room and into a narrow, dimly lighted hallway which led to the bedrooms.

"I don't care what your grandma says," he scoffed. "I don't see Julia as all *that* frail. Seems your grandma has forgotten why we've been appointed the ones to look after her. Julia is a wild one. Out here on the farm, away from the gents, we hope to tame her a mite."

Samantha's insides rolled when her grandfather guided her on past the door which, always before, had led into her assigned bedroom, a room which had been hers since her first summer on the farm. She looked at him in wonder as he stepped up to a closed door at the far end of the hall. It had always been a storage room since it was too small to use as a bedroom.

Samantha tensed as her grandfather swung the door open and stepped aside, allowing her to enter as he mutely watched. Inching her way between the bed and door, she placed her purse on the small bed with its white enamel-painted iron bedsteads and tried to accept what she now knew must be her room.

Once more jealousy tormented her insides, and she hated herself for such an evil emotion. Yet, hadn't Julia taken everything that once was hers? Samantha's grandmother's devotions seemed to be among those stolen properties.

"Your grandma fixed this room up just special for you," Melvin said, nervously pushing his glasses back on his nose. "We even managed to find room to store all the junk that used to be in here somewhere else. Do you like it, Samantha? We got the bed and table at bargain prices from a family who was movin' out of state."

He paused, now kneading his chin nervously. "I guess you understand that Julia needed the larger room, since she is now livin' fulltime with us," he said, apology thick in his words.

"Yes. I understand," Samantha said, almost choking on the words. She forced a smile. "It's lovely. The room still smells of new wallpaper, such a fresh, nice smell."

She looked slowly about her, taking in her surroundings. The room was so small there was only space enough to walk on the one side of the bed which stretched out to the door. There was just barely enough room to store her trunk at the foot of the bed. But where would she even hang her clothes? There was no wardrobe! The bed and nightstand were the only furnishings.

A lone window curtained by white, crisply starched priscilla curtains lay adjacent to the one side of the bed, displaying a full view of the farm. The walls had been freshly papered in designs of tiny yellow rosebuds, and a bedspread on the bed matched with an embroidered backdrop of the same, beautiful design.

Yes, Samantha knew that all this had been done to cushion the shock of having lost her bedroom to another. She tried to understand her loss, but it was hard. She didn't like to know that she had suddenly taken second place in her grandparents' hearts.

Spying her purse on the bed, Samantha let what lay inside it ease her feelings of dejection. The note given her by the handsome, mysterious Troy Gilbert was something that wouldn't have to be shared with Julia! It would be shared with no one. It was her very own secret!

"I'll go fetch your trunk," Melvin said, already out in the hall, walking away from Samantha. "Can't change into jeans without first havin' your trunk to get into."

Samantha silently nodded, then picked up her purse and opened it, to peer downward at the note. Patience was not one of her strongest traits but practice it now, she must. Only after her trunk was secured and she could be left alone to change into her jeans could she dare to chance looking in the strictest of privacy at what was fast becoming her prized possession.

Her heart raced with anticipation. She could feel her cheeks grow hot. Surely she had been chosen from the crowd of people at the depot to be the recipient of this mysterious piece of paper because of the attraction that Troy Gilbert had felt for her while they were passengers on the stagecoach.

Surely he couldn't have placed her in danger by choosing her. Surely he wouldn't. Yet, the remembrance of the vicious attacks upon his person caused Samantha's hair to rise at the nape of her neck. Could she even expect to be sought by these men? Was this note the true cause of the men's wrath?

"Here we are," Melvin said suddenly from behind Samantha, his heavy footsteps and rumble of voice causing Samantha to jump with alarm.

Turning on a heel, she smiled awkwardly up at her grandfather as he dropped the trunk on the bare oak flooring at the foot of the bed. She was grateful that he hadn't noticed her alarm as his presence drew her abruptly from thoughts of intrigue and danger. She clicked her purse shut and placed it back on the bed as Melvin reached to pat her fondly on an arm.

"Supper's waitin'," he said, an eyebrow lifting when he saw a mischievous glint in Samantha's eyes. Shrugging, never able to figure out women and what made them tick, he added, "Change your clothes, then hurry on into the kitchen. Taters and biscuits lose their taste when allowed to grow cold."

"I'll change faster than you can blink an eye," Samantha teased, leaning up to kiss her grandfather affectionately on the cheek.

His solid arms gathered about her waist and drew her next to him. His eyelids were heavy when he looked down at her. "Glad you're here, hon?" he asked thickly.

"You know that I am, Grandpapa," Samantha murmured, seeing her reflection in the thick lense of his glasses, absorbing this rare moment with her grandfather, since he had never been much of one to show affection by way of touching.

"You'll get used to Julia," he said, apology edging the tone of his voice. "It just can't be helped—her bein' here." Then he laughed. "She's put a few sparks in the air since arrivin'," he said. "Kind of good for your grandma and me. Somehow before Julia came, our days ran into nights, without noticin' which was which. That's what old age does for a body, I guess."

Samantha now knew that her yearly trips would no longer be necessary to fill the gap in her grandparents' lives. This saddened her, but she wasn't selfish enough not to be happy that her grandparents were being helped by Julia's sudden presence in their lives.

"Just don't you worry one more minute about how I feel about anything," she said, snuggling against her grandfather's massive chest. "You and Grandmama are all that matters. What's best for you is what makes me happy."

A growl of hunger rising from inside Melvin's stomach caused Samantha to giggle. She broke away from her grandfather and led him to the door.

"Grandpapa, you'd best go on and fill your plate with vittles or you're liable to find yourself serenading the whole countryside with growls from your empty stomach," she teased. "I won't be long. Honest."

Chuckling, Melvin left the room. Samantha's heart began to thump wildly inside her as she closed the door and momentarily leaned against it, breathing hard as she looked at the purse on the bed. At last! She could see just what the value of this note was.

With a bizarre weakness in her knees she approached the bed and once more opened her purse. Visions of Troy's handsomeness danced before her eyes as she, with trembling fingers, removed the folded slip of paper from her purse. Almost breathless from excitement she unfolded the note and placed it before her eyes.

"A *map?*" she whispered, her eyebrows forking. Then her gaze captured what appeared to be some sort of code written above the map. "And *code?* What on earth could it mean?"

She smoothed the paper out on the bed, then lighted the kerosene lamp on the nightstand beside the bed. Moving the lamp so that its light could make her study of the map easier, she picked out the familiar coastline of the southern states. Then once more she wondered about the sprinkling of code.

"Why?" she whispered, kneading the soft curve of her chin. "Why would this be in Troy's possession? Why did

66

he feel the need to part with it in such a way? The men! Surely this is why they attacked Troy! It surely is much more important than I had ever dreamed imaginable!"

Feeling the wide eye of the window hovering so close beside the bed, Samantha felt the need to grab the map and place it behind her back.

"I must hide it," she harshly whispered. "No one must know that I have it. No one, but Troy."

Still holding the map behind her, Samantha crept to the window and lowered the shade, sighing heavily with relief from the secured privacy.

Then her eyes darted about the room, and she wondered where she could hide the map. It had to be someplace where only she would know to look.

Remembering her moments as a child when she had played in this room when it had been used as only storage space, her gaze lowered where an oval braided rug lay so neatly spread over the oak floor beside the bed. If she was calculating right, the loose board was there, beneath the rug. And would the fruit jar still be there? There had been many a time when she had hidden a prized possession there beneath that board, in her very own fruit jar taken from her grandmother's fruit cellar.

But surely the fruit jar had been removed and the board repaired long ago. Yet, she could remember her sore fingertips after struggling to remove the board each time, and she knew that, though it wasn't one that hadn't been properly nailed down, it still had fallen snugly in place between the others.

So perhaps neither of her grandparents had discovered the lack of nails in the board. Perhaps it still lay there, left untouched.

Laying the map on the floor beside her, Samantha went

to her knees and scooted the rug aside, searching with her eyes which board had amused her as a child.

Smiling, she found it, then placed her fingers at the one end where no nails were there to impede her efforts.

"Ouch!" she softly cried as a splinter stabbed a fingertip.

But not to be dissuaded by even that, she once more began working with the board, prying it up with her fingertips, until she finally succeeded at getting a corner of it up.

With a lunge, she slipped her full hand beneath it and eased it on up high enough to see beneath it. The sour smell of damp earth curled up into her nose, and then she caught the shine of the fruit jar which lay only inches away on the earthen floor.

"Good Lord," she gasped. "It *is* still there. After all these years!"

And feeling a child again, she reached and confiscated the jar from its hiding place, brushing a film of dust away from it as she held it out before her. "Oh, jar, what secrets we have shared." She softly laughed. "Well, once more I shall introduce you to a secret of mine, but never before has intrigue been a part of our sharing."

Samantha unscrewed the lid which was rusty from neglect and age and slipped the folded map inside the glass walls of the jar. "Who knows what sort of mystery shall be unraveled by my possessing such a map?" she whispered, returning the lid to the jar and screwing it in place.

She gave the jar a light kiss. "Protect it well, jar. Perhaps this map will be cause for me to meet Troy Gilbert again. Surely he will seek me out, to claim what is his."

The mystery surrounding Troy made him even more attractive to her. Now that Julia was taking her place in her grandmother's heart, Samantha needed something else while in Illinois to busy herself and her idle hours and days.

She hungered for adventure. She felt that if she could get to know Troy she might even, perhaps, find more adventure than even she bargained for.

Smiling, she replaced the board, scooted the rug back in place, then went and removed her jeans from her trunk. She was wondering how long it would take Troy to find her, for surely he would. The map, the code, had to stand for something valuable. Perhaps it could even mean life or death for some poor unsuspecting soul. Perhaps this person could even be Troy—or even—herself!

## Chapter Five

The house smelled heavily of a heady sweetness as cakes and pies had been baked throughout the day. Lincoln had been inaugurated, and it seemed that the whole city of Springfield and the outlying farming community was celebrating.

Samantha's grandparents were playing a lusty role in this celebration. They were getting ready for their very own barn dance to be held this night, on their farm.

Much food had been prepared. The food brought by neighbors would be added to their own, and a feast would be shared by all.

The sky was darkening, the time near for all festivities to begin. Samantha had laid her jeans aside and had opted to wear her frilliest dress with the addition of many layers of lacy petticoats beneath it, to hold the dress way out from her ankles.

Primping at the mirror in what had at one time been her room, she worked curls around her fingers, then pushed them back with a slide, to hang in flames of red down her slender, graceful back. Then with her fingers she brushed minute curls into place across her brow and above her ears.

"No jeans tonight, I see," Julia tormented from across the room as she fastened her own floor-length dress from behind, the bodice so tight and revealing not much of her bosom was left to the imagination. "I would have thought you would offer yourself dressed in jeans and plaid shirt as a male dance partner to the women," Julia continued to chide.

"Don't you wish," Samantha snapped back at her. "You're afraid that you just might have competition this night. Now wouldn't your ego be deflated a mite should the menfolk chose me over you? Or will you flirt and make such a display of yourself that the men won't even get that first chance to see that there are other women besides yourself at the dance?"

Samantha didn't like bantering with her cousin, but Julia just wouldn't let her alone. Oh, the bother of it all! But surely in time Julia would tire of her badgerings and go on her way, to interest herself in things other than her cousin. Hopefully, a man would make himself available to Julia. Ah, now wouldn't that be the answer, though it was not the wish of Melvin and Dorothy June Ainsworth that this should happen. They had hoped to tame Julia, not give her cause to become even more wild than she already was!

"A square dance," Julia groaned. "Imagine! Even in the barn! If my friends in New York would see me participate in such nonsense, they wouldn't believe it."

"No one's forcing you to attend the dance, Julia."

"I must. I am so bored. I shall do anything to ease my boredom."

"Oh, Julia, cut the act of being somebody," Samantha

71

said, swinging around, to face Julia, truly doubting if she could ever be friends with her spoiled cousin. Since Samantha's arrival it had been easier to pass time horseback riding and taking walks by the creek which snaked across her grandparents' farmland than to stay in Julia's company.

Samantha had even gone into town as often as possible on the pretense of shopping while all the time her eyes had sorted through the fancily attired men in search of a tanned face, midnight black hair, and ocean blue eyes, knowing that surely only one man possessed such a combination of heartstopping qualities.

But, alas, she had yet to see or hear from Troy Gilbert, though she had tried to make it easier for him in making herself so readily accessible by being in town, instead of staying cooped up at the farm.

Julia moved across the room with a rustle of petticoats, the silk of her fully gathered dress whipping away from her in soft flutters. Her gold hair seemed to reflect into the golden brown of her eyes as it hung long and free across her bare, pale shoulders, and her lips and cheeks were bright with color. She went to Samantha and reached her tiny tapers of fingers to the shell-shaped gold locket which hung beautifully around Samantha's neck.

"Now I would gather from this lovely piece of jewelry that you have a man friend somewhere who thinks much of you," Julia said, lifting the locket up from Samantha's chest to examine it. "Did you leave a beau behind, in the Carolinas, cousin? Are you even free to dance with gentlemen callers this night?"

Just the thought of Franklin irritated Samantha to no end, let alone Julia's snide insinuation that his gift of a locket had been meant to infer that he was Samantha's beau! She slapped Julia's hand away.

"Who is or who is not my beau is of no concern of yours, Julia," she said dryly. "And as for this locket? It was merely a gift given to me on my birthday. Nothing more, nothing less."

"By a man still," Julia persisted. "Ah, it speaks of romance, cousin. Pure unadulterated romance. Perhaps one day I shall meet the man and steal him away from you."

Samantha could hardly hold her temper intact, her rage was so kindled inside her. But she forced herself to a vow of silence, only circling her hands into tight fists at her side while Julia flipped her layer of skirt and petticoats and strolled leisurely away from her.

Then something grabbed Samantha's quick attention, something she had never noticed before, and she wondered why she even did now when Julia stood over the steady flame that burned from a kerosene-soaked wick behind the protective shield of a glass chimney. The way the shadows were being cast upward and over Julia's tiny-boned face made her, for an instant, take on the appearance of Samantha's dearly departed mother. Had it been the way Julia had looked sad for a fleeting moment when caught lost in thought after losing interest in taunting Samantha?

Or was it just her frailness? Samantha's mother had been frail, even way before the illness that had taken her life.

But then the resemblance had vanished just as quickly when Julia cast Samantha a mischievous glance, an indication that she was ready to once more deliver a raw challenge of words.

"I will wager that I will be the first asked to dance,"

Julia said, laughing scornfully.

Samantha shook her head, trying to clear herself of her momentary crazed thoughts. She placed her fingertips to her temple, wondering why she had compared her mother to this cousin who in no way matched the sweetness of Grace Johnston!

"What?" she said, still fuzzy in thought. "What did you say, Julia?"

"I said that I would wager that I'll be the first to be asked to dance," Julia repeated, cocking her head, to look up at Samantha's statuesque height, envying Samantha this special gift from God. Being short and petite had plagued Julia from the moment she had become aware of men and her need to look lovely for their attention. She had always felt inadequate and wanted to prove that she was not as frail as her appearance showed her to be.

Yet, hadn't this frailty gained her favor with many a man when they thought she was vulnerable and in need of all sorts of attention? It was in bed that she had proved her full worth. In no way had she lacked in any skills while making and being made love to. No. She wouldn't let herself envy her cousin anything!

"I will not give you the satisfaction of playing such a childish game as that," Samantha said icily. "I care not how many dance partners you have this night or whether or not you are asked before me. In fact, I plan to stay as far from you as possible. Play your little game with someone more willing."

Julia's gaze traveled appraisingly over Samantha's silk, low-cut dress. She was admiring its rust color and its lace and gathers and how it flared away from her small waist that almost matched the smallness of her own.

Samantha's gaze traveled appraisingly over Julia's

yellow silk dress, thinking the lace and gathers were quite pretty. She hated to admit to herself that her cousin was beautiful.

Her gaze rose upward, and she found Julia looking back at her in an amused sort of way. "And what may I ask are you finding so amusing?" Samantha asked, placing her hands on her hips.

"I was just looking at your dress, Samantha."

Samantha's eyes blazed with anger. To think that she had just been admiring Julia's dress. How foolish she now felt.

"And what about my dress is so amusing?" she asked hotly.

"I find nothing about it amusing," Julia said, going to the window. She drew the sheer curtain aside and looked toward the barn, seeing people arriving in droves. She dropped the curtain and glided across the floor, toward the door. "I think it gorgeous, cousin," she tossed across her shoulder.

"What?" Samantha gasped, her hands dropping from her waist. She never knew what next to expect from Julia.

Julia stopped and turned in a half swirl to face Samantha. "And mine? Do you approve of my dress?" she asked softly, lifting its skirt out in a display of silken folds.

Samantha laughed beneath her breath, realizing now that they both had at the same time been admiring each other's chosen dress for the night. "Yes. It's quite becoming to you," she said, finding it easier to put aside her ill feelings about Julia, now that Julia had softened in mood and was offering kinder words. In fact, it felt good to be kind instead of hateful.

"Cousin dear," Julia said, going to Samantha to place a

hand gently on her arm. "Shall we call a truce for this evening? I find this constant bantering so tiring."

"A truce it shall be," Samantha sighed, finding this change in her cousin refreshing, but she remained a little suspicious.

"But I still wager that I will be the first asked to dance," Julia said, whipping on away from Samantha, giggling.

Samantha's eyes widened and her mouth dropped open. But she said nothing. She only laughed as Julia took her leave from the room. With a cousin like her, one whose aim in life was to be adored by all men, Samantha knew she had to be on guard at all times, especially if Julia became acquainted with Troy Gilbert. No woman could resist his handsomeness, though a cad he surely was and probably deserved someone like Julia.

Samantha went to the mirror and took one more fast glance at herself. "Could he possibly even be here this night?" she whispered. "News of a barn dance in a community spreads like wildfire. And if he wants the map returned to him, surely he has inquired about me and knows where I am temporarily making residence."

When she saw the splash of color on her cheeks that just thinking of him could produce, she knew that even if he was a rogue, he had awakened feelings inside her that she had no idea she possessed. To kiss him surely would be heaven.

Hearing a fiddle being played from outside and laughter from those already dancing, Samantha rushed toward the door.

"Please let him be there," she softly prayed. "I must see him again. I must talk with him."

But deep down inside her where desire was formed, she

knew that she did want more from him. Much, *much* more.

The night air was warm, almost electric. Excitement was marked by smiling faces, talk, and laughter in those still arriving to the barn dance in their horse-drawn buggies and wagons.

Samantha left the house from the back door in a flutter of skirts. The moon spilled a golden path along the ground, and everywhere Samantha looked kerosene lanterns had been hung either from trees or on posts, lighting her way to the large, red barn, which stood back away from the house.

Empty horse-drawn buggies were secured along the outside walls of the barn, and streamers of light emanated from the cracks in the walls of the building whose roof seemed to now be pulsating from the rising excitement beneath it.

Fiddles and banjoes played. Children laughed, hands clapped and a caller's loud voice rang out above all this with his cries to those couples who chose to join in with square dancing.

Samantha was glad that square dancing would not be the sole style of dancing this night as she preferred the one-on-one dance with a partner, perhaps to an enchanting waltz. But she did enjoy the merriment that square dancing aroused.

From having attended square dances with her grandparents in the past, Samantha understood that the caller was the most important figure of those in attendance. The success of the dance depended on his skill in combining the calls into interesting patterns. As now,

Samantha recognized how the caller was making up rhymes on the spur of the moment as he called. She smiled when hearing him say, "Swing her high, swing her low, don't step on that pretty little toe."

Then she went on inside the barn and stood in awe at the magical setting of color and excitement. At least a hundred lanterns hung about, lighting the barn in bright shafts of gold. The dresses of the women swinging from partner to partner was a patchwork design of brilliant color.

At the far end of the open, drafty room, several men with assorted musical instruments stood on a raised platform with this evening's caller. On the loft overhead, where straw hung from its cracks and over its edges, children sat with their legs dangling, watching the adults at play.

Along a side wall long tables had been set up and on these were an assortment of mouth-watering foods, from baked hams, fried chicken, to all choices of pies and colorfully iced cakes. The heady aroma of these foods combined with the fragrance of coffee filled the barn clean to the rafters, erasing its usual smell of hay and farm seed.

Older women, one of whom was Dorothy June Ainsworth, stood in aprons, gossiping amongst themselves behind the food-laden tables, filling dishes with food for those who wished, while the younger of the women either danced or stood about chatting with other women or beaux.

Samantha inched her way on inside, among those watching, and joined in. She clasped her hands before her in an effort to suppress her anxiety as she scanned the faces of the men, hoping, still silently praying, that he would be one of those who had come to share in this celebration of Abraham Lincoln's success.

In a quadrille formation the couples in the middle of the floor saluted, swung, curtsied, and changed partners as they moved through interesting patterns, in time with the fiddle's throb of music and the throaty calls from the caller.

The caller ordered to "swing your partner," "promenade," and "form a star." But, not seeing the tanned, handsome face that Samantha was looking for, she lost interest and began moving on about the room, speaking soft hellos to those she knew and nodding to others, while her eyes continued to search. She began to feel foolish for even thinking that Troy would be there.

Catching the gold shine of Julia's hair in the crowd across the room from where Samantha now stood, Samantha began to turn and go in the opposite direction, then stopped in midstep as she saw which gentleman it was that Julia had cornered. When Samantha took a step sideways, away from a tall man who was impeding her full view, she knew that her search had, indeed, ended.

Samantha's knees grew weak and her heart skipped a beat when she discovered that she had just succeeded in finding Troy Gilbert! She could feel heat rise to her cheeks in a flush as her gaze fixed on the man who had filled her restless nights with ecstasy-filled dreams. And just as she remembered, he was uniquely handsome with his neatly coiffured midnight black hair worn to the collar of his shirt, his neat sideburns growing halfway down his cheeks, and his eyes which were set beneath finely curved brows.

His deeply tanned face surely had been sculpted by a skilled sculptor with his nose straight and long, the slope of his jaw squared and set hard, and lips sensually full.

This night he was dressed for the occasion in jeans and red plaid shirt, displaying his fine-boned frame, broad shoulders, and narrow hips.

But this night he had not found Samantha but instead her beautiful, spoiled cousin!

Frustration filled Samantha in not knowing what her next move might be. Had it been anyone but Julia, Samantha would have rushed to Troy, to let her presence be known to him.

But with Julia, there would be too many questions later and, also, Samantha didn't wish to openly challenge her cousin for the chance to be with a man—any man. This would please Julia too much to be a part of a game. And, too, what if Troy should choose to stay with the lovely Julia, his interest in her even more important than even the recovery of his map?

Then suddenly Troy looked across the room and locked his eyes on Samantha, their ocean blue now threatening to drown her as he moved away from Julia and began walking toward her.

Samantha swallowed hard, ignoring Julia's surprise as Troy moved closer and closer. She placed her trembling fingers behind her and weaved them together. Her heartbeat grew wild. She was no longer aware of anything or anyone around her except Troy, yet she wondered if she would even have the ability to speak, as hypnotized as she was by the look of his gorgeous eyes.

When he came to her side and placed a hand to her elbow, guiding her from the room and out into the moon-splashed night, she still couldn't find the ability to speak. She was in a state of euphoria.

She had never been speechless before because of a

man, and she hated this weakness in her now. Surely all that he wanted from her was the map! She couldn't fool herself in believing that it was anything more than that. And she had to remember that he was a cad.

The barn was left behind in the shadows as was the sound of the music and laughter of the crowd. Neither Samantha nor Troy had yet spoken a word. Samantha was even beginning to become frightened. Perhaps this man had plans to harm her while forcing her to tell him where the map was. Why hadn't she thought of that sooner? Now that she had, she jerked away from him and stopped to boldly face him, thinking even that she might be better off if she had in her possession her birthday gift, the pistol her father had given her.

Wanting to show that she wasn't afraid, Samantha placed her hands on her hips and straightened her shoulders as she glared up at Troy. "What do you mean by forcing me from the barn?" she hissed, not allowing herself to be swayed any longer by the command of his eyes, though beneath the light of the moon, they had taken on an almost mystical, blue glow.

Troy's lips rose into a half smile as he looked down at her. He lifted a forefinger and traced the gentle, sweet curve of her jawline. "A slight touch to your elbow is called *being forced?*" he said in a husky, deep voice. "My dear, now who are you trying to convince? Me or yourself? I believe you chose to come with me quite willingly."

Samantha slapped his finger away. But there was no denying this strange passion that he aroused inside her. There *was* danger in him realizing this. Surely if he couldn't get the map from her in one way, he would another. She had to be on her toes and be sure that she wouldn't allow him to use her in any respect!

"Don't fool yourself into believing that I came with you because I wanted to," she snapped back angrily.

He goaded her, appearing to be enjoying himself. "Then why did you?" he asked, his eyes now raking over her, seeing that, ah, yes, she was as enchanting as he had remembered her to be. Though set in a stubborn stare, her eyes were lovely in their crisp greens, shadowed by thick, long lashes.

Her face displayed the fine, gentle lines of one born of a beautiful mother, with high cheekbones colored by a flush of pink, and small nose and perfectly shaped lips just ripe for kissing.

In the low-cut dress, her bare, white shoulders led his eyes on downward, to where her breasts lay magnificently large beneath the bodice of her rust, silk dress.

His loins ached with the need to draw her into his arms and confess to her that she had affected him as no other woman ever had before. But her behavior was making it difficult, and he knew that he would have to play the game that most women needed to play so that men would not think them too forward.

"The *only* reason I left the barn with you was to make sure no disturbances were made to destroy my grandparents' social function," Samantha said, becoming unnerved under his even closer scrutiny as his eyes scorched her flesh where her cleavage lay heaving. It was quite evident that his interest did not lie in the gold locket but in the part of her anatomy that had drawn many a look from men. This not only unnerved her but annoyed her as well.

"I imagine you would have preferred that I asked you to dance. Would that have pleased you more than being here alone with me?" he teased, now peering intensely into her eyes.

"Why should I want anything of you?" she gulped, her defenses crumbling as his gaze began to melt her insides into wanting him as she had never wanted a man before. She eased her hands from her hips, and her breath caught in her throat when his warm hands reached and captured hers.

"You know why. Don't deny it," he said huskily. He released her hands and locked his arms about her waist, yanking her against him.

"I don't know what you mean," Samantha said in a voice that she didn't recognize as being hers. She began shoving at his chest.

"Release me," she said. "Release me at once."

Troy ignored her struggles and harsh words. Instead, he lowered his lips and captured hers fully in a fiery kiss while he urged her hips closer, enabling him to place his heated manhood against her.

Samantha felt a crazy spinning begin inside her head and slowly twined her arms about his neck, returning with fervor the kiss that she had so hungered for. It was everything and more than she had dreamed of. It caused a rush of desire to spiral through her, and she became lost to all reality.

She no longer wanted to fight him. He was causing such wondrous sensations inside her that she couldn't refuse him anything any longer. She wanted this. She wanted him.

When his tongue snaked between her teeth and met hers in a sensual dance inside her mouth, Samantha felt herself beginning a strange floating, as though she were being swept away on a soft fluff of clouds, on wings of rapture. There was no map. There was no dangerous men who might even kill for the map. There was no spoiled cousin to ruin Samantha's summer. There was only *now*, in Troy's arms. Even the threat of his manhood pressed solidly against her didn't dissuade her from enjoying the pleasure of his kiss.

His hands swept around and molded her breasts through her dress as his lips lowered and placed a kiss where her deep cleavage began.

Samantha sucked in her breath, becoming mindless and not understanding the message being sent from where she felt a sweet pain rising between her thighs. As his fingers caressed each breast, her heart thumped more wildly against her ribs. Her breath came in short gasps as he reached a hand around and began unfastening her dress. But when it became loosened, enabling him to slip a hand down its bodice to fully cup her breast, she was jerked out of her euphoric state of mind.

Samantha stepped quickly away, breathless, and stared wide-eyed at him. "I don't know what came over me," she said in a rush of words. "Never before have I let a man touch or kiss me in—such—a way."

"Then I am honored to be the first and to be in the company of such a lady," Troy said, gallantly bowing at the waist, yet all the while watching her with a careful eye.

"Are you mocking me?" Samantha gasped, working at securing her dress from behind. She had never been so flustered! Even her nimble fingers failed to accomplish such a simple task as that of snapping her dress back in place. Her eyes felt hot, surely matching her cheeks which felt aflame. Her heart pounded; her knees were awkwardly weak. And her lips! They felt bruised from his kisses, yet she hungered for more. She even wanted his hands on her breasts again. Never had anything felt so wonderfully delicious!

"Mocking?" Troy said, taking a step toward her. "Surely you know that I am not."

Samantha wanted to scream at him, to accuse him of only wanting the map. He would eventually get around to asking for it. She did know that. But first he probably wanted to have some fun with her before taking the map and then leaving, to never be heard from again.

"No matter," she said dryly. "I must return to the dance. Surely there are more honorable gentlemen there than you. Do you always rush women so?"

"Oh? My kissing you makes me less honorable?"

"You did more than kiss."

"Ah, and so I did. I petted you just a mite."

"You touched my breast with a bare hand," she said in a hush.

"As I would like to do also with my lips."

"Sir! *Please—*"

"It is sir to you now? Have you truly forgotten my name?"

Samantha turned her eyes away. She would not let him know that his name was etched in her memory forever. She refused to even allude to how they had met or the map that they strangely shared. Yet, somehow could this even be helped?

Breathing easier now that her dress was finally secured in place, she jerked her head up and challenged him with the flashing of her eyes. "How did you find me? Why are you here?" she snapped. "Where are you now making your residence? You seemed to be a highwayman of sorts. That is where I first saw you, you know."

85

"Whoa!" Troy chuckled. "Only one question at a time." His gaze moved on past her and to the sparkle of water ahead, where the creek snaked across the Ainsworth property, gurgling over and around its rocky bed. Long shadows of cedars grew weaker and finally disappeared along the banks of the creek where the moon could not penetrate their thick, upper branches.

Troy nodded toward this spot where complete privacy seemed to be beckoning. "Let us talk further after making ourselves more comfortable beside the creek," he softly encouraged, reaching for her elbow.

Fearing what his touch might start anew inside her, Samantha flinched and refused to let him assist her, yet she was willing to follow his suggestion. She wasn't quite ready to return to the dance, where Julia surely stood waiting to hound her with questions, though Samantha did have room to brag that this handsome man had chosen her over her spoiled cousin. In a sense, though, that would be a nontruth. Samantha knew that Troy had an ulterior motive for having chosen her. But Julia would never be given the opportunity of seeking out such a truth! It still was Samantha's own secret to be shared with Troy and no one else.

"All right," she agreed. "We can talk. But for only awhile longer."

She followed alongside him, hearing the dried vegetation crunching underfoot as they reached the small spread of trees. The maples and oaks blended in well with the evergreens, making a large umbrella under which they could be lost from the rest of the world.

Samantha once more felt vulnerable, now so far from everyone else. But the warmth of his arms and the passion in his kisses had shown her that the true threat here were her feelings and reactions toward him. She had responded so shamefully, and she must not allow the performance to be repeated.

But could she truly place a barrier between them, should he approach her again? Ah, the sweetness of the feelings he had the skills to arouse! Now awakened to them, she would forever want more.

Troy gestured with a hand toward a clearing beside the rippling splash of water. "Will this do?" he asked.

"It's fine," Samantha said, trying to force a chill into her words. She gathered the skirt of her dress and her petticoats up into her arms as she eased to the ground and sat down close to the water. Little did he know that she sat on this exact spot earlier in the day, dangling her bare feet in the water and idling her moments away, thinking of him, hoping to see him, to be with him.

Never had she dreamed that they would be together and in such a sensual way. Oh, to be kissed by him again. To have his fingers touch her breasts again.

She drew her knees up to her chest, feeling a blush rise when a trace of her ankles showed where her skirts and petticoats slipped up and away from them. Yet how foolish. Hadn't he already seen and felt an even more private part of her anatomy? The shame of it. Should her grandmama ever find out!

"Now where were we?" Troy said, settling down beside her. He picked a sprig of grass and thrust it between his lips.

"You were going to tell me how you found me," Samantha said, not really caring. All that mattered was that he was there with her and she with him, though it would probably be the last time. Once she agreed to give him the map—

Yet, he still hadn't mentioned it, which puzzled her.

Troy scooted closer to her where a shaft of moonlight escaped through the trees and onto her face, illuminating her loveliness. He took the blade of grass from his mouth and flipped it into the water. "I've a friend. A farmer. He lives up the road a mile or two," he said. "That's where I am visiting for a spell. When he received his invitation to the barn dance, he extended it to me. So here I am. That's how."

"You knew not of me before your arrival?" Samantha asked, disappointment heavy in her words.

"Now I didn't say that." He chuckled, leaning toward her.

"Then you did inquire of my whereabouts?"

"I would be daft not to."

"And why is that?" she murmured. She expected now to hear the word map spoken.

"When a man is so taken by a woman, he would do everything in his power to find her."

"That day in the stagecoach. You were—truly—taken by me?"

His eyes spoke what his words didn't. Their lips seemed like magnets, drawn to each other. And it was with intense joy and repeated pleasure that Samantha welcomed his. As his kiss strengthened and his arms embraced her, Samantha leaned fully into him, pressing her breasts against his powerful chest of steel.

She clung to him, giving herself up to the ecstasy of the moment, letting her senses fully ignite, with no thoughts of denial this time. Her response had turned her wild and weak, and when his hand crept between them and dared a touch to her breast, she let him.

Desire shot through her, over and over again, as his

kiss scorched her lips, and his fingers once again released the snaps of her dress. A soft moan rose from deep inside her as he lowered the bodice of her dress and freed her breasts to the cool touch of the breeze and the heated flesh of his hands.

And then she placed her hands to the back of his head and lowered his lips to the taut tip of a breast. She shook with passion as his tongue flicked over and around it before his mouth began a slow sucking sensation which threatened to cause her to become insane with passion.

Each place he touched sent ripples of sheer pleasure through her flesh. Samantha looked down at him through a drunken sort of haze.

"How am I expected to resist you when you steal my senses from me?" she whispered, her heart beating so wildly she thought surely he could hear its thump.

"You aren't expected to do anything but let me love you," he said thickly. "Let me teach you how to love."

"Do I appear as one so inexperienced that I require being taught?" she whispered, pouting.

The moon's reflection caught in the shine of the shell-shaped locket which lay against her chest. Troy's fingers went to it and faintly touched it. "I would hope that there has been no man before me," he tested, now turning the locket from side to side, seeing its fancy designs.

Samantha tensed, seeing how he had become so quiet as he studied her locket. She remembered Julia's teasing her about its being a gift from a beau. Was this also what Troy was thinking? Now she wished that she had given it back to Franklin.

"This locket," he said, looking hauntingly into her eyes, "I now recall having seen you wear it that day in the stagecoach. Is it so important to you that you wear it everyday? Did a special man give it to you?"

Samantha eased his hand away from the locket and covered it with her fingers. "No. No special man," she murmured.

"Your parents, perhaps?"

"No. Again you are wrong."

"Then, who?"

Samantha's eyes widened. "Why do you persist with this?" she asked, now feeling uneasy. She quickly secured the bodice of her dress up and over her breasts, fumbling with the snaps at the back of the dress, trying to make herself presentable enough to return to the dance. Again she had let him almost seduce her.

Where were her morals? Surely she had none! She rose quickly to her feet, attempting to brush the wrinkles from her dress.

"What are you doing?" Troy asked incredulously. "Where are you going?"

"I must return to the dance," she said, already taking steps away from him. She refused to look at him, knowing that he had a strange hold on her. She feared loving him. She had always wanted to love a man who was free to love her in return. Surely this man and his mysterious map were not free in any sense of the word.

Troy pushed himself up from the ground and took long steps after her. "Samantha," he growled, grabbing her by a wrist, stopping her. He spun her around to face him. "Was it something I said? Was it my comments about the locket?"

"No," she said softly, looking up into his eyes, seeing a mixture of hurt and accusation in their blue depths.

"Then why?"

"Troy, my absence will be noticed," she explained.

"My grandmama and grandpapa will begin to wonder and worry."

"That is the true reason?"

"Yes."

"But we were—"

She cast her eyes downward as a blush rose to her cheeks. "I know," she said in a bare whisper. "And we were wrong. I have behaved quite poorly this night. What must you think of me?"

He placed a forefinger to her chin. He forced her eyes upward to meet his soft stare. "What do I think of you?" he said huskily. "My darling, I do believe that I love you."

"But we only just—did—meet."

"Does that truly matter?"

"But it's such a futile thing, Troy."

"And why would you say that?"

"Can you deny that you are a man of mystery? I doubt if I will ever know the whole truth about you."

"Ah, but you will."

"Truly?"

"In time," he said, drawing her fully into his embrace, hugging her tightly. "Yes, Samantha, in time."

"But when? What is it that you are involved in, Troy?" she asked, relishing this moment while in his arms. She placed her arms about him and let her cheek rest on his powerful chest.

"I cannot say," he said thickly. Then he eased her out of his arms and clasped his fingers gently to her shoulders. "The map. It's time for you to return it to me, Samantha."

Samantha tensed. Her face became drawn, and she started to doubt all of the beautiful words that he had just spoken to her. As she had suspected, he had only truly one purpose for his words and actions. The need for the map was his prime reason for even living, it seemed!

"Map?" she said, shaking herself away from him. "I do not know anything of a map." She would refuse to give it to him. Perhaps later, but certainly not now.

She would show him that she was not one to be used. Love! Hah! He didn't know the meaning of the word. She once more turned and began to stomp away from him. She had read him right from the very first! He was a most untrustworthy, unlikable man.

But thinking these things caused a gnawing ache at the pit of her stomach. She stifled a low sob as she began running away from him, ignoring how he was softly crying her name from close behind her.

"Samantha! Damn it, wait up!" Troy said, once more grabbing her by the wrist. He blocked her further approach by stepping in front of her.

Samantha struggled, wincing as his fingers dug into her delicate flesh. "Let me go!" she softly cried. "All you truly want of me is a darn map! How could I have been so foolish to think that there was something special forming between us—that your sole interest in me was *because* of me. I was wrong! Release me! This minute!"

Troy ignored her rush of words. Instead he crushed her lips beneath his. He kissed her long and hard, his hands holding her tightly in place against him.

Samantha couldn't fight him off as the warmth spread through her like wildfire. His kiss was so hot and demanding that when he freed her, looking down at her with passion-heated eyes, a bizarre weakness overcame her. She took a step back away from him, not wanting this erotic spell to weave between them. She would not be used. She had to keep her self-respect intact, at all costs!

"Samantha," Troy said, reaching a hand toward her. "I'm sorry if my concern over the map caused you to doubt my feelings for you."

"I still don't know anything about a map," she lied, hating to be so devious.

"How can you say that?" he said, raking his fingers through his hair, frustration building inside him.

"Because it is true," she said, nervously biting her lower lip, lies not coming easy to her.

"But I gave it to you that day."

"Oh? Was that a map?"

"God, Samantha, surely you looked at it. Surely you saw—"

"No. Not at all."

The moon revealed a figure approaching in the darkness. Samantha's back became rigid, her jaw set, as she saw the flutter of the yellow dress and the shine of the gold hair. Julia! Julia had become impatient waiting for Samantha's and Troy's return and had come in search of them. The nerve! This summer was going to prove to be one that was filled with annoyances.

# Chapter Six

"Samantha? Troy? Is that you?" Julia asked, peering more intently toward the two still figures in the moonlight. She dared not move onward, beginning to think that perhaps she had traveled too far pursuing her cousin who had managed to divert a man's attention away from herself. And Troy Gilbert, of all men and, of all places, here in Illinois! Troy had amused her but only a few times while in New York. His head seemed to always be elsewhere, his business seeming to be even more important to him than women. Strange that he was now in Illinois. And he had quite successfully evaded her questions as to why he was here. Just as Julia had thought that he was getting ready to disclose his reasons, Samantha had drawn him away from her. Julia had thought that he might even ask her to dance, though a square dance was not the kind she would have preferred sharing with him. But a dance could have led them into something much more intimate. Then there had been cousin Samantha's interruption! Why had Samantha been able to draw Troy Gilbert away? What was his

94

attraction to her? And where had they even been now?

Troy was the first to respond to Julia. "Julia? What the hell are you doing this far from the dance?" he growled, stepping away from Samantha, going to Julia to take her hands in his as she met his approach.

"I came in search of you," Julia teased, fluttering her thick lashes up at him, only glancing furtively toward Samantha.

Samantha's insides twisted into a tight knot, seeing the familiarity between Troy and Julia. Surely their short time together at the dance hadn't given them the chance to get this acquainted. It had to mean that they knew each other from another place, another time.

Jealousy tore away at Samantha's heart. First Julia stole Samantha's grandparents' undivided devotions. And now even Troy's. Wasn't anything sacred to Julia? Feelings for a cousin were not, to be sure!

Samantha stood frozen on the spot, hearing the continued exchange of affectionate words.

"Don't you know the dangers of wandering unescorted out here, so far from the dance?" Troy continued to scold. "Julia, you are from the large city of New York. You don't know the art of defending yourself out here in what not long ago was a wilderness."

"But I had to find you," she murmured, once more giving Samantha a coy glance. "And also my cousin. Harm could also come to you two, you know. What on earth are you doing out here all alone?"

Troy gave Samantha a quick glance from across his shoulder, then dropped Julia's hands as though they were hot coals when he saw the seething jealousy flashing in Samantha's eyes. Samantha had already doubted him for one reason. She didn't need another!

He stepped back away from Julia and went to Samantha, sliding an arm about her waist. "We were just soaking up the moonlight, weren't we, Sam?" he said, smiling awkwardly down at Samantha, seeing that her jealousy-filled anger was still intact.

Samantha jerked away from him. "Don't call me Sam," she hissed. "Sam is a man's name. I am much more than that."

Troy chuckled and once more slipped his arm about her waist, holding it firmly in place when she tried again to be free of him. "All right," he said. "Samantha. I agree that that name is much more befitting a lovely lady."

Julia glided toward Troy, then stood on tiptoe before him and placed a hand to his cheek. "Troy, *darling*, you deserted me so ungentlemanly at the dance," she said, openly pouting. "Don't you see a need for an apology?"

She turned her gaze upon Samantha. "My cousin Samantha stole you away from me. Well, we now can return, and you can continue telling me why you are in Illinois and not in New York. What sort of business could tear you away from your ships? There are no large bodies of water here to sail your handsome ships."

Samantha was fast growing numb while listening to this exchange of dialogue between Julia and Troy who appeared to be more than mere friends. He was from New York and the owner of a line of ships? Then what else? What had brought him to Illinois? What was his connection with Julia? The mystique of the man increased twicefold, and the intrigue that followed him around was even more fascinating to Samantha. Yet there was Julia.

"Julia Ainsworth, do not concern yourself with me," Troy said, easing her hand from his cheek. "It is I who should still be scolding you for venturing so far, alone, away from this night's social activities."

Julia tossed her hair haughtily back from her shoulders, angrily folding her arms across her chest. "Troy Gilbert, will you please refrain from treating me as a fragile, porcelain doll!" she fumed. "You know how I hate that. You men are all alike. Just because I am petite you fear the slightest wind might just blow me away."

Troy chuckled. He placed his hands to Julia's shoulders and turned her in the direction from whence she had just traveled. "Now get on with you," he said and laughed, giving her a pretended spank on her behind. "Samantha and I will follow along after you to see to your welfare."

Julia cast Samantha an ugly stare across her shoulder, feeling like she was being treated like a child and Samantha the woman. Somehow she knew that Samantha and Troy had met before, and more than friendship had formed between them. But friendships—any sort— could be spoiled!

Troy fell into step beside Samantha. "You're so quiet," he said, once more inching his arm about her waist.

"And why shouldn't I be?" she snapped. "It seems that knowing you becomes more difficult by the moment."

"Why do you say that?"

Samantha let his arm remain about her waist, knowing that if she removed it, he would just put it there again. In some way, she was beginning to know him.

"From the very first, you've behaved oddly," she said softly. "And now I find out from my cousin, no less, that you are a man of the sea. It has made me aware of just

97

how little I know you."

She looked at Julia who was stomping way on ahead. Then she looked up at Troy. "It is this lack of knowing you that fills me with shame for what nearly happened between us," she said in a whisper, only loud enough for Troy to hear. "A complete stranger! I let myself share such intimate kisses and touches with—a—mere stranger!"

"You know that we've become more than that," he said huskily.

"In a sense, yes. In a sense, no," she said with a strain in her voice. She placed her fingertips to her temple. "Lord, I am so confused. I don't know what to think about anything. You've succeeded at totally scrambling my brain!" Then she glanced up at him. "How is it that you know my cousin so well?" she asked in an accusing tone. "New York is a large city. Strange that you two should have managed to find one another among the swarms of people who live there. Stranger still that you should manage to find one another even here in Illinois!"

"Fate, I suppose," Troy teased.

Samantha's eyes widened. "Do not be so smug," she hissed. "From what I hear, Julia has quite a string of beaux dangling like puppets. If you are among them, I—"

Troy swept her around to face him. He drew her body into the curve of his. "Darling, please put your mind to ease about that," he reassured.

"And why should I?" she gulped, his powerful hold on her once more a threat to her thumping heart.

"Because she was never one I would choose to escort anywhere," he explained. "But I can't say as much about my gentlemen friends. You see, her reputation precedes her. My friends quite freely boast of their conquests of your beautiful, free-spirited cousin."

Samantha felt a blush rise, wondering if even her own reputation was now in question. Would Troy tell of his near conquest to all his gentlemen friends? Well! She would have to see to it that she would give him no more fuel to add to the fire. He wouldn't get as much as even another kiss from her.

Troy leaned his face down into hers. "Again you are so quiet," he murmured.

"You speak so openly of Julia and how she would never be a lady of your choosing, but yet you seemed so truly concerned about her welfare."

"Only because she tends to need protecting."

"Yes. She tends to use her frailty to her advantage," Samantha mocked.

Troy kissed the tip of her nose. "Now, now," he teased. "Do I hear a lingering hint of scornful jealousy in your voice?"

"That is not a pleasant trait, I know that," Samantha quietly confessed. "But Julia has such a way of getting under my skin."

She sighed heavily. "And to think that I must tolerate her this entire summer," she said.

"You will be in Springfield for that length of time?"

"It seems so wrong that you are only now asking me that," she murmured. "Yet you haven't seemed to have the need to ask anything about me." Her face clouded. "You only asked about the darn map."

The words had slipped out before she knew it. She gasped and stared up into his sparkling eyes.

"Yes. The map," he said hoarsely, searching her face for hidden clues of truth. "You do still have it, don't you? You were only jesting before when you said that you didn't.''

A crackling of a twig close by sent Samantha's eyes away from Troy's face. She looked in the direction where she had last seen Julia storming away, back to the gathering of people, and she saw that she was no longer in sight. Then who was it making movement in the darkness? Even now, there was a rush of feet.

Suddenly a lone, large figure of a man lunged forward out of the darkness and grabbed Troy around the neck and wrestled him to the ground. Samantha tried to scream, but no sounds would surface from the depths of her throat. Horrified, she watched as Troy and the man began exchanging blows, with Troy now on the top as the man was sprawled on his back.

Samantha was trembling with fear, but she just couldn't stand by and watch. She had to help. Rushing forth, she caught sight of the man's face in the moonlight. Though blood was trickling from his nose and mouth, she quickly recognized him to be one of the men who had attacked Troy at the depot! Again she was reminded of the map. It surely was the reason for these assaults upon Troy. The importance of the map was profound, it seemed.

Forgetting the delicate material of her dress and petticoats, she fell upon the man's back who had now succeeded in holding Troy on the ground. She grabbed his hair and gave it a yank, causing him to emit a frenzied yelp of pain. Not seeing his swift movement, Samantha suddenly felt herself flying backward, to land in a painful thud upon the ground.

Dazed, she leaned up on an elbow and watched as Troy pushed the man off him and struggled until he was once more straddling him, punching the man's face, knocking him senseless.

And then Troy rose shakily to his feet, rubbing his jaw. Blood curled from his lip, his hair in complete disarray as he looked down at the unconscious form of the man.

"Troy?" Samantha said, rising to a sitting position. Her head was still fuzzy, stars flashing before her eyes. The man had succeeded at rendering her almost unconscious with his powerful shove against her chest. She now understood the danger that surrounded the map. This made her not want to part with it until she understood its full meaning. And once she did give it to Troy, she would never see him again!

Troy suddenly turned and found Samantha in her dazed condition.

"Samantha!" he gasped. He rushed to her and fell to his knees beside her. He framed her face between his hands and studied her closely. "God! Are you hurt?"

He saw no visible signs of injury, only that a comb had fallen from the one side of her coiffure, and her hair was spilling in red cascades across one shoulder.

Samantha licked her lips and blinked her eyes, then softly laughed. "I think I'm still in one piece," she said. "For a moment there I thought my head was a part of the firmament. Stars were dancing quite readily before my eyes."

"What happened, Samantha?"

"Didn't you see?"

"I believe I was a mite involved," he chuckled.

"So was I," she giggled, glad now to be able to laugh about it.

"Samantha, what on earth did you do?"

"I jumped the man. I pulled his hair. I wanted to get

him off you."

"You—did—what?" he said throatily.

"I couldn't just stand there watching," she said in an innocent, sweet voice.

Troy's thumbs caressed the underside of her chin. "My little defender," he sighed. "What am I to do with you? You could've been killed, you know."

Samantha leaned up and twined her arms about his neck, drawing him closer. "I was so afraid for you," she murmured. "That man was one of those who attacked you at the depot."

"Yes. And the rest may not be so far behind. We've got to get out of here."

Samantha's eyes widened with remembrance. She leaned away from Troy. "Lord!" she gasped. "I forgot about him."

Troy's eyes filled with puzzlement. "Who?" he asked, taking a glance over his shoulder to make sure the man was still unconscious.

"Marion Yarborough," she said anxiously.

"Who the hell is Marion Yarborough and why do you mention him now?"

"He was among those men at the depot! He is a part of this plot against you."

"Who is he? How do you know him?"

"He is a most wicked man," Samantha hissed. "He's caused my grandparents some problems in the past and, I'm sure, continues to, even now. But why is he wanting to see harm come to you?"

"There are many things that I cannot yet tell you," he said thickly. "Right now, we must get out of here. We must return to the dance and pretend that nothing has happened."

Samantha placed a finger to Troy's lip and smoothed the trickle of blood away. "You nor I can return like this," she murmured. "Look at you. Look at me!"

"It can be easily remedied," he said. He bent and rescued her comb from the ground and handed it to her. "Can you replace this in your hair without the aid of a mirror?"

"Yes, I believe so," she whispered.

"Then do so," he said, raking his fingers through his own hair, straightening the midnight black strands back in place. He took a handkerchief from his pocket and patted smudges of dirt from Samantha's face as she got her hair in shape again, then cleaned his own face with the handkerchief.

Samantha felt with her fingers, checking her hair, believing that it was once more presentable. Then she brushed the debris from the skirt of her dress, smoothed the gathers down and felt almost as good as new except for the ache that she was starting to feel in her bones.

"Let's move," Troy said, grabbing her by a hand. "It's imperative that we act as though nothing has happened."

Speed was put into their steps, and soon the sounds from the fiddle and laughter from those enjoying the festivities were readily welcomed as the barn came into sight.

Troy stopped and stood over Samantha, taking her hands and holding them solidly against his chest. "Remember. We must act as though nothing has happened," he once more warned. "I don't want to draw undue attention to myself."

"Troy, I wish that you would fully explain."

"Later," he said, his head jerking up as Julia approached from the shadows. He released Samantha's hands as Samantha spun around and away from him.

"It took you two long enough," Julia chirped, edging up next to Troy. She gave him a coy look. "But now that you are here, isn't it time that you dance with me?"

Troy's eyebrows forked, then he gave Samantha a half smile. "I must," he whispered, only loud enough for Samantha to hear. "Remember? We must look as though nothing has happened."

"That has nothing to do with her," Samantha whispered back, fuming.

He leaned into her face. "I can't draw attention to myself. Remember?" he softly argued.

"Dancing with her is the answer?" Samantha argued back.

"Knowing her, she would cause a commotion if I don't dance with her," he growled.

"So you let her blackmail you into doing it?" Samantha snapped.

"Not exactly."

"Oh? So you dance with her because you want to?" Samantha accused. "Again I must say how strange it is that you and she have managed to find one another in Illinois."

She cast Julia a sour glance. "Take him. He's yours," she spat. "Somehow he is suddenly less attractive to me!"

Samantha flung the skirt of her dress around and stormed away from Troy, confused, hurt, and angry. One moment she believed he loved her, then the next, she doubted him all over again!

"I should've helped the man knock Troy mindless!" she whispered beneath her breath. "He deserves everything he gets. Even Julia!"

She entered the barn, let her eyes seek out an available dance partner and boldly invited a man with strawberry-colored hair to join her in the square dance.

Whipping her petticoats about her ankles she smiled and let her feet move to the beat of the fiddle's lusty music.

"Swing your partner," the caller shouted. "Lift your feet. Ain't your dance partner sweet?"

Samantha gave Troy a smug look as he looked at her from across the room, yet inside, she was one large ache of hurt.

# Chapter Seven

The dance was over. Everyone had departed, and Troy left way before everyone else because of Samantha's stubborn refusal to even talk with him again. Samantha now dejectedly entered her grandparents' house along with her grandparents and Julia, waiting in the dark for her grandfather to light a lamp.

She placed a hand to the small of her back, a cruel reminder of the scuffle in the dark. Somehow she had even forgotten about that because of her bitterness while she watched Troy and Julia. How could one understand such a man? First he professes to having no interest in Julia and then he sweeps her away to dance with her!

Samantha fumed even now, thinking about how he had so possessively held Julia about the waist as he had danced with her. It certainly didn't appear that he was suffering because he felt forced to dance with her. His blue eyes danced right along with his feet as he had swung the fragile cousin around and around the dance floor.

The fire skipping along the kerosene-soaked wick of the lamp began emitting a soft, golden glow about the living room, revealing a room in complete disorder.

"Damn!" Melvin gasped.

"Heaven's sake!" Dorothy June uttered softly, covering her mouth with her hands.

"My goodness!" Julia whispered.

Samantha's hands went to her mouth and smothered her own soft cry of alarm. Her gaze swept around the room, seeing how the chairs had been overturned and tables knocked over. Nothing had been left untouched. Even the framed pictures had been thrown from the walls.

Tears sprang forth from Dorothy June's eyes as she began walking dazedly about the room, picking up the pictures from the floor, knocking broken glass from the frames. "Who could've done this?" she cried. "Why was it done?"

Samantha went to her grandmother and took her gently by an arm. "Grandmama, you're going to cut your fingers," she said. "Please wait. Grandpapa and I will take care of this for you."

"It was that damn Marion Yarborough," Melvin growled, moving about the room, standing up the overturned furniture. "You noticed that he didn't attend the dance. He was too busy wreaking havoc here in our house. He's tried everything else to scare us into sellin' out to him. It don't surprise me none that he'd do this."

Samantha gave her grandfather a shadowy glance, having her own suspicions as to the one responsible for this. Yes, it could be Marion, but for reasons other than what her grandfather was thinking. Or had it been Troy? Both men would do such a deed to get their hands on the map!

She blanched, looking toward the door that led to the

107

hallway which in turn led to her room. The map! Was it still there? Or had the search been successful?

"You must alert the authorities at once," Julia said, lifting the skirt of her dress as she inched around the clutter at her feet. "The responsible one—this Marion Yarborough—must be placed behind bars."

Samantha wanted to flee to her room to check on the map, but she also wanted to see just what her grandfather was going to do about Marion. She would keep her suspicions about Troy to herself. Up until now, her grandfather had done absolutely nothing about Marion Yarborough's antics. He seemed to be afraid of him.

Samantha hoped that one day she would understand. Her grandfather was a stocky man, well capable of fending for himself. He even had many opportunities to sell his farm acreage for twice what it was worth, which would enable him to move completely away from this community where Marion Yarborough had such a strong hold on so many lives.

But strangely enough, her grandfather had held on to his property, almost taunting Marion even into these terrible acts of meanness, since Marion sorely wanted the land for himself.

"Grandpapa, surely you are going to alert the authorities, aren't you?" Samantha tested, seeing how a stubborn set to his jaw had tightened the wrinkles around his lips.

He removed his spectacles and went and placed them on the fireplace mantel, then turned and once more surveyed the room. He slipped his hands into the sides of the bib of his coveralls and hung his thumbs inside, on the coarse material, as his fingers spilled over, on the outside.

"We ain't got no proof it was Marion," he growled, screwing his face up into a frown.

"But you're sure it was," Dorothy June softly argued, going to him, looking up into his faded blue eyes. "Don't let him get away with it this time, Melvin. It's got to stop. I can't take much more of these shenanigans."

Melvin drew her gently into his arms and clutched her to his chest. Over her shoulder he gazed first at Samantha and then at Julia, giving Julia a longer, lingering, contemplating look. Then he shook his head and held Dorothy June out away from him.

"We ain't got proof, Dorothy June," he said firmly, yet quietly, so only his wife could hear. "There's not one thing about this mess that throws absolute, factual guilt Marion's way. Don't you see? The authorities would have to wonder why we were accusing Marion. Questions would lead to more questions that we don't want to answer. Surely you can see that."

Dorothy June choked back a sob and shook her head. "Yes, I see," she murmured.

"And ain't this the time to tell Samantha about Doc Raley?" he said, still only loud enough for Dorothy June to hear. "Ain't tonight proof enough that Marion is capable of almost anything?"

"I'm so frightened, Melvin," Dorothy June whispered back.

"Yes. I know," he said, once more hugging her to him. "Damn that man for ruinin' this night for you."

"When will it end? Maybe we should sell him the land."

"Not 'til hell freezes over," he growled. He patted her back. "Now you take Samantha to her room and tell her 'bout Doc Raley," he said. "Me and Julia will begin

109

takin' care of this mess."

"Whatever you think's best, Melvin."

"I'm not sure anymore," he grumbled, then stepped back away from her as she went to Samantha. Hate for Marion filled his every pore. So many years! But true, fulfilled revenge would perhaps take many, many more.

Samantha hadn't been able to make out the words being exchanged between her grandparents, but she knew that somehow she was a part of these whisperings because her grandmother was now guiding her by an elbow away from the room.

"Grandmama, what is it?" Samantha asked, glancing back over her shoulder at her grandfather and his somber mood. Then she went willingly on to her room, anxious as her grandmother lighted a lamp and placed it on the nightstand, beside the bed.

With a wild heartbeat, Samantha looked quickly about her, then down at the oval, braided rug. Nothing had been disturbed in this room. This puzzled her. Both Troy and Marion had to know that she would surely hide the map in her room, not elsewhere. And seeing that her room had been left untouched, she began doubting that the map was the cause for the destruction in the outer room. Perhaps Marion Yarborough didn't even suspect that she knew about the map or had it in her possession. Perhaps he had caused the havoc in the Ainsworth house for reasons understood by her grandparents. If so, then she had been wrong to accuse Troy! Yet, she doubted him for many reasons. It was only logical that she would think him capable of this miserable deed!

Dorothy June went to the bed and patted it. "Come and

let's talk, honey," she said, her face pale and showing added signs of strain.

"Talk? Why? What about?" Samantha said, not budging from where she now stood. At a time like this, what could her grandmother have to say to her that was so important? It was as though the destruction in the living room had something to do with this intimate talk. But why? So many things seemed to be making less and less sense.

"Just come and sit down beside me," Dorothy June encouraged, reaching a hand to Samantha. "We'll have a talk just like we did when you were little. Remember? So much was shared between us when your grandpapa was out hoein' in the garden. It was a time just for us."

"Yes. I remember," Samantha said, sighing. She moved on across the room and took her grandmother's hand, once more cringing when she felt the hardened calluses on each palm. It didn't seem fair that her grandmother should work so hard, but the Ainsworths had been too proud to accept any monetary assistance from Craig Johnston, their daughter's rich husband. They had even refused money to pay for Samantha's needs while she had spent her summers there.

They had always professed to having enough food to pass around to anyone who might be sitting at their supper table. They even tithed regularly, giving the church ten percent of everything their farm netted them in proven dollars. Samantha had always admired this about them, thinking they had to be the most unselfish couple on the entire earth! And damn that pitiful excuse of a man Marion Yarborough for causing them such heartache.

"Well, then let's just pretend that this is one of those

times," Dorothy June said, placing Samantha's hand on her lap as Samantha sat down beside her.

"But, Grandmama, this doesn't seem a fit time," Samantha softly argued. "I feel that I should be helping Grandpapa."

"Julia can help," Dorothy June said, clearing her throat nervously as she gave Samantha a searching look, not knowing how to tell her what she should have known many years ago. Doc Raley. One day Doc Raley would reveal it all to her. It had been decided long ago that Julia would not be the one taken into this sort of confidence. Only Samantha. Samantha was the one with the level head. Samantha was the strong one of the two girls. She would understand just why such a secret needed airing. It was imperative that somebody know, should something happen to her grandparents. They were the only ones, beside Doc Raley, who had known from the beginning. Yet, two others had known. But they were now dead.

"I'm sure cousin Julia is a lot of help," Samantha said scornfully, lifting her fingers to the comb in her hair and slipping it off, letting her hair flutter free and down to her shoulders.

"Don't be so hard on your cousin," Dorothy June softly scolded. "She is from another sort of life than either you or I. Though you are from a wealthy background, it was that of the Carolinas. Those from New York are a different sort, Samantha. But I don't have to tell you that."

"Yes, I would say that Julia is quite different," Samantha said, laughing softly. "And I prefer the way I was taught my particular morals in Charleston."

Her eyes wavered, her face taking on a blush of pink as she remembered the brazen ways in which she had behaved not even an hour ago while with Troy. She had even bared her breasts to him! The shame of having done it made a sick sort of feeling ripple through her insides. yet, she knew that, should he kiss her again in that special way, she would be guilty of letting him do it again. His hands. His lips! Even now she could swoon.

Then she remembered whose company she was in and felt a renewed shame, knowing that her grandmama would surely disown her if she knew the hussy who sat beside her, one who pretended to be such an untouched, innocent lass!

"Yes. My sweet Samantha," Dorothy June crooned, leaning over, to fondly pat Samantha on the cheek. "You are so much that I see good in young women these days. One day you will make the right man a perfect wife."

Once more Samantha felt a blush rise. She smiled awkwardly down at her grandmother and was glad when the hand was removed from her cheek. Her grandmother's smile had faded, and she took on a sort of melancholy look. Even her crisp blue eyes dimmed.

"Grandmama, what is it that you have to tell me?" Samantha asked, raking her fingers through her auburn hair, smoothing away its tangled curls.

Once more she looked toward the undisturbed oval rug, again relieved. This map. What was its purpose? And when should she return it to Troy? He might even be capable of killing for it. Would she even become a victim? Was she playing a dangerous game with a man she knew nothing about, only that he was the owner of a fleet of ships which sailed from New York? New York was so far from Illinois! Almost even a different country. Why, oh why?

"Honey, I'm not quite sure how to tell you this,"

Dorothy June began, now nervously clasping and unclasping her hands on her lap. "But I must. And now."

"Grandmama, what is it?" Samantha asked, seeing how her grandmother's hands worked so fitfully together. "What is it that you are finding so hard to say?"

"You must know. I must tell you. And, yes, now is the time," Dorothy June persisted. She looked quickly up at Samantha. "If anything should happen to me and your grandpapa, it's imperative that you go to Doc Raley in town to listen to what he has to tell you."

"Doc—Raley?" Samantha murmured, her eyebrows arching with wonder. "What could he have to say that you can't?"

"He is keeping to himself a family secret, something so confidential that only you are to know, upon the death of me and your grandpapa," Dorothy June said, tears sparkling at the corners of her eyes. "We didn't feel that the truth should be allowed to die along with us."

"Grandmama, what truth?"

"Samantha, you will find out. Later. Just you go to Doc Raley. That's all I can tell you now. I don't want to say any more about it."

"Grandmama, surely you can't expect me to not persist in asking what this is all about? Please tell me now. I can't stand the suspense."

"Samantha, you must respect my wishes," Dorothy June said softly. "It is only necessary that you know this secret only after your grandpapa and I have passed on."

"Grandmama, you surely don't truly expect anything to happen to you just yet," Samantha scoffed. "You and Grandpapa have many years left."

Then Samantha's face shadowed. She looked across her shoulder, in the direction of the living room. "No," she gasped. She directed her gaze back at her grandmother. "You don't think that Marion Yarborough is *that* sort of threat, do you?"

"Samantha, that man is capable of anything," Dorothy June murmured.

"But if you so fear him, surely the authorities—"

Dorothy June placed a forefinger to Samantha's lips. "No. Never," she said flatly. "Now you must accept your grandmama and grandpapa's way of doing things. It is our decision to take this one day at a time. Should harm come to us, then you know what to do."

"Grandmama," Samantha protested, easing her grandmother's finger away from her mouth.

"Hush," Dorothy June said, rising from the bed. "Should anything happen to us, go to him, Samantha."

"After I go to the authorities," Samantha stormed, jumping from the bed. "I should even do that now, no matter what you say."

"No. If you do, you will be going against our wishes," Dorothy June said icily.

"But, Grandmama—"

"Just do as you are told, Samantha," Dorothy June said, lifting the skirt of her dress and walking toward the bedroom door. "Now I must go and see to that mess in the living room. Come and help if you wish." She turned and gave Samantha another steady stare. "Just remember, Samantha," she murmured. "Doc Raley."

Samantha stood numbly by as Dorothy June fled from the room. She was stunned. She was now faced with two puzzling mysteries! First there was the map and now this secret held by Doc Raley!

A web of fear began weaving about her heart. Should that evil man—

But then she scoffed at the thought. Surely Marion Yarborough wouldn't be that foolish! He wouldn't go that far to get what he wanted.

Samantha took one last look at the rug, then went after her grandmother to do what she could at this time. But what about later?

# Chapter Eight

Restless, unable to sleep because of all of these perplexing emotions and fears, Samantha rose from her bed. Feeling around in the darkness of the room, she found her silk robe at the foot of her bed and slipped it around her shoulders.

She stole silently from her room, hoping that a breath of fresh air and a stroll in the moonlight might help to clear her head. Creeping breathlessly on past the other closed bedroom doors, she sighed with relief when she reached the back door, unnoticed.

Stepping on outside, she cautiously looked from side to side, seeing only weaving shadows as the leaves in the giant oak trees moved overhead with the gentle breeze. The moon had lowered in the sky. Clouds had formed dark streaks across it, making the glow no longer bright.

But Samantha moved idly onward, barefoot, toward the barn, now hearing its silence, almost in a profound way, after the full night's activities and merriment. She curved her lips down in an angry pout, remembering once again how Troy had catered to Julia. In a sense, Julia had won after all, for it was because of her that Samantha had refused Troy even the courtesy of a smile before he had angrily left the dance. She had even been his reason for leaving before anyone else. Unless, he thought he could find the map in the house while she was not there.

But, then, she decided that it had been Marion Yarborough who had ransacked the house. She wanted to continue hoping that she could trust Troy. But how could she when he had given her so many reasons not to?

She once more thought of how she had so badly treated him at the dance. "Perhaps I was a bit too harsh with him," she whispered. "He had said that he had to dance with Julia."

She clutched the flimsiness of her robe about her, wondering about her sanity in coming out into the night air with such little attire, and barefoot, of all things!

And was she placing herself in danger? What if Marion Yarborough would still be lurking, waiting.

"But, no. He wouldn't be so foolish as to return and do more meanness this same night," she argued with herself.

She shivered and hugged herself with her arms as she turned and began walking back toward the house. Though she felt safe, she still felt foolish for having left the house so late at night.

She hastened her footsteps, then jumped with alarm and let out a soft cry when a hand slid about her waist and stopped her. She jerked her head around, then sighed with relief when she saw that it was Troy. He had apparently been standing in the shadows of the barn where she couldn't see him.

"Troy!" she whispered harshly. "What do you think you're doing?"

118

He spun her around to fully face him. "I began worrying about your welfare," he said thickly. "I came to keep watch." His eyes raked over her. "God, woman, what do you think you're doing out here, dressed like this?" he grumbled.

"How I'm dressed is no concern of yours," she hissed, stepping back away from him. "Even I am no concern of yours. Or are you even telling me the truth? Is it Julia you've come to protect? Or did you even come to meet her in the dark to continue with your little tete-a-tete?"

"I told you why I am here," he growled, taking her by a wrist, yanking her next to him. "You. You are the only reason."

She wanted to argue further, say that his only true interest in her was the map—the darn, mysterious map—but she would not be the first to make mention of it. That would be stepping right into the trap that he was perhaps even setting.

His lips searched for hers, and he gave her a sweet, soft kiss. Then he looked at her with his eyes shadowed by his dark, thick lashes. "Let's go to the barn and talk," he said hoarsely. "It's warmer there. And I believe we could use the privacy with you dressed in—uh—that fashion."

"And when we are there, you do plan to do more than talk, don't you?" she scoffed, not wanting to feel the thrill that his kiss had stirred within her. "Isn't seduction on your mind?" She placed her hands on her hips. "If that is the case, why not let Julia fill those needs? Or had she planned to? It wouldn't surprise me at all to see her slip from the back door at any moment now, with her eyes set on the barn. Much can be shared in the hayloft, you know."

"Oh?" Troy chuckled. "You speak from experience, do you?"

Samantha's face grew hot with a flush. "Don't put words in my mouth," she snapped.

"My darling, you're the one who made mention of a hayloft," he teased. "Not I. But I am game to give it a try if you are."

"Never!" she said, tilting her chin haughtily.

"All right then," he said, lifting his shoulder in a shrug. "Let's at least go into the barn and have that talk that I suggested—*only* suggested."

"We have nothing to discuss."

"You know better than that."

"And to what are you referring?"

"Feelings, Samantha," Troy said huskily, taking one of her hands in his to very gentlemanly kiss its palm. "Feelings that we have for one another." His eyes searched her face for hidden answers.

"Feelings?" she said, jerking her hand away. "Ha! What do you know about feelings? And what makes you think that I have any for the likes of you? You made it quite plain tonight that you preferred Julia over me. Was she a delightful dance partner? You appeared to be thoroughly enjoying yourself. Not once did you look my way."

"As did you while flitting yourself from man to man," he growled.

"And you would have expected me to stand aside, like a wallflower, watching?"

"Wallflower? You?" he chuckled. "Never, my darling."

"Then you musn't act so annoyed about my dancing," she said stubbornly.

"As you shouldn't about my dancing with Julia. I told you why I had to do it. She would have surely caused some sort of scene. I could not draw attention to myself."

"Ah, such a man of mystery," Samantha said scornfully.

Troy stepped closer to her and looked down at her, his jaw set hard. "Tell me something," he said. "Why are you so bitter toward me? What have I done to cause you to behave in such a way?"

"You even have to ask?" she said, laughing.

"If it's Julia, then you are wrong," he said shallowly.

"It's much, much more," she said, turning her back to him. Her heart was hammering against her ribs, his closeness almost drowning her in sensual sensations. It was hard to actually remember the reasons why she should be angry with him.

But the map! The mystery surrounding it! She had to keep reminding herself that the map was his reason for his interest in her. It would take a lot of persuading on his part for her to forget this assumption.

Troy swept his arm about her waist and began leading her on toward the opened door of the barn. "Then we have to find out just what you're talking about," he said gruffly, tightening his hold as she began to squirm. "And you might as well accept that you are going to accompany me to the barn. If I have to pick you up bodily from the ground and carry you there, you are going to go and have that talk with me."

Samantha pushed at his strong arm. "Let me go," she softly cried. "You are impossible, Troy Gilbert! What will you do next? Take me by force sexually?"

"Perhaps." He chuckled, almost dragging her through the barn door to where a ladder led up into the loft. "That

121

idea is intriguing."

"You wouldn't!" Samantha gasped. She squinted her eyes, trying to see through the intense darkness. "It's so dark. Surely you do have plans for me which will not be pleasant," she argued. "Troy, release me or I shall scream."

He slipped a hand over her mouth and held it in place, fumbling with his other one as he began climbing the ladder, forcing her on upward in front of him, her body warm against his. "I don't think so," he said. "Do I even have to gag you so that you will at least listen to what I have to say once we reach the hayloft floor?"

Samantha tried to jerk her head, to free her lips of his hand, but found the effort useless. So she proceeded on upward, glad that the cracks in the roof emitted a few rays of soft moonlight downward, revealing the wide bed of spread straw which Troy was now guiding her down upon.

"I'll never understand you," she said dryly. "Everything you do puzzles me."

She looked slowly from side to side, feeling their complete aloneness. "And now that you have me here, what are you true plans for me? Will you even torture me to get the truth out of me?"

"What truth?" he teased.

"Surely you know."

"I'm not sure."

She still refused to say the word map to him. "All right," she said, shrugging. "If you want to continue with this game, so shall I. I have all night. It doesn't matter where I spend it. I wasn't able to sleep in my bed, anyway."

"And why was that?" Troy asked, reaching to lift

122

layers of her hair from her shoulders, scooting closer, enabling him to get a whiff of its jasmine smell. "Could it have anything to do with me and what we share between us?"

Again she slapped his hand away. "You won't trick me into saying anything that I would regret later," she said hatefully.

"Like you love me?" he teased, now placing a finger to her jaw, tracing it. "Is that what you would have to be tricked into saying, Samantha?"

Of course she had not been referring to love but to the darn map. She shivered and swallowed hard as his finger roamed lower, down the slope of her neck, and then to where her robe was tied in front. Something willed her to let him untie the robe. It was a power he seemed to have over her from the beginning. This passion she felt for him could not easily be denied. Even now, as his fingers were easing her robe and even her gown away from her shoulders, she could not refuse him.

She shuddered and melted into his embrace as he drew her into his arms and began running his hands along the satiny lines of her hips, down to her thighs, and then around to where her gown clung and revealed the softness of her womanhood. She emitted a soft moan when he began softly caressing her there, through her gown. She twined her arms about his neck and urged his lips down to hers, letting her tongue make entry into his mouth where their tongues met in a flicking fashion, setting her even more afire inside.

Sighing, Samantha squirmed into his embrace, relishing the feel of his muscles wrapped around her now as he held her tight. He kissed the hollow of her throat, and then down to where her breasts swelled from the low bodice of the revealing, silk gown.

When his lips pressed against her flesh where the deep cleavage lay, Samantha moaned sensuously. She threw her head back in ecstasy as he lowered her gown away from her breasts and let his tongue taste the sweetness of each. From breast to breast his lips traveled, his hands cupping them, causing the nipples to become more hardened and more accessible to the teasing touches of his teasing teeth.

"God, you're beautiful," Troy said huskily, now looking into her eyes as he wove his fingers through her hair. "And I don't see you fighting me now. I don't hear your protests, Samantha."

"Don't give me the chance," she said throatily. "Troy, just love me. Love me fully."

"Before, you said that you didn't want—"

"That was before," she softly argued. "This is now."

"You won't be sorry? You won't accuse me of seducing you?"

"Troy! I can't believe that you are actually testing me. Don't you see? I have given you permission. What more do you need?"

"I need assurances. I don't want to be the cad that you have accused me of being."

"You have already proven me wrong, my love," she said, cupping his chin gently in her hand.

"How did I do that?"

"By not taking me by force. By asking me. I surely was wrong about you, in every way."

"That's all I needed to hear," he said thickly, then drew her roughly against him, easing her on her back, on the thick bed of straw, while his lips kissed her and his hands touched her every sensitive, quivering crevice.

The bed of straw became a cradle of pleasure, a place where feelings could flourish, rise to heights even unexplored before.

Drawing his lips away, Troy once more silently questioned her with his eyes. Samantha looked up at him and nodded as his hands responded by slipping her robe completely away from her, and then slowly he worked her silken gown down, over her thighs and her ankles.

Troy cupped her swelling breasts in each hand and lowered his lips to a taut, dark nipple, softly kissing it. Then he positioned himself lower over her and let his tongue dance along the full length of her body, causing a guttural sigh to rise from somewhere deep inside Samantha.

She writhed and curled her fingers through his hair, forgetting all notions of ever refusing him again. She needed him as surely as night must turn to day.

When his tongue began probing sensuously where her thighs were tightly closed, Samantha's breath momentarily ceased. She looked down at him, wide-eyed, as she filled up with a sweet pain that tormented her. She knew that somehow only Troy knew how to satisfy this sensation.

"Darling, let me," Troy said huskily, looking up at her through eyes hot with desire.

"I'm not sure," she softly protested, sensing that her surrender could truly brand her as a wanton.

Troy's fingers began a slow caress along her flat abdomen, on upward, to once more cup her breasts. He softly kneaded and kissed her navel, then rained kisses downward, stirring a passion so keen she was filled with a spiraling of euphoria.

She closed her eyes, bit her lower lip and allowed her

thighs to part, an open admission of her permission for him to do with her what he liked.

"This will make what follows easier, less painful," Troy whispered.

Samantha looked wonderingly down at him and sighed, entering heaven it seemed. The sensation his tongue was now stirring inside her was so delicious. She sighed and writhed as his tongue flicked, searched.

And just as she felt she would burst into a million pieces of wondrous delight, he moved fully over her. His lips quivered as he lowered them to hers in an utter sweetness, his hands framing her face, his man's strength quite evident as he pressed it hard against her abdomen.

Her hands went to the buttons of his shirt and began releasing them while thrilling to his continuous kiss. Needing to feel skin against skin, she slipped his shirt off, then let her fingers explore his powerful chest and its tight curls of hair which circled his nipples.

Her fingers toyed with his nipples, feeling their hardened rubbery texture, and then her hands traveled lower, where the waist of his jeans fit so snugly. Her heart pounded and her pulse raced as she unsnapped the first snap, and then the next, feeling the hardness which lay just beneath. Daringly she ran her hand over this hardness through the coarse texture of the jeans, drawing a throaty groan from deep inside Troy.

Drawing away from her, Troy looked down at her with passion-heavy lashes over his ocean blue eyes. He guided her hands, urging them to continue loosening his jeans.

"Darling, lower them," he said in a deep huskiness. "Then I shall introduce you to sensations you never imagined."

"How could I feel any more delicious than I do now?"

she whispered.

Troy chuckled. "Trust me," he said.

"I want to," Samantha sighed, placing a hand gently to his cheek.

He captured that hand and lowered it to where he throbbed almost unmercifully. "Do you feel it?" he asked throatily.

"Feel what?" Samantha innocently asked, yet she felt how his largeness now even seemed almost alive!

"Remove my breeches," he said in a husky demand.

"I do feel so suddenly wicked." She softly laughed.

"Wicked ladies do wicked things," Troy teased. "Proceed, my lady. Send my heart into a tailspin."

Following his lead, she completed unsnapping his jeans, then slowly scooted them down over his hips while he removed his shoes. When his swollen need was fully revealed to her, she sucked in her breath and became swallowed whole by a rush of wonder and building fear. Such largeness could surely tear her apart! Was she even willing now to continue with this? Seeing him had brought her to her senses, yet there was a hidden desire coiling inside that aroused her.

He rolled her over on her back and anchored her beneath him while his lips quivered against hers in another gentle kiss. Samantha's world began melting away as his kiss grew more demanding, his hands urgent on her body. And when she felt his manhood graze her thigh, she once more tensed, and barely did she breathe as one of his knees parted her thighs and flowered her open to him.

Troy buried his lips along the delicate line of her neck and embraced her long and sweet as he began inching himself inside her. Suddenly he made one quick lunge and broke through her thin membrane which had proven to him that she, indeed, had never before been taken by a man.

The pain caused a soft cry to flow from between Samantha's lips, then she sighed as this pain miraculously changed into pleasure. Her hips strained upward, and she twined her arms about his neck, welcoming his timely eager strokes inside her, each one kindling a more hungry passion to course through her veins.

"God," Troy groaned, beads of perspiration now glistening on his brow. He gave her a meltingly hot kiss, his hand working feverishly on her breast.

Samantha lifted her legs and locked them about Troy's muscular male buttocks, breathless as she gave herself up to the rapture.

Together they plunged themselves into unfathomed depths, swept away by sensations as torrential as the tides.

"I love you," Samantha whispered, flushed with excitement. "Oh, how I do—love—you."

Once more he kissed her, his tongue surging between her teeth. She returned the kiss, feeling sensations she never had experienced before. It was a splash of warmth, heating up, as though a million bubbles of ecstasy exploded inside her as her body became a mass of sensual shivers.

She was mindless with pleasure for a brief moment, and then the feeling eased away, leaving her relaxed and at peace with herself as never before. Yet Troy's thrusts continued. She sensed that he was still searching for his own release so she continued to cling, happy that he was receiving pleasure from her.

In Samantha's mind's eye she suddenly saw Troy

dancing with Julia, laughing with her, joking with her, enjoying her. Jealousy threatened to spoil this moment of bliss, but Troy's throaty moan of pleasure, accompanied by sensual quiverings as he plunged harder into her, made her mind deliver itself back to thoughts only of him and the present moment.

Then it was over, and he relaxed on top of her, holding her in bondage with the tight grip of his muscled arms.

"Darling, are you disappointed?" he whispered into her ear.

"Disappointed?" she whispered back. "In what way?"

"Surely you know what I am asking."

"Yes. I know."

He drew a fraction away from her. His fingers were trembling as he smoothed some wet locks of her hair from her brow. "Well? Are you?" he persisted.

"It was beautiful," she sighed.

"The pain at first entry. Did it last long?"

"I don't even recall any pain, Troy," she softly teased.

A contented smile was his reply to her as he was happy that she had enjoyed it and that she had never been with another man before him. When this damn thing was settled between the North and the South, he would ask her to marry him. She was innocent as a babe. Yes, he would marry her.

Samantha trembled in a sudden chill as a gust of air whipped downward through the wide gaps in the roof. Troy saw this and gathered her clothes and handed them to her. Then he hurried into his own clothes, watching her silhouette in the darkness, seeing the gentle curves of her hips. When she turned sideways to flutter her silk gown over her head, he was given the full view of her perfectly rounded breasts which thrust out gracefully from her chest.

A renewed ache rose in his loins as he needed her again, but he knew that had to come later. Now was the time to convince her that he must have the map. He couldn't understand this game that she had chosen to play! She didn't seem to be the type to just idly toss away something that seemed so important. Somehow he had to get the map back in his possession. Many lives depended on his securing it. If the wrong person studied it and could decode it—

"There. That's somewhat better," Samantha said, laughing softly as she pulled her robe closed in front. "But still, these silk things just aren't enough to ward off further chill. I must return to the house, Troy."

Troy slipped into one shoe and then the other, still watching her. He was hesitant to mention the map again. He knew just what to expect of her. She would accuse him of making love to soften her into relinquishing the map to him. As he could see it, there would be no true way to convince her otherwise, so he would just have to take the chance that she would understand later, if not now.

He reached for her and pulled her gently into his arms. "Darling," he whispered, burrowing his nose into the flaming red of her hair. "I hate for you to go. I wish we could spend the full night together."

"A hayloft is not my idea of where to spend the first full night with the man of my choosing," she murmured, twining her arms about his neck, clinging.

Troy drew partially away from her and looked studiously down into her eyes. "Samantha, I must know where the—" he began, but was interrupted when a scraping noise at his side drew his eyes quickly around just as Julia's head appeared at the top of the ladder, peering over it and up into the hayloft.

"So this is where my cousin drifted away to in the middle of the night," Julia said, smiling coyly from Samantha to Troy. "My, oh, my. What *are* you two up to here in this drafty hayloft?"

Samantha's gaze jerked around, looking incredulously at Julia as she stepped on up from the ladder, into full view in her clinging, quite scanty lace-trimmed, silken nightgown. Even with only the moonlight streaming through the cracks in the roof, every sensual crevice and curve on Julia's body was exposed to the viewing eye through her attire. Samantha's face flamed with color, embarrassment and anger fusing inside her.

"Julia, what are you doing here?" Samantha hissed. "And—and dressed in such a way?"

Then Samantha grew numb inside as her gaze moved back to Troy, silently accusing him. She had been right from the first! Troy was only out here because he had originally planned to meet Julia and have his needs fulfilled by *her.* Samantha felt used, humiliated and very, very foolish.

Whipping herself away from Troy she brushed past Julia and down the ladder, closing her ears to Troy's protests of her sudden exit. Samantha cringed when she heard Julia's soft, wicked laughter. Tears then trickled from the corners of her eyes as she rushed on to the privacy of her room.

Throwing herself across her bed, she punched the mattress with her fists, now aware of a soreness between her thighs, bluntly reminding her of her wantonness. She had given up her virginity. And for *him?*

## Chapter Nine

The day was warm, the sun bright, the sky a ceiling of a crystal clear blue as Samantha, dressed in her jeans and plaid shirt, rode her horse. Hatless, she let her hair lift and fall upon her shoulders as she sent the brown mare into a steady gallop, feeling the need this morning to put a few miles between herself and Julia and the memories of the previous night. Though Julia had arrived back at the farmhouse shortly after Samantha, revealing that nothing illicit transpired between them, it wasn't proof that a rendezvous hadn't been planned earlier between Julia and Troy. It had been only chance that Samantha had been the first to arrive, and Troy had succeeded in seducing her instead of the woman who he had most obviously preferred.

"Oh! How could I have fallen into such a trap?" she harshly whispered. "I not only lost my virginity but also my pride!"

With her face flaming red from humiliation, she flicked the horse's reins and thrust her knees into its side.

"Take me away! Far away!" she shouted to the mare. She groaned as the bouncing of the horse made her muscles ache from the scuffle with the man the previous night. Also, to her chagrin, she still felt the raw soreness between her thighs.

She frowned darkly, wondering how such marvelous feelings which could have arisen from this part of her anatomy now pained her so. While with Troy the pain had blended into such a sweetness that she had momentarily lost her sense of time *and* place.

"And to whom I was even sharing this with?" she argued to herself. "But his eyes were like the sky is today, so blue and mesmerizing!"

The flat land of blowing Indian grass stretched out before her was only disturbed now by the sudden presence of a lone horseman heading her way. Samantha drew her reins, squinted her eyes and followed the approach of the man, not yet able to make out his full features because of the distance between them. But Samantha couldn't help but feel a trace of fear, realizing that her aloneness could put her in jeopardy. In her haste to leave the farm, she had even forgotten to bring her pistol with her. Why hadn't she remembered the dangers of traveling so far from the farm?

But she knew why. Troy Gilbert. Continual thoughts of him caused her to do many foolish things.

"Troy. Maybe the lone horseman is Troy, headed for the farm, in an attempt to confuse me even more," she whispered.

She leaned forward in the saddle, steadying herself as she peered more intensely at the figure moving toward her. The man didn't appear to be as tall and lean as Troy. But he was as impeccably dressed, in a dark frock coat, vest, and tight, matching breeches with a white ruffled collar at his throat, where a neat cravat had been tied. Only the complexion and hair coloring that showed beneath his tall top hat now proved that this man was not Troy. In fact, didn't the man closely resemble—

"Good Lord, no!" Samantha gasped. "Not Marion Yarborough. What have I led myself into? Two traps in two days? When I return to the farm, I must insist that Grandmama lock me in my room because I seem to have lost all ability to protect myself from my lack of logic."

Her first instinct was to swing her horse around and flee, but on second thought, she knew the futility of trying. Marion was much too close, and if his original plan this day was to seek her out for questioning or pray tell whatever else, she knew that he would manage this, no matter the obstacles! Wouldn't he be surprised that she was so approachable, almost being handed to him on a silver platter as she waited for his arrival to her side!

The closer he drew to her, the more Samantha tensed, her heart wildly pounding. How long had it been since she had met him face-to-face, for any sort of conversation? Wisely, in the past, he had not approached her, but he had always looked. God, how he had looked. It had always been as though he had been studying her, looking for more than the eye would allow. But Samantha knew not what. It hadn't been so much a lustful look, because he had done the same since before her womanly curves had grown into full bloom.

Then what?

A shiver of disgust coursed through her as Marion drew rein next to her. As always before, Samantha was filled with loathing for this man of unpleasant features with his shifty, almost colorless eyes, and his annoying half smile that was caused by a scar which drew his upper lip into a constant, tight curve at the right corner.

Slight of height, the weight he displayed was quite noticeable. As it was, pity the poor stallion on which Marion sat!

"Mr. Yarborough, why have you stopped while on your outing?" Samantha said dryly, tilting her chin haughtily. "What about me do you find so interesting?"

She met the challenge of his stare, though fear was now circling her heart. Never had she seen him look so threateningly toward her. In his eyes she could see a coldness, a daring, as he set his lips in a narrow line. And as his right hand went to the pistol belted at his hip, Samantha could hardly suppress the weakness growing in her knees nor the throbbing at her temple.

"Why did you stop when you saw my approach?" he growled.

He gestured with a wide sweep of his hand toward the outspreading of open meadow. "You have all this land on which to travel," he added. He leaned forward in the saddle. "Or do you know that I would eventually be seeking you out?"

"I don't know what you're talking about," Samantha said, swallowing hard.

"Where is it, Samantha?" he snarled. "You *do* have it, don't you? I would have more than likely found it hidden away in your room had you and your grandparents stayed away from the house for a while longer last night."

"Then it was you!" Samantha gasped, paling. She wrapped the reins around her hands, now truly believing it best that she try to flee! This evil man was capable of anything. And it was most certain that he did somehow know that she had the map. At all costs, she could not allow him to have it! She now knew that she had to give it to Troy, no matter how angry she was at him. Rather Troy than Marion Yarborough!

"I will not deny that it was I who searched your grandparents' drab farmhouse for the map," he brazenly admitted. "I knew that I would not be accused. Your grandfather quakes in his boots at even the mere thought of me and the power that I possess in this community."

Momentarily forgetting the map, Samantha went into the defense of her grandfather, even now forgetting her fear of Marion. "Hah!" she snapped, inching her mare closer to Marion's classic, black stallion. "If my grandpapa so fears you, why doesn't he sell his property to you? Do not mistake fear for *gallantry*, Mr. Yarborough."

Done! She had spoken well! Yet, she did so while not even understanding her grandfather's motives. First he showed fear; then hate seemed to become even an ally where Marion Yarborough was concerned. And now it appeared that Samantha wouldn't know why until she met and spoke with Doc Raley.

But even this could not come about until the death of Samantha's precious grandparents.

"I care not about why your grandfather behaves irrationally as he does from day to day," Marion scoffed, suddenly grabbing Samantha's reins from her, startling her into almost falling from her horse. "The map is the true issue here. Where is it, Samantha?"

Samantha steadied herself. "Return my reins this minute, sir," she hissed, now jerking at the reins. "My grandpapa will not keep quiet if you harm me. He will even kill you. I am sure that he is quite fed up with your antics. To even touch me is to set his wrath upon you!"

Marion chuckled amusedly, holding her reins firmly away from her. "That old man?" he said. "With his weak eyes hidden behind gold-framed spectacles? He couldn't see to aim a gun, much less shoot it."

"You speak of his being an old man," she said icily. "You're as old. Your fine clothes and the fact that you are not forced to wear eyeglasses does not make you appear to be younger or more agile than my grandpapa. Sir, you are fooling yourself into a grave should you further rile my grandpapa."

Marion still appeared to be smiling, yet he emitted a low growl and grabbed Samantha by the wrist. "Enough of this useless bantering," he said. "I want that map. You will go and get it for me or I will kill the whole lot of Ainsworths, you included."

Samantha flinched as his fingers dug into her flesh. "Sir, I know of no map," she bravely lied. "Why would I?"

"Must I remind you that I do not have the need of spectacles?" he snarled. "My eyes are perhaps even keener in vision than yours at your ripe, young age."

"So? What does that prove?" she argued, her head jerking up to see, over his shoulder, another rider on the horizon, quickly approaching.

"I saw Troy Gilbert give the map to you at the depot," he said. "Now try again denying that you do not have it. He wouldn't still be hanging around if you didn't."

"My word!" Samantha uttered, giving him a sour glance. "You think I cannot attract a gentleman's attention for myself?"

Her heart began to race as she was now able to make out who was fast approaching. Troy! There was no mistaking the midnight black of his hair as the sun danced upon it, nor the masculine way in which he sat in the saddle, attired in his smart frock coat and matching breeches and white silk shirt, appearing to be even whiter against the tan of his face. Only a short while ago Samantha would have been angered by his entry into her life again, but now he was sorely welcomed!

She focused her attention back on Marion, hoping that he hadn't noticed her staring into the distance. She wouldn't want him to know about Troy until Troy was upon him.

"If you thought that I had this map, why would one of your cohorts attack Troy in the darkness last night, while he was in my presence?" she challenged.

Marion chuckled. "We not only want the map," he said, "we also want the man who composed it. He could be useful, this man who owns a vast fleet of ships."

Samantha shook her head in confusion. "I don't understand," she murmured. "How is it that you even know Troy Gilbert?"

"You think that I would tell you anything?" he scoffed. "It is you who will give me answers."

His eyes squinted and his face lined with anger, he dismounted his horse and grabbed Samantha by an arm, jerking her to the ground where she stumbled and fell clumsily against him. Marion's other hand steadied her and, while doing so, crushed his fingers into her breast.

Samantha let out a loud yelp of pain, then with her free hand formed into a fist, punched Marion's chin. She flinched and suppressed another cry of pain, knowing that she had probably caused much more pain to her own knuckles than to him. But she was glad that she had been brave enough to at least try to defend herself.

Marion's head jerked with her blow, surprise showing

in his eyes. He then threw her roughly to the ground and fell to his knees over her, straddling her. "So you are a spitfire as well as a liar," he growled.

He held her wrists tightly to the ground, his gaze raking over her. "And you're almost as beautiful as your mother was," he said thickly.

"My—mother?" Samantha gasped. "How is it that you—knew—my mother? Why would you even make mention of her?"

Marion's eyes took on a haunted emptiness. "Never mind that," he said. "All I'm interested in is the map. The past is the past. The present is all that matters."

Samantha eyed him closely, completely puzzled over his mention of her mother, yet as he had said, the present had to be dealt with. She had to try harder to free herself from this evil man, though Troy surely would help her since she could now hear the horse's closer approach. Even Marion heard the horse because he jumped to his feet and yanked Samantha up, shoving her toward her horse.

"I'll deal with you later," he threatened, quickly mounting his horse. Without even looking to see who was only a few hoofbeats away, he rode off in a fury, leaving Samantha looking numbly after him.

Then she swung around just as Troy jumped from his horse to walk briskly toward her.

Flashes of the previous night materialized in Samantha's mind's eye, once more angering her. She rushed toward her horse, determined to not talk with Troy, no matter what. Seeing him again made her even more determined to not return the map to him. She would even *burn* it first!

Grabbing her horse's reins and fitting her foot into the

stirrup, she swung herself up and into the saddle just as Troy reached her.

"Samantha," he said, placing a hand on her horse to calm it as it nervously pawed at the ground, snorting. "Who was that? What was that all about?"

"It's no concern of yours," she said dryly. She gave him an icy look yet melted inside from his closeness, his handsomeness, his eyes that set her pulse to racing. She slung her hair back from her shoulders and looked away from him.

"Get out of my way," she said blandly. "I've better places to be than here and, indeed, better company to keep."

Troy yanked her reins from her hands. "You're not going anywhere until I get some answers," he growled.

"This is too much," Samantha angrily spat. "Why do you men persist in bothering me? Why do you persist in thinking you can get your way by force?" She jerked the reins until they were once more in her possession. "My horse's reins, sir, are mine. And I intend to use them, to get myself as far from you as I can."

"Samantha—"

Samantha glared down at him. "Step aside, Troy," she hissed. "Or I shall be forced to command my horse to run right over you."

Troy chuckled. "Now you wouldn't do that," he dared. "You don't even want to go."

"I didn't wish to be with or talk to Marion Yarborough, just as I don't wish to be with you," she said stubbornly.

Troy took a step backward, his face taking on a somber tone. "Marion Yarborough?" he said hoarsely. He looked into the distance, now only barely able to see the figure of a man on horseback, riding hurriedly away. "So that's

140

what that was all about. That sonofabitch was trying to force you into telling him about the map. It looks like they'll stop at nothing to get it in their possession."

Troy glared up at Samantha, once more taking hold of her reins but not succeeding at keeping them for long, for she, just as quickly, jerked them away from him. "Samantha, it's time to place all fun and games behind us," he growled. "You must give me that map."

Samantha's face grew red in color as hurt fused with anger inside her. "Fun? Games?" she said shallowly. "Is that all I ever was to you?"

She sank her knees deeply into her horse's sides, flicked her reins sharply, and sent her horse thundering away from Troy. She hated him! How could she have ever loved and trusted such a man? He didn't deserve love from any woman, most certainly not from her.

Seeing his mistake and realizing the importance of convincing Samantha that she was wrong about his feelings for her, Troy knew that talk of the map must be placed aside, though each day that passed meant possible disaster. But she was important. She would be his lifetime commitment once this feud between the North and the South was settled. So she had to come first now, no matter the outcome. He loved her. God, how he loved her. There could never be another woman who could take her place in his heart.

Rushing to his horse, he quickly mounted it, then hurried it onward, following Samantha, who seemed quite skilled with horses since she had already managed to be only a speck on the horizon.

"Hah!" Troy shouted, ducking low as his horse picked up speed. He kept his eyes on Samantha, making sure that Marion Yarborough didn't reappear on the scene, to cause her harm again. But it had appeared Marion was gone, for at least the time being. But what about later? Samantha, with her free spirit and stubborn streak, could get herself in a lot of trouble. If only she would part with the map!

Drawing closer now to her, Troy saw that she was headed for trees. Fearing losing her there, Troy urged his horse on even faster, slapping its mane with the reins, almost unmercifully. Troy would not let her go this time without convincing her that he loved her. He would speak of the map to her again, on the morrow. One more day and then it would be returned to him, and he could go on about his business. If what he had heard from what was usually a reliable source was true, his future was in jeopardy. Trade with the southern states was a necessity! Surely Lincoln wouldn't—

But if Lincoln *did,* Troy had to make the best of the ugly situation. And damn it, he couldn't take Samantha into his confidence about this, even if she was from one of the states which, only this day, had joined others, to be called the Confederate States of America! Only a few knew. She could not yet be added to this list of few.

Seeing her now become almost swallowed whole into the island of trees, Troy almost panicked. Yet, in only a matter of moments, he was also there, but slowed by the thickness of the brush and the crowded trees.

Hearing the soft whinny of a horse not far ahead, Troy tensed. He peered sharply ahead and caught the reflection of water, and then saw Samantha standing beside a tranquil creek while her horse drank thirstily at her side. When Samantha turned and let her gaze meet his, Troy knew that something had compelled her to wait, to meet his approach head-on.

Dismounting, Troy walked the horse the rest of the way until he was standing face-to-face with Samantha. He slapped his horse's rump, urging it to drink beside Samantha's horse, then reached a hand to Samantha, taking one of hers in his. He felt her fingers stiffen, yet there was a trembling in them which proved to him that she did still care and was moved by his presence.

"Samantha, why do you always want to run away from me?" he asked, his voice low and strained. "I love you. Surely you have to know that."

Samantha's eyes shifted, her insides turning to jelly as she realized how hard she had to fight to keep her feelings in check. "You prove your love in such strange ways," she murmured. "Even now you are here for all the wrong reasons."

"Why did you stop and wait for me?"

"It was not of my choosing. My horse had become too lathered by my overtaxing him. That's all."

"And you expect me to believe that?" he chuckled, glancing over at the perfectly cooled body of her horse.

"You believe what you choose to believe," she said bitterly, easing her hand from his. She turned to her horse and ran a hand down its mane. "And now that my horse is in better shape, I shall move on. I've had enough of you and your lies for today."

In one wide step, Troy had his hands at Samantha's waist and had spun her around into his arms. "Damn you," he said huskily. "If words don't work, action sure as hell will."

He crushed his lips down upon hers, his hands on her neck as he held her tightly into place. Squirming, Samantha pushed at his chest but felt the spiraling of her senses. His kiss was so utterly delicious.

143

Slowly the fight left her, and she found herself slinking her body into the curve of his. Her hands crept along the hard lines of his chest, on around, until she was clinging to him from around his neck. When his tongue moved between her teeth in a sensuous warm wetness, she let her tongue meet his and flick against it. And as his hands lowered from her hair and began unbuttoning her shirt, she was too carried away on another rapturous cloud of ecstasy to protest. She had needs, just as he did. Even feeling the wickedness of her needs seemed to add to the excitement that was building inside her.

Then for some reason unknown to her, Marion Yarborough's words began tormenting her: that she was almost as beautiful as her mother. Had he known her mother before even her father? Had her mother known this man in a wild and wanton way? Did Samantha inherit such a trait? Such a thought caused her to shiver violently, hating Marion Yarborough so.

Troy drew away from her and gently framed her face between his hands. "Are you all right?" he asked, studying her face and how it seemed to be blossoming in color. Her green eyes even appeared to have taken on a troubled expression, making them lose their crispness. "Surely my kissing you doesn't distress you, so that you shudder because of it."

Samantha laughed softly. "No," she said, reaching to touch his cheek. "I have tried hard to wish that were so, but it wasn't because of the kiss. It was something quite unrelated to you."

His fingers lowered once more to her shirt, and he opened it so that her breasts were now fully exposed to the heat of his eyes. He cupped them both and smoothed his thumbs over her hardened nipples, hearing a deep

144

sigh escape quietly through her parted lips.

Samantha closed her eyes and sucked in her breath as Troy placed his lips to a breast and softly kissed its taut tip. Her fingers circled into fists at her side, plagued by the sweet pain that was awakening between her thighs.

He gazed at her, a half smile playing on his lips. "You don't seem to appear to have gotten enough of me now," he teased, his fingers grazing the softness of the side of her breasts.

Samantha stiffened. She shoved him away from her, his words breaking the sensuous spell that had begun to spin a web around them. "What *was* I thinking," she said, her fingers already fastening the buttons of her shirt. "Troy Gilbert, you do have a way with women— even those who despise you!"

Troy kneaded his chin, an eyebrow arched. "Despise?" he chuckled. "So now you despise me?"

"That's what I said," Samantha said, now stomping toward her horse.

"Then I guess it doesn't matter if—I—do—this—" Troy said, going to her. He gathered her up fully into his arms and carried her toward the creek.

Samantha's eyes were wide. She began pummeling his chest with her fists and kicking her legs. "What are you doing?" she fumed. She looked down at the water, where he had stopped. "Let me go, Troy. If you do what I think—"

Troy swung Samantha over the water, then suddenly released her. She emitted a scream as she fell. The water was a cushion as she splashed into it, her bottom settling into the sandy bed of the creek.

"Ouch!" she yelled, then glared up at him as she pushed herself back up. "You're crazy!" She looked

145

down at her water-soaked jeans and shirt, feeling her feet squishing around in her leather boots as she left the water and stood on the banks of the creek.

"Why did you do this to me?" she demanded.

"To shake some sense into you," Troy said, suppressing a laugh behind his hand. Then as he saw how her wet clothes clung to her sensuous curves, he became aroused.

Samantha gestured with a sweep of her hands over her body. "And this is how you do it?" she shrieked. "You get me soaked to the skin?"

"One way to remedy that," Troy said, going to her and lifting her damp strands of hair from her shoulders, "is to just take your wet clothes off and dry yourself beneath me."

"Oh!" she softly cried, slapping his hands away. "Just get away from me."

"Come on, Samantha," Troy persisted, his fingers now once more working with the buttons of her shirt. "Surely you can take a joke."

"Joke?" she argued, again slapping his hand away. "You have a rotten sense of humor." She looked down at herself, wiggled her toes in her boots, then looked back up at him with soft wonder in her eyes. "What am I to do? I can't let my grandparents see me like this."

"Do you mean wet?"

"You know that I do."

"Then do as I suggested. Remove your clothes. Dry them beneath the sun while you and I—"

"Never!" she hissed, backing away from him. Then her breath was stolen from her as she lost her footing and felt herself once more falling, but this time from her own doing, not his, as she clumsily fell backward, back into the water.

Her legs tangled as she hit the bottom of the creek, causing her to twist around and settle facedown in the water. Though her ears were beneath the surface of the water, she could hear Troy's roar of laughter. This spurred her anger even more. She pushed herself up from the water in a flash, coughing and wiping the wetness from her eyes, then spun around and faced him.

"I hope you're enjoying yourself," she hissed, flinging her wet hair from her shoulders with a jerk of her head. She began twisting the tail of her shirt as she once more climbed to flat, dry land. Then she became aware of her one exposed breast, where the shirt had fallen open from the shock of her fall. She began to cover it, but Troy was too soon there with his lips lowered over the nipple.

As usual, Samantha could hardly resist his kiss, and seeing him so close to the water was just too much of a temptation to ignore. And wasn't he too preoccupied to notice what she had planned for him?

When he placed his lips at the hollow of her throat to kiss her ardently there, Samantha softly put her hands at his chest and—then—shoved.

Troy let out a cry of surprise as he tumbled sideways into the water. Samantha burst into laughter, especially after seeing the dumbfounded look on his face as he now sat in the water, looking up at her. His hair had never been as black as it dripped water from it onto the brown wool of his frock coat. His eyes had never been as blue nor as wide. At this moment, Samantha had never loved him as much. He seemed like an innocent child, having been gotten the better of by a buddy, not the woman he professed to love.

Wiping a laughter tear away that was trickling down

her cheek, Samantha stooped to her knees and gazed directly into Troy's eyes. "Why, darling, how clumsy you've suddenly become," she teased.

"Samantha, do you know what these clothes cost which you've just now ruined by your impish ways?" Troy growled, lifting the tail of his coat, wringing water from it. It reeked of wet wool. "It'll probably shrink so fast I won't be able to even get it off."

"Then hurry and take it off now, my love, before it does," Samantha further teased. "Isn't that what you suggested I do?"

"You witch," Troy said, chuckling. His lips rose into an amused smile, his eyes twinkled. "But, yes, you're right."

He struggled out of his wet coat and threw it up on dry land. His cravat was next and then his shirt. And when he reached beneath the water and removed his shoes and socks, Samantha began to wonder just how far he was going to go. She watched as he rose to his feet and unfastened his breeches.

"My breeches must be slipped off real quickly," Troy said, still half smiling up at her. "I can already feel them tightening in a delicate area. We mustn't have that."

Samantha's heart fluttered and her face reddened as he slipped his breeches down, revealing to her the part of his anatomy which already sent her blood to warming at merely the sight of it.

Embarrassed, she straightened to a full standing position and turned her back quickly to him. But when she heard the splash of water, she took a sideways glance and saw him leaving the creek, and he was already beside her with his hands at her waist, forcing her around to face him.

"It's your turn to remove your wet clothes, Saman-tha," he said huskily. "We don't want you to catch a death of cold by wearing them."

She looked up into his eyes, wanting to fight him off, but she was becoming mesmerized all over again by his nearness, this time even more because of his total nudity. She didn't dare look down, knowing that he was ready for her with his rod of steel. Even now she felt she needed to accept him inside her, the pulsating between her thighs becoming so severe. It was no longer a sweet pain. It was a dull ache.

His lips came down gently on hers as his hands removed her shirt and lowered her jeans, stopping at her boots.

Troy lifted his lips from hers. "Darling, your boots," he said in a husky whisper.

Under his spell, Samantha bent and yanked first one boot off and then the other, tossed them aside, then watched as Troy stooped before her and eased her jeans on away from her.

Then he playfully tugged at one of her ankles until she bent to her knees and into his embrace, and he lowered her on down to the ground. Their bodies locked together in a lovers' embrace.

Samantha's hands traveled over his sleekly muscled shoulders, down his smooth back, and then slowly around, to where his curling chest hairs tapered down to his waist. She didn't have to lower her hands any farther to feel him. His maleness was pressed hard against her abdomen, where he was teasingly, slowly gyrating it into her flesh.

A thick, husky groan rose into the air as she opened herself to him, and he entered her in one motion. He held her as though in a vise as he began his eager strokes. His lips were reining kisses along her face, and then they found her lips and kissed their petal softness.

Samantha's soft moans repeatedly surfaced from inside her. She clung to him, her hips straining upward, meeting his eager movements. And then they shared the quiet explosion of their love as their bodies shook and quaked together.

Still floating, Samantha basked in the afterglow of their intense lovemaking.

Then Troy drew away from her and looked down into her eyes, his own eyelids heavy, still so passion filled.

"I love you so," he said thickly. "Marry me, Sam. After this nonsense with the North and South is over, marry me."

Samantha's mouth dropped open in surprise. "Marry—you?" she whispered, ignoring the fact that he had called her by her dreaded nickname, Sam. Somehow, she even liked the way he had said it.

He ran a thumb beneath her chin and on down, so that his hand fully cupped a breast. "Well? Will you?" he asked, now lowering a kiss to the taut nipple. "Perhaps we wouldn't have too long to wait."

"Why wait?" she murmured, her heart beating wildly.

"By asking that, is that your way of saying yes?" he asked anxiously.

Samantha wanted to fully trust him and his offer. To marry her would be full proof that he had made love with her because of her, not the map that he wanted to reclaim from her. Then she became suspicious all over again, realizing that he said they would marry later.

She eased from his arms and scooted away from him. "I didn't say yes," she murmured, reaching for her wet jeans. "I asked why must we wait, if you truly want to marry me?"

Troy rose as he leaned up on an elbow to face her. "There's too much unrest in the country right now," he said thickly. "If there's a war, who's to know what will happen? I wouldn't want to wed you just to make you a widow."

Samantha blanched. "Widow?" she gasped. "Troy, I never thought about the danger to you that a war between the North and South could bring." She shivered involuntarily and threw herself into his arms as he rose and drew her upward.

"I won't be in any danger if I have anything to do with it," he grumbled. "Nor will any of my acquaintances. But Samantha, if this is to be seen to, I must be on my way."

He held her partially away from him, looking longingly down into her eyes. "You see, I hadn't planned to be in the Springfield area so long. I've much to do—people to contact."

Samantha once more eased into his arms and pressed her cheek against the bare flesh of his chest. "I don't want you to go," she whispered. "It may be forever before I shall see you again."

"That's true," Troy said thickly. "That's why wedding plans must be delayed."

"Yes. I can understand," Samantha murmured, her eyes clouding with tears. She could hear his heart thudding hard against his chest and could tell that her nearness did have a continuing sensuous effect on him. She now truly believed that he loved her for her own sake.

"Do you honestly understand, Sam?"

"Yes," she sighed. Then she giggled. "You're calling

me by my nickname, and I don't even want to object. Somehow it makes me feel closer to you."

"Don't think that I could ever think of you as less feminine by calling you that," he said and chuckled. His hands ran down the sweet, gentle curves of her body. "God, are you beautiful."

Samantha's breath caught in her throat when his fingers found the core of her being and began to caress it. She enjoyed the warmth spreading through her body. Yet, she couldn't let this begin again between them. She had other plans.

Slipping away from him and once more reaching for her jeans and quickly slipping into them, she looked coyly up at him. "I must return to my grandparents' house," she said, watching a keen disappointment wash across his face.

"Just like that? So quickly?" Troy softly argued.

"Yes. I must."

"I must leave also," he said. "But let's be together just awhile longer, Sam. Who knows when we will—"

Samantha's jeans were in place and fastened and her shirt slipped over her shoulders, yet not buttoned. She went to Troy and placed a forefinger to his lips to seal them of further words. "Shh, my love," she murmured. "We'll meet again. soon. Even tonight, if you'll agree to."

He eased her finger away from his lips. "Tonight?" he said, forking an eyebrow.

"I'll have a surprise for you if you'll meet me at the barn right after sunset," she said, quickly buttoning her shirt. She wanted to tell him that she planned to give him the map, but she felt it would make their meeting more exciting if there was an element of surprise involved.

Yes. It was best to give him the map. He had proven enough to her these past moments for her to feel free and finally give it to him. Perhaps his possessing it could even speed up their plans for marriage.

"Surprise?" Troy said, bending to rescue his own clothes and begin dressing. "What sort?"

"You'll see." Samantha giggled. "If you'll come to meet with me."

"*If?*" He chuckled. "I'll be there, Sam. I'll be there. I like surprises." He had to wonder if the surprise could be the map. If not, he would have to insist that she give it to him this night anyway, no matter what the outcome. He had waited long enough.

# Chapter Ten

Samantha knew the difficulty of sneaking into the house in broad daylight, undetected. The house was so small. There would surely be someone in either the living room or kitchen, the only two rooms that fed into the hallway which would lead her to the privacy of her bedroom.

If only she could avoid meeting Julia head-on before changing her wet clothes and soggy boots! Wouldn't Julia have fun tormenting her about how she happened to be in such a mess!

"Oh, well," Samantha sighed, stepping up on the front porch and heading toward the door. "I do what I must."

Her heart warmed with thoughts of what then happened shortly after that. Guilt would not spoil her memories of their sensual embraces this time. They would eventually be married.

Holding her head high, her hair in knotted damp strands on her shoulders, she stepped on into the living room. She stiffened when she found everyone there, sitting comfortably around the room in their chosen

154

chairs. Her grandmother was knitting, Julia was embroidering, her grandfather was deeply engrossed in reading the early afternoon newspaper.

So far no one had noticed her standing in the shadows. She barely breathed. All three would probably jump her at once.

"So it's happened," Melvin growled, still staring at the newspaper that he held up close to his eyes.

"What's happened, Melvin?" Dorothy June asked, not missing a stroke with her knitting needles, click-clacking them together while keeping her eyes focused on her handiwork.

"War," Melvin grumbled. "There's to be war for sure now."

"Why is that?" Dorothy June asked, still clicking away. "What's in the paper that makes you say that?"

"It's the damn southern states," he said. "They've done the damnedest thing."

"What now?" Dorothy June sighed, resting her knitting on her lap to look toward him. "Why can't they accept Lincoln and what he feels is best for the country? He's such a dear, smart man. I don't understand how anyone can dislike him. He only wants to free those poor slaves."

Melvin folded the newspaper and turned it over, scanning that page now placed before his eyes. "It's more than the slavery issue," he said. "It's also the economic rivalry between the North and South, the damn jealousy between the commercial and planting sections of the country. Slavery has become the most talked about issue because it's absolutely necessary to carry on the plantations of the South."

"Tsk, tsk," Dorothy June said, slowly shaking her

head. "It's so sad. Those poor folk. They're caught right in the middle of this senseless feudin'."

"There's more to worry 'bout now besides the slaves," Melvin grumbled, adjusting the spectacles on his nose as he placed the newspaper on the table beside his chair. "It's the white folks who'll soon be needin' your sympathies and prayers, Dorothy June."

Dorothy June leaned forward, her ocean blue eyes wide. "Why do you say that?" she asked, now seeing Melvin's concern in the way his face had become so intensely drawn, his eyes shadowed in troubled thought.

Melvin tapped the newspaper with the fingers of his left hand while taking a half-smoked cigar from his overall pocket with his other. "It says here in the newspaper that the southern states have seceded from the Union and have set up their own separate nation called the Confederate States of America," he said thickly. "A Jefferson Davis has been named the president. Can you beat that? They've got the gall to even call another man president with Lincoln in the White House in Washington! Those responsible for such nonsense should first be horsewhipped then hung!"

He scraped a long fingernail across the tip of a match causing flames to hiss and dance in a small golden glow, then he lighted his cigar. He flipped the match into the dead ashes of the fireplace, then settled back in the chair, staring off into space, fearful of the future for many reasons.

Dorothy June's shoulders slumped. "Good Lord," she whispered. "There will be a war for sure now. How dreadful, Melvin."

Julia set her embroidery work aside and rose from her chair, a picture of gentle frailty in the soft flutter of her blue silk dress with an abundance of white lace at its low bodice. "I don't look to war as dreadful," she said, smiling down at her grandparents. "I think a war will be exciting."

Melvin's eyes shot upward. "Exciting?" he gasped. "Don't you know how many men could be killed from both the North and the South? There's even mention of a possible blockade of the southern states. If so, there would not only be war by land, but also by sea. Julia, your head is in the clouds if you think this is in any way exciting."

Samantha was still in the shadows, almost too numb now to even move. She had absorbed all of her grandfather's words and had expected to hear of the formation of the Confederate States of America. Her father was even leading this movement. But—a—blockade? What sort of blockade? How could it affect Johnston Oaks? And war? Oh, God, she was fast remembering Troy's words and why their marriage must be delayed.

Unable to stand not knowing the full details that the newspaper article had disclosed, Samantha took a quick wide step and let herself be seen. "Grandpapa, the newspaper," she said, hurrying to the table to grab it. "I must see it. I must read it. I want to see for myself every word written about this new development."

"My word!" Dorothy June gasped, seeing Samantha's complete disarray. "What on earth happened to you, Samantha?"

"Yes, cousin Samantha, what sort of mischief have you been involved in today?" Julia said, viewing Samantha closely and smirking. "Not one inch of you appears to be dry. Do you make it a habit to go swimming fully clothed?"

Samantha's face grew hot with embarrassment. She avoided Julia, then smiled awkwardly at her grandmother and her grandfather. "Seems I took a spill," she said, running her hands over the wetness of her jeans. "I had stopped to refresh my horse at the creek and darn if it didn't nudge me from behind and knock me in, boots and all."

Julia gave Samantha a coy look. "A likely story," she scoffed. "Surely you can come up with a better one than that."

Samantha spun around on a heel to boldly face Julia, but her eyes were again drawn to the newspaper, and she decided that anything that Julia had to say was nothing to concern herself over.

"You go to your room and change into something dry," Dorothy June said, rising to go and smooth Samantha's hair back from her shoulders. "And look at your lovely hair. It'll take hours to brush the tangles from it."

"Grandmama, dry clothes and my hair will have to wait," Samantha softly argued. "I must read the newspaper. Do you forget father? He and Johnston Oaks may be in danger."

"The blockade could cause your pa pressures," Melvin said, flicking ashes from his cigar into an ashtray. "But I doubt if things'll go that far. Lincoln will take care of this latest problem. You'll see. The Confederate States of America will be dissolved, just as quickly as they were formed. Things just can't be allowed to get this out of hand. Surely no one wants war."

"Except for Julia," Samantha grumbled, giving Julia an ugly glance. She carried the newspaper to the light of the window and began reading. Then she saw a map on one of the pages of the newspaper which was an exact replica of the one that she had in her possession, except that the words written in code at the top were missing. The other difference was the dots on this newspaper map. Ice filled her veins as she read the names of the cities out loud that each of these dots represented.

"New Orleans, Galveston, Savannah, Mobile, Wilmington, Pensacola, and—*Charleston*," she whispered. "All major southern ports."

Her gaze moved upward, registering shock. "My God," she said. "It does appear there may be a blockade. The North plans to cut off the southern exports and European imports. Father will—be—ruined."

"Naw. It won't be allowed to happen," Melvin scoffed. "Things'll turn around. Don't worry yourself so 'bout it."

Samantha was once more thinking about the map in the jar hidden beneath the flooring in her room. How was it that Troy should know in advance about a blockade? Surely that's what his map did represent! But what was his connection with it? And the code at the top. Did it mean good or bad things for the South? Surely it wasn't good. Troy could only be working for the North since he was in the North.

Her gut twisted as she now realized that he must be her enemy. There was no way that she could give him the map now. In fact, what was she to do with it?

In dire need of seeing and studying the map again, she placed the newspaper aside and tried to appear as calm as possible as she began edging her way from the room.

"It's about time you decide to go to change those clothes," Dorothy June said. "Leave the talk of war to

159

the men, Samantha. We women have our place in society, you know. Now go change into something frilly. I'll brush your hair for you."

The reference made by her grandmother that women had their place in society made Samantha realize just how far apart they were in their viewpoints about life. Samantha did not feel at all like one who should be sheltered while a man—or men—shaped her destiny for her. She felt quite responsible and in charge of her own future, a future that now surely did not include Troy.

"I'll be awhile, Grandmama," she quickly interjected. "Please don't bother worrying over my hair. I can take care of it."

"You now act awfully anxious to be alone in your room," Julia said, taking a step toward Samantha. "Perhaps I should accompany you there and assist you in your change of wardrobe. I could even brush your hair."

Dorothy June clasped her hands together before her, looking adoringly toward Julia. "Why how sweet and thoughtful of you, Julia," she said. "This is what I like to see in my babies. Devotion."

Samantha's eyes rolled upward, not believing how gullible her grandmother could be at times. Then she gave Julia a sour look. "Julia, how sweet you are," she mocked. "But must I remind you how small my room is? There's only room for one at a time. I'm afraid I must decline your generous offer and tend to my own comforts all by myself."

"Ah, too bad," Julia said and softly laughed. "If only walls could talk."

Samantha circled her hands into fists at her side, her heart racing. "What are you implying?" she said dryly. She couldn't help but wonder if Julia had been snooping and had found the hidden jar.

"Oh, never mind," Julia said with a jerk of her head and swoosh of skirts as she made a quick spin and left the room ahead of Samantha.

"What on earth was that all about?" Melvin said, pushing himself up from his chair. "There was much unsaid between you and Julia, Samantha. Want to tell me about it?"

Samantha's eyes wavered as she let her fingers relax from their fist position. "Julia talks in riddles," she said and shrugged. "I don't have any idea of what she was talking about this time."

Dorothy June once more began fussing with Samantha's hair. "Samantha, go on to your room," she said. "You're going to take a chill. I just know it."

"All right, grandmama," she murmured. "I do feel a bit chilled."

"I'll fix you a cup of hot chocolate and bring it to you."

Samantha placed a hand on her grandmother's arm. "No. That won't be necessary," she murmured. "Please. Just let me change clothes and then I'll want that hot chocolate, but not in my room. I'll come to the kitchen."

"Whatever you say, honey," Dorothy June said, an eyebrow lifting, giving Melvin a harried look of wonder.

Samantha kissed her grandmother's cheek, then rushed on away from her, feeling a keen sense of relief in finally being alone. She could hardly wait to see the map again. Yet, hadn't she almost memorized everything about it? It did appear to pose a threat to her father.

"Father!" she suddenly said to herself. "I now know what I must do! I must return to the Carolinas and take the map to Father! Perhaps he can decipher the code and somehow prevent whatever threat it might be. Yes. I

161

shall leave today, as soon as I can pack my trunk. I mustn't let Troy even guess what I'm doing."

She remembered their planned rendezvous for this coming night. A gnawing ache circled her heart as she knew that he would be waiting for her in vain. From the very first their relationship had seemed doomed. They were casualties of war, before any battle had even been fought on land or sea between the North and the South.

"A battle of the heart already fought and lost," she softly cried, muffling her words and sobs behind a hand.

Then she wiped a tear from her cheek, lifted her chin stubbornly, and hurried on into her room. Closing the door behind her, she looked toward the braided oval rug, and her heart skipped a beat when she saw that it was crumpled aside, baring the loose board.

"She has been snooping!" Samantha gasped. "Damn that Julia. What did she hope to gain? Perhaps—"

She covered her mouth with her hand, her heart sinking to her feet. "Oh, no," she gasped. "Surely she didn't know that Troy wanted this. She wouldn't give it to him!"

Falling to her knees she eagerly began to pry the board up with her fingers, cringing as her fingertips became inflamed with soreness. And then suddenly the board was up enough for her to see the jar, and it still held the map safely inside it.

"Thank God," she whispered. She reached for the jar, squeezed it through the opening, and quickly unscrewed the lid. Her fingers were trembling as she reached down and removed the folded paper from inside it.

She went to her bed and unfolded the paper, stretching it out upon the bed and peering downward at it. Her heart pumped fast as she once more studied it, knowing that it did represent the southern states. It surely did have something to do with the hinted blockade. But what?

Her gaze moved to the top of the page, seeing the code. She slowly shook her head. "There's no way I can figure that out," she sighed. "There's only one thing to do. I must return to Johnston Oaks. Immediately. Surely father can make something of it. But if not, at least it won't be in the hands of an enemy."

The creaking of the door behind her took Samantha by surprise, and she didn't have time to hide the map. Then Samantha rose quickly to her feet, anger flashing in her eyes when she discovered Julia entering the room.

"What do you want now?" Samantha hissed, placing her hands on her hips. "Doesn't the wish for privacy mean anything to you?"

Julia looked on past Samantha, seeing the map. Her lips lifted in a mocking smile. "Just as I thought," she said. "It was you who put the map in the jar." Her eyes challenged Samantha. "And the map is why you were so eager to come to your room. Why, Samantha? What does it mean? Where did you even get it?"

At least there was one thing to be thankful for. It was obvious that Julia hadn't yet surveyed the newspaper and realized that this map was almost an exact replica of the one that was a part of this day's disturbing news. But then there was the fact that Julia had invaded Samantha's privacy by coming to the room and finding the map while Samantha was on her outing.

Samantha took a step toward Julia and blocked her further entry into the room. "Who do you think you are, by coming into my room to snoop while I was gone?" she snapped. "And how did you even know about the hiding place beneath the board?"

Julia stepped on around Samantha and sat down on the edge of the bed. She picked up the jar and screwed the lid back onto it. "I was bored, *bored*," she said. "So I thought I'd just check my old hiding place that I found while visiting grandmama when I was a child." Her eyes took on a mischievous glint as she looked up at Samantha. "But I now know that it wasn't solely my hiding place. You also knew about it. What a shame. And a map? When did you hide it there, cousin? Why did you have the need to remove it now? What is there about this map that is so mysterious?"

"You knew about this loose board all these years?" Samantha gasped. "I thought it was my secret, and all along you knew?"

Julia giggled. "Seems that way, Samantha," she said. She placed the jar on the table and reached for the map, but Samantha was quickly there, with the map already in her possession.

"Julia, you must not tell a soul about this map," Samantha warned. "It could even mean a matter of life or death." She implored Julia with her eyes. "Promise me, Julia, that you won't tell."

Julia rose with a flutter of skirts from the bed. She smiled coyly up at Samantha. "And what is my reward, cousin, for such a promise? For my silence?" she asked in a low whisper as she leaned up into Samantha's face.

"God, Julia," Samantha said hotly. "Must you always want something from people? Can't you ever just give? All I want is a mere promise. Is that too much to ask?"

Julia shrugged and stepped away from Samantha. "Like I said. I'm bored," she said matter-of-factly. "I need something. Anything to help pass my dreary days and nights while I'm forced to live here in the country."

She clasped her hands together and looked toward the ceiling. "Lord how I miss men. In New York, there were so many. While here—"

Then Julia's face took on an impishness as she fluttered her skirts hurriedly back to Samantha. "I want *him* as a reward for my silence," she quickly blurted.

Samantha blanched. "You want who?" she dared to ask, already knowing the answer.

"Of course you know of whom I am speaking," Julia taunted.

"Yes. I guess I do," Samantha murmured.

"Well? Is it a deal?"

"Julia, I thought it was you who always said that a man—any man was yours just for the asking. If this is true, why do you feel the need to bargain over Troy?" Samantha said icily.

"Because he is worth it," Julia said and laughed. "And because for once, a man has not wholly given in to my charm. Seems you've gotten in the way, cousin."

Julia gave Samantha a studious stare, raking her eyes slowly up and down her full length. "But I must say, I do not understand why Troy's attentions were drawn more to you than me," she pondered aloud. "Surely there's something more than mere looks, cousin." Her eyes settled on the map. "Perhaps even—the—map? Does Troy Gilbert want the map?"

Samantha's insides flamed with heated rage, yet she wouldn't let this get out of hand. She had to draw attention away from Troy's connections with the map, and quickly. And wasn't Julia only interested in the man? Anything else to her was trivial.

"You can have him," Samantha quickly blurted, aching inside with the thought of Troy and Julia intimately together. But it was the only way. And Troy was beyond her own reach now, because he was the enemy.

But she also knew that it was easy to tell Julia that she could have him because Troy would know Samantha had left with the map and he wouldn't even be available for Julia. He would most surely follow Samantha.

"What?" Julia gasped.

Samantha spun around on a heel and placed the map inside her purse. "You can have Troy Gilbert," she said shallowly, now removing her boots. "He is yours to do what you wish with him. I care not for the man. He is a man of questionable character." She looked up at Julia with a gleam in her eyes. "Yes, you two should make a perfect pair. Have fun, cousin Julia."

"My word!" Julia said, then left in a rush from the room, slamming the door behind her.

"Whew!" Samantha whispered, wiping a bead of perspiration from her brow. "And now how am I to tell Grandmama and Grandpapa that I must return to Johnston Oaks?"

Her eyes brightened. "It will be simple," she said. "They would have to even want me to return home before war breaks out. And war is inevitable. The newspapers shout the news of war."

She shook her head. "Yes. It will be easy. And I must leave before nightfall. Troy must be made to wait alone in the barn *this* night."

# *Chapter Eleven*

Troy paced in the darkness just inside the open barn door, occasionally stopping to look toward the farmhouse, wondering what was taking Samantha so long. She had sounded excited about this meeting. She had even suggested it. So then why didn't she come?

A soft breeze fluttered straw down from the hayloft overhead, a horse whinnied from its stall, and in the far distance a loon bounced its hysterical sort of cry from across a body of water.

And then the banging of a door was added to the night noises, causing Troy's heart to skip a beat and then race as he slipped from the barn and watched a female figure gliding beneath the moonlight, along the gravel path.

But then Troy's anxiety waned as he watched the demure figure walk casually in the other direction from where he stood.

"What the—" Troy wondered aloud, raking his fingers through his hair in frustration. He set his jaw firmly and walked in hurried, wide strides away from the barn, toward the continuing moving silhouette. And once he was upon her, he stopped short, seeing it was Julia.

"Troy! Thank God it's only you," she said, breathing hard. "When I heard footsteps, I was afraid to look."

Troy glanced toward the house, then back at Julia. "Have you seen Samantha?" he asked thickly. "Is she still in the house?"

Julia's lips formed a pout. "Oh, I see," she said. "You're only here to see my cousin. I should have known."

"Well? Where is she?" Troy persisted.

"Did you two have a planned rendezvous?" Julia said bitterly. "Samantha made a bargain with me. You are to be—" Then she placed a hand over her mouth, catching herself before finishing her statement which would reveal that Troy had been the bargain.

"You were saying?" Troy said, lifting an eyebrow quizzically.

"Oh, nothing." Julia giggled. She stepped to his side and locked her arm through his. "All that matters is that you're here. Let's walk together, Troy. It's such a beautiful night. It's a shame to waste it."

Troy eased his arm from hers. "I think not," he said dryly.

Julia's eyes widened, stunned that this man would continue to ignore her. "It's because of Samantha, isn't it?" she said icily.

"You know how I feel about her, Julia. I've not kept it a secret."

"I also know how she feels about you."

"Then why don't you run along and leave me to my waiting. Samantha will be along any minute now."

"You surely don't know how she feels about you or

168

you wouldn't be wasting your time waiting on her."

"Oh? And what is that supposed to mean?"

"It means that she detests you, Troy," Julia said with a toss of her head. "She sees you as a rogue."

"A—rogue?" he said hoarsely. Then he laughed. "Yes. At first that's how she saw me. But not now. We have an understanding."

"Hah! Some understanding," Julia scoffed.

"All right, Julia," Troy said, growing annoyed. "What are you implying now?"

"If she understood you so well and cared so deeply for you, why did she leave today, to return to the Carolinas, apparently without a word to you of her departure?"

Troy felt the color drain from his face and his stomach lurch. "She *what?*" he gasped.

Julia shrugged. "She is now surely many miles out of Springfield on a stagecoach, on her way home, to Johnston Oaks," she said. "It was a quick decision on her part. The newspaper's mentioning some sort of blockade seemed to prompt her decision to return to her father."

"Blockade? Newspaper?" Troy said, clasping his fingers tightly to her shoulders. "What newspaper?"

"Today's," Julia said, grimacing as his fingers dug into her flesh. "Troy, you're hurting me. Release me at once."

Troy dropped his hands to his side. "Sorry," he apologized. He kneaded his brow. "I didn't take the time to read the paper this afternoon. I was meeting with friends. I didn't know that news of the blockade was out, for all to know. Damn. *Damn.*"

"It is only a rumor," Julia corrected. "Why concern yourself about such nonsense?"

"Rumors of war and blockades are not to be taken

lightly," he warned. He eyed her guardedly. "Samantha left when?"

"Only a few short hours ago."

"She didn't mention me to you?"

"She mostly talked of secrets," Julia said, watching him closely for his reaction.

"What sort?"

"Something about a map," she murmured, never having thought to keep such a secret all to herself, though she had promised. Promises were made to be broken.

Once more he grabbed onto her shoulder. He leaned down into her face. "A map?" he said hoarsely. "What about a map? Did you even see it?"

Feeling the burning pain his fingers were inflicting upon her shoulder, Julia shoved his hand away, then glared up at him. "I don't know why I'm telling you anything," she said. "It's apparent you have no interest in me. I think I shall be on my way, Troy Gilbert. I am the one who is wasting time with you."

He grabbed her by a wrist and yanked her roughly to him. "By God, woman, you're going to tell me about the map," he snarled. "And *now*. Did you actually see it?"

"Yes," she said weakly, tears sparkling at the corners of her eyes. "And now that I've told you, please let me go. Or do you enjoy hurting women?"

"Did Samantha take the map with her?" he growled, drawing her even closer, ignoring the hurt in her eyes.

"Yes," she said, sniffling. "I saw her—place—it in her purse."

Troy released her, spun around, and rushed away from Julia, his thoughts scrambled with confusion. Why had Samantha left so abruptly, without even a good-bye?

Then a thought struck him. "She must think I'm an enemy," he said beneath his breath. "God. What has she got planned for the map? Who does she plan to hand it over to? Thinking I'm an enemy of the South, she could even hand it over to the authorities once she reaches Charleston."

He knew that the danger wasn't so much in what she wanted to do but more in whether anyone would accost her before she had the chance to do it.

"I must get to her first," he said, swinging himself up into his saddle, urging his horse quickly away, into the darkness.


The moon was a silver curve in the black velvet sky as Samantha looked up at it from the stagecoach window. So far the journey home was a lonely one. Even now no one shared the coach with her. The only sounds were the wheels rattling over a dirt road. The aroma of the night air dew smelled faintly of some distant flower bushes, perhaps lilacs.

In her travel suit of a heavy, dark cotton and a matching hat with braided ribbons brightening its brim, she thumped her fingers nervously against the purse on her lap. She was plagued by her recent good-byes. Leaving her grandparents so soon had been sad, almost even too hard. Strange how seeing them standing at the depot, watching her leave in the stagecoach, made her feel as though it was the last time she would ever see them.

But she had later scoffed at this. It was the talk of war that had caused her apprehensions. Yet at the back of her mind, she kept seeing the threatening face of Marion

Yarborough materializing. What if he—

"No," she whispered. "I mustn't even think about that. I've enough to worry about."

She settled back against the plump cushion of the seat but was unable to relax, though she was trying hard. Too much was changing in her life; foremost were her mixed loyalties, to the North and the South: the North because she had spent so much time there, with her grandparents. But her fiercest loyalty was to her father and the South, because her father had so much to lose by a war!

Samantha didn't want to hate Troy for what he was guided to do, in his own personal war against the South, which, in turn, would be a war against *her*. He had his own loyalties, and had she not taken the initiative to turn her back on their relationship, she had to believe that he would have—as soon as he had gotten the map from her.

Not wanting to think of Troy, or Julia, for that matter, Samantha tried to focus her thoughts on her father. She felt a tinge of guilt where her grandparents were concerned in thinking about her father's part in the organization of the Confederate States of America. Her grandparents loved Lincoln and everything that he stood for. They would, for sure, look on Craig Johnston as a traitor.

The sound of an approaching horse drew Samantha from her reverie and to the window. The moon was not bright enough for her to see, but it seemed to be a lone horseman coming quickly upon the stagecoach from behind.

Fear inched its way into her heart as she remembered Marion Yarborough and his determination to have the map. Could he have managed to find out that she had left Springfield? Had he even been hiding in the shadows, watching her board the stagecoach? To what extent would he go to get the map in his possession?

Samantha's hand went to her purse and felt the hard lump which lay just beneath its leather surface. Her pistol. She didn't yet have a need to use it, but if her life became threatened, she would. She had listened only halfheartedly to her father's warnings before her departure from Johnston Oaks. But she could defend herself. Quite readily! And she would!

The hoofbeats were growing closer. Samantha continued to watch, now holding onto her hat as it threatened to be blown off by the wind.

And then her heart beat faster when she finally got a look at the lone horseman's face as he led his horse into the light of one of the glass-enclosed lanterns which flanked the sides of the stagecoach. There was no escaping Troy, it seemed, for there he was, as big as life itself, ordering the stagecoach driver to stop the stagecoach at gunpoint.

The jolt of the coach coming to such a sudden halt threw Samantha clumsily from the seat. She fell in a heap on the floor, wide-eyed and dumbfounded at this newest dilemma she had managed to get herself in. And Troy! Of all people! Was he a highwayman as she had at first expected? It surely took much practiced courage to stop a stagecoach by gunpoint.

But, of course, she knew that she was the prime reason this time. And it had to have been cousin Julia who had spilled the beans as to where she was, and probably even why!

Upon falling, her purse had been thrown aside. She went to her knees and began searching for it in the coach's dark interior, her pulse racing more by the minute. She recoiled in pain as she banged a knee against the wooden base of the seat. She worked at her hat which now hung by only a tied satin ribbon from around her neck, where it had fallen from her sudden jolt.

"Darn it," she mumbled, deciding to just untie the ribbon and let her hat become the first casualty of this war that would begin real soon between her and Troy. She would not let him take advantage of her again.

"Where is that purse?" she said, tossing her hat aside and once more frantically feeling around for her purse. The pistol. She must have the pistol to thrust it into his face, to show him who was the smarter of the two.

But just thinking of his handsomeness and her feelings for him tore shreds of her heart away. To never be kissed or held by him again could be almost the same as to be forced to live in exile for the rest of her life.

But what must be, must be. She would learn to accept what fate handed her in life, though without Troy, she would only be half alive.

Samantha became aware of the sudden silence of the stagecoach wheels, now replaced by voices exchanging angered words. She stiffened her back and put an ear closer to the door to listen. She couldn't make out the words, but when she heard her name called out, there was no mistaking that. She began to tremble, Troy's voice touching her so familiarly. If only she could find the blasted purse!

Ignoring his order to step from the coach, Samantha once more desperately groped in the darkness for her purse, but just as she found it, Troy was there, still on horseback, throwing the door open before her wide eyes. He glared down at her, yet still aimed his pistol up at the stagecoach driver.

"Damn it, Sam, come on out of there," Troy growled. "I won't be able to hold my gun on the driver all night."

Samantha swallowed hard, looking sheepishly up into his eyes. Having been caught off guard so suddenly by his presence at the door, she was unable to grab her purse.

Then she regained a small portion of her courage. "I refuse to move," she said. "Who do you think you are, Troy Gilbert, stopping the stagecoach in such a way? You will be hanged for sure."

"I won't be around long enough for that to happen," he said, glancing from her back to the driver. "Now move. You're coming with me."

Samantha looked toward her purse and held her breath as her fingers crept toward it.

"And give me that purse," Troy suddenly ordered. "I won't give you a chance to tear up the map before I have it once more safely inside my pocket."

Samantha's mouth fell open. "The map? My purse?" she whispered shallowly. Then a mischievous smile played on her lips. Yes, he would think the map would be inside her purse. That's why she had placed it elsewhere—a place that no man would think to look.

But then her smile faded. The pistol! It was inside the purse. If she forfeited the purse to Troy, then she would be defenseless. She would be at his mercy. And she knew the danger of that.

"Well? Hand it over," Troy said, gesturing with his free hand. "Then we'll settle our other disagreements later, once we're alone."

"All right," Samantha said, her fingers almost like jelly they were so weak. "You can have the purse." She lifted the purse slowly from the floor, working with its latch, finding it stubbornly stuck.

175

"No need to try to retrieve the map before handing the purse my way," Troy warned. "Sam, just give it here so we can be on our way."

"We?"

"You heard right."

Samantha angrily shoved the purse toward him. "Take the purse," she said hotly. "But if you think I'm going anywhere with you, you're foolish. I refuse to budge from this stagecoach." She nodded toward the purse now in his hand. "You've got what you came for," she said sullenly. "Now leave me be to continue on my way. My father needs me. Not you."

"Right now I'll be the judge of who needs who," he growled. "Seems my gun helps in the persuasion, wouldn't you say?"

"If you don't force me one way, you do another," she hissed, struggling with her petticoats as she worked herself up from the floor.

"I don't believe I remember ever forcing you to do anything," Troy said dryly. "Seems you were willing, Sam."

"Why, you cad!" she softly cried. "Now you accuse me of—of—being a loose woman?"

"No. I didn't mean to imply that."

"You did so. Now you look to me as you—as you did cousin Julia. To whom have you bragged about your conquest of me?"

"No one," he growled, suddenly reaching to grab her around the waist, jerking her roughly onto the saddle with him. "But I just may if you give me any further problems."

Samantha wriggled and fought him but felt his grip of steel about her waist and knew that her struggles were in vain. She had no choice but cling to his arm as he directed his horse away from the stagecoach and into the darker reaches of the woods.

"My trunk," Samantha screamed. "My possessions. They will all be lost to me, Troy. Please don't do this."

She felt the hardness of her pistol as it pressed against her back. With every bounce of the horse, it pained her.

"That's just like a woman," Troy chuckled. "Worrying about her frilly dresses when her hide is in jeopardy. Even your fancy hat, Sam. Aren't you going to cry over its loss?"

Samantha cast a quick look over her shoulder. The hat! Why hadn't she known it was needed to protect her swirl of hair atop her head and what lay hidden in its folds of curls! Even now the whip of the wind threatened to loosen it! She placed a hand to her hair and desperately fought in keeping it in place.

Troy led his horse onward around trees, beneath low branches and then into a clearing where the outline of a house came into view. Samantha tensed as he drew rein before it and quickly dismounted. He lifted his arms toward her.

"Come on," he said gruffly. "Let's get on inside."

"Whose place is this?" Samantha whispered, looking cautiously about her as she eased from the saddle on to the ground.

"Never mind that," Troy said, nodding with his head toward the door. "You go on inside. I'll secure the horse out back." He gave her a warning look. "And don't try escaping. You wouldn't get far."

"You think not?" she said, stubbornly squaring her shoulders.

"I wouldn't try it," he chuckled, gazing at her layers of

177

petticoats beneath her dark travel suit. "Your petticoats. Surely they would tangle about your ankles."

"No petticoat has ever slowed me down," she argued back. "Especially when having a need to flee such a rogue as you."

"Yes. A rogue. I believe I've heard that before," he said, sighing. Once more he nodded toward the door. "Go on, Sam. We'll talk this out after I see to the horse."

"My name is Samantha," she stormed. "I no longer wish to be called by my nickname by a man I loathe."

She swung her skirt and petticoats around and walked heatedly toward the door, yet with all intentions of going in the opposite direction just as soon as he got out of sight, behind the house. In the dark, she could find many places to hide. She would hide until hell froze over. She would not let him force her to do anything, ever again.

Watching out of the corner of her eye, she slowed her pace, and when he disappeared around the corner of the house, she made a quick turn and began running as fast as her feet would take her across the clearing and quickly into a clump of trees.

Breathing hard and feeling a sharp, knifelike pain in her lower right side from her exertions, she stopped and leaned her back against the trunk of a tree. She wiped nervous perspiration from her brow and upper lip, then cautiously checked her hairdo, sighing with relief when she found that, for the most part, her swirl of hair was still in place, protecting what was hidden inside it.

"I must hurry onward," she breathlessly whispered, wishing that her heart would quit pounding so hard. It was as though her whole body was one massive, combined heartbeat. She even felt light-headed from its threatening thundering at her temple. And her knees.

They were weak and rubbery as she once more began to run. She lifted her skirt and petticoats high above her ankles and jumped over fallen branches, scratching her way through tangles of blackberry brambles. And then to her surprise Troy was suddenly there, blocking her way.

"Where—did you—come from?" she asked, panting hard. "I thought you were—"

"I knew you'd try this," he growled. "So I watched."

"And you even let me get this far, on—purpose?"

"Well," he said, chuckling, "you did run faster than I expected."

Samantha took a quick step toward him and began beating her fists against his chest. "You rogue!" she shouted. "I hate you! Why do you continue to do these things to me?"

He tried to grab her wrists, but she began fighting him off, giving him a shove, causing him to trip backward over a log. As he fell, he pulled her along with him. She began flailing her arms and screaming, then found his fingers clasped firmly over her mouth as he managed to get atop her, to straddle her.

"God, woman, do you want to bring the cavalry with your screaming?"

Samantha tossed her head back and forth, trying to free her lips, but he continued to hold his hand in place.

"Now just blink your eyes twice in succession if you agree to no more screams," he scolded. "Only then will I remove my hand."

Anger flashed in her eyes, yet she did as he asked because she knew that she had no other choice. One blink and then quickly another, and she felt relief to have charge of her own lips. She wiped at them with the back of a hand, not wanting to have the taste of him on them.

She wanted to hate him. She would wish hard that it were so, to make being with him easier and not hellish torture with the usual hungry want of him.

"That's more like it," Troy said, reaching to smooth a stray lock of hair back from her eyes. "Now we can return to the house and settle a thing or two between us."

Samantha knocked his hand away and crept her fingers upward, to once more check the swirl of curls atop her head. When finding this still, thankfully, in place, she tried to shove Troy away from her.

"Troy, there isn't any way I can budge without you making the first move," she argued. "Why aren't you getting off me?"

Troy's gaze took in her loveliness, though this was a poor time for him to be caught up in any sort of fantasy of her. Yet, didn't being angry make her even more desirable? He loved the way her cheeks flamed in color and the way her green eyes sparkled in the soft shaft of moonlight. Her lips, seductively parted, were drawing his downward—downward—

He crushed his lips down upon hers and eased from his straddling position to lie fully atop her. His hands went to the soft, straight line of her neck where his thumbs then reached to trace her gentle jawline.

Samantha pushed at his chest and grumbled beneath her breath as his lips continued to press against hers, and his fingers were setting fires where they touched.

The screech of an owl overhead broke the momentary lover's spell that Troy was trying to weave between them. Troy drew away from her, clearing his throat nervously. He helped her from the ground, his eyelids heavy in passion's grip.

"Let's get back to the house," he said thickly.

"Yes, let's," Samantha said scornfully. "The sooner the better. Perhaps then you will let me resume my travels south."

"Only if what I am after is given me," he said, giving her a harried look.

Samantha shook dried leaves and grass from her skirt. "My guess is that you are speaking of not only one thing, but two," she snapped. "First, you will satisfy your sexual appetite and then you will demand to have the map." She gave him a sour look. "Am I right Troy?" she demanded. "Or do you wish for one of those more than the other?"

Troy took her by an elbow and began leading her back in the direction of the house. "Sam, did anyone ever tell you that you have one damn suspicious mind?" he said flatly.

Samantha's eyes widened. She laughed loosely. "Suspicious?" she said. "Now why on earth would I have cause to be suspicious, Troy?"

# Chapter Twelve

The house was dark and cold. Samantha stood trembling and hugging herself as she watched Troy light a kerosene lamp, its fire hardly visible behind its black-smoked glass chimney. But it emitted enough light for Samantha to see that the one-room house had been abandoned for sometime and was only sparsely furnished with drab, colorless pieces of odds and ends of furniture.

Dust lay on the tables and along the hardwood floor. A broken mirror at the one end of the room caught the light and reflected it down upon an iron bed with a tattered and torn, filth-laden mattress. Samantha grimaced with the thought of having to lie on the bed, imagining the bedbugs that were surely hidden away in its seams.

"This will do in a pinch," Troy said, holding the lamp up, surveying the room more closely. "At least we won't be bothered here. It's apparent that the owners are long gone and could care less about this place or who borrows it for awhile."

"It's filthy," Samantha snapped. "Even rats wouldn't

spend a night in this place."

"We may not even have to," Troy said, removing her purse from inside his frock coat. "If what I'm looking for is in here, perhaps we can even leave here before sunup."

He weighed the purse in his hands. "So you armed yourself for your journey to the Carolinas," he said. "A pistol. Yes, that was a smart move on your part, but it didn't help you yet, did it?"

"If the stagecoach hadn't stopped so quickly, causing my purse to fly from my lap, you would be nursing a leg wound at this very moment," she said dryly.

He opened the purse and withdrew the pistol, looking at it thoughtfully. "So you say you would have shot me with this, huh?" he murmured.

"Given the chance, I still will," she threatened.

"I'll have to be careful, won't I?" he teased, his blue eyes taking on a hint of amusement. "This isn't a toy pistol, that's for sure."

He checked the bullets in the chamber. "Yes," he confirmed. "Fully loaded and one has my name on it." He laughed softly and dropped the pistol back inside the purse. "But enough about the firearm," he said. "I'm interested in what else is in this purse."

One item at a time he removed the articles of the purse, even once more removing the pistol when he didn't find the map. He continued with his search, placing all of Samantha's personal articles on a table, until nothing was left. Scowling, he turned the purse upside down and shook it.

"No need to tear it apart at the seams," Samantha said, smiling confidently up at him. "It's quite empty."

"How can that be?" Troy growled, angrily throwing the purse across the room. "Julia said that she saw you

183

put the map in your purse. Where is it, Sam? Time is wasting!"

Samantha's face flamed with color. "So it was Julia who informed you of my departure," she said angrily. "She even broke her promise to me and told you that I still had the map. I should have known that she couldn't be trusted. She'll never change."

Troy went to Samantha and took her by the shoulders. "I don't give a damn about Julia or her personality," he fumed. "I want the map. The news of a possible blockade has now been splashed all over the newspapers. I've got to return to my ship. I've many plans to make."

"I'm sure you have," Samantha accused. "And against the South. Try and deny that, Troy."

"I cannot deny or explain anything at this time," he growled. "My silence will protect many men. I've no other choice."

"The denial is proof of just which side you are loyal to," Samantha hissed. "And if you think I'm going to hand over the map to you, you're daft. I am sure now that your ship will be among the first to block the entrance to the southern ports."

Troy wanted to tell her the truth; that all she surmised was false. But he was afraid to breathe a word of the truth to anyone, until the men who volunteered to travel with him were safe and sound on his ship. Only then would he be free to explain his true plans for this nonsensical war!

"You can think what you want, Sam," he said thickly. "I'm sure I'd be wasting my words to ask you to trust me."

"Yes, quite," she snapped, folding her arms stubbornly across her chest.

"And you won't willingly hand over the map?"

"Never!"

"Then I must insist that you undress, one article at a time, and let me search you to find the damn map."

Samantha's eyes widened in alarm. "What?" she gasped, dropping her arms to her side.

"You heard me."

"You wouldn't."

"Just watch."

"I refuse."

"Then I'll have to do it for you," he growled, reaching to unbutton the top front button of her suit jacket.

"You stop that this minute," Samantha said, slapping him across the face. When she saw the deep frown quickly form as he glowered down at her, his hand rubbing where she had left her hand print in red on his cheek, she took a step backward.

"You she-devil," Troy snarled, then took a step forward and grabbed both her wrists and, unable to curb the power within him that commanded him to kiss her, he kissed her hard and long, his hands traveling down the straight line of her back, across the soft flare of her hips and to her buttocks. He yanked her into the hardness of his body, letting her experience along with him the risen strength of his sex, throbbing to be set free from its tight confines.

"Love me," he whispered, now sending butterfly kisses down her neck, to the sensitive hollow of her throat.

A soft whimper of delight filled the still night as Samantha was becoming torn with emotion. "Please," she said in almost a gurgle. "Why do you always confuse me so? First you love me, then you don't. How am I even supposed to understand you? Lord, Troy, you are—my—enemy. How can you also be my lover?"

"Let me show you," he whispered huskily into her ear.

"No," she softly argued. "Just let me go. I didn't ask to come here. You forced me."

"And I would again."

"I know. Don't you see? That's why we shouldn't. And the map—"

"To hell with the map," he said thickly, inching her toward the bed.

She darted a sidelong glance toward the bed. She shuddered involuntarily. "Not there," she harshly whispered.

"We'll spread our clothes."

"Troy, please," she said, breathing hard, too caught up in shared passion to care any longer about anything. She had vowed to not let this happen again. But fighting this thing she felt for Troy was a never-ending battle, her heart always overruling her common senses.

He looked down at her, his eyes dark with need. "Let me undress you," he said, stopping at the edge of the bed.

Something seemed to click inside Samantha's mind. He had ordered her to undress earlier, one piece of clothing at a time, to search for the map. Was he using a different sort of tactic now to get her to do so? Was he trying to get her to cooperate by sending her mind in a senseless spiraling of rapture by his skilled ways of lovemaking?

Suddenly her bubble of ecstasy burst, and she knew what she had to do. She fluttered her thick, sultry lashes up at him. "Darling," she purred, placing her hands at the lapels of his coat. "Let me undress you first. Surely you wouldn't mind, would you?"

"I would be daft, wouldn't I, if I objected to such an offer as that," he said, chuckling.

"Then just you stand there and let me do you the honors," she murmured, pursing her lips up at him in a mock kiss. "I will make this an evening you will never forget."

She wanted to giggle when she saw how this comment made his face express even more anxious need. When he soon discovered that she had made a fool of him, what then? Surely he would hate her!

Samantha knew that it was going to be hard for her to carry out this charade because of her extreme attraction to him. She had to have a strong will. She had to keep thinking of how important it was for her to return to the Carolinas. Even if she didn't have the map in her possession, the need to be with her father at such a time was a driving force inside her. She knew how much Johnston Oaks meant to him; even to herself, though she had always been eager for her visits to her grandparents' house.

Now the thought of making yearly visits to Springfield was less important in her mind: partially because of Julia and partially because Samantha felt that she had finally grown up into a mature adult, no longer needing the fussing over by this older generation of grandparents.

She deftly unbuttoned Troy's shirt after having already tossed his frock coat and cravat aside. She let her fingers stray inside the shirt to tease the flesh of his chest, watching him all the while for his emotions to show in his delicious blue eyes. If he didn't remember this night, she would. She would be denying herself the man who she loved. In her heart, she wanted this one last time with him. But she knew that it could never be. He

187

was her enemy. He was her enchanted enemy.

Dropping the shirt to the floor, Samantha splayed her fingers across his chest and eased her lips to one of his nipples, sucking on it, savoring at least this much of him while she could. She heard his intake of breath. She could feel the pounding of his heart against his chest. Even her own heart wouldn't be still as it threatened to overcome her in unleashed passion.

But then she proceeded with her plan. She smiled awkwardly up at him as her fingers lowered, to his waist, to slowly unfasten his breeches while he managed to remove one of his shoes, and then the other, kicking them far away to the other side of the room. When he lowered his breeches on down away from him, she smiled victoriously up at him.

"It is now your turn to undress," he said thickly.

"Get on the bed first," Samantha said, her voice trembling as she glanced toward the pistol that now lay only a few inches from her fingers. She had to move quickly while his back was to her as he got on the bed. The pistol. She had to use it on him. Hopefully she would only have to threaten him, not shoot him. When it came right down to it, could she?

He gave her an amused smile, then placed his back to her and walked toward the bed. In a flash, Samantha had the pistol. With a pounding heart and trembling fingers she aimed it in his direction.

"Troy, darling," she said, her voice shaking almost as much as her hands. "Darling, turn around."

Troy turned and looked in her direction, then froze in his steps as he saw the pistol. "Sam, God, what are you doing?" he gasped, his face suddenly ashen in color. "Why do you have that pistol pointed at me?"

"I don't have any choice," she said, now kicking his clothes into a heap at her feet. "I must do what I must, Troy. So often it isn't what I'd like."

"Why are you doing this?" he said, seeing her now picking his clothes up. "And what are you doing with my clothes?"

"Troy, I knew what you were up to," she said sullenly. "You were only catching me off guard so you could find the map on my person. Well, I beat you to the draw, darling. You are now at my mercy."

"Yes, I want the map," he said thickly. "But I also want you. Do you think me that devious?"

"I know how badly you want the map," she said, inching her way toward the door. "Well, darling, the only one who is going to get it, is my father. Then we shall see what its importance is."

"Sam, gave it to me," Troy said, taking a step forward. "It won't be worth a damn to your father. I am the only one who knows its full value."

"That's a lie and you know it," she scoffed. "It's obvious that Marion Yarborough knows as much about it as you, or he and his cohorts wouldn't want it so badly in their possession."

"He wants it for all the wrong reasons," Troy growled.

"Well, we shall see what the reasons are, won't we, darling, when my father studies it."

"It may be too late by then," Troy said, inching even closer to her. He reached a hand toward her. "Give it to me, Sam. Damn it, don't go through with this. I never expected you to—"

She laughed bitterly. "No. You wouldn't expect me to be this brave," she said. "Or should I say that you wouldn't expect me to say no to you when you had my

189

heart racing like mad. On both counts, you are wrong."

When he took another step toward her, she raised the pistol and aimed directly at him. She placed a hand on the trigger. "Don't come any closer," she said, inching toward the door, with his clothes in a bundle in the crook of her left arm.

"Where are you going with my clothes?" he gasped, his eyes wide. "God, Sam, you wouldn't!"

"Yes, I would," she said blandly. "And, yes, I am. Like I said, Troy, I do what I must. This is a must. Without clothes, it will be hard for you to follow me." Once more she laughed. "And without a horse, it will be even harder."

"Sam, even my horse?" he asked, raking his fingers nervously through his hair.

"Without it I wouldn't get far, now would I?" she teased.

"You won't anyway," he growled. "Don't you know the dangers of women being alone at night, especially on horseback?"

"I won't be alone long," she said. "I know the route the stagecoach takes. I will once again, very soon, be its passenger."

"Sam, reconsider," Troy said, gesturing with a hand. "You're being foolish."

"I've been foolish, it seems, from the first time I laid eyes on you," she argued. "I let myself lose all thought of right and wrong while with you. Now I know that I should have practiced more restraint. You weren't worth my losing my virginity."

Tears splashed from her eyes as she swung around and began running blindly from the house, stumbling over debris on the ground as she circled around to the back, to untie the horse. She looked about her and, seeing a thick cluster of forsythia bushes, she threw his clothes into it, mounted the horse, and soon was on her way.

Samantha ignored Troy's angry shouts from the doorway, yet she couldn't help but take one last look his way. She couldn't suppress a giggle when she saw how funny he looked standing in the doorway, with the light of the kerosene lamp silhouetting his figure in its nudity. Then she grew somber, hating the situation they were both in. She could never love another! Never!

# Chapter Thirteen

Samantha rode hard until she felt that she was far enough away from any threat of Troy. She stopped and swung herself from the horse, knowing that if she were to travel any further, she would have to do something about her petticoats.

With her pistol secured into the waistband of her skirt, she slipped out of her petticoats, then took time to get her breath before once more tackling the horse and the miles that stretched out before her. If only she had her jeans, then she would be able to maneuver even more freely. But she would have to make do.

Soon she would once more be a passenger on the stagecoach, and in a few days, she would be at Johnston Oaks. She had to wonder how her father was and what he was up to. He was the restless sort, always involved in politics one way or the other.

But this latest venture of his! She couldn't let herself approve. How could she, when it was causing her separation from Troy!

Knowing that she must move onward, having wasted

enough time, she took a step toward Troy's horse, then stopped, tense, after hearing what had sounded like a soft whinny from another horse not so far away. She looked cautiously about her, seeing the stars beneath the canopy of the maple trees and the weaving shadows of the leaves as they danced and played along the ground.

"It's only the wind," she scoffed to herself. "Now isn't the time to begin imagining things."

She lifted the tail of her skirt and fit a foot in the stirrup, then hurried herself on up and into the saddle. She flicked the reins and nudged the horse's side with her knees, glad to once more be moving. Troy had been right. She was vulnerable out here so far from Springfield, so very much alone. But surely she wouldn't have to travel far. And if she didn't catch up with the stagecoach while it traveled along the road, she would as it stopped at its first inn, for a full night. Though empty, it would have to make its scheduled stops. There was always a chance of acquiring passengers at each designated inn or depot along the line.

"Hah!" Samantha shouted, now finally on the road. She followed the spill of the moonlight, gladly accepting its path of light. Then once again she tensed, this time hearing hoofbeats, and not those of the horse on which she was riding. There was another, and not so far behind her. It seemed to her that this horse had materialized from out of nowhere!

As the hoofbeats drew closer, Samantha ducked her head and took a quick look behind her. It was a man. A lone horseman. Any man was a threat this time of night. Oh, if she had only been able to get dressed in breeches and shirt! She could have pretended to be a man. She should have even exchanged her clothes for Troy's. Why hadn't she thought to do that? With her skirt flapping in the wind, even up above her knees, revealing her thighs, how could a man even resist accosting her if he was of an evil mind and heart!

"I must travel faster," Samantha said, directing her eyes ahead, peering into the darkness, hoping for signs of the stagecoach or even a house at the side of the road.

But seeing neither, she was fast becoming afraid. It was obvious that this rider in the night was not being dissuaded by the speed in which she was now traveling. As she speeded up, so did he. And as she whipped her horse from the road and into the shadows of a tall cedar tree, so did he.

Samantha's heart did a fast pounding as she watched the horse draw closer. She now knew that she was the object of the man's pursuit. And she knew of only one man besides Troy who would specifically be singling her out to follow and to confront: Marion Yarborough. It surely was Marion Yarborough, coming to carry out his threat to her.

Samantha's hand went swiftly to the pistol at her waist and grabbed it. Steadying her hand with the other, she aimed it and waited for the horseman to stop before her. Barely breathing, she watched Marion Yarborough's face materialize beneath the soft light of the moon, seeing the ugly scar lifting his lip into its sickening grin.

"Halt!" she cried, trying to hide the strain in her voice, due to her rising fear. "Don't come any closer." She steadied her pistol with her other hand, her finger ready to press onto the trigger, if needed.

Marion was now close enough to see the threat of the pistol. "So I see you are prepared for any sort of mischief on the trail," he said thickly. "I never bargained for that."

"No. I guess you would not," she said coolly. "Now go on your way, sir, or I shall be forced to shoot you."

"I doubt if you would have the courage to shoot anything," he scoffed, edging his horse forward. "All I want is the map. Give it to me and I will let you proceed on your way, unharmed."

Samantha's eyes widened. She laughed beneath her breath. "You will let me proceed on my way?" she mocked. "Sir, don't you think that you've got that a little backward? It is I who have the gun pointed in your direction. Are you daft? One pull of the trigger and you could be dead."

"Have you ever shot a man before, Samantha?" Marion asked, laughing sarcastically.

"No," she said, hating herself for having stammered. But she was losing more courage by the minute. She hadn't expected him to be this daring. She had thought that with one look at the pistol pointed in his direction, he would turn around and ride in the opposite direction.

"It is quite messy," he mocked. "Most women faint at the sight of blood. Do you?"

Samantha straightened her back and set her jaw stubbornly. "I have never fainted in my entire life, over anything," she spat. "Nor would I over the spilling of your blood, sir. I would be performing a service for my grandparents, I am sure."

Suddenly, before Samantha could pull the trigger, Marion dashed his horse forward and gave her a brutal shove, knocking her from her horse and to the ground. She landed with a thud, momentarily dazing her. Then she was aware of hands gripping her wrists and a face hovering over her, glaring down at her.

"I've wasted enough time with you," Marion growled. "Now. Where is the map?"

"Why—do—you think I even still have it?" she gasped, shaking her head to clear the fogginess that seemed to be swirling inside it.

"I followed you from the depot. I was ready to take you from the coach when I saw Troy Gilbert do the deed for me," he said. "I then followed both of you to the house and was ready to enter when I saw you leave. I would have jumped you then, but thought I would give chase later, to give you time to get confidence that you were no longer being followed. You see, I knew about the pistol. I just didn't think you would have time to draw it to use against me."

Samantha struggled against his hold. "Troy? Did you harm him?" she hissed.

"Now don't tell me that you really care," Marion said from between clenched teeth. "What a way to leave a man. Tsk, tsk. A man without clothes is a defenseless man, wouldn't you say?"

"Then you *did* harm him," Samantha cried. "You beast. You ugly, evil beast!"

"Would you settle down a mite and cooperate if I told you that I left Troy Gilbert untouched?" he said, loosening his grip on her wrists.

"I wouldn't believe anything you'd say," she snapped.

"Then I won't tell you that I didn't bother to look in on Troy, even though I would've loved seeing him squirm under my close scrutiny while I teased him with the barrel of my pistol."

"Then you didn't hurt him?"

"No. Not with you in my sights to travel after."

Samantha sighed. Then she eyed him with daring.

"Release me and I shall give you the map," she lied, now seeing her pistol within reach, only inches above her right hand.

"So easy?" he said, his eyebrows arching. "Why would you?"

"I'm weary of this battle over just a mere slip of paper," she murmured. "I'm anxious to get to my father. I don't wish for any more delays."

"Where is it? I shall get it myself."

"You will leave me be if I tell you?"

"Yes. I have no need of you," he said thickly. His gaze raked over her. "I would love to have a taste of what lies beneath that skirt, yet a man doesn't rape his own—"

His words were cut off by his own choice, puzzling Samantha. "Your own what?" she asked, rubbing her wrists one at a time as he finally released his hold on her. "One other time you behaved so strangely—when . . . even mentioning my mother in the same breath. Why would you?"

Marion rose to his feet and towered over her. "Never you mind," he growled. "Now. Tell me where the map is. I must have it."

"It was in the trunk that stayed with the stagecoach that I was abducted from," she said matter-of-factly. Once more she eyed her pistol, then him.

Marion fell to his knees and slapped her across the face. "You bitch," he snarled. "Do you expect me to believe that? Just as I am sure Troy suspected, you wouldn't place something of that importance away from your person. Now, try again. Where is that map?"

He clenched his fingers onto her shoulders and held her roughly against the ground.

Recovering from his one blow, Samantha felt the

strength to begin fighting him anew. She doubled up a fist and crashed it against his chin while one of her knees arched upward and landed into his groin. He fell away from her, yowling, and when he did so, she grabbed her pistol and rose quickly to her feet to stand over him. But she didn't expect him to recover from his own pain so quickly and was stunned when he flipped over and grabbed the tail of her skirt, jerking her downward.

Screaming, Samantha fell in a tangle atop him and, while doing so, her finger involuntarily squeezed the trigger of her pistol, and the silence of the night was marred by the crack of gunfire.

Marion winced and grabbed at his chest. Samantha's heart skipped a beat, realizing that she had shot him. She crawled away from him and looked at him, stunned, seeing how quietly he now lay, with blood curling down the front of his fancy frock coat.

"Good Lord," Samantha said, still afraid to move. She wanted to check to see if he was dead, but she now knew that she had to get away from there, and fast. Though it was an accident that she shot him, the thought of it sickened her. It was one thing to use the pistol as a threat. It was another to actually use it.

She stared down at the pistol, still clutched into her right hand. She wanted to toss it clean away from her, but she knew that still she had to carry it, to provide even more protection for her further venture. And why was she feeling bad in having shot Marion Yarborough? He deserved even worse! He stood for everything that was evil. And wouldn't her grandparents be able to live a more peaceful existence now, with him no longer around to pester them?

"Good Lord! I'm thinking that he *is* dead," she

whispered. Upon closer observation she could see now that he was breathing. And if he was breathing, perhaps he could recover much too quickly and become a threat to her one more time.

"I must get out of here," she said, pushing herself up from the ground. Her fingers went to the swirl of curls at the top of her head. Yes. The map was still encircled inside it. Strange that two men had wanted it and had never suspected just how close they had been to it.

Smiling, she crept toward her horse, taking quick glances over her shoulder at Marion, making sure that he wasn't following her. And then with aching bones and a throbbing head, she once more swung herself up into the saddle and rode off, thrusting her pistol once again into the waistband of her skirt.

Samantha was relieved to now be in the family carriage, safely in Charleston, though she would have preferred not to be in Franklin LaFontaine's presence so soon. Her father had asked Franklin to meet Samantha at the depot.

"And you say that Father is so involved in business matters that he couldn't meet my stagecoach?" Samantha asked, casting Franklin an annoyed glance and seeing that she hadn't been mistaken when she thought him to be a shallow, unattractive person. Having been with someone as exciting as Troy made her feel Franklin to be more boring than she remembered. Yet he was her father's loyal companion. She did at least give him credit for that.

Franklin straightened the maroon cravat at his throat, then fussed with the tail of his immaculate frock coat which lay against his upper thigh. "It's talk of the possible firing upon Fort Sumter that has your father's mind occupied," he said. "You know what that could mean to Charleston."

"It could mean many things," she said bitterly. "Mostly bad, I would think."

"There are mixed feelings about this," Franklin said, frowning toward her. "Samantha, I am sure that your loyalties are mixed, especially now that you have once more spent time up North. But do your father a favor and keep these loyalties to yourself."

Samantha's eyes grew wide. "Then you have always known?" she murmured.

"How could one not?" he said dryly, his lips drawn into a narrow line of disapproval.

"How is Father?" Samantha asked, who, for the last several nights dreamed of his being lost at sea. She wanted to ask Franklin about the blockade but felt that was something best spoken about only to her father.

"He is doing well enough," Franklin said, his eyes now absorbing her and the way in which she was dressed for her arrival back to Charleston: A pale pink cashmere shawl with wide, knotted fringes was draped casually about her shoulders, worn over a dress of primrose faille with a white satin collar at her throat and cuffs at the long sleeves.

Partially exposed from behind a corner of the shawl was the definite gleam of gold of the locket that he had given her for her birthday, and pride shone in his eyes for her having chosen to wear it this day, which surely had to mean that it meant something very special to her.

His gaze went upward, seeing how beautifully her hair had been readied where it showed from beneath the bonnet that she wore with lacing around the inside of the brim, matching the coloring of her dress.

The sides of her flaming red hair were waved, and the back of her hair was coiled up and held in place with a slide. Also at the back, gorgeous, loose ringlets hung from the tight coil to her collar.

Her cheeks were rosy with excitement, and her green eyes never seemed to be crisper. Just the sight of her made his insides turn to mush, and the urge to touch her fingers had to be fought against, for he knew that she would not approve of this in public. She was a genteel, southern lady, with manners and delicacies that no woman of the North could match. And she had yet to be taken to bed by a man. Hopefully, he would be the first.

Samantha tried to ignore his appraising look by focusing her attention elsewhere, wondering about this new Charleston that she was seeing. The last leg of her journey had been filled with listening to the bold talk of the gentlemen who traveled the stagecoach with her. She had heard that General Beauregard had roughly six thousand men of all ages and degrees of training manning guns at Charleston Harbor as well as at James Island and at the tip of Morris Island.

Established militia companies had been called out and now occupied Charleston. The men had scoffed about how some were fuzz-cheeked boys who had run away from home to bear arms while others were old men who had come to take a hand in the great event, bored with what life had handed them.

To Samantha's amazement, the town was ablaze with excitement: Flags waved from the house tops, and the heavy tread of the soldiers could be heard in the streets. It seemed to her that southern patriots, even those who were ignorant and strangers to manual labor, had moved guns and dug emplacements, waiting for the command from General Beauregard.

A tremble coursed across Samantha's flesh. It was just becoming nightfall and great bonfires were casting leaping shadows of orange up into the darkening sky. Long parades snaked through the streets, drums rolled, and the hooves of horses clattered.

"I don't like what has happened to Charleston," she said, drawing her shawl more snugly about her shoulders. "There seems to be a hunger for blood. Don't the people see? It will be the blood of their brothers and fathers! How could they wish for war?"

"It has been said that unless you sprinkle blood in the face of the southern people, they will be back in the old Union in less than ten days," Franklin said matter-of-factly. "This is why this excitement is being created in Charleston. They have to want it for the Union to be defeated."

"I don't want to even think about it," she said, shuddering. "I just want to go home. I suddenly am so much more worried about Father than ever before."

"You need not worry," Franklin said, shrugging. "His age will keep him from having to serve in the war."

Samantha cast Franklin an annoyed look. "There are more things to worry about than who is and who isn't going to actually be doing the fighting," she spat. "Franklin, my father is one of those who makes the rules. He has the ability to say who will and won't fight. I fear for his soul, Franklin. Not so much his life."

"Samantha, what a horrible thing to say," Franklin gasped. "You talk blasphemy, as I see it."

"I say what I feel. You know that, Franklin," she

sighed. "Yet, now? It would be too hard to put my feelings into words. So much is at stake here. So much. . . ."

Her words trailed off to a nothingness with visions of Troy dancing before her eyes. Would war somehow bring them together again? It seemed not. But if so, they would not be able to meet as friends. Yes, her father had helped make the rules—rules that affected her future more than she could ever tell him.

She settled back against the seat as the carriage moved on away from the city and on a country road, as night now fell in its total blackness. Samantha hated this darkness! She had longed to see Johnston Oaks in its loveliness on her arrival home, wondering just how long it would remain untouched should war erupt sometime soon. So many memories were locked up inside the walls of the mansion. Would they be shattered into bits and pieces with one blast from a cannon?

Samantha hung her head in her hands and shook it slowly back and forth. She had always thought that her father was one of the most intelligent men on the face of the earth. But somehow now she thought less of that assumption. While thinking that he was making way for a better South, he was possibly leading the way for the total destruction of his entire past.

The wheels of the carriage were a steady drone, rocking her to sleep. It had been such a tiring, long trip from Illinois. Surely she would never feel rested again.

Softly dozing, Samantha dreamed in flashes. First she was in the arms of Troy, then her father. And then she was beckoning for her grandparents to come to her but they couldn't! They were being engulfed in flames, screaming! And then Julia's hysterical, mocking laughter sent gooseflesh across Samantha's skin, awakening her to a startled alertness.

"Where are we, Franklin? How much farther?" she asked, wiping sleep from her eyes.

"Don't you recognize the bend in the road, Samantha?"

"I've been asleep. I am somewhat disoriented."

"Soon we will be turning into the Avenue of the Oaks," Franklin said, smoothing the sleeves of his coat.

"It seems forever, Franklin."

"You were gone from Charleston only a short while. Why did you cut your visit short, Samantha?"

"You have to ask?" she said bitterly. "With the talk of war, you really have to ask?"

"I had hoped—" Franklin said and stopped, clearing his throat nervously as his forefinger eased his cravat away from his neck.

"Franklin, surely you didn't think that I was returning because of you."

He laughed awkwardly. "Samantha, when a man gets my age and is not wed, he doesn't truly expect miracles," he said. "I had only hoped."

"I returned because of Father," she said blandly. "Only because of Father!"

## Chapter Fourteen

Johnston Oaks stood dark on the hill overlooking Ashley River. All shutters but a few had been closed for the night. Pale, golden light emanated from those few windows facing the gravel drive on which Samantha was traveling.

Anxious, she scooted to the edge of the seat and peered intensely at the mansion. Though she had been eager to leave the Carolinas and travel to Illinois, there was no denying the rapid pounding of her heart in being home again. Not only were her loyalties to the North and South torn, but also feelings over her family and who she wished to live with.

First she ached to be with her father and then in the next breath she longed for her grandparents.

But now circumstances beyond her control had changed all of this, and she had to admit that it wasn't only because she had blossomed into a mature woman but also because it seemed to her the country was struggling itself, with its own sort of maturity.

The barking of a dog broke through the silence of the

night, alerting Samantha to another love.

"Checkers!" she cried, laughing as she saw her Collie materialize out of the darkness, ahead, bounding toward the carriage.

Checkers became almost wild with excitement when he came alongside the carriage and saw Samantha. He continued to run beside the carriage, panting, keeping his dark eyes devotedly focused on Samantha. When the carriage pulled to a halt before the grand steps of the mansion, Samantha rushed from it and, forgetting her expensive attire, she dropped to her knees and heartily hugged her dog.

"I've missed you so," Samantha whispered, running her fingers through the thick softness of Checkers' brown-spotted fur. "You're a ray of sunshine for me during this foreboding time. I love you, Checkers. You are always faithful, aren't you?"

The banging of a door and approaching heavy footsteps drew Samantha quickly to her feet. Expecting to see her father, she tried to not show her disappointment when she saw Jewel, her personal maid, instead.

Jewel waddled down the steps, her fleshy arms outstretched. "Samantha, honey," she said in her southern drawl. "Ah've been so worried. There's so much meanness goin' on. When we received your wire that you were travelin' south, my ol' heart ain' been the same since."

Samantha welcomed Jewel with a fond hug. Jewel returned the affectionate gesture, squeezing her so hard that Samantha let out a cry followed by a low, sultry laugh. "Jewel, I'm all right. As you can see, I'm all in one piece," she said, almost able to place her chin on her maid's head, Jewel was so short. "You shouldn't worry so about me. Don't you know that I'm a survivor?"

Jewel stepped back away from Samantha and looked her carefully up and down. "Yes'm. I sees you're jus' fine," she said, nodding her head. "But were your travels trouble free? There's plenty talk of highwaymen."

Samantha's face clouded in remembrance. She still wondered whether Troy managed to flee from the drab, abandoned house. And had Marion Yarborough died from her inflicted gun wound?

"No. No problems, whatsoever," she lied. "It seems that I met problems though, when I arrived in Charleston. The whole city is buzzing with soldiers and guns. What is to be expected to happen to us all, Jewel?"

Samantha looked on past Jewel, up the steps and to the closed, massive oak door. "And where is Father?" she asked, now feeling a keen disappointment that he still seemed to be purposely avoiding her. But why? Had her stubborn decision to travel on to Illinois against his wishes caused him to bear a grudge against her? This was no time for a father to behave so childishly. This was the time for alliances, even if it was only between a father and a daughter. Johnston Oaks's survival depended on such alliances. They were the two lone survivors of the long line of Johnston ancestors left to protect the plantation from the ravages of war.

Jewel looked nervously up at Samantha and then toward Franklin as he stepped up next to Samantha. "Massa Craig ain't here," she said, her dark eyes wavering.

"Where is he?" Franklin interjected. "He told me nothing of plans to leave." He looked toward the house, disbelieving.

"He was called away. A messenger boy said somethin'

'bout General Beauregard needin' Massa Craig's quick attention on an important matter—somethin' to do with Fort Sumter.''

"Fort Sumter?" Samantha said shallowly, fear once more plaguing her. "Did the messenger boy say anything else?"

Jewel's gray ringlets of curls swayed, and her wrinkled neck stretched with the quick action of her head as she shook it back and forth. "No, ma'am," she said. "He said nothin' more. But Massa Craig left a message 'fore he left.''

"And? What is the message?" Franklin said with authority, sliding an arm about Samantha's waist, which she abruptly rejected by stepping away from him.

"Massa Franklin, you're to stay here with Miss Samantha until Massa Craig returns," Jewel said. "He wants you here with Miss Samantha, to look afta her."

Samantha spun around and faced Franklin. "That isn't necessary," she said dryly. "I'm capable of taking care of myself as my recent travels proved, Franklin."

Jewel stepped up to Samantha and placed a hand on her arm. "Now, Samantha, honey, you mus' do as yo' pappy wants," she said softly. "If yo' don', it will be ol' Jewel who'll be punished. It's up to me to see that his orders are followed. You knows that, Miss Samantha."

Samantha's heart wrenched as she truly understood Jewel's plight. Though Craig Johnston was a man sorely loved by Samantha, she knew that he had a black side to his heart. When any slaves stepped out of line, the punishment could be severe. Samantha had shivered and softly cried to herself many a time when hearing the snap of the whip and the scream of those upon whom the whip had been used.

208

"All right, Jewel," she quickly said, placing her hands to Jewel's wide, dark cheeks. "Franklin can stay. I won't object."

Then Samantha took a wide step toward Franklin. "But I won't remain in your company, sir," she said icily. "I will retire immediately to my room. Will you see to my trunk? And will you inform me of my father's return to Johnston Oaks?"

Franklin's face flamed in color with humiliation and his lips pursed as he glowered back at Samantha. "I am not your servant," he snapped. "And if my company is not preferred, you cannot expect me to inform you of anything, though I will be awaiting your father's arrival in the library, as he requested."

"Whatever," Samantha said, shrugging. She lifted the tail of her skirt and petticoats up into her arms and began climbing the stairs. "Jewel, please ask Joshua to see to my trunk. And please inform me the moment Father arrives. I will try to catch a wink of sleep. I'm afraid there may be a few sleepless nights ahead if shots are fired upon Fort Sumter."

"Yes'm," Jewel said. "Yo' covers is turned back on yo' bed. A lamp is lit in yo' room. And fresh water is poured in yo' basin for refreshin' yo'self. Anythin' else, just ring for me, honey."

Jewel's continued devotion warmed Samantha's heart. Stepping up on the porch, she cast Jewel a smile across her shoulder. "I'll be just fine," she reassured. "I just need to refresh myself and try to get some rest. Just be sure to awaken me when Father arrives back home."

"Yes'm," Jewel said, nodding.

Samantha momentarily forgot her ladylike ways and gave a brisk whistle toward Checkers. "Come on, boy," she encouraged. "Come with me and keep me company."

She wanted to tell Franklin that she felt safer in her Collie's company than she did in his. Somehow the thought of being under the same roof with this man whose eyes spoke of more than mere friendly affection toward her sent a message of caution to her brain. She had always suspected that, given the chance, Franklin would behave less than gentlemanly toward her. The thought of his kiss, which surely would be a wet and slobbery one, made a bitterness rise up into her throat. Should he— She would shoot him first!

Checkers scampered to her side, and together they went on inside the mansion, greeted by the clean, refreshing smell of lemon oil furniture polish and the soft shine of candles lighted on wall sconces along the wall which led Samantha on to the majestic, winding staircase.

Without stopping to absorb this setting which reflected the influential Johnston heritage, she glided on up the staircase and to her room.

Sighing, she slipped her shawl from her shoulders and draped it over the back of a plushly upholstered, yellow velvet chair. Her gaze moved about the room as she touched everything familiar while removing the hat pin from her hat.

As always the bedroom's colors of pale pinks and greens with the soft pink rosebud-bedecked wallpaper, lacy curtains at the windows, and white, four-poster, canopied bed seemed to relax her and make her troubles seem far removed.

But then she remembered and compared this room to the one that had been given to her at her grandparents' house. The same old jealousy of Julia was once more there at the front of her mind, plaguing her, when she envisioned her spoiled cousin in what had been Samantha's room for so many years.

"What am I doing?" she whispered, plopping her hat on her dressing table. "Why am I even thinking about Julia? She can in no way interfere in my life here at Johnston Oaks. I've more important things to worry myself over."

Stepping up to the mirror which hung over her dressing table, Samantha glanced up at the swirl of hair at the top of her head. "And now, Troy my love, I can remove the map and be safe while doing it," she murmured. "When Father returns, I shall finally see what the mystery is about that miserable piece of paper. Surely he can decipher the code. He's smart about these sorts of things."

With eager fingers, she worked with her hair, loosening it, then smiled mischievously when she plucked the tiny, folded paper from the deep folds of her hair. "Ah, there you are." She softly laughed.

She eyed it questionably, wondering whether or not she should unfold it and take another moment to study it, then shrugged. She had grown sorely tired of worrying over it. But one thing that she liked about having it in her possession was that she felt closer to Troy because it had been his.

"No need to look at it again," she said, laying it aside. "I will know no more now than before."

Checkers came up to her and offered her a paw, his dark eyes pleading for attention. "Poor baby," Samantha said, kneeling, running her fingers across his fur, laughing at how static electricity caused his fur to cling even after she withdrew her hand.

Looking toward a window, Samantha's smile faded when she saw the orange cast to the sky, in the direction of Charleston. "The bonfires," she whispered. "The way the people were massing in the streets, those fires will burn all night."

She gave Checkers another pat and saw that this was all that was required to make him content, for he went to her bedside and curled up on the thick carpet, placing his head between his paws and closing his eyes.

Samantha eyed him wearily, the aching in her joints and the burning of her eyes making her realize just how tired she was. "Checkers, you have the right idea," she sighed. "I need to go to bed."

She removed the pins from her hair and let it flutter down and across her shoulders. "And I don't think I'll even undress."

Her thoughts returned to Franklin and her earlier fears of his being here at Johnston Oaks when her father was gone. It would be best not to let herself be caught in a sheer nightgown. It would make things much too easy for Franklin.

"And I want to be dressed appropriately for Father's arrival," she whispered. "We've much to talk over."

Once more she looked toward the window. "Damn it," she uttered. "Where *is* he? Why did General Beauregard call him at this late hour?"

She would not let herself get tangled up in thoughts of the romantic Creole general who was now in command of the Confederate forces. This man was as responsible as her own father for Charleston's state of affairs. Though she was forced to be loyal to her father and his beliefs, she felt that he and General Beauregard were wrong.

"Oh, why even ponder over it?" she argued to herself

as she removed her shoes. "As always, I must do what I must, and I must stand behind my father all the way, no matter the pitfalls that may lie ahead."

She rid herself of her petticoats, then slinked down onto her bed and sighed. "Home. It seems I was never even gone," she whispered. But when her thoughts were suddenly filled with Troy, she knew that the past several weeks had, indeed, been real enough. She missed Troy. Every lonesome heartbeat rang out his name.

Sleep eluded Samantha. She rolled on her bed from one side to the other, then just finally left the bed and began to pace. "Where is Father?" she whispered. "Is he even all right?"

The bells of a nearby church pealed four in the morning. Samantha tensed, not realizing it was this late. A knock on her bedroom door drew her quickly around, and in a rustle of skirt she hurried to the door and opened it. Seeing her father standing there, his red hair tousled and his green eyes troubled, brought a rush of tears to Samantha's eyes. She threw herself into his arms and sobbed against his massive chest.

"I was so worried, Father," she softly cried. "Where have you been for so long? What have you been doing?"

"Let's go to the roof, Sam," Craig said hoarsely. "I've already directed Franklin there."

Samantha eased away from him, her eyes wide. "The roof?" she questioned, wiping the wetness from her eyes. "Father, why? What's happening?"

"Come," he urged, taking her by an elbow. "I'll explain while we go to the roof."

Barefoot, Samantha followed alongside him, shivering

213

from fear. She wasn't sure if she wanted to hear any explanations. There could only be one reason to go to the roof and stand at the widow's watch platform which faced Charleston Harbor: It would be to view something. Samantha dared not think on what she would see. It surely would change her life.

The hallway was only dimly lighted by candles, and the staircase which led to the third floor was even darker as Samantha groped along it with her father.

"Samantha, in only a matter of minutes, Fort Sumter will be fired upon," Craig said, tightening his hold on her elbow as he felt her teeter at his words.

He continued. "I've been meeting with General Beauregard and his men this evening," he explained. "It ran into morning because General Beauregard decided to send Col. James Chestnut to deliver a written surrender ultimatum to Major Anderson at Fort Sumter. Major Anderson rejected it. Major Anderson said that he would evacuate Fort Sumter on April fifteenth holding his fire in the meantime unless fired upon, or unless he detected some sort of hostile intent that would endanger the fort. He further stated that his agreement to hold fire might be altered if he received other instructions from his government—or additional supplies."

Craig paused in his story to help Samantha up to the roof where Franklin already stood leaning his hands onto the rail, looking intensely out at Charleston Harbor.

Samantha felt pinpricks of apprehension tingle across her flesh as Craig guided her to stand between him and Franklin. Her mouth was dry, her stomach felt weak. She had no alternative but to become an observer, so she hugged herself against the chill blowing in from the harbor and also looked toward the harbor, listening to her father's further explanation.

"Colonel Chestnut decided that Major Anderson was allowing himself too many ways out, offering terms that were manifestly futile. So Colonel Chestnut wrote out a formal declaration, stating that he had the honor to notify Major Anderson that the Confederate troops would open the fire of their batteries on Fort Sumter in one hour."

"And at what time was this promise made, Father?" Samantha asked softly, trying to keep her lips from quivering from pent-up emotions.

"Three-thirty," Craig said hoarsely. "It took me almost the full hour to return home and to alert you and Franklin of what is to happen."

At almost the instant Craig spoke his last word, the opening shot of what was to become known as the Civil War, a shell fired from Fort Johnston, exploded over Fort Sumter.

"The signal for all Confederate batteries to start their bombardment," Craig said, matter-of-factly.

Tracking the shell by its burning fuse, Samantha thought it looked like a firefly in the night. But it wasn't the peaceful glow from a firefly. It was the hellish beginning of a war.

"And so we fool on, into the black cloud ahead of us," Samantha whispered, tears once more blurring her vision, but not enough to keep her from seeing the confident smiles on the faces of both her father and Franklin, nor the hardy handshake that they shared as the sky brightened above Fort Sumter.

"The beginning of the end for Old Abe," Franklin shouted.

"Yup, I think so," Craig boasted. "But one thing

worries the hell out of me."

"What's that?" Franklin asked, offering Craig a cigar as they began descending the stairs from the roof.

Craig accepted the cigar and nervously turned it between his fingers of one hand while assisting Samantha down the dark stairs with the other. He squinted through the darkness, watching his footing. "It's the failure of our diplomats Mason and Slidell on the British ship the *Trent* that concerns me. Damn that Charles Wilkey of the *U.S.S. San Jacinto* for stopping the *Trent* from reaching Europe to persuade Britain and France to take up the southern cause. Wilkey even did this without orders to do so. He even took Mason and Slidell prisoners to Boston."

"No need to worry yourself over that," Franklin encouraged. "Great Britain intervened. They showed him Wilkey's act violated the principle of freedom of the seas because England is a neutral nation. Great Britain threatened war, and the North gave in and released the prisoners. Surely Britain will now, for sure, look to us as the side to be loyal to."

As they left the staircase and were now in the bright lights of the parlor, Craig led Samantha to a wing chair where she eased herself down into it, still numb from the war becoming a reality this night.

"I think this calls for a glass of champagne," Craig boldly stated, going to the liquor cabinet where a bottle had already been opened and three tall-stemmed glasses waited. "Tonight even you will join in the celebration and share drinks with the men, Sam."

Samantha was surprised, yet glad. She hoped the sting of alcohol could help her to accept the fate of the night.

"Do you think the rumor of the blockade will now become fact, now that Fort Sumter has been fired upon?" Franklin asked, accepting his glass of champagne handed him by Craig.

Samantha almost spilled the glass that had just been handed to her when she heard mention of the blockade. The map! In the confusion of the firing upon Fort Sumter, she had forgotten about the map that she had been so anxious to show her father!

She stood up and moved toward her father, placing the glass of champagne on a table, not interested now in drinking at all. She felt alive again. And once her father saw the map, how would it change things in his eyes? Would he still be as confident or would this map be cause for his alarm?

"Father," she said, hurrying to his side to place a hand on his arm. "I've something to tell you."

Craig brushed her hand aside. "Sam, this isn't the time for idle chatter," he scolded. "Now you just sit down and enjoy your champagne while Franklin and I continue to discuss the affairs of state."

Samantha felt anger rising inside her. She circled her fingers into tight fists at her side and set her jaw solidly. "Father, I have to talk to you. I have something to show you," she demanded. "What I am talking about is not idle chatter."

"Sam!" Craig shouted, pointing toward the chair. "Sit. You are not behaving like a true lady should."

"I will not be ordered to sit like one does a dog," she spat back. "When will you treat me as an intelligent adult, Father?"

Craig leaned down into her face, emitting a soft growl. "Sam, like I said. This isn't the time," he fumed. "Why

217

must you always show yourself in front of Franklin, of all people? He will lose all interest in you."

"Ah, if only he would," Samantha testily argued back. "Then perhaps I could get the attention I deserve from *you*."

She went to the far corner of the room and sulked, wondering how she could get his attention. The map. Yes, she would have to get the map. She sneaked away from the room, took the steps two at a time, and rushed on into her bedroom and grabbed the map. When she returned to the parlor, she received an ugly stare from her father. She took this as a warning, so she stood idly by, waiting for the right moment to intervene in the continuing conversation about the blockade.

"The blockade is a big joke," Franklin said, downing another glass of champagne. "Britain will help us to break it if Old Abe tries to pull that on the South. After all, Britain owes nothing to the North. On the other hand, the South is an important customer for British manufacturers and shipping services."

Craig settled down into a chair and casually crossed his legs, eyeing Samantha out of the corner of his eyes, scowling toward her disobediences. "The South produces half of the world's output of a commodity that is processed voluminously and lucratively in English mills. Cotton," he bragged. "Cotton is king. The export of raw cotton truly makes England hostage to the South. It can hardly be otherwise, since almost a quarter of Britain's population is engaged in the textile business."

"Yes, the owners of the great mills of England's Midlands would be ruined if the cotton supply is interrupted," Franklin said. "And thousands of British mill hands might starve if the shuttle looms come to a halt for lack of raw materials."

Craig chuckled, lifting an eyebrow amusedly as he placed his empty glass on the table beside him. "You might say the destiny of the world hangs on a thread," he mocked. "Never did so much depend upon a mere flock of down!"

Bored and angry, Samantha stomped to stand before her father. Methodically she unfolded the map and placed it before his wondering eyes. "Father, if you don't listen to what I have to say, at least look at this," she said bitterly. "And after seeing it, tell me what you make of it."

Craig took the map from Samantha and looked studiously at it, slowly kneading his chin. "Where the hell did you get this?" he finally said, challenging Samantha with the flashing of his green eyes.

Sighing with relief, glad that her father was going to finally let her have her say, Samantha eased down to the floor and propped her elbows on his knees, looking up into his face. "It's like this," she said, then continued with her tale of how she came about having the map and the importance that it appeared to have.

Then she asked, "The code, Father. Can you decipher it? Surely it means something valuable to the North and even something evil for the South, for it was a northern gentleman who had first possession of it."

She could not—would not—speak Troy's name. She did not want to condemn him. She would keep his name hidden deeply inside her heart, for only her own benefit. She could never cause him undue harm.

Franklin rose from his chair, stooped over Craig's shoulder, and also studied the map. "Hmm," he said. "It *is* a map drawn of the southern states. It does have something to do with the blockade, I am sure. But I'd say it's rubbish. Anyone can draw a map and say that it means something. I say toss it into the fireplace and set a match to it. We have no need of it, do we, Craig?"

"I would like to decipher the code," Craig said. "It has to mean something or why would one bother to place the words in code? Why would men fight over it?"

"Well?" Samantha asked anxiously. "Can you, Father?"

Craig studied it for awhile longer, then handed it back to Samantha. "I think Franklin is right," he said. "I don't see any benefit whatsoever that this map might be to us."

Samantha rose to her feet, stunned, her eyes wide with disbelief. "But the code, Father," she said. "Surely you can't dismiss it as unimportant."

Craig rose from his chair and meandered toward the liquor cabinet and, once there, poured himself another glass of beverage. "One man's code is not another's." He shrugged. "Only the man who set it down on paper could tell its full meaning."

"But men fought over the map," she softly argued, waving it in the air. She didn't want to stress the danger she was in because of it. Apparently there was no need to say anything more about it. As usual, her father showed no interest in anything that she, a mere daughter, would have to say. Now if a son had discovered such a map, it would be a piece of gold in her father's hands!

"If men fought over the map, it was because they knew not what was on the folded paper," he said nonchalantly. "Now go on your way, Sam. And take the map with you. Its mystery is yours to amuse yourself with. I don't care to bother myself with such nonsense."

"Oh!" Samantha said, stomping a foot angrily. She began to spin around to leave the room, when Joshua rushed into the room, unannounced.

Craig almost dropped his wineglass at the suddenness of Joshua's entry. "Joshua!" he scolded, steadying his hand as he placed the glass back down on a table. "What is the meaning of this interruption? You know you should never enter a room at Johnston Oaks without first being announced."

Joshua humbled himself by bowing his head respectfully though this seemed strange coming from such a powerfully built man. But just as Samantha had been taught her own place in the household, that of being a mere lady, Joshua's learning his own place had been beaten into him twicefold. He even had a few scars on his back to prove it.

"Massa Craig, you knows I wouldn't break rules 'less I had somethin' mighty important to tell," he said, now lifting his dark eyes to look nervously toward his master. His gray hair made his face appear darker and his shabby, faded cotton shirt and breeches strained where his muscles abounded. He was a walking powerhouse, a credit to Johnston Oaks Plantation.

Annoyance making Craig's one cheek twitch, he went to Joshua. "What is it?" he grumbled. "Tell me, Joshua. Lord! It's the wee hours of the morning!"

"It was dem guns explodin' in the distance and the fire of the sky," Joshua said in his deep voice. He looked over his shoulder as though he expected someone to be there to grab him. "It's some of my people. They got plumb scared, jumped from their beds and ran off into the swamps!"

Craig was taken aback. It had been sometime now since

221

a slave had tried to escape from his plantation. They knew the punishment for such a deed. The thought of that should have scared them more than gunfire that was in no way yet a threat to them.

"How many?" Craig said throatily, kneading his chin.

"I'd say twenty," Joshua said, again lowering his eyes. "Massa, let ol' Joshua go get 'em. They can't be far."

"Take as many men as you need, Joshua," Craig said, nodding. "And I'll be waiting. You know the penalty."

"Yassa," Joshua mumbled. "I knows plenty."

"Do your best," Craig said, patting Joshua on the shoulder. "And you'd best explain to all those who stayed behind to get used to gunfire because a war is now being fought, Joshua."

"Yassa." Joshua nodded, then turned and left the room in a loud shuffle of feet.

"Damn!" Craig shouted, flailing his arms into the air. "If it's not one thing, it's another. You can't tell me the damn slaves ran because they were scared. By hearing the gunfire, they thought Lincoln himself had probably come to free them."

He went to a window and looked from it, seeing the first streaks of dawn lighting the sky. "I'll show 'em," he said beneath his breath, clasping his hands tightly together behind him. "They can't be permitted to even think of escape."

Samantha swallowed hard and slipped from the room, hurrying to her bedroom to try and prepare herself for the slaves' return. She knew what to expect and dreaded it.

"Sometimes I hardly know my father at all," she whispered. She closed her bedroom door and leaned heavily against it, her heart heavy.

Then she held the map before her eyes, astonished again at her father's disinterest in it. Now she doubted if she would ever know the true meaning of the code. But just because her father scoffed at its importance didn't mean she would discard it. Perhaps one day . . .

Weary from many things, Samantha felt the sudden need to escape in her own way. Sleep. But first, what should she do with the map? She knew not to leave it where it could be found easily should the wrong person come across it.

"The loose brick in the fireplace in the parlor," she whispered. "I shall place it there tomorrow when no one is looking."

Voices from outside made Samantha's heart jump with fright. It seemed that Joshua hadn't had to go far in the swamp to find the slaves. He had already returned.

The sound of the whip's snap made Samantha begin a violent trembling. She placed her hands tightly over her ears and closed her eyes, yet nothing could stifle the screams that followed from the slaves who had no choice but accept their punishment.

# Chapter Fifteen

The blockade had become a reality. Lincoln had declared the coast from Virginia all the way to Texas blockaded. He had ordered United States Navy warships to scatter along the stretch of seashore, particularly at seaports, for the definite purpose of stopping and capturing all ships that attempted to go in or out of southern harbors, whether they were Confederate ships or English ships or those of any other foreign country. The southern leaders had said the South would not be defeated but "choked to death."

Yet in euphoric optimism the Confederacy concluded that the insatiable British need for cotton would compel England to come to their aid with diplomatic recognition, loans, and war material. They believed that if the blockade did choke off Confederate exports, Britain would send a fleet to break the stranglehold and ensure her steady supply of raw cotton. England's economic interest would be the guardian of the South's independence.

Craig Johnston, along with other southern leaders, had

decided to create a cotton shortage to speed up the day when Britain would intervene in their behalf. Local cotton brokers and state government officials voluntarily declared a cotton embargo. This was "cotton diplomacy" carried to an extreme, but only a few appreciated that fact.

Confederate Attorney General Benjamin urged the South to ship as much cotton as fast as possible to secure credit in Europe for sorely needed weapons and munitions. But in the heady aftermath of the victory at Fort Sumter, most Southerners ignored his plea. They gambled on a cotton shortage, and wrongfully so, because an immense surplus existed. The southern states had produced and exported bumper crops. This glut of cotton had led many European brokers and speculators to stockpile cotton imports from the South.

The cotton embargo turned out to be a blunder. And the South had been wrong about Britain's intervening in the war for any reason. Britain refused to intervene unless the South could show that it might win a final victory, which the South could not.

"Johnston Oaks will fall to ruin if my ship the *Magnolia* cannot be allowed to leave the harbor because of this damn blockade," Craig said, pacing his study, Samantha wide-eyed in silence as she stood watching. "So there is only one thing to do, Sam."

Samantha was amazed that he was including her in any of his plans. But the threat to Johnston Oaks was surely the cause. He needed her, as he would have needed a son. She was all he had. He had finally come to realize that when he faced the reality of what the war was already bringing to their private lives. So much was already backfiring for the once smug Craig Johnston. Now

Samantha could see doubt in his every worried expression.

Samantha, dressed in a low-cut, flowing silk dress, her hair swept back and held in place behind her ears by slides, went to her father. "What are you planning?" she asked, relighting his cigar that had grown dead between his lips.

Craig squinted his eyes and puffed on his cigar until its tip was once more a glowing orange. He nodded a thanks to Samantha as she blew out the match. Then he withdrew the cigar and stared from the window, in the direction of Charleston Harbor.

"Though that damn Lincoln tried to make escape impossible at the harbor by sinking those useless, old New England whalers filled with stones across the bar of Charleston's main shipping channels, the tides and currents have already scoured the harbor open and blockade-runners are back in business," he said. "That has to be our next move, Sam."

Samantha blanched and her knees became rubbery. "Father!" she gasped. "Are you saying—"

He turned on a heel and faced her. "Yes. We will convert the *Magnolia* into a blockade-running vessel. I refuse to let Lincoln outsmart me. We must do everything within our power to save Johnston Oaks Plantation. Are you game, Sam?"

"Me?" Samantha said in an astonished murmur. "You really want me?"

"I will need every able-bodied hand possible to make this work," he said thickly. He placed his cigar in an ashtray and went to Samantha to frame her face between his hands. "In the past, I've scoffed at your worthiness because you're female. But with much thought and

226

deliberation I realized just how strong a female you are. Not many a lady would travel as you have, unescorted, between the North and South."

His eyelids grew heavy. "Sam, I need you at my side," he murmured. "Franklin must stay behind and keep an eye on the slaves at his plantation as well as ours. One by one they've been slipping away, fleeing north. No warnings are heeded any longer by me."

He looked momentarily away from her, his face shadowed with worry. Then he once more looked determinedly down at her. "And, Sam, I don't want to leave you behind. You'd be safer with me, for many reasons."

Samantha wondered if he was silently referring to not trusting Franklin where she was concerned, though he would never admit it. Or was he referring to the threat of the northern blue-uniformed Billy Yanks who continued to fight their way south, though her father had earlier bragged that no blood would be spilled on southern soil?

She swallowed hard, accepting any reason just to be recognized by him. "I'll do whatever you wish," she said. "You know that, Father. Now, what are your plans?"

He swung away from her and resumed pacing, his eyes watching his footsteps, his hands clasped tightly behind him. "The damn British," he growled. "The cowards. If they had done as expected, none of this would be necessary. As it is, only a few British entrepreneurs are involved in the South's plight, and their sympathies with the South are primarily concerned with making money. Nothing more. Nothing less."

"Yes. I know," Samantha sighed, easing down into a chair, drained from confused worry.

"We must elude the federal squadrons at all cost with our *Magnolia*," Craig said. "She will carry our cotton cargo to the neutral ports in Bermuda. We will there exchange cotton for European war materials delivered to Bermuda by transatlantic merchantmen. Damn the United States Navy. If it's not stopped, it will jeopardize the entire Confederate war effort, let alone destroy Johnston Oaks!"

Samantha rose slowly from her chair and inched toward her father. "Father, are you saying that we will not only be selling our cotton but also transporting ammunition and firearms?" she asked.

"That is in the plan," he growled. "We must do our part for the southern cause, Samantha. How better a way than to help supply war material to our fighting men?"

"Father, that will be dangerous in many ways," she said. "The *Magnolia* could be blown clean out of the water if a spark of fire would touch the—"

"Sam, enough!" Craig roared. "Do not question what I do or plan. We must do what we must."

Knowing how often she used that same phrase, she silently agreed with a nod.

"And, Sam, you will become the son I never had while traveling by my side on the *Magnolia*," Craig said hoarsely.

"What?" Samantha quietly uttered, her eyebrows forking.

Craig's eyes raked over her. A smile lightened his mood. "Yes, you will dress in breeches and shirt, with your hair hidden beneath a hat." He chuckled. "No one will ever suspect a lady travels on the *Magnolia*."

\* \* \*

The nights were dark, the seas were wide, and Craig Johnston was an expert at navigating among the numerous sounds, bays, and inlets that dotted the shoreline. The *Magnolia* had run the blockade with such ease and consistency that Craig had begun to mock the efforts of the United States Navy.

Five months had passed. Craig and Samantha had retraced the perilous journey numerous times between the Bahamas and Charleston, taking out cotton and bringing back arms, ammunition, medicines, and clothing for the Confederacy.

Once again the *Magnolia* was ready to elude the federal squadrons. The *Magnolia* was a lean, low ship, a three-masted steam frigate. Its shallow draft enabled it to dart into cover or inlets where the deeper-draft federal ships could not follow.

The line of the *Magnolia* was sharp and narrow, its length nine times the beam, so that the hull could knife through the water. Its profile was kept low to make the vessel inconspicuous. Its hull always rose only a few feet out of the water, and her superstructure had been made to be rudimentary.

On deck, funnels could be telescoped down to hide them, and the hull had been painted a dull gray, to blend with the fog and sea. The crew quarters were spartan. The cargo space was the first consideration.

The *Magnolia* could make headway under its full set of sails, but its primary motive force was steam. Its engines were big and powerful, with enough brawn to push the craft to a top speed of eighteen knots.

It was a moon-bright night, clear and calm, dangerous conditions for a runner. The *Magnolia* was laden with seven hundred bales of cotton. Craig stood on top deck, with Samantha at his side looking the part of a man in loose-fitted cotton breeches, shirt, and wide-brimmed hat, where her hair lay hidden beneath.

Samantha clung to the railing, peering toward the twinkle of lights aboard the federal ships. Lights had become a critical role in this game of hide-and-seek. The runners used the well-lighted ships of the federal squadron as guide markers. All lights had been blacked out on the *Magnolia*, only a dark shadow now against the black waters of Ashley River.

Craig lifted his telescope and peered through it, at the river entrance where the enemy ships lay in wait, menacing shapes on the horizon. Nine hundred barrels of gunpowder awaited the *Magnolia* in Nassau. If on the return voyage the vessel came under heavy fire from the federal gunboats, a shell penetrating the hull this time could cause the gunpowder in the hold to blow the *Magnolia* to splinters.

"When can we leave, Father?" Samantha whispered, shivering in the chill of the sea air.

"When the moon disappears from the night sky," Craig whispered back. "Only then will it be safe to leave these waters."

They waited, tense and quiet. Then when the moon had slipped easily away from eyesight, Craig hauled anchor slowly and carefully, so that the chains did not rattle. The *Magnolia*, her lights blacked out with not even the glow of a cigar allowed, and her sidewheels barely turning, steamed, inching down the narrow inlet, toward the Atlantic, forced to sail at an unfavorable angle to the wind. Ahead, anchored in the channel, two federal warships threatened to bar her way to freedom. The *Magnolia* hugged the shore where the ship was practically invisible, and the noise of her engine was drowned by her breaking waves.

The ship was loaded with cotton to the gunwales. A special steam-powered machinery on the waterfront had been used to pack it tightly into bales so that not an inch of space had been wasted.

The engine-room hatchways were covered with tarpaulins at the risk of suffocating the stokers, and even the tiny light in the compass housing was shielded. Orders were passed in whispers, and except for the throbbing of the engine and the soft slap of the paddle blades which sounded deafening to Samantha, the *Magnolia* steamed on in silence.

The crew on deck crouched low, behind the bulwarks, expecting at any moment to be challenged by a Yankee gunboat. Samantha bravely stood her ground beside her father on the bridge, proud that he had thought to include her in the excitement. Their eyes strained together in the darkness, watching, breathing shallowly.

Craig occasionally requested a sounding. The ship slowed and stopped, and a shadowy figure in the forechains heaved the lead and reported the depth of conditions of the bottom. The readings were guideposts in Craig's mind, and they prompted adjustments in the *Magnolia*'s course.

As the ship then proceeded to cut through the darkness, Samantha's breath caught in her throat. She grabbed at her father's arm, digging her fingers into him. "There's one of them," she harshly whispered. "A Yankee ship. On the starboard bow."

Craig peered into the gloom, seeing nothing. "Sam, where?" he whispered back, and before she could reply he also made out the black, motionless bulk of a gunboat on the starboard side. He held his breath, expecting the red flash of a Yankee gun and the war of an explosion. But the *Magnolia* passed unnoticed within one hundred feet of the foe.

Samantha had just begun to breathe freely again when she heard the pilot whisper, "Steamer on the port bow!"

"Hard aport," Craig growled, and the *Magnolia* once more eluded a Yankee gunboat, creeping by unobserved.

But soon another enemy ship appeared out of the night. It was steaming slowly across the *Magnolia*'s bow. "Stop her," Craig ordered. "Stop the *Magnolia* at once."

The *Magnolia* lay dead in the water as the enemy vessel glided past. Darkness had once again shielded the *Magnolia*, and she was now free to ride on out to open sea.

"Father, we did it," Samantha said, her voice now above a whisper.

"Never feel too confident," Craig scolded. "You know better than that, Sam. Perils await us everywhere. We must keep alert at all times."

"Yes, I know," Samantha answered. She inched her hat back a fraction from her brow and wiped a spray of seawater from it. Her thoughts had not been allowed to stray much; to wonder about Troy and where his ship was taking him. She had wondered at times, when she had viewed an enemy ship, if he could possibly be its captain.

She had to wonder if he ever thought about her and how the war was treating her.

She had only allowed herself occasional longings to see him again. The memory of his kiss and touch never faded. It was guarded inside her heart by a wall of sweet sensuality. One day she hoped that he would come to her and scale this wall, himself, to take what was his alone for the taking.

A full day out to sea and night had once more fallen in its screen of blackness. As the *Magnolia* headed west across the open ocean, the crew kept a constant lookout for the United States Navy warships.

Trailing tatters of smoke from her two rakish funnels, the *Magnolia* slipped along under the moonless night, under the power of its steam engines and a full set of sails. Armed with a large pivot gun and a thirty-two pound howitzer, it made a formidable enough fighting vessel.

Samantha was in her private cabin this night, stretched across her bunk, wishing that she could just once shed her man's apparel. Even now it lay like a sack on her. But she had to be prepared at all times for any sudden attack to the *Magnolia*. If by chance the *Magnolia* was taken by the enemy she had to look the role of a man for as long as possible. She had been repeatedly warned by her father of the appetites of the crew of any ship that had been away from seaports for a spell. And wouldn't the northern Billy Yanks just love to ravage a southern lady? A shiver of fear coursed through her at the thought.

She fell into a restless sleep, then woke with a start to the sound of scurrying feet overhead on top deck. Startled, she jumped from the bunk. With trembling fingers she placed the drab hat she had become so acquainted with tightly on her head and shoved her red tresses beneath its edges.

Having slept in her shoes, she was ready to hurry to top

deck. Her feet would hardly carry her fast enough as she wondered what was going on. When she reached the top rung of the companion ladder, she saw that night was fading fast, and she could almost feel the pulsating fears of those on board as dawn began to brighten the eastern sky.

One step on deck and Samantha saw the reason for concern etched on all the faces around her. Out of the gray, misty gloom of low-lying fog emerged the somber phantom form of an enemy ship. The moment of trial was at hand. Firmness and decisions were essential for the emergency.

"Get back to your cabin, Sam," Craig softly ordered as he saw her approach. "This time there's sure to be open firing."

"Father, I refuse to run like a scared rabbit back to shelter," she flatly stated, stubbornly taking her position beside him on the bridge.

Everyone became deathly quiet as the *Magnolia* slipped on through the water and passed near the enemy ship. Samantha became filled with excited astonishment when the *Magnolia* wasn't discovered. But just as the crew began to breathe more easily, flares sent up by the federal vessel lit the fog-laden sky and exposed the Confederate runner.

The enemy ship angrily opened fire, firing broadside after broadside. It was time for Craig to choose between surrender and fight, shouting to his engineer for full speed.

Samantha stood frozen, stunned by the mounting danger. She watched as shots whistled through the *Magnolia*'s rigging, and shells exploded around her while her father's proud, dutiful ship continued to churn the water to foam with her paddles.

Suddenly the *Magnolia* shuddered from a hit, throwing Samantha to the deck where she lay momentarily dazed. Then her eyes grew wild, searching for her father. When she found him, she saw that he was tending to two of the crew who had been wounded while others of the crew were fighting a fire that had been started in the bales of deckside cotton.

Crawling, Samantha reached for her father and spoke his name, then cowered back away from him as the forked tongue of the fire suddenly leaped into the newly tarred rigging and ran rapidly up the shrouds. The intricate network of the cordage was traced, the many threads of flames twisting and writhing, setting everything in its path to a fiery inferno.

Another blast of gunfire and the *Magnolia* shook with the blow and groaned as though it were human as it began to slowly sink.

"Father!" Samantha screamed, no longer able to make him out because of the dense, black smoke swirling about her.

The great mainmast suddenly teetered, reeled, and fell over the ship's side into the sea, and Samantha saw only momentarily the broken foremast that was falling toward her.

# Chapter Sixteen

Blinking her eyes nervously, Samantha aroused from what had felt to be the deepest sleep ever in her life. Then her eyes shot widely open, remembering her father's burning ship and the falling mast.

"No," she cried to herself, seeing the strangeness of her surroundings. She knew that she was no longer on her father's ship. She rose slowly to an elbow and peered through the semidarkness, a whale-oil lamp's light on a far wall emitting enough light for her to make out the sleeping figures of men on the floor all around her.

Her nose twitched. She sniffled. There was a mixture of aromas in the air. She could smell tobacco, rum, and perfume, and other aromas unidentifiable to her. But the most identifiable of all was the murky aroma of body sweat curling her nose, emanating from all those around her.

Running her hands on the floor beside her she gathered bits of fuzz between her fingers and knew this had to be cotton. She became aware of the slapping of water against wood, the creaking of ropes, and the drone of voices overhead.

I'm in the hold of a ship, she finally realized. And most certainly not the *Magnolia*'s. The *Magnolia*'s was not this spacious nor fine. She could see grand oak beams smoothly varnished that ran along the ceiling, and a hint of copper shone from a far wall where steps led up to where there was more light.

"Father!" Samantha suddenly gasped, paling. "Where is he?"

Her gaze once more absorbed the stretched-out sleeping figures about her. She recognized the man closest to her. He was one of the *Magnolia*'s crew. One by one, Samantha studied faces. They were all a part of her father's ship's crew.

"But Father?" she murmured, rising to a sitting position. "Is he among these who are sleeping? And on whose ship are we?"

A stab of fear pierced her heart. "We've been captured," she whispered. "Lord, we've been taken aboard the United States Navy warship."

Instinct drove her hands to her head, checking to see if her hat was in place. She sorely needed it now to protect herself against the evil men of this enemy vessel.

"It's still there," she sighed, only finding a few stray locks of hair that had fallen from its edges. She was glad now that her father had wisely chosen a hat for her. He said one that fit the tightest would be an anchor for her hair, and even a severe blow to her person shouldn't knock it from her head.

"My head," she murmured, aghast that she could find no swollen bumps or a head wound. "But surely the mast hit me. I saw it falling."

Then she recalled at the last moment of her consciousness aboard the *Magnolia* a set of strong hands dragging her aside as the mast crashed beside her. "Father," she gasped. "It must've been Father dragging me to safety. I must have fainted from fright! The first time ever in my life to faint, and it had to be when I needed to stay conscious and aware the most."

But she hadn't, and now she had to see just what her fate and her father's would be. First she had to find her father among the men who were without a ship, now held hostage on another.

Hostage? She wondered. She saw no armed guards, and that the hatch which led from the hold was open and also unguarded. Strange. She would have expected to be placed in shackles upon being taken prisoner!

At least I have that to be thankful for, she thought, yet she was deeply saddened over the loss of the *Magnolia* and whatever lives that had traveled to the bottom of the sea on it.

Going to her knees, crawling, she went from man to man, searching faces, beginning to fear the worst: that her father was not among the survivors. She grew frantic at the thought. In an almost crazed fashion she crawled to the remaining sleeping figures and looked upon their faces. Tears clouded her vision as she reached the last and again saw that it wasn't her father.

Then she looked toward the open hatch and anger welled up inside her. "He's not dead at all," she whispered, wiping tear streaks from her face. "He's been separated from us purposely and possibly even tortured."

Such a thought gave Samantha a reviving of strength, fueled by anger. She set her sights on the ladder that led up and through the hatch, determined to find her father,

238

no matter what she had to do to accomplish the deed. It wasn't fair that he should be singled out and punished for doing what he had to do for his survival.

Yet, she was reminded that these past months he hadn't only been transporting cotton but materials of war, as well. Surely, word of the *Magnolia*'s activities had reached Washington, and it had become a target long ago. That was no pleasant thought. If the name *Magnolia* had become familiar on the enemy's lips, then Craig Johnston's had also. He would be treated as any other prisoner of war, even though he hadn't fought on the battlefield and fired that first shot against the enemy. To Samantha, he was innocent until proven guilty! The sinking of the *Magnolia* had taken with it all evidence that could be held against her father. No traces of gunpowder could now be sniffed out in the corners behind the bales of cotton! Samantha would, herself, argue her father's case!

Scurrying up the ladder, Samantha kept her eye on the opened hatch. She couldn't be caught off guard and forced to return to the hold. She wanted to find the captain and demand to be taken to her father and then demand her father's release!

With a thudding heart threatening to spoil her plans, she paused just before climbing on out. She breathed deeply and listened to its shakiness as she exhaled.

"I must get hold of myself," she whispered, feeling the violent trembling of her fingers. "And I must remember to play the role of a man."

She lifted a hand to her face and raked her fingers across it, then inspected her fingertips, relieved to see their blackness. The smoke from the *Magnolia*'s fire had settled onto her face, giving her a most perfect disguise to hide behind.

She tested her hat, making sure that it was still firmly in place and that no hair escaped from it. She even pulled its wide brim lower, over her eyes.

Then she gazed down at her attire. The looseness of her shirt helped to hide the swell of her breasts, and the breeches were, thankfully, just as loose and even hung low and over her shoes which helped to hide their female's smallness.

Gathering courage, she set her jaw hard and climbed on up to top deck where darkness hung like a black shroud over the ship. Groping through the darkness, Samantha met a crew member head-on. Keeping her face lowered somewhat, she knew that she must speak in as deep a tone as she could manage to the sailor, who was dressed in heavy cotton breeches and cotton shirt that was half unbuttoned, revealing a muscled, hairy chest. Afraid to look at his face, not knowing whether or not he would treat her roughly, being that she was a captive, she still kept her face lowered.

"Sir, take me to your captain," she said gruffly. "I must have a few words with him."

"Sorry. That's impossible," the sailor said. "The cap'n is in conference now with his associates. Just get back down below. You can speak with him later." He paused and placed a hand to her shoulder and lowered his face, trying to look up into hers. "Ye all right?" he questioned. "You're the first to stir of those brought aboard from the sinkin' vessel."

Samantha was taken aback, not understanding why he was being this nice. He even sounded sincerely concerned. And why hadn't he been upset with her for having left the hold, since surely that's where the *Magnolia*'s crew had been forced to stay as prisoners.

Then she became aware of his lingering hand on her shoulder and tensed, hoping he wouldn't feel the lack of muscle there and realize that she wasn't a man after all.

Easing his hand away, she took a step backward. But she would not return to the hold quite yet. She had to see to her father's welfare. He could even be mortally injured. He surely needed her.

"I must speak to the captain of your ship now," she said with more determination, hardly even recognizing her own voice, it was so low and throaty.

"Like I said, young lad, you can't," the sailor insisted. "If it's food you're needin', some vittles will be served you later. Now run along with ye. I've more to do than stand here chattin'."

Again Samantha was amazed at his lack of forcefulness for not having thrown her bodily back into the hold. This gave her courage to become even more confident. He did seem an easy one to deal with, even if he was a Billy Yank!

"I won't budge until I have my say," she grumbled.

"Tell me what's botherin' you, lad," the sailor said. "Are you ailin'? Do you require medical attention?"

A sudden thought struck Samantha. If she were to say that there had been a deadly epidemic of sorts springing up among the crew of the *Magnolia*, which had just been discovered before the *Magnolia* sank, *that* could get her the attention and fast. The captain of the ship would want to know all the details.

Samantha pretended a groan and grabbed at her head. "Yes. I'm ailing," she said. "I need to see the captain, to warn him of the epidemic."

She almost laughed when hearing this sailor's surprised gasp. Instead she emitted another most pitiful groan.

"Epidemic did you say?" the sailor said, his voice

suddenly high-pitched. "What are you talkin' 'bout, lad?"

"The crew of the *Magnolia*," Samantha groaned.

"Holy Jesus!" the sailor said thickly. "Follow me. You'd bes' tell the cap'n firsthand 'bout this epidemic thing. We may have to leave the lot of you on the next shore available."

Samantha hid a smug smile behind a hand as she kept her face lowered, following along behind him. He was making sure that much space was left between them, as though she, personally, was the carrier of the black plague. Soon he would discover that he had been made to look like a fool. Samantha didn't plan to carry on with this talk of epidemic once she was brought face-to-face with this ship's captain. Time was not on her side. She had to be taken to her father, see personally to his needs.

When the sailor guided Samantha to the master cabin, she tried to retain the courage that had led her this far, knowing that continuing to play the role of a man was not in her favor. Once under the scrutiny of the ship's captain, in brighter lights, would he see the gentle slope of her jawline, her long, feathery eyelashes, the shape of her lips which were not that of a man?

Hopefully, the black of the smoke would be the mask required, yet, she knew the chance she was taking by having boldly lied to the sailor. Once he discovered that it had only been a ploy, what sort of punishment would he encourage the ship's captain to use on her?

Then another thought struck a chord of fear in her heart. What if she were forced to remove her hat in the presence of the captain?

Suddenly they were at the door to the cabin, and Samantha forced her worries to the back of her mind. She stiffly stepped inside a brightly lighted room where cabin lights fueled by kerosene revealed beautiful walls of oak paneling. The cabin had plush leather furniture, shelves with the shine of crystal behind glass, and along the far wall, a large bunk was prominent with spread blankets and pillows.

In the middle of the cabin, Samantha saw several men positioned about a round table upon which had been spread a map and half-filled glasses of beverage.

The men were all expensively attired in satin, embroidered waistcoats worn over crisp, white shirts, with cravats at their throats, where most displayed diamond stickpins.

Some men were mustached, others were not. Some puffed on cigars, others pipes. The room had a soft cloud of smoke hanging from the ceiling, and intermixed was the strong, identifiable aroma of alcohol.

A throaty laugh rumbled from one man, a chuckle from another. And then suddenly one of the men caught sight of Samantha standing there with the sailor.

"Cap'n?" the sailor said, stepping behind a man whose back was still to him and Samantha.

Samantha swallowed hard, knowing that her moment of reckoning was at hand. She looked intensely toward the captain, who had yet to make any signs of having been spoken to.

Then Samantha looked harder at him, seeing the midnight black of his hair that reached his collar top. Her gaze lowered, seeing his muscled shoulders and strong back.

"Troy?" she whispered before she realized that she had done so. Her knees became suddenly weak, and her head became giddy as her whisper reached his ear, and he turned suddenly around to face her.

Troy rose so quickly from his chair it flipped over and fell in a loud crash to the oak flooring. "What *is* this?" he gasped, stepping toward her, studying her closely. "How—did—you—"

Samantha panicked. She knew that he had recognized her, black face and all. Though she was quite shaken by being suddenly thrown in his presence, she had to gain control of the situation and make sure he didn't speak her name.

"Sam?" he blurted. "Is it you, Sam?"

Samantha sighed with relief. She had forgotten that he had begun calling her by her nickname. She was still safe from the other men discovering that she was female—so far.

The sailor stepped between Troy and Samantha. "Sir, I wouldn't get too close to the lad," he warned. "He's said his crew has some sort of—"

An amused glint showed in Troy's eyes. He interrupted the sailor. "Lad, did you say?" he said, lifting an eyebrow. "Oh, yes. I see. Sam. You're speaking of this lad, *Sam.*"

The sailor's eyes showed confusion. He tilted his head and looked from Samantha to Troy. "You know this lad, sir?" he questioned.

"Quite familiarly," Troy chuckled, his lips lifting into a wry smile. "Where'd you find him?"

"He's part of the crew taken from the sinkin' ship, the *Magnolia.*"

"*Is* he now?" Troy said, now circling Samantha, taking a good look at her.

Samantha was over her shock in seeing Troy, and her old anger was renewing in strength. Troy was the one responsible for the sinking of the *Magnolia.* Apparently he had even been the one to shout the command of the first shot fired upon her. Troy was the captain of this ship Samantha was now forced to be on: a northern warship that surely had hunted until she had finally found and sunk the beautiful, dutiful ship, the *Magnolia*.

"Sir," the sailor persisted. "I think you'd best listen to what I have to warn you 'bout."

"Does it have to do with this lad here?" Troy asked, nodding toward Samantha.

"Why, yes," the sailor said. "It does. Bes' you listen, too."

"I'll listen to what the lad has to say in private," Troy said thickly, his eyes locking with hers. He gestured with a hand toward the men who sat gawking from the table. "You're all dismissed for now. We'll talk later. I must talk to this lad alone to see what the problem is."

One by one the men scooted their chairs back and filed on past Troy and Samantha, eyeing them both questionably. And once the sailor who had brought her there was gone and the door closed, Samantha and Troy were left completely alone.

Samantha jumped as Troy yanked her hat from her head, feeling her hair flutter in flaming reds to her shoulders. She began to tremble when he tossed the hat aside and began to weave his fingers through her hair, all the while looking at her with fire in his eyes.

"Samantha, how is it that you were aboard that Confederate-runner ship and dressed in this way?" he said hoarsely. He reached a hand to her face and with his fingertips rubbed some black from her cheeks. "God. You could have been burned alive aboard that ship."

Samantha composed herself from the initial shock of seeing him again. She shoved his hand away. "Thanks to you and your warship, my father's ship burned," she hissed.

"Your father's?" he gasped. "And you are blaming me?"

"Why else would you think I would be on board a ship dressed in such garb, if not with my father? It was he who suggested it, to protect me, a woman aboard a ship with men."

"I can hardly believe this."

Samantha suddenly remembered her main concern, the reason she had so boldly come to this master cabin to meet with the ship's captain. "I demand to be taken to my father at once," she said icily, ignoring his continuing incredulous stare.

"What do you mean?" he said, his eyebrows forking.

"Don't act innocent," Samantha hissed. "You're holding my father prisoner, separate from the rest of the crew. Don't deny it. Take me to him, Troy."

Troy ran his fingers through his hair. "Sam, honest to God, I don't know what you're talking about," he said thickly. "Your father? On my ship? Being held prisoner?"

"He's not in the hold. You surely have other plans for him," she said hotly. "That's not fair, Troy. He's no criminal. He was only doing what had to be done to keep our plantation alive."

Troy placed his hands to Samantha's shoulders and softly shook her. "Now you listen to me," he said gruffly. "Your being here like this is mystery enough to me without my becoming more confused by your ramblings about your father. Cut it out, Sam. If your father wasn't among those in the hold of my ship, he's not on my ship at all."

Samantha shook herself free. She took a bold step closer to Troy and spoke up into his face. "You're a liar," she accused. "You just won't admit to what you've done because you want to punish him even more by keeping me from him."

Troy grabbed her wrists and held them to his chest. "Sam, you're not hearing anything I say," he growled.

"Nor are you hearing me," Samantha bluntly returned. "Being the captain of a United States Navy warship has caused you to become deaf when it benefits you, it seems."

Troy dropped her wrists, shock registering in his blue eyes. "What—did—you say?" he gasped, his cheeks flushing pink.

"Ha! So now you will try to play coy and even deny that," she accused. She took wide steps to the table and pressed her palms on its top as her eyes scanned the map. "And what have we here?" she said scornfully. "Future plans for hunting down and sinking more Confederate runners? Which drawn lines on this map are the travel routes of the *Magnolia?* Just how long did you follow her before firing at her?"

Troy was stunned by her words and her fierce accusations. But slowly he began to understand just why she would believe he was the enemy. From their very first meeting he had been forced to withhold the truth from her. And now? For her to think that his ship had fired upon her father's?

Yes, it did fit in, yet why didn't she already know that it wasn't he who was responsible? She had surely even seen his ship come to the rescue of the *Magnolia.* Hadn't she even been helped from the burning *Magnolia* by his seamen? If she wasn't aware of these things it had to only mean that for some reason she hadn't been conscious at the time!

The thought of her having been injured in any way coiled his insides painfully. His gaze raked over her, seeing that she appeared fit enough. Yet, wouldn't she pretend to be all right, to look strong, to succeed in what she was doing? Yes, that was like her; her fiery spirit taking charge of her life in her moment of frustration, when surely it must seem as if her whole existence was threatened by this damn, illogical war.

Samantha swung around and glared at him, flinging her hair back from her shoulders with a toss of her head. It was hard being so near him, trying to hate him when her heart cried out just the opposite. In her dreams it had been so different. But how could one forgive or love an enemy?

"Well? What do you have to say for yourself?" she said coldly.

She felt her pulse racing, unable not to see his handsomeness, his tanned face making his blue eyes even more vivid beneath his thick, black lashes. His nose was nicely shaped, his lips widely sensuous. And his jaw was relaxed, puzzling her since her words should be angering him.

"I think you'd best sit down before I tell you the way it *really* is," Troy said, taking her gently by an elbow, urging her toward a chair. He now knew that news of her father was not good, for her father surely was dead having gone down with his ship.

Samantha edged away from him, refusing to be caught up in his soft words and expecting only more lies from him. "The *Magnolia* is gone and perhaps even along with it the future of Johnston Oaks Plantation," she said bitterly. "So I really don't care to hear why you were compelled to destroy my future. All I care about now is my father. Troy, I'm not asking much of you. All I want is to be taken to my father." She would demand her father's release later. First she had to see that he wasn't being treated poorly.

Troy was determined that she listen and, God, how could he tell her about her father without devastating her? He placed his hands to her waist and jerked her against him. He held her snugly in place by the imprisonment of his arms and looked down at her, his loins aroused by her nearness, though the timing was bad for any sensual feelings to be exchanged between them.

"Damn it, Sam," he growled. "You've got to listen. You're going to listen!" He felt her body tense against him and ignored her hands trying to shove him away.

"No matter what you do, you will not get away this time," he grumbled. "You've got to hear what I have to say."

"All I want is to be taken to my father," she hissed. "Release me at once, Troy Gilbert."

Troy knew that he had no choice but to get to the truth quickly, no matter the hurt it would inflict upon her heart. She gave him no other choice but to be blunt, though cruel it would be. As he saw it, now was the time.

"Sam, as I've tried to tell you over and over again, your father did not board this ship with the others—if he's not among those in the hold," he blurted. "That surely must mean that he—" His eyes wavered, seeing her crisp green eyes softly pleading with him as the truth began to slowly take hold inside her brain. He continued, though every word became painful as it slipped between his lips, knowing that he was going to cause her a deep,

249

torturous pain, when she realized the truth and accepted it as that.

"It must mean that he rode the *Magnolia* on its last voyage, to the bottom of the sea," he quickly finished.

Samantha's heart sank. She now believed that he was telling her the truth. There was no need for him to lie at such a time. And he did sound sincere. He even showed remorse over having to tell her. It now became real to her: Her father hadn't left his ship and now lay, graveless, at the bottom of the sea.

A quick knot formed in her throat, threatening to choke her, and an emptiness plagued her insides. And then her heart suddenly had a tearing sensation, paining her as nothing had ever before in her life.

"No," she finally managed to whisper. "It just can't—be."

"I'm sorry," Troy said, lowering his eyes. He released his grip on her and let her step free of him.

"Sorry?" Samantha uttered, a crooked smile lifting her lips awkwardly. "You—are—*sorry?*"

"Sam, I—" he began, then was shocked by her sudden attack of fists pelting his chest.

"It's all your fault!" she screamed, suddenly blinded by rage.

"You killed my father," she cried. "Why, oh, why, Troy? Why did it have to be you?"

Her fists now ached from the blows against his chest of steel. Tears rushed from her eyes, and a weakness overcame her. She felt light-headed, and as her knees went limp, she found herself falling.

Troy grabbed her and carried her to his bunk and placed her easily on it, then gently brushed strands of her hair that were wet with tears back from her eyes.

"Darling," he said hoarsely.

His heart ached, seeing her lying there so limply, having fainted from the shock of discovery of her father's fate. It was hard to comprehend how any father could include a daughter in such a dangerous scheme as blockade-running.

Yet, knowing Samantha, she had probably insisted. He had many questions to ask her, one of which was what she had done with the map.

Samantha stirred. Slowly opening her eyes she found Troy there, looking sympathetically down at her. For a moment she forgot why she was there and relished his closeness. Then reality came to her in a flash as she remembered that she had just found out that her father was dead.

Turning her face away from him, she softly cried, too wounded inside to get into it further with him.

"Sam," Troy murmured. He placed a forefinger to her chin and urged her to once more face him. "You're wrong. I am not responsible for the sinking of the *Magnolia*."

"Troy, how can you—continue—to deny—"

He sealed her words with a finger at her lips. "Because what I say is true," he demanded. "My ship came upon the northern warship firing upon the *Magnolia*. My guns scared the warship off, but it was already too late for your father's ship. It was already sinking. I did all I could, and that was to take as many survivors as possible from the *Magnolia*."

"Troy, why try to fool me with your made-up story?" Samantha sobbed, wiping her eyes free of tears.

"How can I convince you that what I say is true?"

She once more turned her eyes from him. "You

can't," she whispered.

"Not if I even told you that my ship and crew work hard to help the blockade-runners?" he murmured.

Samantha stiffened, her eyes widened but still stared at the wall.

"The map, Samantha," Troy continued. "I can now tell you why I couldn't let anyone get their hands on it."

Samantha was barely breathing but still she refused to look at him, though her heart was pounding, his words convincing her more and more by the minute that she had accused him wrongly.

"I am telling you in the strictest of confidence," he said. "And I still want the map. If it falls into the wrong hands, my men's lives could be in jeopardy."

He paused, then continued. "You see, I had heard rumors that the southern ports were to be blockaded by an order from Lincoln if the South fired upon the North. At the moment it was only a rumor, but rumors too often become reality, especially if the man behind the rumor is Abraham Lincoln. As you know, Sam, I am a businessman from New York. I own a line of ships that have been heavily into trade with the South for many years now. I saw a loss of revenue if my ships could not enter or leave the southern ports. I decided to recruit men that I knew I could trust and who would be willing to partake in the dangerous venture of assisting blockade-runners since I had even begun to hear rumors of the formation of secret groups planning to be ready to become runners if the blockade became a reality."

He placed a finger to her chin and directed her eyes up. She still looked very sad, yet he still had to think of convincing her of the truth. He continued. "When we met on the stagecoach that day, Sam, I was on my travels, recruiting men. The map? It was to show the men where

252

we would be traveling by sea. The code? It is the name of all the men who agreed to partake in the adventure. Those men are safely aboard my ship, with me, now. But should the map fall into wrong hands and the men are hunted and caught, they would be imprisoned and possibly even worse."

Samantha's pulse raced. She wanted so to believe him! It sounded all so logical. Slowly she reached a hand to him, and between them hardly a breath was taken as she clasped onto one of his hands, their gazes locked.

"Sam?" Troy said hoarsely, hopeful questioning in his eyes.

Samantha felt the magnet of his eyes, pulling her to him. She rose to a sitting position, hesitating a moment, then threw herself into his arms. "Oh, Troy, I'm so glad," she softly cried. "All these weeks and months, I thought you surely were—were my enemy."

Troy clung to her, burying his nose into her hair, not caring that it was tangled and smelled of smoke from the burned ship. He cared not even that her face was black and tear-streaked. He only cared that she was here with him, and she finally knew the truth and believed him.

"Will you be all right?" he softly asked, gently caressing her back through her shirt. "So much has happened in your life so quickly. You've lost—so—much."

"My father," she sobbed, pressing her cheek hard against his chest. "I can't believe that he's dead. Those damn Yankees."

"Are you going to be all right?" he insisted.

"Yes. In time," she said, a tremble coursing through her as she suppressed another bout of sobs.

"Poor baby," Troy crooned, now rocking her as though she were a baby.

Though Samantha was torn apart with grief, she couldn't stop herself from giving him a slight smile when she remembered how she had last seen him. He had looked comical standing silhouetted in the door of the abandoned house, stark naked.

"How did you find your way back to Springfield after I stole your horse, Troy?" she asked, wiping her eyes free of tears.

"So you remember how you left me, do you?" he said, chuckling.

"That was mean of me," she murmured, sniffling, tears still threatening to spill with the lingering thought of her father's passing. "But had you told me that night what you just told me, all of that would have been unnecessary."

"You should now understand why I couldn't."

"But even my father couldn't decipher the code, Troy. He said one man's code is not another's."

"That's true most of the time. But with such men as Marion Yarborough out there, wanting to make a name for themselves in the community, no code is left untouched."

"Why Marion Yarborough?" she said, shuddering, remembering how she had left him to die with her inflicted wound.

"He's the type who would turn his own mother over to the law if it would draw attention to him. He's a glory seeker, Sam. And I suspect he would work for either side, the North or the South, if it could benefit him in any way."

"Troy, did you—uh—happen to see Marion Yarborough after that night?"

"No. Why do you ask?"

She didn't want to get into that. Not this night. There

were already too many things to sort out in her mind. "No reason," she murmured.

She cuddled against him, drawing from his strength and accepting his comforting, realizing that she was once more free to love him. There was no reason not to. Their loyalties were for the same cause: hers to save her father's plantation which had now become hers; Troy's to his business, which, in turn, led him to aid the South.

"It feels good, Sam," Troy said huskily.

"What feels good?" she asked, trying not to let her father's untimely death spoil this brief moment of heaven while in Troy's arms.

"Being with you again."

"But the circumstances?"

"Yes. I know."

"What are we to do now, Troy?"

"I know what I'd like to do," he softly teased.

"Troy!" she teasingly scolded. "Not with a lad."

"Huh?" he said, drawing away from her to question her with his eyes.

She placed her hands to her breeches and held the cotton material away from her legs. "Me." She softly laughed. "I'm the lad in question."

"A lad with a mighty dirty face," Troy said, winking at her. He set his lips to the tip of her nose and softly kissed her. "If you'd like, I'll kiss the smudges away."

"Troy, please," Samantha sighed, closing her eyes, his hot breath causing fires to flame inside her.

Then she was plagued with guilt, her father's face flashing before her eyes. She crept away from Troy and rose shakily to her feet. "This isn't the time," she murmured. "My father."

"Yes. I understand," Troy said, following her lead, also rising from the bunk. "What you truly need is some time alone."

"Yes. That would be best."

"You can stay here in my cabin. I'll have a fresh basin of water sent in so you can refresh yourself."

"I would appreciate that, Troy."

His gaze traveled over her. "But, darling, seems you'll have to stay dressed as a man awhile longer," he said. "One thing I don't carry on board my ship is a lady's wardrobe."

"I'm glad of that," Samantha said and managed to softly laugh.

"You are?"

"That proves that you, at least, don't carry women on board for your companionship," she said, unable to keep from once more easing into his arms, to hug him, to touch him, to realize that he was real and that she was with him.

When his hands slipped inside her shirt to her breasts, to softly cup them, a warmth began melting and spreading upward, between Samantha's thighs. She desired Troy so, she hurt with the want. But she couldn't indulge in this while she sorely missed her father.

She reached and guided his hands from her shirt. "I do need to be alone," she whispered. "Troy, please?"

Troy cleared his throat nervously. "Yes. That would be best. I'll leave now, but I'll check in on you later," he said, moving toward the door.

"Thank you," Samantha said, tears once more blinding her.

He nodded and left, leaving her alone with her grief.

"Oh, Father," she softly cried, hanging her face in her hands. "What am I to do with Johnston Oaks now that you are gone? You *were* Johnston Oaks."

# Chapter Seventeen

The sea had a strange calm to it. The sky was overcast with billows of clouds. Charleston Harbor was only a few hours away. Troy was going to check on Samantha, having left her alone for quite awhile. She seemed to finally accept her father's death, as much as could be expected in this length of time, but he knew that she was fearing for her future. Troy wanted to assure her of their future together, but the war was like a solid wall of steel between them, keeping them apart.

Samantha stood brushing her hair, thankful for at least that luxury, though minor it was since it was Troy's own more stubby, bristly man's hairbrush that she was using. She had yet to dress in her clothes borrowed from one of Troy's crew who was smaller in build.

At the moment she was dressed in only the long-sleeved denim shirt with its buttons yet to be secured. Barefoot, she strolled around the ship's cabin, realizing by its expensive furnishings and decor just how wealthy Troy had to be. The highback chairs were of the best leather, and the table on which lay the large map with its markings of arrows and lines representing ships, islands, and the southern coast of America had a round marble top. The oak paneling which covered the wall shone from a fresh waxing, and the wall lights were of copper as well as the beams at the ceiling which were outlined by copper strippings.

Placing the brush handle to her chin, Samantha stood contemplatingly over the map, studying it. It was more detailed and, of course, much larger than the one she had hidden behind the loose brick of the fireplace at Johnston Oaks. On this map she could make out Cuba, the Bahamas—

A light tap on the door drew Samantha's head around. A smile brightened her face, thinking it was Troy, since he had yet to check on her. Thus far he had kept his distance, respecting her need to be alone. But Charleston Harbor was not that far away now, and she knew that their remaining time together was short. She hungered to be with him—fully with him. Perhaps it would be the last. The war so quickly snuffed the life from so many.

Dropping the hairbrush onto the table, she rushed to the door and swung it open. She looked adoringly up into Troy's eyes, thrilling from the message of passion that she received from their crystal clear blue depths.

"You shouldn't have to knock on your own door," she said, grabbing his hand, guiding him on inside. She closed the door behind him, then melted into his arms and clung to him. "Darling, I feel guilty having kept you from your own bunk. Where did you sleep?"

"In the cabin adjoining this one. Only a wall separated us," he said.

"You've been so understanding, Troy. How can I ever repay you for your kindness?"

"I can think of a way," he said chuckling. He lifted her chin with a finger and lowered his lips to hers, becoming almost mad with desire seeing her in only the gaping shirt, revealing her swells of breasts and the silken curves of her bare legs.

He kissed her gently, his fingers slipping the shirt from around her shoulders and then on away from her, fluttering downward to rest at her feet. His hands trembled as he let them trace the satin soft outline of her hips, on upward, across the flat surface of her belly, and then to her breasts. Gently kneading them, they seemed to swell in his hands. The taut tips grew hard as he circled his thumbs over and around them.

Samantha groaned, her pleasure mounting as spirals of rapture floated around inside her.

"Is it too soon after?" Troy asked, easing her lips from his.

She sealed his lips with a quick kiss, then whispered, "Don't ask that, Troy. Let's just block out everything from our mind but us. We soon will be forced to part."

"Must you return to your plantation? There's much danger in that. Without your father—"

"That's why it's imperative that I do return. It is for Father that I must do this thing. I must carry on where he left off."

"God," he said, looking alarmingly down at her. "You don't plan to become involved in blockade-running again, do you?"

Samantha giggled softly. "No," she reassured. "But perhaps I can see to it that our cotton is carried by someone else's ship to the Bahamas. I must try, Troy."

"I'll feel guilty as hell agreeing to return you to Johnston Oaks if I discover later that harm has come to you because of this."

"If you didn't return me, I would find other means," she said. Then she worried. "But, Troy, it is I who would suffer the guilt if anything should happen to you and your beautiful ship while you are chancing my return into Charleston Harbor. There are many warships, and surely your ship is sought because of what you do against the North."

He shrugged. "My ship maneuvers quite well, no matter where I steer it," he said. "Do not fret. Charleston Harbor is truly no more dangerous to me than the high seas."

Samantha snuggled back into his arms, oblivious to her nudity, feeling natural to be that way with the man she loved. "I will worry about you every waking hour and through my restless nights," she murmured. "How shall I ever know how you are?"

Troy wove his fingers through the softness of her hair. It smelled clean and looked so flaming red after its washing.

"I shall manage to elude the warships at Charleston Harbor more than once," he said huskily. "I will return to your arms, my love, as often as I can."

"But the dangers?" she again said, trembling as her rapture mounted, heated by his passion-burned lips.

"Does my ship show any signs of having lost battles with the warships, darling?"

"Not that I could see."

"Then you must realize just how dependable it is. Do not worry your pretty head over my safety for one moment longer. It's foolish. Almost as foolish as our standing here talking instead of making love."

"But, Troy, how can we?" Samantha teased, stepping

back away from him, looking coyly up at him.

"That's a crazy question," he chuckled. "Why would you ask it?"

"My love, one cannot make mad love while fully clothed." She laughed, her gaze moving slowly over him. "Now am I right, or wrong?"

A low rumble of a laugh rose from inside Troy. He slipped one shoe off and then the other, then proceeded undressing, all the while watching her. His eyes bespoke the pleasure of what he saw, thinking she never looked as seductive as now with her face flushed with risen passion and her eyes a sort of hazy green from need.

When he tossed his last garment aside, Samantha began moving backward toward the bunk, gesturing with beckoning hands for him to come to her. In three wide strides he was there, sweeping her fully up and into his arms, holding her close to his rapture-filled, pounding heart.

"I love you so," he said huskily, the fingers of his left hand circling her left breast.

"I could never love anyone but you," she whispered, consumed by her pounding heart and flooded by desire of him. When his lips pressed down upon hers, she twined her arms about his neck and enjoyed—fully enjoyed. And as he lowered her to the bed and stretched out above her, she writhed sensuously as he wasted no more time on preliminaries. He placed his man's hardness inside her and began his eager strokes.

Lifting her hips to him, she met each thrust with abandon. His lips were teasing her breasts, going from one to the other. And as his tongue flicked out and touched her taut nipples, Samantha moaned.

Troy stroked. Samantha writhed. He kissed her long

261

and hard, his fingers now clasped onto her buttocks, digging into her flesh as he lifted her even closer.

Almost mindless with pleasure now, Samantha's heart raced, keeping time, it seemed, with Troy's thrusts. Her insides were awash with a warm mushiness, and then she felt the rapture mounting, making her breathless.

She snaked her tongue between his teeth and then threw her head back away from his in a guttural sigh. All colors of the rainbow suddenly splashed inside her head as she felt herself reach the pinnacle of joy, making her momentarily oblivious of anything but total pleasure.

When her senses returned, she clung to Troy, realizing that his own release was near by the familiar way in which he was now reacting to his continuing, eager thrusts. First his muscles tightened and his jaw became hard set. Then his body would loosen into a soft quiver, repeating this a few more times until he seemed wracked by explosive spasms, headed off by a throaty groan, until he finally lay, fully spent, beside her.

Samantha traced his masculine facial features with a forefinger, softly smiling at him as she lay on her side, facing him. "Darling, how can you command your ship now that you've exhausted yourself so," she teased. "Perhaps the tale is true."

He leaned up on an elbow, taking her fingertips and kissing them each, sucking them one at a time between his lips. "What tale are you speaking of?" he said throatily, his pulse still erratic from his brief moment of mind-boggling pleasure.

"The tale that it is bad luck to have a woman on board a sea-sailing vessel," she said, once more feeling the tingling between her thighs with his sensual way of kissing and sucking her fingertips.

"Ah, yes, the dangers are many," Troy teased back. "Seems even the ship itself is seduced by this lovely lady's presence."

"Sam," Troy whispered huskily, now placing his lips over the tip of her breast, softly nipping it with his teeth.

Samantha closed her eyes and held her head back, her hair spread beneath her like a halo of red against the white of the blanket beneath her. Her fingers dug into the flesh at his muscled shoulders and the wondrous feelings aroused inside her were so beautiful that she felt as though she were in another world.

Troy laid his head on Samantha's breast and let the passion once more mount, and this time they reached the peak together in a quiet explosion of shared love.

They were drawn suddenly apart by a loud burst of thunder and by the sudden crashing of waves against the sides of the ship.

"What the—" Troy gasped, jumping from the bunk.

"Seems we've run into a storm," Samantha said, looking toward the porthole. Daylight seemed to have changed to dark, and it .was still only afternoon.

Troy gathered his clothes up from the floor and hurried into them. "A storm could be a blessing, Sam," he said.

Samantha rose to her feet and put her shirt on, quickly buttoning it. "A blessing?" she asked. "How?"

"I was fearing arriving into Charleston Harbor before nightfall," he said. "The storm could be the answer."

"How on earth?" Samantha queried, now slipping on the borrowed breeches.

"We can elude the warships under cover of the raging storm," he boasted. "We've used this tactic before. It's dangerous. Yet it could be our only way."

"You had had doubts?" Samantha asked, paling.

"I would never have admitted it," he chuckled. He reached for the man's cap and placed it on her head and gently scooted her red tresses beneath it. "Now shall we step outside and see what our true challenge is?"

"You won't force me to stay below because I'm a female?" she tested.

His eyes raked over her, amusement rich in them. "Now I would argue that statement," he chuckled. "I see no female, only a young lad with green, innocent eyes."

Fully dressed with her shoes on, Samantha laughed and swung her arm about his waist. "Let's go," she said. "I'm ready for anything as long as I'm with you."

"Whoa, there," Troy said, stepping away from her as he suppressed a laugh.

"Why?" she asked, placing her hands on her hips. "You said that I could go with you."

"Darling, not arm in arm," he said. "Now wouldn't that cause eyebrows to raise!"

"But they surely know I'm female by now."

"No. I didn't share this secret with them. Too many have been without a woman for too long to take the risk. They have thought I gave my cabin up to a wounded, young lad. That's all."

Another crash of thunder and the tossing of the ship which caused Samantha to be thrown into Troy's arms alerted them to the worsening of the storm.

"Damn," Troy snarled. He eased her away from him, his face shadowed by a deep frown. "Maybe I'd best insist that you don't accompany me topside after all."

"Troy, I refuse to stay hidden away in this cabin any longer," she argued, stomping away from him. She yanked the door open and walked on past him, her eyes locked on the companion ladder.

"All right," Troy growled, moving to her side. "But be careful, Sam. One wave and you could be swept overboard. I'll be too busy to keep an eye on you."

"I'm a survivor, Troy."

"I've noticed," he answered.

Together they went topside. Samantha clung to her hat. The lightning was awesome as it forked across the heavens that were black as night. The sea was rumbling, and the wind whistled harshly, making the masts creak ominously as the sails bellied against its force.

The ship tumbled back and forth beneath the powerful shock of the waves, and Samantha was tossed away from Troy, throwing her against a coil of rope, momentarily stunning her. Troy rushed to her side and helped her to her feet.

"Sam, go below!" he shouted, the howl of the wind deafening his words.

"No! I want to be with you when we enter the harbor! Maybe I can help! I helped Father dodge the warships."

"If this storm develops any more thrust behind its winds, no ship will be left to sail into any harbor!"

Suddenly the rain began to fall cold and hard, a steady pelting downward. The water swelled around the ship, the lurid flashes of lightning lighting up the sea and sky. The ship shuddered and groaned, and the masts weaved.

A shout sounded from somewhere on the deck. "Ship starboard!"

Troy tensed. "God! We're there. We're approaching the harbor!" he said, worried. "The wind has carried us there more quickly than I anticipated!"

Samantha hugged herself and shivered as the rain drove down upon her. She looked wildly about her, feeling the hand of doom upon her shoulders. But she would not show her fear. She ran alongside Troy to the ship's bridge and stood boldly with him as he spoke commands which led the ship past the haunting bulk of one warship and then another, thanking God that the lightning had subsided and that the sky remained dark.

It seemed an eternity, but Samantha was finally able to breathe more easily. Troy's ship had weathered the storm and the threat of the enemy ships. It now sailed quietly close to land, and when Samantha recognized the bends and curves of Ashley River, she emitted a soft shout of victory.

She gave Troy an appraising look and had to fight the urge to hug him. She had to heed his warning about such an outward show of affection since she was a lad in the eye of the crew!

But then she was surprised when he grabbed her hat from her head and tossed it away from her, letting her hair spill out across her shoulders in its brilliant red streamers.

"Troy!" Samantha gasped, looking cautiously about her. "Why did you do that? I thought—"

The rain was only a fine drizzle now. Troy's face was shining with wetness as he drew her into his arms. "The charade is no longer needed," he said thickly. "You are almost home, Sam. It doesn't matter if the crew now sees that it was a vivacious lady who shared my cabin with me these past two days now, does it?"

"They're liable to mutiny," she teased. Her gaze settled on the tall shadow of a house high on a hill in the distance. Sadness engulfed her, for when she saw Johnston Oaks, it had always been the same as seeing her father. It just wouldn't seem right arriving home without his open arms welcoming her return. But it was something that she would have to get used to. This was for forever.

The ship ebbed its way along the shoreline until they reached the dock which stretched out from the lower grounds of Johnston Oaks Plantation. The anchor was dropped and the gangplank lowered, and Samantha and Troy left the ship, forging their way through a heavy fog which now hung low over the land. Only a lone pale light showed from the parlor window. All other shutters had been closed to the storm.

"I hate to carry such bad news back to Johnston Oaks," Samantha murmured. She looked all about her, seeing no activity whatsoever. Even the slave houses were mutely dark. The whole atmosphere was ghostly.

A shudder coursed through Samantha as she climbed the front marble steps and led Troy on inside to the dark foyer and hallway. "Come. I saw light in the parlor," she said, shaking her hair of its droplets of rain. "Perhaps Franklin is there. I imagine he's seeing to things after the storm."

"Who is Franklin?" Troy asked, forking his eyebrows.

"You really don't want to know," Samantha said blandly.

"Oh?" Troy said, raking his fingers through his hair, straightening it. "Now you really have my curiosity aroused."

"He would wish to call himself my suitor, but he has been warned against it," Samantha scoffed, stepping into the parlor of expensive velvet chairs and gilt-trimmed mirrors and picture frames. A fire burned low on the grate of the fireplace. Samantha was fighting against getting caught up in missing her father. So much around her spoke of him and his presence. The feeling was almost overpowering, as though he would step into the parlor, a cigar thrust between his lips, his eyes dancing upon seeing her.

"Are you trying to tell me that he pursues and you flee?" Troy asked, chuckling. His eyes flicked around the room, seeing its grandness, having already been awed by the expanse of the estate grounds and its many outbuildings. There had to be many slaves. There were acres and acres of land planted with cotton.

Samantha swung around and faced him. She looked quite bedraggled in her rain-soaked attire, yet seductive still as the bold outline of her breasts was prominent against her clinging shirt.

"The locket that you've seen me wear and accused of being special to me?" she said softly.

"Yes?"

"It was a gift from Franklin," she explained. "His name is Franklin LaFontaine. He is—he was—my father's best friend and most faithful companion. He has pursued me for sometime now, but my feelings for him are those of silent loathing."

"Why did you wear the necklace?"

"Didn't you see how lovely it was?"

"Yes."

"Then you know why. A woman loves beautiful jewelry. That necklace is among the prettiest I have ever seen. I could not help but want to wear it."

"Samantha, honey!"

Jewel's deep voice, so drawn with its southern accent, came suddenly into the room as Jewel appeared at the doorway. "Miss Samantha, why are you here? Why are you dressed in such a manner? Where is yo' father and who is this man?"

Jewel's rush of questions took Samantha aback. Her head was swimming with which question to answer first.

Samantha gave Troy a nervous glance, then met Jewel's further approach. She took Jewel's pudgy hands in hers and squeezed them fondly. "Jewel," she began, and then poured out the sad story to her. And when she was through, she matched Jewel's tears as they both silently wept.

Jewel hugged Samantha. "My baby," she sobbed. "You've been through so much."

"I'll be all right," Samantha reassured. She cleared her throat nervously and went back to Troy and placed her arm about his waist. "Now tell me, Jewel, how are things here at Johnston Oaks? Has Franklin kept things in hand for Father, as he promised to do?"

Jewel lowered her eyes. Her fingers played nervously with the tail of her apron. "Miss Samantha, how can I tell you?" she murmured.

"Tell me what?" Samantha asked, her back tensing.

Jewel now desperately wrung her hands, her dark eyes wavering. "Everythin' has fallen apart since 'dem guns grows louder and louder," she cried. "Even Massa Franklin done run, Miss Samantha."

"What?" Samantha gasped, teetering. "What do you mean? Where has Franklin gone?"

"I doesn't know where but he's gone and no one is left on the plantation," Jewel said, nodding her head frantically.

Samantha was numb. She placed her fingers to her suddenly throbbing temple. "This can't be," she said. "I have only been gone a few days."

"Das' not all," Jewel said, looking toward the one

open window.

"What else?" Samantha gasped, almost panicking with worry.

"Joshua hasn't been able to keep our people from runnin' off, either," Jewel choked out. "He's done been left to tend to the cotton pickin' all by hisself."

Samantha shook her head. "This is all a nightmare," she softly cried. "I just can't believe it's happening. First my father and now all of this? Johnston Oaks is truly doomed."

She swung around and with pleading eyes looked up at Troy. "What am I do to?" she cried. "Troy, it's all but lost to me."

Troy drew her into his arms and comforted her. He spoke tenderly into her ear. "Sam, I'd stay and help but I can't," he said. "I'd even take you with me. But I can't. The one alternative is that I will urge you to go back north, stay with your grandparents. You're not safe here. Anything could happen."

"I can't leave," she sobbed. "My loyalties are still to my father which means to the plantation that he so valued. I can't give up. I must at least make an effort to save it."

"With no help, it's useless, Sam," he argued. "Surely you can see that."

"Joshua is still here," she said stubbornly, wrenching herself free to go and stare from the window into the swirling grays of the fog.

Troy went to her and clasped his fingers onto her shoulders. "Sam, Joshua is only one man," he said hoarsely. "One man can do only so much. Why not let Joshua see to your safe return to the North?"

"No. I plan to stay right here," Samantha said between

clenched teeth. "Nothing you say or do will change my mind, Troy."

Troy looked across his shoulder at Jewel, then lowered his face down into Samantha's. "Then I guess I have no choice but to leave you here, do I?" he whispered.

"No. I guess not."

"I really do have to go, Sam. My ship will surely be detected in the cove."

She threw her arms about his neck and clung to him. "Be careful," she murmured. "Troy, please return to me. I love you so."

"Nothing could keep me away," he said thickly.

"I will forever be watching for you, my love."

"Sam, one more thing."

"Yes, darling. What is it?"

"The map. I'd like to have it now. It still could bring harm to my friends should it fall into the wrong hands."

Samantha grew cold inside. Her heart skipped a beat. "The—map?" she stammered.

"Yes. I know that you still have it, Sam. I remember your saying that your father had seen it and had said that one man's code isn't another's. He could have only seen it after you brought it here from Illinois."

Samantha jerked away from him, her eyes flashing angrily. "Again I've been a fool," she hissed. "You only cared for me and brought me safely home so you could get your hands on the damn map. You even made love to me, all the while using me, to get me here for the map."

Her words lifted into hysterics. She pointed toward the door. "Get out!" she screamed. "You've never cared about me at all, only the map and the men it protects! How dare you, Troy Gilbert! How dare you!"

Troy took quick steps toward her. "Sam, you're

wrong!" he said, trying to take her hands in his, only having them denied him.

Samantha looked toward Jewel. "Jewel, go and fetch Joshua," she flatly ordered. "Tell him that we have someone here in the house who needs to be removed."

Troy's face darkened with anger. "Sam, I'll be back," he snarled. "You'll listen then. For now? I must return to my ship. I must get my ship back in safer waters."

"Yes," she said dryly. "Protect your precious cargo of men at all costs. Just be sure to let the men in the hold go free. They don't belong to you."

Troy shook his head and stormed from the house.

"Do I still go and get Joshua?" Jewel innocently asked.

"No. That's no longer necessary," Samantha sighed. She ducked her head and headed toward the staircase. "Draw my bath, Jewel. I need a cleansing for many reasons."

"Yes'm."

Tormented with grief and overwhelming loneliness, Samantha moved slowly up the sweep of staircase, hearing the silence of the house. It was as though she was imprisoned inside a tomb.

Then softness brushed against her leg. She jumped, startled, then looked downward and saw the wide, dark eyes of her collie. He whined and lifted a paw to her.

"Oh, Checkers," Samantha softly cried, dropping to her knees to hug him. "At least I still have you!"

# *Chapter Eighteen*

Only one look from her bedroom window made Samantha quickly aware of what was more important than the pleasures of a bath. Something had to be done about the absence of slaves on her plantation. If not, the cotton would rot right on its stem.

"The slaves must be found and returned to Johnston Oaks," she whispered, leaning against the marble windowsill. She looked down at her attire. She was dressed in such a way that would make travel into the swamps easier. Yes! In her man's attire she would personally go with Joshua. Together they would see to the slaves' return. Together they would keep Johnston Oaks Plantation alive!

Swinging around, determination causing fire in her eyes, Samantha rushed from her room, down the staircase and on outside. She found Joshua chopping firewood, then quickly told him her plan.

"It ain't safe, Miss Samantha," he growled, stacking wood. "If'n Massa Craig was alive he wouldn't approve of me takin' you into the swamps for no reason. You be his gentle, sweet girl. A swamp and its snakes ain't no place for a lady."

His dark eyes raked over her and filled with amusement. His lips rose into a soft smile. "Yet I ain't seen no lady dressed like that before," he chuckled. "Whea' on earth did you fin' those clothes, Miss Samantha? They ain't fit fo' such as you."

"Never mind how I'm dressed," Samantha scolded. "It is what I choose to wear to go in search of our laborers, for you see, Joshua, we *are* going, no matter what you say."

"Must you always be so stubborn?" Joshua said. "With yo' pappy gone, what is to become of you with you bein' so headstrong 'bout everythin'?"

Samantha placed a hand on Joshua's arm. "Joshua, I am now owner of Johnston Oaks," she murmured. "It's up to me to see to its welfare. I know that I will fail in this endeavor if the slaves aren't found and brought back to work the fields." Her eyes wavered. "I need your help, Joshua. Just pretend I'm Father. Listen to me, as you did to him. We must work together, Joshua, to make this work."

"I'll go into the swamps alone," he argued. "You stay behind. I'll see to it that the cotton is picked one way or the other, Miss Samantha. I jus' don' want you goin' into those swamps."

"I'm going, Joshua," Samantha said, stubbornly lifting her chin. "No matter what you say, I'm going. I can't sit back and watch and wait. I must see to it that things happen. I want to make them happen."

A rush of feet drew Samantha around. She saw Jewel running, panting hard, toward her. In her haste, Samantha had forgotten to tell Jewel of her plans and left the house before first warning her. In Jewel's dark eyes, Samantha could see fear and worry. With quick steps she met Jewel's further approach.

"I'm sorry, Jewel," she apologized. "I didn't think to tell you that I would be taking my bath later. I didn't mean to cause you worry."

Sweat beading her dark brow, Jewel stopped to catch her breath. Then she hotly scolded Samantha. "Land sakes, chil'," she said. "You do give me a fright. First you're here and den you ain't. You musn't move around so quickly, from place to place. You mus' tells me whea' you be at all times. It ain't like befo' dem guns exploded in the sky. Things ain't safe now, no how you look at it."

Samantha leaned down and hugged Jewel. "I'm sorry," she apologized. "I just didn't think. I'm just so worried about things, Jewel. So much is suddenly my sole responsibility."

"Yes'm. Ah knows," Jewel said, patting Samantha fondly on the back. "But still, you mus' tell ol' Jewel befo' jumpin' hea' and thea'."

Samantha giggled. "All right," she murmured. "I promise."

Jewel leaned back away from Samantha, eyeing Samantha and then Joshua. "And what's you up to now?" she asked, feeling a conspiracy between her husband and Samantha. "I see trouble wrote in yo' eyes. What you two about?"

Joshua's thick gray brows folded into a frown. "It ain't somethin' I think bes'," he growled. "Miss Samantha, it's her idea."

Jewel folded her plump arms across her chest, giving Samantha a scalding look. "What's got yo' mind workin' now, honey?" she grumbled. "Ain't it enough that you're safely home?"

Samantha clasped onto Jewel's shoulders. "Jewel, don't you hear—even feel the silence of Johnston Oaks?" she said shallowly. "It needs life brought back to it. Joshua and I have got to go in search of—of—those who have run off. It won't be only for the benefit of my plantation but also for those who surely are lost somewhere out there in the swamps, hungry and cold. Please understand. Joshua and I must at least try and find them."

Jewel placed a hand to her throat, her eyes wide with alarm. "The swamp?" she gasped. "You and Joshua ain't goin' into the *swamp!*"

"We must, Jewel," Samantha urged. "We really have no choice."

"There are snakes," Jewel said, swallowing hard. "There are—are—even the Kiawah Indians. You mustn't, Samantha." She looked fearfully toward Joshua. "Joshua, tell her that she can't."

"She now be the mistress of Johnston Oaks," Joshua said throatily. "I am now her overseer. What she orders, I do."

Jewel turned and headed back toward the house, her head hung, softly mumbling to herself.

"Let's go," Samantha said, nodding toward Joshua.

"Soon as I get my rifle and knife," Joshua grumbled, meandering away from her.

Samantha paced, looking about her. She was glad that the fog had lifted but disappointed that the sun was missing from the sky. Threatening, billowing clouds rolled across the gray sky. The air was close and moist, making it hard to breathe.

Samantha combed her fingers through her hair and

shook it to hang long down her back, then fell into step next to Joshua as they moved across the cotton fields and along the very edges of Ashley River. Too soon the water grew swampy, the heavy beards of moss on the trees impeding the way, yet Samantha and Joshua moved deeper into murky, rot-infested land, where the smell was acrid, even enough to burn the nostrils.

The black water of the swamp reflected the stately cypress trees and splashes of vibrant color of the creepers overhead, bright as any butterfly's wings. Purple clusters of wild flowers grew in the moistness of the thickets beside the water, and gnarled roots of trees rose and fell, twisting from the swamp as though giant, swollen fingers maimed by a disfiguring ailment.

The denseness of the trees were lilac in shadow. Wild cotton blossoms now sparkled along the shore, and an occasional scent of arrowroot was in the wind.

Samantha cringed as one of her shoes sank deeply in mud, suctioning her more deeply into it as she fought to pull herself out of this muck. "Joshua," she softly cried, reaching for him as her other shoe began to sink in the mud. "I'm stuck in the mud. Help me. It seems to be pulling me further down into it."

Joshua turned and gave her a harried look. Resting his rifle against a tree he went to her and placed his hands to her waist and, being the strong man that he was, he had her free with only one lift upward.

Laughing softly, Samantha stepped to dry land and shook her feet, sending mud in thick splashes all around her. "I guess I'd best be more careful where I step," she said, giggling.

"You sure you want to go on?" Joshua asked, again sporting his rifle, clutching onto it tightly. "I ain't yet seen no sign of no one."

"You give up way too easily," Samantha scoffed, feeling her shoes were lighter now that she had shaken the mud free of them. Then her heart went erratic, her eyes froze in place as she caught sight of a huge snake coiling down a tree's limb, right above Joshua's head.

Joshua saw Samantha's sudden stillness and lock of eyes. He could only think of one thing that would cause her to gape so when looking overhead in a tree. It had to be a snake.

"Jis' stand still, Miss Samantha," Joshua softly warned.

"But, Joshua, if you move—"

"Yes'm. Ah knows."

He spun quickly around on a heel and shot his rifle just as the snake loosened itself from the tree and, as it was in midair, dropping toward Joshua, the bullet tore its head from its body."

"Lord!" Samantha gasped, placing her hands to her mouth, watching the snake fall to the ground, its body still twitching.

Joshua stepped on the snake's head and burrowed it deeply into the mud, then gave Samantha a lingering, questioning look. "That's only one sort of creature to fear," he said thickly. "Now that I shot my rifle off, you can be sure the Indians will come searchin', to see who's done the shootin'."

"The Kiawah have never caused us problems," Samantha scoffed, stepping on around the snake which now lay lifeless at her feet. "Why should they now?"

"We're trespassing on land they see as theirs, Miss Samantha."

"Hogwash!" Samantha spat. "The swamps surely

aren't that important to them. How can they be to anyone?"

"It's their home, Miss Samantha. Just like Johnston Oaks Plantation is our home. They respected your ownership. They want what respect is due them."

"The more reason for us to find and return the slaves to Johnston Oaks," she argued. "Surely their lives are in danger. They have to be looked on as intruders also by the Kiawah."

"Yes'm," Joshua humbly said. "You're probably right."

"Then let's go on searching, Joshua," Samantha said flatly. "The day is only so long. I never thought to have Jewel fix us food to bring with us. Already I'm feeling an emptiness in my stomach."

"Then we'll head back 'fore nightfall?" Joshua asked testily. He feared that she would think that he was a coward, when, in truth, he worried only for her welfare. He had caught a glimpse already of a lurking Indian wearing only a breechcloth and carrying a rifle. Hopefully the Indian would see that he had nothing to fear since there were only two intruders in his territory, one even being a woman who sported no firearms.

Joshua didn't want to alarm Samantha quite yet with this news. He knew that her alarm would show, and this could transfer to the Indian and possibly cause him to move in haste and perhaps even alert many others!

"We'll see," Samantha said. "If by then we see no trace of my slaves perhaps it would be best to return home. I am beginning to realize the dangers of being here."

She looked toward the sky, only able to see shafts of gray through the roof of the trees, yet enough to know the chances of a storm were great. A storm now would be the worst luck possible.

"And if the weather grows more threatening, Joshua, I'll agree to turn back," she said hoarsely. "If we must, we may have to pick all the cotton by ourselves, Joshua. Do you think that's possible?"

"Anything is possible if your heart is in it," he said, taking her by an elbow to guide her onward.

A look of remorse splashed across Samantha's face, momentarily clouding her eyes, with the mention of the heart and feelings. She was remembering her last moments with Troy and how her heart had been once again torn to shreds when she discovered that his feelings for her were not sincere. He continued to use her, not caring about her at all. He seemed to be quite skilled in telling nontruths—as skilled as he was at stealing hearts.

Samantha was glad that she now had a purpose in life, something that would offer her escape from torturous thoughts of him. He didn't deserve her thoughts. He most certainly didn't have the right to her kisses and so much more that she had willingly shared with him.

How foolish she had been! She had always thought herself much smarter than that. In the future, she had much to prove to herself where men were concerned. None would fool her again!

Forcing her thoughts to the present and to the task at hand, Samantha moved on alongside Joshua, listening and watching the abundance of wild life and water fowl which seemed to be this swampy area's only inhabitants. In this semitropical forest and murky lagoon she caught glances of an occasional whitetail deer, raccoon, opossum, and the bold, staring eyes of an alligator shimmying along just beneath the surface of the water, frightened more than not of the presence of humans.

A brown pelican swept down from the sky and splashed into the water. Sandpipers scurried back and forth at the water's edge, seeming to be misplaced here, where mud took precedence over sand.

Pines, palmettos, oaks, and sweetgum trees were the nesting place of an assortment of colorfully winged birds, and the air was filled with the cries and chatter of all these, echoing from tree to tree.

A sudden flash of lightning followed by a loud clap of thunder commanded a sudden silence in the trees. Not even a leaf fluttered. It was as though the earth was suddenly standing still, ominous in its silence.

"Just as I thought," Samantha said. "A darn storm. What lousy timing!"

"We'd best find shelter," Joshua said. "We've come too far now to turn back. The storm would hit before we made it safely back to Johnston Oaks."

"But where can we find shelter, Joshua?"

"We'll find somethin', Miss Samantha," Joshua encouraged, grabbing her hand, running with her.

Overhead the sky was dark—a starless night. The swampy waters were unruffled by not even a passing breeze. The dark woodlands hung like purple curtains, shutting out the world beyond. The earth, wrapped in a spell of hushed and profound repose, reflected the quiet of the heavens bending over it all.

And then again a lurid lightning flash lit up the sky and forest, and in the lightning's vivid sheen could be seen a thatched hut just up ahead.

"Over there, Joshua!" Samantha yelled, pointing. "I see a hut! Maybe we can—"

Joshua stopped dead in his tracks and turned to face Samantha, after also seeing the dwelling. His eyes were narrow with warning, his gray hair more definable against the dark backdrop of cloud and trees. "That's a Kiawah Indian wigwam," he softly cautioned.

"Perhaps it's abandoned," Samantha said, anxiously looking on past Joshua. "I see no one, and the hut is in bad disrepair as though no one has lived there for some time. Surely we can find shelter there until the storm passes, Joshua."

Joshua raised his rifle, keeping it poised for shooting as he turned to scrutinize the hut more closely. He peered then into the forest that surrounded it, remembering having seen the one Indian. Seeing no one and convinced that the hut was abandoned, he relaxed the muscles at his shoulders and walked on toward it.

"Do you think it will be all right?" Samantha asked cautiously, following close behind him. "Do you think we'll be safe enough?"

"We'll see," Joshua grumbled.

Tearing creepers away, he made a path for Samantha to follow, then stepped up to the hut and let his eyes rove over it. It was a round wigwam, its framework of saplings covered with slabs of elm bark, with some bare spaces where the elm bark hung lazily down away from the sapling pole.

Samantha moved inside onto the bare earth flooring, seeing a firespace in the center made from a circle of rocks. A gray blanket of ash lay in the firespace, and above it light fell in small patches from the smoke hole in the roof.

Ceramic dishes with colorful designs painted on them lay broken along the floor, and a discarded, moth-eaten blanket lay crumpled along the far wall.

Samantha nodded to Joshua as he entered. "It appears that no one has lived here for some time," she said, wondering why she felt the need to whisper.

"Appearances can be deceiving," Joshua warned. "The Kiawah are known to wander from place to place." He looked toward the dead ash in the firespace. "Who's to tell how long those ashes have been cold?"

Lightning once more flashed from cloud to cloud. Thunder caused the earth to tremble violently beneath Samantha's feet. A shudder coursed through her as she had always feared storms.

"I wish there was a fire in the firespace right now," she said, hugging herself.

Joshua chuckled. He leaned his rifle against the inside wall of the hut. "At least I think that can be arranged," he said. "I'll get some firewood. I won't be long."

Samantha reached a hand toward him. "Joshua, do you think you should?" she asked softly.

"I'll only be right outside. There's plenty of dry wood there, Miss Samantha. Don't worry 'bout me leavin' you here for even one second. Maybe yo' pappy ain't here to scold me should I let somethin' happen to you, but I'm sure his spirit is."

Chuckling, he stepped outside. Samantha's teeth chattered, the air having suddenly turned cold. She had to wonder about the slaves and how they were managing to survive all alone. They had grown used to being taken care of. Having lived in shacks at Johnston Oaks Plantation, at least they had never been without shelter, warmth, clothing, or food. So far from Johnston Oaks, surely some were starving as well as freezing to death.

And the Indians? Had the Kiawah tolerated the intrusion of the dark-skinned people? Only time would tell.

## *Chapter Nineteen*

Things were much too quiet. Samantha looked toward the door of the hut, wondering what was taking Joshua so long. He had said that he would only be right outside gathering wood. Why couldn't she hear his footsteps? Why wasn't he already back inside the hut, starting a fire?

The sudden rustle of leaves outside made a quivering breath of air escape Samantha's lips. She relaxed her shoulder muscles and smiled to herself, feeling foolish for her moment of worry. Joshua was still there, and soon a fire would be warming Samantha's bones.

Taking a step toward the door, thinking how she could assist Joshua, Samantha stepped on some broken ceramic pieces, causing her to teeter awkwardly when she lost her balance.

Laughing, she steadied herself, and when footsteps at the doorway made her expect to see Joshua with an armload of firewood, she took another step forward, then stopped with alarm. Her heart skipped a beat, her insides froze when she saw the sudden presence of a Kiawah

Indian blocking the doorway, his bow drawn tautly with an arrow readied in it.

"No," Samantha gasped, her gaze taking in the full threat of the Indian, his massiveness displaying muscles of steel at his shoulders, arms, and bare thighs. He wore only a breechcloth, and his copper skin shone as though it was waxed. His coarse, black hair hung in a long braid down his back, and his headband of colorful designs showed a lone eagle's feather positioned into it.

But it was the darkness of his eyes and set of his squared jaw that frightened Samantha. She knew that he was looking at her with intense hate and mistrust.

Then another thought struck her. "Joshua!" she worried aloud. She tried to look past the Indian but couldn't see further than how the door perfectly framed him.

"Come with me," the Indian flatly ordered. "My warriors wait in a canoe. You will be taken to our village. My warriors will draw lots for you. Then you will die."

Samantha blanched. She took a fierce step backward. "Why?" she asked. "Why do you see a need to kill me? Where—where—is Joshua? Did you already—kill—him?"

"An arrow found its way into the brown-skinned man," the Indian bragged. "And if you don't come with me, your white flesh will have blood also spilled on it by my waiting arrow."

Samantha shook her head remorsefully. She clasped a hand over her mouth, feeling ill. Joshua. Sweet Joshua. Dead! And now even she was doomed.

A flash of lightning lighted the hut momentarily, revealing Joshua's rifle's barrel that still stood against the wall where he had left it. Somehow she had to get it. But she knew that the Indian's arrow would be quicker than her hand. Somehow she had to trick the Indian into lowering the arrow, to even disarm the bow. She had to convince him that she could be trusted.

"There will be no need to use your bow and arrow again," she said dryly. She lifted her chin boldly. "I will go with you peacefully. I will not put up a fight. I realize that you are strong. I see your muscles. I would be foolish to try and fight such a man as you."

Samantha watched closely for his reaction. She was glad to see his jawline soften and his eyes waver. She then thought to say more to persuade him. If an Indian had the same feelings for females as did the white man, then she knew she could use compliments that most men loved to hear. It was hard being rational, though, with Joshua's death hanging over Samantha, causing her such heartache. But she must do what she could to protect herself.

Seductively weaving her fingers through her hair, lifting it from her shoulders, Samantha gave the Indian an inviting gaze. "Why must your men draw lots over me when it was you who found me?" she teased, now running her hands down the sleek curves of her body. Even in the man's clothes the thrust of her breasts, her tiny waist, and the curves of her thighs were quite definable as she drew her clothes tightly over her, her hands traveling up and down her body.

Out of the corner of her eye she again focused a moment's attention on the rifle. Only inching along she backed herself toward it. Then she was able to breathe easier when the Indian removed the arrow from his bow and lowered both to his side.

"You are right," he grumbled, his dark eyes gleaming. "You will be my woman." He looked her up and down.

"Take off the ugly clothes, woman. Let me see what you hide beneath them."

Samantha swallowed hard. Her fingers went to the top button of her shirt, yet she worked her way closer to the rifle. Only two more steps and she could grab it!

Looking toward the Indian she saw lust now in his eyes. Hoping to mesmerize him more, she loosened the last button and slowly opened her shirt, cringing when she saw his eyes feast on the ripeness of her breasts.

But as she hoped, her slow, sensual movements so mesmerized him, she was able to turn quickly and lunge toward the rifle, panting as she made contact with the cold steel of its barrel.

Wrapping her fingers around it, she struggled to flip it up so that she could shoot it. But rough hands at her waist, stopping her, caused her breath to be knocked from inside her as she felt herself being jerked around and held firmly against the steel frame of the Indian.

"So you try to fool Lone Cloud?" the Indian growled. "You will pay for that, white woman. Now I will give you to my warriors. You will be taken by many instead of one."

His fingers went to her breasts and brutally squeezed them both. "My warriors will enjoy you. Fully." He laughed. "Then maybe I will also."

He gave her a hard shove toward the door. "Now go!" he snarled. "My warriors have waited long enough in the canoe. The rains will come soon. We must reach our village quickly."

Samantha stumbled from the hut, her heart pounding from fear. A lurid lightning flash lit up the sky. Thunder cracked as though a giant whip snapped in the heavens. Rain began to fall, softly at first, then hard like steel pellets in its fierceness.

"Move along!" Lone Cloud shouted, giving Samantha another rough shove.

Samantha began to run blind through the thicket. Then when another flame of lightning lighted the sky and earth and showed Joshua lying on his back only a few feet from the hut, she stopped dead in her tracks and stared sadly toward him. His eyes were peacefully closed and his one hand was clutched onto an arrow that had pierced his upper right chest. Blood had spilled down the front of his shirt. His face was gaunt and pale.

"Joshua!" Samantha softly cried. She took a step toward him but was stopped by the steel grip of the Indian's hand at her wrist.

Swinging around to face the Indian, Samantha screamed at him, struggling to be set free. "You beast!" she cried. "Let me go to him! Maybe he's still alive."

Lone Cloud tightened his hold on her wrist, which inflamed Samantha's wrath. With her free hand she raked her long fingernails across the Indian's face, then doubled her fist and hit him in the jaw.

Growling, the Indian released her wrist, but only to strike her with a powerful blow across her face, causing her to crash to the ground in pain.

Stunned, Samantha rubbed her throbbing lip, then, feeling a wetness there, looked down at her fingers and saw them covered with blood. He had burst her lip open. With rage, she looked up at him, just in time to see him reach for her and grab her roughly up by an arm.

"Go!" he grumbled. "And if you try fighting me again I'll kill you! My warriors will then take turns with your body."

The thought repelled Samantha. She couldn't even

288

envision such a distasteful scene. Surely he just said this to frighten her more.

With her hand covering her throbbing lip, Samantha worked her way through the ground tangle, now slippery from the rain. In only a matter of moments she caught her first sight of the canoe moored along the shoreline of the black, swampy waters. Two other Indian braves, also dressed in only breechcloths, sat waiting, oars ready to shove the canoe out into deeper water.

With a hardy shove, Samantha was forced into the canoe. Lone Cloud shoved her again, making her lie down on the canoe floor, where he rested a foot on her left thigh, holding her in place.

Some Indian words were exchanged between the three Indian braves, and soon Samantha was aware of motion and the splash of water beneath her as the canoe began speeding away from the shore. She trembled and silently prayed. It seemed as though she was a part of a different world. Was there truly a Civil War being fought? Was there a man named Troy Gilbert who commanded a great ship and who carried with him her heart?

All of these things seemed so far removed from her now, being taken to a fate she dared not let her mind dwell on.

When a great bolt of lightning tore from the heavens and spliced a towering oak in half alongside the swamp, crashing it to the ground, Samantha tensed and tried to look from the canoe. All she could see now was a sudden squall of rain, blotting out everything within sight. The high wind raged. It tore shrieking through the trees. The torrents of rain seemed to fall horizontally. The wind whipped the water about the canoe into giant combers.

The Indians began exchanging loud shouts as the

canoe began to heave and pitch. A wild spray of water splashed in the canoe and onto Samantha's face, momentarily choking her. Then she eyed Lone Cloud as his foot jerked from her thigh, and then his body pitched into the water when a tree's limb came crashing down onto his head.

The canoe bounced. It heaved. And suddenly it tipped over, spilling everyone into the murky depths of the swamp. Samantha became entangled beneath the water in some debris. She fought and struggled, feeling her lungs almost bursting with need of air. She looked to the water's surface, seeing only an ominous blackness. Then finally she loosened herself from the slimy, underwater tangles and swam quickly to the surface.

When she broke through, she gasped for breath. She choked and coughed, and wiped frantically at her burning eyes, all the while treading water. And when she was able to look around her, she discovered the overturned canoe close by and the bobbing, lifeless bodies of two Indians, one of which was Lone Cloud.

Desperate, Samantha looked on about her. Where was the third Indian? As long as even one was still alive and knew of her whereabouts, she would live with the threat of again being abducted.

And then she saw him. A crocodile was toying with the body at the water's edge. Seeing this sent a spasm of fear through Samantha. It appeared that the crocodile had made its choice of lunch. Samantha had somehow been spared. But she knew that she could be next on the menu, so she had to get away before being detected. She did have one thing in her favor: The storm had abated. Only a fine drizzle now fell from the sky. A rainbow was even bending its way across the water in its soft colors, where the sun was peeping its way through the heavy tree cover overhead.

Watching the crocodile closely, Samantha swam as silently as possible to the canoe. Soundlessly she turned it right side up, scooped the oars out of the water and placed them in the canoe, and then slithered herself up and into it, breathing hard with the effort.

Easing herself onto the seat, she labored with her breath. She wrung the water from the ends of her hair then flipped it over her shoulder, then wiped her face dry with the palms of her hands.

Her tongue discovered the swollen, split wound on her lip where it still unmercifully throbbed. She blinked her eyes to clear them of a lingering stinging from the saltwater of the swamp. And then she fully composed herself, squaring her shoulders, lifting her chin, knowing that it was up to her to retrace the route of the canoe and find her way back to Joshua. Perhaps it still wasn't too late for him. At least the arrow hadn't pierced his heart.

With oars in hand, Samantha steered the canoe around the lifeless bodies floating in the water. And then she moved onward, her shoulders and arms straining with each pull of the oar.

Shafts of sun streamed down upon her. Birds sang and flew from tree to tree along the shore. Everything seemed greener, freshly bathed from the rain, and a fresh smell of newness hung heavily in the air.

But the sun pulling the dampness from the earth caused an oppressed mugginess to close in on Samantha. She perspired and moaned, each lift of the oar now a painful pull to her body.

"Will this nightmare ever end?" she whispered harshly to herself. "Lord, I should have heeded Joshua and Jewel's warnings. I should have never entered these swamps. How do I even find my way out again without Joshua, should he be dead?"

She began scanning the land with her eyes. "Surely I'm almost there," she said. "The Indians didn't carry me this far from the hut."

She sank the oars and pulled them through the water. She groaned and panted. Her perspiration rolling into her eyes would momentarily blind her. And then through the trees she caught her first glimpse of the wigwam.

"Let Joshua still be alive," she softly prayed, her heart pounding with fear. "Oh, please let him still be alive."

Paddling the canoe close to the shoreline, Samantha eagerly watched around her, fearing more Indians. But seeing none and eager to get to Joshua, she dropped the oars to the floor of the canoe and splashed out into the water, wading ankle-deep in mud and onto land.

Cringing from the clinging mud, she broke into a run and ran in the direction of the hut. Low tree limbs slapped her in the face. Thorns from creepers tore at the flesh of her arms and legs. Then she stopped with a start when she reached the spot where she had last seen Joshua.

"Joshua?" she gasped, seeing only bloodstains on the ground where he had been.

Looking frantically around her, Samantha's heart stormed within. Had Indians taken him away? Or had he left under his own power?

Hurrying inside the hut, remembering the rifle, again Samantha stopped with a start. The rifle was also gone.

"Could he have been only slightly wounded?" she said, kneading her brow. "Did Lone Cloud render him momentarily unconscious by a blow to the head after shooting him with the arrow?"

All of these questions were spinning around inside Samantha's brain, confusing her. Now she didn't know whether to stay or leave. What if Joshua had regained consciousness and had wandered further into the forest in search of her? And, if he didn't find her, would he return here, to see if she had wandered back, to check on him?

"What should I do?" she softly cried.

Her aching limbs and throbbing temples made her aware of what she mostly needed. Rest! Her eyelids were heavy, her knees weak. Perhaps if she just rested for awhile, then everything would settle in place inside her brain, and she would know what her next move would be.

Slumping to the earthen floor of the hut, brushing broken ceramic ware aside, Samantha couldn't help but stretch out, though the floor was damp and cold, even through her clothes.

Clutching her shirt closed in front and trembling, Samantha's eyelids grew heavier and a numbness grabbed hold of her. Never had she been so tired, so frightened, so alone.

# *Chapter Twenty*

The touch of a caressing warmth on her face and a soft golden glow waving before her closed eyes caused Samantha to awaken from her fitful sleep. Upon opening her eyes she discovered not only a warm fire burning in the firespace but also eyes watching her. Seeing their ocean blue set against a darkly tanned face framed by midnight black hair she thought she must be dreaming. She fluttered her eyes and wiped at them, not wanting to wake up for even if Troy were there in a dream, it would be better than not at all.

"Sam? Darling?" Troy said, reaching a hand to smooth some loose locks of hair back from her eyes. "Are you all right? I didn't awaken you because you were sleeping so soundly."

The feel of his fingers on her flesh and the deep masculine tone of his voice was evidence that Samantha wasn't dreaming at all and that he was truly there. Tears burned at the corners of her eyes as she leaned her face into his hand.

"Troy," she said softly. "How can you be here? How

did you find me?"

"It wasn't easy," he said thickly.

"Why did you even try?"

"The way I left you—with you so angry, I could hardly bear it. I didn't even get my ship away from Ashley River before I commanded its return to Johnston Oaks to make things right with you."

"And? You found that I was gone in search of my slaves?"

"Jewel told me. I then came in search of you."

Samantha lowered her eyes and sniffed. "Did Jewel tell you that Joshua was with me?" she murmured.

"Yes. She did."

Her eyes implored him. "Troy, Joshua was shot by an Indian with an arrow." She choked. "I'm so concerned about him. I don't—don't know where he is. I was abducted by some Kiawah Indians and when I got free of them and returned here, where I last saw Joshua, he was gone. What if other Kiawah Indians took him away?"

Troy settled down beside her and drew her into his arms. "He's all right, Sam," he reassured.

Samantha eased away from him and searched his face with her eyes. "How—how—would you know that?" she asked, still unable to believe that Troy was there, suddenly out of nowhere. She was too happy to recall any of the angry words last exchanged between them. He had proven his sincere love for her by being with her now.

"Sam, I found Joshua here earlier," he explained. "He's alive. A bit disoriented, but well. I assured him that I would find you and urged him to return to Johnston Oaks to get his wound patched up."

Samantha's insides relaxed. She placed her cheek against Troy's chest. "Thank God," she sighed. "If

Joshua would have died it would have been all my fault. He didn't want to come into the swamps. He warned me of the dangers."

"But now you both are all right," Troy said, nuzzling his nose into the slender taper of her neck. He paused, then spoke again. "The Indians. How did you escape, Sam?"

"It was during the storm," she said, shuddering with the memory. "The canoe capsized. Somehow I—I was the only survivor. I returned here—to check on Joshua. Once I was here my exhaustion got the best of me. It was then that I went to sleep."

Again she drew away from him. She questioned him with her eyes, then said, "How did you know to find me here?" she murmured. "You said that you had already been here the one other time, when you found Joshua."

"Seems my search for you took me in a circle." He chuckled, then grew somber as he placed a finger to her swollen lip. "Something then compelled me to check inside the hut when I found myself here again. Thank God I did, Sam." His eyes narrowed. "Your lip, darling," he questioned. "How was the wound inflicted?"

Samantha ran her tongue over the swollen, sore lump. "Lone Cloud," she said, again shivering. "He hit me. He had plans to even—do—worse." She threw herself back into Troy's arms, trembling. "Troy, the storm saved me. If not for it—" She tensed when she heard a low growl of thunder and the splash of rain again beginning.

"Prepare yourself for another storm," Troy said hoarsely. "We might be forced to spend the night here."

Samantha eyed Troy, worry etched onto her lovely face. "What if the Indians—" she murmured.

"I'm sure we don't have to worry any further about

them, at least for now," Troy said, smoothing a tear into Samantha's cheek. "I know something of the Kiawah. It is said that they fear storms—that they look to it as an evil spirit sent to punish them. I'm sure all Kiawah are now back in their village, hiding away in their wigwams until the storm is over."

"Yes, I remember how Lone Cloud feared the storm," Samantha said, nodding. "And isn't it strange how the three who abducted me didn't survive the last storm? I was—the only—one spared."

"I'm sure it had nothing to do with spirits," Troy chuckled. "Surely the Indians' heads were hit by the canoe as it overturned. Something simple as that."

"A tree's limb fell and knocked Lone Cloud from the canoe," Samantha said contemplatingly. "One other was taken—by—a—a—crocodile. The other, well, perhaps the canoe did inflict his wound."

"No matter," Troy said with a shrug. "At least they were rendered harmless to you. And you are here safely in my arms."

Again Samantha snuggled, relishing his closeness and the cozy warmth of the fire. "But are you going to be safe, Troy?" she asked. "Where is your ship? Should you be gone from it so long?"

"My ship is anchored at Johnston Oaks," he said. "To any passing ship it is only a ship rendered helpless by the blockade. No one will be the wiser."

"But your crew? Won't they wonder about your absence?"

"I alerted them as to where I was going. They know I'll be gone awhile."

"And you truly think we will be safe enough here for the night, Troy?"

"With me you are always safe," he said, framing her face between his hands. He lowered his lips to hers and only softly kissed her, fearing to cause more pain to her lip.

Samantha's stomach emitted a loud grumble. She giggled from embarrassment, but she was starved. She had been foolish not to bring nourishment along. But she hadn't planned to be gone from Johnston Oaks this long.

"And I even have a remedy for *that*," Troy said, laughing softly as he stood and walked away from Samantha.

Samantha rose to her knees and watched him wonderingly. "You have a remedy for what?" she softly queried. Then her eyes grew wide as she saw him lift a small rattan basket from the dark corner of the hut. She placed her hands to her mouth and laughed when she recognized the picnic basket that belonged to Jewel's kitchen.

Troy placed the basket on the floor before her. "Jewel was worried more about your stomach than anything else," he said, his face alight with amusement.

"Do you mean you've carried that with you all the while searching for me?" Samantha asked incredulously. "Even through the storm?"

"Well, I must admit that I had momentarily abandoned it," he said chuckling. "I stashed it beneath the cover of some low brush just outside the hut after discovering that you weren't safely with Joshua. I couldn't let it impede my search for you."

"Then you were lucky for two reasons to be led by accident back to this hut," Samantha replied and giggled.

"Food and you," Troy laughed. "Yes. It worked out perfect, except for—" His gaze moved over her, stopping at the dried mud on her shoes and ankles.

"Except for?" she said, lifting an eyebrow quizzically.

"I think you could enjoy the food and my presence even more if, let's say, you rid yourself of some of the mud."

His eyes danced and his smile sent sensuous ripples through Samantha. She was fast forgetting all her plights, then looked down at herself. In her relief to find Joshua there she had forgotten how she looked. Her shirt gaped open in front, breeches that she wore were spattered with mud and swamp debris, and mud was dried and caked on her shoes and even up onto her bare ankles.

Her fingers went to her hair and felt the knots. She smiled sheepishly at Troy. If he loved her now in her horrid disarray, his love was truly sincere.

"I do look a sight, don't I?" She giggled, combing her fingers through her hair. "I'm sure I smell as horribly."

Her gaze swept over him. His white-ruffled shirt was opened down the front to reveal his well-muscled chest covered with soft swirls of black hair. His breeches were tight and showed the strength of muscle in his lean thighs. Still wet from the rain his hair was even blacker than midnight and in need of combing. His ocean blue eyes were causing Samantha's insides to stir. He was giving her a maddening grin with his white flash of teeth set against his tanned, handsome face.

"Even that could be remedied," Troy said, taking Samantha by the hand, urging her to her feet.

"And how would you suggest that be done, my darling?" Samantha teased. "I see no bathtub. I see no bubble bath."

Troy's fingers went to her shirt and eased it down and over her shoulders, setting her breasts free. He lowered his head and flicked a tongue over a taut nipple, drawing a nervous sigh from inside Samantha. Then he straightened his back and tossed her shirt aside.

"Troy, what do you think you're doing?" Samantha murmured, breathless as he now loosened the buttons of her breeches.

"The rain will be our source of bath this evening, darling," Troy said thickly. "Fully undress. I shall also."

Color rose to Samantha's cheeks. "You're not serious," she said, softly laughing.

Troy jerked his shirt off, displaying the full magnificence of his chest. "Quite serious." He chuckled. "Aren't you game?"

"But should the Indians return—" Samantha said, becoming feverish as she watched him lower his breeches, stopping first to remove and kick his shoes aside.

"Like I said, I don't think we have anything to fear of the Indians. The thunder is a constant reminder of the approaching new storm. And I didn't see any signs of Indians before arriving to this hut the second time."

"But, still, Troy, I don't know."

"Trust me," Troy said huskily, now fully nude. He ran his fingers over the swell of her breasts and then lower to where her stomach lay flat.

As though under a spell, Samantha removed her shoes, then held her arms out away from her sides to let him lower her breeches on down, away from her. She trembled sensually as Troy placed a hand fully over her soft vee of curls between her thighs, letting a lone finger slip up inside her.

Melting, she crept on into his arms and clung to him, feeling the hardness of his manhood tease her abdomen as it lay against her.

"I love you," Troy whispered, then gave her a soft kiss, careful not to inflict added pain to her wounded mouth. His fingers eased up to cup a breast.

Samantha's senses were reeling, her heart thumping erratically against her chest as Troy swept her up fully into his arms and walked toward the door.

"I wish I could kiss you. Really kiss you," he whispered. "But I don't want to hurt your injured lip."

Feeling drunkenly content, Samantha welcomed the cool splash of rain on her upturned face as Troy stepped on out of the hut. Thunder groaned in the distance. Shreds of lightning flashed overhead where night had settled in with its velvet dark sky.

"I can't believe this," Samantha laughed as Troy placed her feet to the ground. "Nude in the rain with the man I love? I would have never thought it possible."

The rain glistened on Samantha's body, mirroring her natural, enchanting beauty. Troy's eyes glittered as he reached both hands to her and began trailing them over her body. Lower he went, from her bare slim shoulders and delicate collarbones to her round breasts, where water glistened like diamonds.

Unable to deny himself such temptation any longer, Troy leaned down and flicked his tongue onto her breast and then placed his lips fully over it, drawing the hardened nipple between his teeth.

Samantha threw her head back, moaning softly. She wove her slender fingers through his thick, wet hair and drew his lips even harder against her, aware of his searching hands as they traveled on lower across her abdomen and then rested on each of her hips.

"Enough," Troy said from between clenched teeth.

"Darling, let's go back inside. I must fully have you. Now."

Clinging, their bodies wet against the other, they went back inside the hut. And after the floor was cleared and their clothes spread beside the fire for a cushion upon which to make love, they stretched out beside one another, their eyes sweeping over the other with a silent, urgent message. Then they embraced long and sweet. Troy was the first to break away, showering heated kisses over Samantha's taut-tipped breasts and then burying his lips along the vulnerable line of her neck.

"Love me," Samantha softly cried, her hands moving frantically over him, stopping at his sleek, muscled buttocks. When he anchored her fiercely against him and gave her a meltingly hot kiss, she forgot the pain of her swollen lip and became swallowed up in the desire that was shooting through her.

Clinging to him, she welcomed him atop her. He exhaled a thick, husky groan as he entered her. She writhed in response, her body turning to hot liquid beneath him. The burning ache between her thighs flamed higher as he plied her with his eager thrusts. His fingers were wild on her breasts, his lips and tongue dancing at her throat and then down, to again claim a taut nipple.

Weak with desire, Samantha became swept away by an undercurrent of sensation as torrential as the tides. Her hands became urgent on his body as she was imprisoned beneath him in an exciting bondage.

He thrust himself inside her, over and over again. She surrendered wholly to him as her hips lifted to meet him. And then the familiar searing flame of rapture shot through her, setting her afire with trembles, welcoming his harder thrusts as he, too, reached the pinnacle of joy.

Afterward they clung together, still on a cloud of rapture, then Troy rose away from her and stepped into his breeches.

Samantha eased up onto an elbow as Troy removed a bottle from the rattan basket. "Wine?" she marveled. "Surely Jewel didn't—"

"No. Not Jewel," Troy said, settling down beside her. "This is my own treat, though I did take it from the liquor cabinet in your study at Johnston Oaks."

"My word." Samantha giggled. "You do think of everything, love."

Removing the cork, Troy gave Samantha a mischievous stare, then tipped the bottle, pouring some wine onto one of her nipples.

"What are you—" she gasped.

Before she could get any further words out, Troy was already licking the wine from her nipple, and even lower, where a few drops had fallen to her flat abdomen.

"Never tasted better," he said huskily.

"What? Me or the wine?" Samantha teased, his lips and tongue again stirring her insides to molten lava.

"Both," he teased back.

Samantha took the wine bottle from him and placed it on the floor beside her. Then, sighing, she crept into his arms and clung to him. "I love you so," she whispered. "I'm so alive when I'm with you."

"You're glad that I saved you?"

"I could've found my way back alone."

"Oh, now listen to you. My strong, adventurous woman."

"I could have. I only stopped to rest. That's all."

"Then you wish I hadn't searched for you?"

Samantha eyed him hazily. "You silly man," she laughed. "You know the answer to that."

"What about the slaves? Are you going to give up the search?"

"I have no choice but to," she said and pouted. "Surely the Kiawah Indians have dealt with the slaves in their own way."

Troy traced her swollen lip with his forefinger. "Damn the Indian who did this to you," he growled.

"Troy, just hold me. Make love to me all night. Make me forget everything but you."

"Darling, that would be my pleasure."

# Chapter Twenty-One

Tired, dirty and wet, Samantha walked alongside Troy, finally away from the swamp. Weaving their way between the heavy heads of cotton plants, Samantha looked anxiously toward the slaves' quarters, worrying about Joshua. When she saw a slow spiral of smoke rising from the fireplace chimney at the side of the colorless cabin, Samantha sighed with relief. Joshua was surely all right. Still, she hurried her steps, wanting to see firsthand that he was well enough. In her mind's eye she could still see him stretched out, lifeless, on the ground with the arrow piercing his chest.

"Sam, what's the hurry?" Troy grumbled as he hurried his pace to keep up with her. "God! I've never seen a woman with such energy. We've just walked miles and you're still perky and ready to go some more."

Samantha cast Troy a sideways glance. "I must check on Joshua," she said anxiously. "Though you said that he was all right, I've just got to see for myself."

"Seems your slaves mean a lot to you," Troy said softly, taking her hand, clasping onto it.

"Yes. They do," Samantha murmured. "I've always respected them. They've always been my friends. Especially Joshua and Jewel. They've almost been substitute parents."

"Yes. I've heard of such attachments before." Troy nodded. "As for me, I prefer a business relationship."

"Oh? And in New York you have such dealings?"

"Why, yes," Troy said. "I have a maid and a butler. I pay them quite well."

Samantha gave him a questioning look then went to the cabin door and lightly tapped her knuckles against it. When the door slowly opened and Joshua was there, shirtless, with a clean, white bandage wrapped neatly about his chest, contrasting so against his sleek, dark skin, Samantha took a wide step and eased into his arms.

"Thank the Lord," she murmured, hugging him. When his powerful arms fit around her, she felt a keen peacefulness settle over her. Her father was gone but she had the next best thing. She had Joshua.

Joshua peered on past Samantha's head at Troy. "Thank you fo' findin' mah baby," he said hoarsely. "I lets her down out thea' in the swamp. Dem Indians got de bes' o' me. Had you not come along—"

Troy took a step forward and placed a hand firmly on Joshua's muscled shoulder, seeing such wisdom in the dark man's eyes and strength in the set of his powerful jaw. "She's home safe," he said thickly. "And what happened with you out there couldn't be helped. You did what you could. It could've happened just as quickly to me."

"Ah owes you a debt, no mattah' what you says," Joshua said. "Jus' names it. Ah'll do it."

Troy dropped his hand away from Joshua, then

reached out and drew Samantha up next to him. "Just take care of Samantha while I'm gone," he said. "Don't let her do anything foolish, like again going in search of the escaped slaves. Keep her close where you can keep an eye on her."

Samantha nudged Troy in the ribs. "Troy, I appreciate both your concerns, but I can darn well take care of myself," she argued. "I believe I've proven that more than once."

"Well, now I would argue that," Troy said, frowning down at her. "Had I not found you—"

"I would have been just fine," she scolded.

Joshua intervened. "Jewel's been worryin' sick," he said. "Bes' you go and shows her that you're home safe, Miss Samantha."

"Yes. Best I do," Samantha said, briefly taking one of his hands, squeezing it affectionately. Then she swung around and, with Troy beside her, hurried on, toward the house. Samantha's eyes were drawn to the moored ship. Some of Troy's crew could be seen on top deck, idling about, the ship itself an intrusion as far as Samantha was concerned. Soon it would be carrying Troy away from her. And then when would she even see him again? Fitting her body next to his, she clung to him about his waist. "I wish you didn't have to go," she murmured.

"Let's just be thankful for another full day ahead of us," Troy said hoarsely, studying his ship with a sharp eye. "I must delay my ship's parting until tonight. Only then will it be safe to escape from these waters."

"Even then it's not safe," Samantha softly argued. "You know the dangers. The northern warships are like giant octopuses, their tentacles outspread, ready to ensnare any ship that is not one of them."

307

"I'm skilled at maneuvering," Troy said smugly. "Don't worry your sweet self over it for even one more minute."

Samantha gave him a heavy-lashed look. "I shall always worry about you when you're out of my eyesight," she said glumly. "I wish there had been no declaration of war. Nothing good, whatsoever, will come of it. Why didn't everyone see? President Lincoln wanted only what was best for the country."

Troy stopped and swung around to face Samantha. "Samantha, you're speaking in favor of the northern cause," he gasped. "Do you even dare to, while standing on southern soil?"

She reached a hand to his cheek, feeling the fresh stubble of facial whiskers. "From the very beginning, I had mixed loyalties," she explained. "You know that I spent summers up North."

"Yes. But your father—"

"He had his beliefs. I had mine," she stated flatly.

Troy's gaze swept over her. Though she was covered with smudges of mud and her hair was a tangle of unbrushed knots, he couldn't help but admire the tantalizing cleavage of her full breasts where her soiled shirt gaped open in front. Her cheeks were glowing, her eyes sparkling, her long tapering calves and silken thighs damnedly hidden beneath the man's breeches.

"We've only a few hours left before I leave," he said huskily. "What say we don't spend them in talking about the war. Didn't you promise me a hot tub of water, a thin cheroot, and a bottle of wine?"

Samantha slinked up next to him and twined her arms about his neck. "Darling, I believe I promised you more than that," she teased, licking her lips seductively. "Or have you forgotten?"

"But what about Jewel? Will you mind that she knows that we are—uh—sharing more than a bath?"

"She won't even know that we're sharing a bath. I shall instruct her to pour two separate baths, in two separate rooms. Then I shall sneak into your bath with you."

"You're a scheming wench," Troy laughed huskily.

"You'd rather I'd be different, love?"

"Darling, don't ever change," he said, lowering a soft kiss to her lips. Then he ran a finger across the bruised scar on her lip. "Does it hurt, hon?" he quietly asked.

"Only when you don't kiss it," Samantha purred.

"I'll kiss it all right," Troy chuckled. "You'll beg me to stop."

"Never," she laughed, now walking alongside him and up the fine marble steps of Johnston Oaks. Her eyes wavered as she looked about her; she missed her father so. Yet he was everywhere: in the shadows of the porch, the windows staring down at her, and at the massive oak door, awaiting her safe arrival home. He *was* Johnston Oaks. How could it ever be any other way?

"Hon?" Troy said, seeing her suddenly sad. "What is it?"

Samantha was shaken from her reverie by his words. She didn't want to spoil these last hours with him by letting him see how desperately she missed her father. It was a private hurt, not to be shared, not even with the man she loved.

"Nothing," she quickly blurted. "Nothing's wrong. Let's hurry on in the house. Let's have Jewel get those tubs ready for us."

"And a thin cheroot?" he asked, lifting an eyebrow.

"And a bottle of wine," she softly laughed.

"And then," he said, winking at her.

Her hair quickly washed, brushed and hanging in lustrous waves down her back, and wearing a clinging, silk robe, Samantha crept from her room and along the upstairs hallway. It had been hard to convince Jewel that no assistance was needed while she took a bath.

But Jewel had agreed not to check in on Samantha for awhile after Samantha had assured her that sleep and rest were desperately needed after her ordeal in the swampy forest. This gave Samantha the freedom to slip into the room assigned to Troy where, hopefully, many sensual hours would be shared with him. A slow ache circled her heart when she thought of later good-byes.

The aroma of cigar smoke floated beneath the closed bedroom door and down the hallway, meeting Samantha's approach. She smiled to herself. Three of Troy's wishes had been granted: the tub of water, the thin cheroot, and wine; and now for Samantha to make her appearance to complete his fantasies.

With a turn of the doorknob, Samantha slipped on into the bedroom, met by a room flooded in sunlight, hazed over by the spiraling clouds of cigar smoke.

In the center of the room, Troy sat in a large copper tub, almost comical looking with suds sparkling about his waist, a cigar clamped between his teeth as he held a thin-stemmed glass filled with sparkling, red wine.

The canopied bed was the backdrop with its lace-trimmed spread and canopy and magnificently carved oak headboard and four posters. Two windows were open-shuttered to the beautiful summer day, and the sound of the song birds were soft and sweet.

Samantha laughed to herself as she caught Troy humming, his eyes closed in his perfect contentment. Quietly closing the door she tiptoed across the floor, the deep carpet muffling the contact of her bare feet into its depths.

Her face flamed, her heart pounded. She let the robe slip from her shoulders and flutter away from her. And then she bent over beside the tub and pressed her lips to one of Troy's rubbery nipples. He jumped with surprise.

"Sam." He then laughed throatily, yanking his cigar from between his lips. "God. You gave me a start. You've got to remember that I'm in strange surroundings."

"They shouldn't be strange. Troy. They're mine," she said, tracing his full lips with a forefinger. "And everything I have will one day be yours."

"Oh?" He chuckled, lifting an eyebrow.

"We will be married after the war is over, won't we?" she asked, now taking the wineglass and then his cigar away from him.

"That's what I hope for," he said, watching her now slipping into the tub with him, the circle of suds already clinging to her swollen breasts like sparkling diamonds. He reached for her waist and helped her in to straddle him. And then when he felt her soft buttocks resting on his thighs, he slipped a hand beneath the water and let his fingers move slowly over her, already drunk with pleasure at the mere sight of her.

Samantha's pulse raced. Her face felt hotter when she felt his risen sex probe between her thighs. She wriggled closer to him, tremoring with ecstasy as he easily entered her and began his easy strokes inside her. She moaned longingly, wrapping her arms about his neck to cling

311

to him.

Troy sucked in his breath, her breasts which were thrust into his chest and her lips which nibbled at the flesh of his shoulders almost driving him mad. He placed a forefinger beneath her chin and urged her eyes to meet his, seeing the heat in their depths, evidence that she was in the grip of a growing passion, melting their worlds together, fusing as though one.

"Darling, you take my breath away," Troy said thickly, then crushed his lips down upon hers and gave her a fiery, long kiss, his hands running from her thighs to her hips, and then to her breasts to cup them.

Samantha shuddered sensually as his tongue danced between her teeth and plunged into the warm recesses of her mouth. She felt flaming desire run through her from her head to her toes, licking fires along her veins.

She rocked on him as he continued his even strokes inside her. She went breathless as his lips went lower now, to kiss first one exquisitely tender breast and then the other. Her throat arched backward, her eyes closed in ecstasy.

And then the familiar eruption began like thunder inside her as Troy worked more feverishly with his thrusts, and together they reached that peak of drugged euphoria, their moans of delight vibrating from wall to wall.

"Darling," Samantha sighed, still feeling the tremors of ecstasy floating through her.

"Were you too cramped to fully enjoy it?" Troy asked, looking down at her. Seeing her drugged expression, he was sure that his question was unnecessary.

"Well, yes," she said, smiling coyly up at him.

Troy was taken aback. "But, Sam, you truly seemed to

enjoy it as much as—"

She sealed his lips with a forefinger. "But we've yet to use the bed," she teased. "And it is so much larger. Just think what might be accomplished there if so much was able to be done in this small tub."

He chuckled, his eyes gleaming. "You *are* a wench," he said. "God, woman, you're insatiable."

"I want to store up for the time I won't be with you," she said, pouting.

"If that's what my lady requests, that's what my lady gets," he said, placing his arms beneath her and lifting her up into them as he rose from the tub.

"Steady," Samantha said giggling, clinging, feeling their bodies slick against the other. "Don't lose your footing now, Troy. A crash of any sort could get us discovered. Jewel would come running for sure."

Dripping suds and water, Troy stepped gingerly from the tub, laughing hoarsely as Samantha slipped and slid against him in his arms.

"We're going to get everything wet," he whispered, watching his wet footsteps being left behind in the carpet.

"It'll dry," Samantha reassured. "Don't fret so much, darling. Just relax and enjoy. The sun is already dipping lower in the sky. Soon you'll—be—gone."

"Shh. We're not to speak of that, remember?" he scolded, placing her on the bed. His eyes raked over her, fully absorbing her loveliness. He leaned down over her and flicked his tongue into her navel, then left a trail of kisses downward.

Samantha barely breathed as she felt his lips on places where only he had become familiar. Like a puppet being guided by strings she opened herself fully to him and closed her eyes, letting the pleasure of his lips and tongue

313

fire her passion.

And then his lips were pressed sensually against hers in a hot kiss, and she felt the muscled sleekness of his body entrap her beneath it.

Wrapping her arms about his neck, she arched and moaned as he again entered her, trembling with readiness. Her fingernails dug into his flesh, she rose and fell with his thrusts while his palms moved seductively over her. He teased and stroked the supple lines of her body. Her body was an instrument, he the musician. She felt the urgency building. His mouth was hot and demanding, now kissing her on the soft hollow of her throat.

"I love you so," Samantha whispered, curling her fingers through his hair. "I don't want this—to—end."

But just as she said the words, she felt the delicious splash of wondrous desire flooding her senses. Her body quaked. It shook. And she welcomed the spill of his warmth inside her as he also was swept away, caught up this time in a more gentle passion than moments earlier while in the tub.

Her heartbeat thundering against her chest, Samantha clung to him. He was breathing hard against her cheek. His body still covered her, yet she was happy in her utter surrender beneath him.

"Sam," Troy said softly, now leaning up to look down into her eyes. "I know this will sound a bit crass but I must now leave. Please understand."

Samantha blanched. Her throat went dry. "Lord, Troy," she gasped. "We've not even grown cold from our moments of lovemaking and you announce that you must go? Why? I thought you were going to wait until dark."

He kissed her softly and ran a hand fleetingly across a

314

breast. "Hon, I must alert my crew that I'm even alive," he said chuckling.

"If anyone should doubt that, they should come to me," she softly teased, pressing her lips against one of his nipples, then nipping it with her teeth.

"You know what I mean," he said, easing away from her. "I've already been gone too long, Sam. God! If the guys knew what I've really been about, they'd not only be jealous but would become mutinous."

"Troy, please?" Samantha begged, slinking from the bed and up against him, pressing her breasts invitingly into him. "Please stay?"

"Sam, you know that I want to."

"Well then, stay."

He stepped on away from her and grabbed his breeches and slipped into them, and then into his shoes and shirt.

"You're serious," Samantha gasped, eyeing him disbelievingly. "You are going."

"I really must."

"When do you think I'll see you again?" she asked, pouting, slipping her robe on and tying it in front.

"Are you staying here, Sam? Don't you think you'd be better off going north to stay with your grandparents?"

"I told you before that I couldn't do that. I must stay and protect Johnston Oaks."

"You and Joshua?" he openly scoffed. "The rest of your slaves are gone, Sam."

"You needn't remind me of that," she argued.

"What can you possibly accomplish here, darling?" he said, clasping his fingers onto her shoulders. "Who knows when the military will even take over your property?"

"Father said the war would be fought on northern soil."

"You know how wrong he was about that. Be realistic, Sam."

"I am when I say that I must try and make things work here at Johnston Oaks. It was my father's pride and joy. I can't leave it behind. I just can't."

"I hate leaving you behind, darling," Troy said, drawing her fully into his arms, giving her a fierce hug.

"I'll be all right," she murmured. "I'm a survivor, or hadn't you noticed?"

"Yeah, damn it," he said. "I've noticed."

His lips went to hers and again passion flamed between them, but then he broke away from her and was gone, leaving Samantha staring blankly after him. It seemed he could materialize and disappear with one blink of an eye!

But she did understand why he had chosen to depart so hastily. Any more time spent together would only make the leaving harder.

With a flutter of silk she rushed to the window and, standing on tiptoe, saw his handsome, tall form darting across the lawn, in the direction of his ship. And then something came quickly to her mind.

"He didn't ask for the map," she said in a rush of words. "Not a word was spoken of it between us this time. Does that mean—"

Her heart swelled with a warmful joy. The map was a thing of the past, no longer something to be bartered over. His full interest in her now was—her!

"God, when shall I even seen him again?" she whispered, curling her fingers into painful fists at her side.

# Chapter Twenty-Two

Weeks turned into months. Joshua had worked as though he had been ten laborers in the fields. Then, one by one, the slaves had trickled in from the swamps, having discovered that it was easier to live under plantation rule than fending for themselves, though most had found refuge in the villages of the Kiawah. The fact that the Kiawah Indians had opened their hearts to the escaped Negro populace had changed Samantha's opinion of the Indians. They had understood and sympathized with the plight of the Negro, having themselves been taken advantage of by the white man. Samantha now understood why the Indians wanted to kill her. They had wanted to protect the Negro.

Upon the slaves' first return to Johnston Oaks, Samantha had begun to have hope. She had even managed for awhile to find an occasional blockade-runner who had purchased her cotton in exchange for provisions for the plantation.

But now her hopes were fading. No one would risk being caught to come and help her. She and all who were a part of Johnston Oaks Plantation were isolated. Rumor was that the war had worsened and that the homes in the South were being burned and cattle was being slaughtered wherever the Union soldiers had been. Gunfire in Charleston Harbor was a constant reminder of what might one day happen to Johnston Oaks.

With her hair tied back by a scarlet ribbon, to hang in one long curl down her back, and wearing a fully gathered cotton dress with a low-cut bodice chosen purposely for cooling effect, Samantha was in the cotton fields laboring alongside the slaves. Though she didn't know where she might sell the cotton, she could not leave it to rot in the fields. And she could no longer stand to stay idle in the mansion, fearing that she just might wither away.

She needed the sun, the wind, the smell of the earth, to cleanse her mind of loneliness and heartache. She had lost her father. And Troy hadn't returned as he had promised. She felt as though she had also lost him. Always when she had begun to believe that his love for her was sincere, he would give her cause to feel the fool.

Yet fool or not, she would always love him. And what if he hadn't returned because he was dead? Samantha knew the possibilities of that, yet wouldn't let herself believe it.

With her hands at the small of her back, she groaned and stretched herself, looking up into the pounding rays of the sun. Her face felt scorched, her hair somewhat bleached. She then looked over her shoulder at Joshua as he placed another boll of cotton into the bag that he had slung over his right shoulder. She worried about how much he had thinned from overwork. His eyes were weary, as was the stoop to his shoulders.

Joshua saw her study of him and returned the show of concern for her. "You work too hard, Miss Samantha,"

318

he said, frowning. "And you should be in the house away from the hot sun. It's gonna bake your skin like it was a potato."

Samantha laughed at the comparison. "Lord, Joshua," she said. "What a thing to say."

"If Massa Craig was alive you'd not be workin' day in, day out."

"Joshua," Samantha scolded. "Even when Father was alive, I worked alongside you in the fields."

"Only a few hours at a time," he corrected. "I remember Massa Craig swattin' yo' behind and sendin' you flyin' back in the house."

"Yes. I remember." Samantha giggled. Again she stretched her back, groaning with the soreness. "But things are much different now. I'm the one who sets up the rules. It is up to me to see that Johnston Oaks doesn't wither and die like these cotton plants would if we neglected them."

"Ol' Joshua here thinks time is drawin' near when you'll have to give up," Joshua said hoarsely, humbly lowering his eyes. "We've done 'bout all we can do. Where are we even gonna sell this cotton? The sheds are already strainin' at the seams with what's already been picked and stored there."

"Where there's a will, there's a way, Joshua," Samantha said firmly, squinting and placing a hand over her eyes to shield them from the sun when she suddenly spotted a fancy carriage coming up the road. Samantha tensed. If she was not mistaken, the carriage belonged to Franklin. It was identifiable by its silver-spoked wheels and the proud chestnut leading the carriage.

"My word," Samantha gasped. "After all these months, Franklin has returned. Not one word. And now?

Why? Where has he even been? His whole plantation has been left to waste away."

"Massa Franklin?" Joshua said, also shielding his eyes with a hand to watch the carriage's approach.

"As far as I'm concerned, he can just turn around and go back to where he's been hiding," Samantha said bitterly. "I've no patience with the likes of him."

"Bes' we hear what he has to say, Miss Samantha," Joshua quietly said, beginning to feel the sole responsibility for her welfare, though he never forgot his place as a slave.

"I don't care to hear anything that miserable man has to say," Samantha spat, hurriedly resuming picking cotton, dropping the soft bolls into a bag that she had stretched out on the ground at her feet.

"Now that Father is gone, I have the say as to who comes and goes from Johnston Oaks. He's not welcome, Joshua. He forfeited that right when he turned his back on my father and left Johnston Oaks Plantation unsupervised after he promised Father that he would watch out for it while Father traveled the seas in the *Magnolia*. He doesn't deserve my friendship. I will not offer it to him."

"He may offer help," Joshua argued.

"I don't want his sort of help." Samantha glowered, glancing up, seeing the carriage now pulling up before the house and stopping, its driver one unfamiliar to Samantha. Inside the carriage, she could see movement at the windows, and when the driver stepped down from the front outside seat and opened the door, Samantha once more ceased with her labors and watched.

Samantha took a step forward when she saw a lady alight the carriage, her fully gathered dress a soft color of yellow, her hair matching in its long funnels of golden curls hanging down her delicate back. Samantha tensed. There was much familiar about this lady. It was her petiteness, a frailty which was defined by her tiny-boned arms, shoulders, and waistline. And—her—hair?

Samantha laughed nervously to herself. "No. It's my imagination playing tricks on me," she whispered. "It couldn't be Julia. Why would she be here? Why would—she—be with Franklin?"

Still watching, she saw a man alight the carriage, and her heart fluttered nervously. She felt a light-headedness sweep over her when she saw the man's powerful build, his red hair and cheekwhiskers, and his expensive attire.

"Massa Craig?" Joshua gasped, stealing Samantha's thoughts from her. "It can't be. It surely is his ghost come back, Miss Samantha."

"Father?" Samantha whispered. "How—"

"You see it, too," Joshua said excitedly. "Miss Samantha, ain't it Massa Craig? Tell me my ol' eyes ain't foolin' me."

When the man in question turned his eyes in Samantha's direction, giving her a full view of his face, a soft cry rose from her throat.

"It *is* you, Father!" she yelled, almost tripping on her skirt as she began to run toward him. She steadied herself and never let her eyes leave the bulk of the man as he began limping in her direction.

"Sam!" Craig shouted. "Honey, I'm home!"

Samantha was finding this hard to comprehend. Surely she was dreaming! But the heat of the sun still beating down on her flesh and her father's voice proved to her that this was all very much a reality. Somehow he had escaped the perils of the sea! But where had he been

321

these past months? Why hadn't he contacted her?

But none of these unanswered questions mattered to her when his powerful arms accepted her in them. She fell sobbing against him, clinging, afraid to let go, fearing that he might disappear from her eyesight again.

"Sam—Sam," Craig said, patting her on the back. "Honey, it's all right. I know what you must've been thinkin' all this time. You surely thought I was dead. Honey, I thought the same of you. But word was brought to me that you were safe—that some sea captain had brought you safely home after rescuing you at sea."

Samantha clung to him, yet eased her head away, enabling her to look squarely up into his eyes that were the color of hers. "Father, how?" she asked, stifling a sob. Her eyes searched his face, seeing it flawless. He seemed to be all right except for the noticeable limp as he had run choppily toward her.

"Sam, are you all right?" he asked, cupping her chin in his hand, searching her face. "God, girl, your skin is burned." He looked at her hair and reached and lifted its long, tied locks from her back and inspected it. "And your hair. The ends are split and the sun is bleachin' it of its brilliant reds."

"Father, I'm fine," she reassured. "But tell me where you've been? How did you—you—escape the *Magnolia?*"

"I've been in prison, Sam," he said thickly. "Up in Illinois. In fact, in Springfield."

Samantha blanched. "Prison? In Springfield?" she gasped.

"I was left for dead on the *Magnolia*," he tried to explain. "Somehow when the ship sank I was left to drift on some floating debris. The crew of a northern warship

322

scooped me up out of the water, questioned me, and the next thing I knew, I was in prison."

"Good Lord," Samantha said, feeling ice fill her veins at the thought. Then she rose to elated heights again and once more hugged him. "But now you're home. You're alive. It's like a dream, Father. A wonderful dream."

"Thanks to Franklin," he said, spoiling Samantha's moment of happiness with the mere mention of Franklin's wretched name.

She eased away from her father's arm. "Franklin?" she dared to ask. "What has he got to do with any of this?"

"He helped me escape," Craig explained. "And, Sam, he placed his life in jeopardy while doing so."

"Father, how? I'm so confused," Samantha said, her mind reeling by all that was happening.

"Let's go in the house and talk about it," Craig said, taking her by an elbow, turning her in the direction of the house. "There's a lot I must tell you, and so much of it is not pleasant."

"Father, nothing but you matters right now," Samantha said, leaning into his embrace as he drew her once more next to him. "You're alive. Except for—" She looked down at his limp, wondering about it, as they were now walking toward the house.

"Except for my limp?" he said, completing her words. "Yes."

"Honey, I got that while on board the *Magnolia*," he explained. "A mast half crushed it."

Samantha suddenly had flashes of remembering that day and the strong hands shoving her away from the falling mast. As she had thought, it *had* been her father. It *had* been his hands. He had taken the blow, himself, and had been left for dead because of it. That knowledge filled her heart with a dull ache. If only she hadn't fainted! At one time in her life she could brag of never fainting and since the beginning of the war, she had fainted not once but twice.

"I'm sorry," she softly replied. Then a sudden chill coursed through her when the waiting lady at the carriage stepped fully into view. Samantha had simply forgotten about her in her floating happiness.

Samantha stopped abruptly, her heart pounding with recognition. "Julia Ainsworth?" she said in a strain. "Cousin Julia?" She grabbed her father's arm. "Father, why is Julia here?" She wasn't sure if she wanted to hear the answer. Julia's trip south surely hadn't been made for pleasure. The whole countryside was too torn by war to even travel the roads without the worry of being thrown into skirmishes between soldiers.

"Yes," Craig said thickly. "Julia is here. She traveled from Springfield with Franklin and me."

Now Samantha saw Franklin as he came into view and began helping Julia up the front steps. Samantha looked more intensely toward Julia. Something seemed amiss about her. It was the slow gait in which she walked. The life was gone from her steps, and as Julia suddenly looked Samantha's way, Samantha could see that even Julia's face lacked something. She tensed, seeing that Julia's eyes seemed empty, dispirited. Julia didn't even seem to recognize Samantha.

"What's wrong with her, Father?" Samantha suddenly blurted.

Craig swept Samantha on along, once more headed for the house. "Sam, like I said, I've much to tell you," he said. "Let's go inside. I'm weary from the trip. It's been hectic—one of searching backroads, where no one would stop us. If I had been recognized, I'd have been shot on the spot."

"Oh, Father," Samantha groaned. "That doesn't seem possible, that you'd be—a—wanted—hunted man."

"But I am," he grumbled. "My reputation as a successful blockade-runner precedes me, Sam." He looked over his shoulder at Joshua who still stood in the field numbed by Craig's sudden appearance, as though Joshua still thought Craig an apparition.

"And how is Joshua?" he mumbled. His gaze captured the full setting of the plantation, seeing that not much had changed. Fewer slaves and much cotton left to be harvested, but, otherwise, no cannons had yet been pointed its way and left their mark.

"Joshua has been a godsend as usual," Samantha said, squaring her back. "If not for him, I just don't know, Father. He works from sunup to sunset. He even guards my door at night. You chose him wisely, Father, over the others, to appoint him overseer."

"Yes, he is one of a kind," Craig said, now going up the stairs, toward the front door.

Checkers rushed across the full length of the veranda and began yelping at Craig's feet, wagging his tail anxiously. "Hey, there, Checkers," Craig laughed, stooping to pet him. "Seems you didn't forget this old man either." He ran his fingers through the Collie's fur, patting him fondly, then gave Samantha an apprehensive look. "Hon, let's go on inside. It's best to get all this told. We've much planning to do. Seems as though we'll be leaving by ship again, and soon."

"You don't plan to resume blockade-running, do you, Father?" Samantha asked cautiously. "You have

325

no ship."

"No. No blockade-running," Craig uttered, holding the door open for Samantha to enter before him. "We'll be traveling to Brazil on a ship with Franklin."

Samantha stopped just inside the foyer, stunned by his words. "Brazil?" she gasped. "Why would we travel to Brazil, of all places?"

Craig clasped his hands onto Samantha's shoulders and looked solemnly down at her. "Sam, let's go in the parlor then I'll explain all of these new developments to you," he said.

"All right," she murmured, suddenly afraid.

Following along beside him she went to the parlor, looking anxiously about for Julia, disappointed that she wasn't there. Instead, Franklin came toward her in his usual attire of expensive frock coat and matching accessories, his bald head shining as though waxed and his eyes pale in color, yet gleaming as he took her hand and gentlemanly kissed its palm.

"Samantha, how good it is to see you," Franklin chimed, smiling at her. Then as his eyes traveled over her, seeing her more closely and the neglect of her person, his smug smile changed to that of distaste. Somehow she looked less a lady, yet he knew what lay beneath the cheap cotton dress and still hoped that one day soon he would get a taste of her hidden special traits. She would feel a need to repay him for having rescued her father from that miserable prison. On their journey to Brazil, many hours and opportunities to be alone would be handed them. And Craig would welcome his daughter's union with his best friend and associate. Yes, soon, soon.

"Where is Julia?" Craig asked, slipping his frock

coat off and then his cravat.

Franklin stepped back away from Samantha. "Jewel took her upstairs," he said. "Julia needs to be refreshed, and Jewel is going to get her into bed."

Samantha looked from her father to Franklin, wondering why they were talking about Julia as though she were an invalid. Julia had always come across to all men as helpless, but it had been a ploy. And why was Julia not in Springfield with her grandparents? Samantha was becoming more confused by the minute.

Craig went to Samantha, took her hand and led her to a chair. "You'd best sit down, hon," he said. "It's time you're told."

"Yes, I think it is," Samantha said thickly, eyeing Franklin as he sat down opposite her in a wing chair. Her father sat down beside her on the wide velvet sofa. "Lord, you two act as though you're attending a funeral. You should be happy! You're home."

"I'll begin at the beginning," Craig said. "Just listen, Sam. Don't interrupt. And when I get to the part about your grandparents, just try not to get too upset. What's done is done. Nothing can change what has happened."

An icy coldness splashed through Samantha's insides. "What about Grandpapa and Grandmama?" she said shallowly. "Julia came south with you. Surely, oh, God, no. That doesn't mean—"

"Sam, I'm going to tell you what happened from the beginning. It'll be easier that way," Craig interrupted, giving Franklin a nervous glance, nodding toward the liquor cabinet on the far side of the room.

Franklin understood and went to the cabinet, pouring some sherry into three glasses. He gave one each to Sam and Craig, then sat back down with his own and sipped

327

slowly from it, watching and listening.

Samantha's heart was thumping hard. She clasped onto the long-stemmed glass and stiffened her back, now realizing that she had no choice but to sit patiently, waiting and listening. But a fear so profound told her that something terrible had happened to her beloved grandparents. This day she gained a father but she feared having lost a grandmother and grandfather.

Craig leaned back into the sofa and sighed heavily before entering into his long, eventually morbid narrative. He took a deep swallow of sherry, then rested the glass on his right knee.

"As I told you already, I was rescued from the sea and taken prisoner," he said. "But what I failed to mention was that I was first taken to a military hospital because of my leg injury and my weakness from the time spent in the water."

He paused for another sip of sherry, then continued, his eyes wavering as he looked over at Samantha. "Sam, while still in the hospital, I became acquainted with Julia. She was doing volunteer work. And then one day she again arrived there but under much different circumstances. She was rushed there along with your grandparents after—a—a crazed mob of men burned your grandparents' house. The military hospital was the closest."

Samantha jumped up from the sofa, knocking her glass onto the floor in her startled haste, "No," she gasped. "Not—not my grandparents." She bit her lower lip and wrung her hands. "Father, you're trying to tell me that they are—dead, aren't you?"

Craig handed his glass to Franklin and rose to quickly take Samantha into his embrace. "Sam, I'm sorry," he murmured. "So damn, damn sorry."

Samantha was too numb to cry. She felt in a daze, as though not accepting what he said would make what he said unreal.

"Sam, say something," Craig uttered, leaning away from her, studying her dazed expression.

She shook her head slowly back and forth. "No. I cannot accept what you just told me," she said, almost choking on the knot that had formed in her throat.

"I know," Craig said, leading her back down onto the sofa. "It's all been hard to accept as real. But it is, Sam. Every damn sordid detail of it."

"How?" she said, fighting tears that stung her eyes. "How—did—it happen?"

"There was a rash of lootings and shootings in Springfield and the outlying areas," Craig said, accepting a refilled glass of sherry as Franklin quietly brought it to him.

"This mob of men were retaliating against orders to enlist to fight in the war," he continued. "Your grandparents' farm was among the first involved in this path of destruction. The men showed up there one night and set fire to the house, and from what I could gather from what Julia said, your grandfather tried to defend his family and property and he was shot while doing it."

He hung his head in a hand, then continued. "Your grandmother was badly burned trying to drag your grandfather from the burning house."

"God," Samantha gasped, tears now rushing from her eyes, a painful sick feeling gnawing at her insides.

"Julia was taken and—and—brutally raped," Craig further said. "She was beaten almost senseless. She could hardly relay the story to the authorities. Seems the experience did something to her. She seems dead inside. She may never be the same again."

Samantha brushed tears from her face, anger now replacing her grief. "Did they find the ones responsible?" she said dryly.

"No. They didn't, Sam."

"Did Julia describe the one—who—raped her?"

"She's refused to talk about it," Craig grumbled. "In fact, she rarely says anything. That's why we brought her with us. She's not capable of fending for herself. I hope you can help her, Sam."

Samantha swallowed hard, finding it hard to visualize Julia in any way other than vivacious and alluring to all men who looked her way. And strange that she would be truly defenseless now, having always used that tactic to get men to go to her rescue and become entangled in her web of deception.

"But Julia has spoken out in her nightmares while on the journey south," Franklin interjected.

Samantha jerked her head around to implore him with her eyes. "What did she say?" she asked, determined to find answers, yet not knowing what she would do with them. But maybe one day. Her grandparents' death had to be avenged and she would, hopefully, do the honors.

Franklin leaned forward in his chair, turning his glass around between his fingers. He watched the light reflect in the crystal of the glass, making the glass appear to look as though it were a large, glistening diamond. "She spoke of a man with a smiling scar," he said matter-of-factly. "That's all." He raised his eyes to Samantha. "But I thought that must mean something since she cried the same thing out so many times as she slept."

Samantha's heart skipped a beat, and her eyes widened

with shock. "A scar?" she said. "A—smiling scar? That can only be one man."

She looked anxiously toward her father and grabbed onto his arm. "Father, I know who did it," she cried. "It was Marion Yarborough. He has such a scar. It's at his lip. It makes him look like he's smiling all the time."

"Sam, you don't really know."

"Yes! It has to be! He hated my grandparents."

"Sam, you're getting all worked up. Please settle down," Craig said, patting her hand, seeing the wildness of her eyes. "It won't do any good to come to such conclusions as to who did what. There's no way to prove it or do anything about it. It's impossible to travel back north to point an accusing finger. We're lucky, Franklin, Julia, and I, that we made it back to the Carolinas alive. Forget it, Sam."

Samantha shook her head. "I can't forget it. He did it. He can't get away with it," she almost shouted. "Don't you see? He's wanted to be rid of my grandparents for years. He wanted their land. He found a way, working under the guise of the men in the area who were looting. He must be made to pay. Wire the authorities, Father."

"There's no proof, Sam."

Samantha blinked her eyes nervously. "Julia is proof," she argued.

"Sam, even if she is, you know the impossibility of my contacting the authorities," Craig said. "They would love that. Remember, I am wanted. Forget it, Sam, for all of our benefit."

"I'll never forget it," Samantha argued. She knew that she now had two reasons to return to Springfield. She would, personally, see to Marion Yarborough. It was apparent that her one bullet hadn't stopped him. Well, her next would.

And she also now had the chore of meeting with Doc Raley to see what secret he had held in confidence. He was supposed to tell her upon the death of her grandparents. Somehow, someday, she would see to these two chores that awaited her.

"And, Sam, we've got things to do here," Craig said, rising, going to a window to stare from it. "We must prepare ourselves for our voyage to Brazil."

Samantha had completely forgotten about any mention of Brazil. She went to her father's side. "What is this about Brazil?" she asked. "Why would you even think to go there? We've much to do here. We must continue to fight, to save Johnston Oaks."

Craig turned to face her, his face lined with worry. "Sam, Franklin is part of a new movement," he said. "He is the leader of a Brazilian movement of Southerners expatriating themselves while immigrating to Brazil. It is people like Franklin and I who are leaving."

"But, why, Father?"

"For many reasons. I see a bleak future for we of the South who have fought to have freedom of choice, to have control of our own destiny, and to own slaves. The North is pushing south. One day the South will fall," he said glumly. "I don't want to be here. The Brazilian government is welcoming the Southerners with open arms. And slavery is still accepted there. We will take our slaves and make a new life for ourselves, Sam."

"But, Father, Johnston Oaks?"

"Sam, I believe you're forgetting that I am a wanted man," he said. "If not for Franklin here, I'd probably still be rotting in prison."

Samantha went to stand over Franklin, her jaw set.

"And, Franklin, how is it that you knew about my father and where he was?" she asked.

"Word spreads," Franklin explained. "One prisoner escapes, they tell of other prisoners. It was on a voyage to Brazil when I came across this man who had just escaped the Springfield prison. He spoke of your father. Upon my return to the States, I arranged his escape."

"Then you have already been to Brazil?" she softly asked.

"Your father knew before his last journey on the *Magnolia* that I planned to leave," Franklin said hoarsely. "We didn't tell you because we didn't want you to worry about Johnston Oaks, with my not being there to see to its welfare. This is another reason why he so eagerly took you with him on that last doomed voyage."

"So much is falling into place," Samantha said beneath her breath.

"I've already got a house in Brazil. A plantation house has even now been built and readied for your father," Franklin added. "My slaves have already been transported there." He rose and looked nervously toward her. "My house needs a woman. This would be an ideal time— to—to become my wife, Samantha."

Samantha's insides knotted. She swung away from him so that he couldn't see her look of distaste. He deserved to be treated better by her. She was grateful that he had arranged her father's release. But she was not grateful enough to marry him. That special event would be reserved for just one man: Troy.

She suddenly panicked. Troy! she thought desperately to herself. If she traveled to Brazil, he would never know how to find her! What was she to do?

"It's a must, Sam," Craig said, going to her, hugging

her to him. "If we don't go to Brazil, well, if the South falls, so will I. I'll be shot for sure, Sam. I hope you understand. We must go to Brazil."

"Johnston Oaks?" she choked. "What's to become of it?"

"Perhaps one day we can return."

"But it will go to ruin."

"It will anyway," he said hoarsely. "But at least I'll be alive. I will be safe in Brazil, Sam. I'm not one to run, but things have changed. I have changed."

"It's all so sad, Father."

"Yes. Very," he sighed. "But you are willing to do what must be done, aren't you?"

"For you? I'd do anything," she whispered. "For so long, I thought you were dead. How wonderful it is that you are here. It feels so good to be hugged by you, Father. It makes me feel like I'm a little girl again."

"Ah, if only you could be. Things were so innocent then, baby."

"Poor Julia," Samantha said, again remembering how blankly Julia looked at her. "I guess she will also go with us to Brazil?"

"I see no other way for her."

Samantha eased from his arms and looked up into his eyes. "Father, I guess I still don't quite understand about Brazil. What prompted Franklin to go there?"

"I failed to mention that Lincoln has issued a preliminary Emancipation Proclamation, freeing the slaves of the Confederate States. If we don't take our slaves away with us now, we will lose them for sure."

He went and slumped down in a chair, his shoulders heavy. "The land is being ruined by war. The South is no longer attractive economically, socially, or politically," he grumbled. "We will leave this land of desolation to those who are making it. In Brazil, land is cheap and payments can be long deferred. Slavery still exists, an inducement for any Southerner who cannot tolerate or understand a free Negro population. The lower South is destined to be overrun by Negroes."

He kneaded his brow. "I'm being sought for two reasons, Sam," he said. "For helping form the Confederate States of America and blockade-running. I have no future here, Sam. None at all."

"Say no more, Father. I truly understand. I shall begin preparing for the voyage, even this night."

Samantha was torn by feelings. She was happy that her father was alive but saddened that they had been forced to leave their land, their country. Also, she knew that she now definitely would never see Troy again.

# Chapter Twenty-Three

Samantha swept up the spiral staircase to the second floor and headed for her bedroom, but stopped abruptly when she saw Jewel close the door to another room. Samantha's spine stiffened as she knew that that had to be the room where Julia had been taken. Though Samantha didn't want to think the worst about anybody, she still couldn't believe that Julia was all that harmed mentally. Samantha had known Julia for too long and understood too well Julia's ploys of acting the innocent, frail lady, to draw attention her way. Why would it be different now than before? Surely a rape hadn't affected her so harshly. It was common knowledge that Julia welcomed a man, any man in her bed. Perhaps even such slime as Marion Yarborough.

With her lips set in a narrow line she decided that, before going to her own room, she would first go to Julia and ply her with questions. Somehow Julia would be drawn out of her pretended state, if it *was* pretense. It would be Julia's dislike of her cousin that would be the cause for her to lose her composure. Julia would not stand by, wordless, and let Samantha get the last word!

Jewel waddled toward Samantha, her dark eyes showing worry in them. When she met Samantha's approach, Jewel took Samantha's hands in hers. She looked up into Samantha's eyes. "That po' baby," she sighed. "She jus' don' show no spunk at all. What are we gonno do, Miss Samantha?"

Samantha cringed. Again it was happening. Julia was managing to twist whomever she pleased around her little finger. And in doing so, she was again going to cause another's loyalties to switch from Samantha to herself. Samantha could see the writing on the wall. Jewel would feel that Julia needed her the most because Julia was pitifully ailing.

The same old jealousy gnawed away at Samantha's insides, and she hated herself for such a weakness, yet she was unable to shake it, knowing that she had already lost Jewel's devoted attentions to Julia.

"Julia will be all right in time," Samantha found herself saying, her loyalties to Jewel causing her the need to reassure her lest Jewel fret and stew when it surely wasn't needed.

"But she jus' stares into space as though nothin' matters to her," Jewel said. She released Samantha's hands and walked away from her, slowly shaking her head back and forth.

"Po', po' baby," Jewel continued to say. "Po', helpless baby."

"That does it," Samantha hissed, storming to the door which housed Julia behind it. Taking a deep breath and quietly clearing her throat, she barged on into the room, catching Julia completely off guard.

Samantha watched, wide-eyed, as Julia made her last

337

bounce on the bed, laughing, very much full of life. And when Julia discovered Samantha there she slipped from the bed, scarlet-faced, clasping her hands nervously together before her.

Samantha straightened her back, her green eyes flashing angrily as she moved further into the room after closing the door behind her.

"You are despicable," Samantha hissed. "Julia, how long did you think you could get away with this charade?"

Julia dared Samantha with her eyes. "Charade?" she said icily. "What on earth are you talking about, cousin?"

Samantha stopped directly in front of Julia and looked down at her, again glad to be the taller of the two. Julia had always hated having to look up at her cousin. "You can ask that?" Samantha said incredulously. "Lord, Julia, you have everyone fooled. Why are you doing this?"

In her delicate, lace-trimmed yellow silk dress, Julia swung away from Samantha and went to a window, staring down from it. "I have my reasons," she said quietly. "This time I have more reason than ever before to draw attention to myself, Samantha."

Samantha couldn't believe that Julia was actually confessing to her game of deceit. She was almost speechless from the confession. But determined to find out what was behind Julia's needs, she went and stood beside her and let her gaze follow Julia's dedicated stare downward. A numbness settled over Samantha as she saw that it was her father who was the recipient of the look of stardust now in Julia's eyes.

"No," Samantha gasped. "You wouldn't, Julia. Not

my—father!"

Julia's head jerked around, her facial features soft and beautiful as never before. "Samantha, now do you understand?" she murmured.

"I hope I don't," Samantha said dryly.

"I love him," Julia whispered, desperately clasping onto Samantha's hands. "Honest. I do."

"Julia, no. I can't believe it. Why?"

"I've never met such a gentleman before," Julia said, dropping her hands away from Samantha. She again faced the window, leaning on its sill, straining her neck to follow Craig as he walked toward the stable. "And the way he looks at me? It's as though he loved me from our first eye contact."

"Lord, Julia," Samantha said, covering her mouth with a hand. "Don't play games with my father. Why, he's even your uncle."

Julia now challenged Samantha with flashing eyes. "Not by blood ties, he isn't," she snapped. "I shall have him, Samantha, if he wants me, no matter what you say, think or do. I've never felt this way about a man before. I can't let him go. I shall never feel the same about a man again. I know it."

"If you love him so much why are you playing such a cruel game with him?" Samantha hissed.

"Don't you see, Samantha? I must show that I am shattered by the rape. Your father expects it. He seems the sort that would even want to marry a virgin," Julia said in a rush of words. "And I'm so young. I must win his love to even make him forget that he is old enough to be my father."

"I won't let you get away with this," Samantha warned. "I shall tell Father everything. He will even send you north on the next stage. Your game is over."

"I wouldn't do that if I were you," Julia said, lifting the skirt of her dress, prancing to the dresser to lift a hairbrush from it. In slow, even strokes she began brushing her long curls into smooth golden strands down her back.

"And why shouldn't I?"

"Your father has been a lonely man. Am I right, Samantha?"

"I can't deny that. Mother has been dead for some time now."

"Do you wish to see him be alone forever, Samantha?"

"I'd rather see him alone than with you."

"You're being a mite selfish now, aren't you, cousin?"

"Ha! You can say that? You've been nothing but selfish all of your life, Julia. You've always wanted everything your way. Your parents spoiled you because they weren't able to have any more children."

"Was that my fault?" Julia idly shrugged.

"No, that wasn't. But now you are a mature adult who knows better."

"Wanting your father. Is that so wrong? What's selfish about that? I'm thinking of him. I want to make him happy."

"Who are you trying to convince? Me or yourself?" Samantha chided.

"Samantha, please," Julia sighed. She placed the brush back on the dresser and stretched her arms above her head. "Please leave me be. It was such a tiring trip. I do need to rest."

"Poor, poor Julia," Samantha tormented. "And, yes, I'll leave you. I have to have a private conference with my father."

Julia's eyes grew wide, her face losing its peach color. She rushed to Samantha and grabbed her arm. "You can't, Samantha," she pleaded. "I *do* love him. I will be faithful to him. Give me a chance. Let me prove this to you—to him."

"If you fail in the test, my father will be the loser," Samantha said, her voice breaking with worried emotion.

"I won't fail him," Julia said, begging with her eyes. "And, Samantha, Brazil is such a desolate place."

"Ah-hah!" Samantha exclaimed, jerking away from Julia. "Now I understand. You're worrying about how few available gentlemen there will be in Brazil for your flirtations, so you will snare my father for your needs before even reaching Brazil."

"Oh, why must you be so suspicious?" Julia sighed.

"With you, one must always be on one's toes," Samantha scoffed. Then she smiled smugly. "I don't know why I'm worried so much. My father is a smart man. He won't let himself be fooled by the likes of you."

"You just won't believe me, will you, Samantha, that my feelings are sincere about Craig?"

Samantha blanched. "And he is now Craig to you?" she said incredulously. "He is no longer Uncle Craig?"

"It would not seem appropriate to address one's future husband as 'uncle,' now would it?" Julia said smoothly, her eyes innocently wide.

"Lord," Samantha gasped, then jerked with a start when a light tapping on the door drew her thoughts away from her cousin.

Julia's hands went to her cheeks which were suddenly aflame with color. "Samantha, maybe it's him," she anxiously whispered. Then her hands went to her skirt, straightening its folds. "Do I look all right? Oh, I must. I

341

never want to disappoint him."

Stunned, Samantha watched Julia in what appeared to be real concern over her appearance. There was an anxiousness about Julia that Samantha had never witnessed before. Could her spoiled cousin truly have fallen for a man twice her age? A man who hadn't let himself show feelings for women, not even his one and only wife?

The knocking persisted. Julia inched toward the door.

"And how are you to explain your sudden recovery?" Samantha asked, laughing softly.

"Craig will be so glad to see that I am better, he won't question it," Julia murmured, placing her hand on the doorknob. She took a deep breath then slowly opened the door, swallowed by heartbeats in seeing Craig there, looking down at her with his crisp green eyes charged with the same dark emotion as always when he looked at her. It stirred her insides so to be looked at in such a way, spreading warmth throughout her. She swallowed hard as she lifted a hand toward him.

"I'm so glad it is you," she said sweetly. "As you see, I have recovered my full faculties. I knew you would be happy for me."

Craig took her delicate hand in his and lifted it to his lips, mesmerized by her loveliness, again seeing so much in her that he saw in his late wife. Was it her eyes? Her hair? Her frailness? No matter. It was the same as reliving his younger days, when freshly in love. Ah, how he had missed the tingle, the aliveness that being in love brought to one's life. He hadn't let himself fully love his wife after realizing that there had been a man before him who had taken her virginity away. He had been wrong to deny himself the passion that she had offered him after

342

their wedding night. And with Julia, could he even dare to think of the possibility of such shared passions?

But he did know that with her he could forget that she had lost her virginity. It had been forcibly taken! It had not been of her doing! She even deserved to be protected from any future such assaults.

He devotedly pressed his lips against her hand, then let her draw it back to herself. "Julia, my dear, how relieved I am to see you so improved," he said, not wanting to let himself fully wonder about the suddenness of this recovery. All that mattered was that she had snapped out of her trancelike state. Now he could tell her how he felt about her. And it had to be soon. With the uncertain future that lay ahead of them all, time did not afford one to pursue a lady slowly.

Julia gave Samantha a guarded glance. "It is because of Samantha," she murmured. "She said so much to me to make—to make me remember."

Craig smiled at Samantha as he stepped on into the room. "Sam, hon, you must feel really grand, seeing what you've been capable of doing," he said. Then he frowned at Julia. "I only hope that you haven't recalled the—uh—painful moments of the past months." He was afraid that the rape could cloud her thoughts of ever trusting a man again. Ah, what waste, if that were the case.

Julia lowered her eyes. "One cannot forget such a thing all that easily," she said softly. Then her eyes lifted, all wide and blue. "But I no longer will let it affect me. Truly I won't."

"Ah, I am so glad," Craig said, stepping up to her, placing his powerful arms about her, drawing her into his embrace. "God, I'm so glad, Julia."

Samantha stifled a sob, seeing the longing in her

father's eyes, understanding such longings. She now realized that she had already lost him to Julia. Yes, he had been given back to her in life. Could she lose him again so soon? She knew this to be so, for she had never seen her father be attentive to any lady before, not even his *wife*.

She inched on past the embraced couple and out into the hallway, closing the door quietly behind her, leaving a part of her heart where her father stood, surely now lost to her, this time forever. And she would not talk with him about Julia; tell of Julia's flighty, loose ways. He had made his choice, be it right or wrong, and he would have to learn to live with it. Samantha had never been her father's keeper and now was not the time to start.

Julia's insides melted as Craig's steel arms enfolded her. Her eyes turned up, drinking in the sight of him. She had always searched for the proper man in whose presence she could feel fully protected. It was especially so now, after having been so cruelly raped by the evil man in Springfield. It had not been altogether a charade of weakness these past weeks while she was in Craig's presence. The rapist had placed a keen fear into her heart and had caused her to carry this fear with her day and night. Her waking hours as well as her restless nights had been filled with the man with the smiling scar. When he had taken her sexually, it had been with such hunger he had become brutal, almost ripping her apart with his maddening thrusts. She knew that it would take a gentle, caring man to erase such a nightmare of pain and degradation. Ironically, she had found such a man in Craig Johnston, and hopefully, he would love her in the same way as she now loved him.

"Are you truly all right, Julia?" Craig asked throatily, now seeing her eyes pooled with tears.

"I am now that you are here," she murmured. "Do you know how I've grown to feel about you?"

"How could I? You were unable to even say, until now. It's a miracle how you've snapped out of it so quickly."

She lowered her eyes. "What happened to me in Springfield," she whispered. "It is a thing that nightmares are made of."

"Then you do remember, Julia?"

She again lifted her eyes to his. "How could one possibly forget?" she softly cried.

"I will help you forget," Craig said, his lips softly trembling. "That is, if you will let an old man such as myself."

"Old?" Julia said, lifting a hand to place it tenderly against his cheek. "Never. To me you are anything but old."

"What are you saying, Julia?" Craig asked huskily.

"I am saying that I want you, only you, to be the one to fill my days, and nights. Yes, you, you alone, can help me forget."

"Julia, you are my—my—niece."

"Not by blood ties."

"You are so young."

"Only in age."

"You—you are so beautiful."

"Enough to kiss?"

"Do you want me to kiss you?"

"Do you want to?"

"Hell yes."

"Then please—please do."

His lips lowered softly and slowly to hers and kissed

345

her with such a lazy warmth, her knees weakened. She twined her long fingers through his thick red hair, and for the first time in her life knew the true joy of a kiss. Before it had always been a part of a game; seeing just how many men she could make fall in love with her.

But now all games were a thing of the past. There would only be one man, and she wondered how she deserved him. She was aware of how long his bed had been empty.

"Julia," Craig whispered as he drew his lips away from hers. His hands framed her face, his eyes glazed. "My sweet, sweet, Julia."

"Do you want me?" she whispered, her eyes wide and innocent. "I mean fully want me? I feel it in your kiss and in the trembling of your hands."

"Will you marry me, Julia?"

"Yes, oh yes," she softly cried.

"Though the asking is so sudden?"

"I understand. We musn't waste any time. Who knows what the morrow will bring."

"Exactly my thoughts, Julia."

"When shall we marry?"

"Before the ship leaves for Brazil. It will be a simple ceremony."

"But before then—do you want me?" she softly asked. "I understand needs. I am willing, Craig, if you wish to take me sexually."

"I wish to," he said and laughed. "But things will be properly done between us. We shall hurry the marriage ceremony along. By this time tomorrow evening we can share our love as man and wife."

"I shall make you a good wife," Julia sighed, quivering as he softly kissed the tip of her nose.

346

"I shall be a devoted husband," Craig answered.

Samantha went to her bedroom window and stared up at the black velvet stretch of sky where stars sparkled like sequins. She gasped when she saw the streak that fell suddenly toward the earth.

"A falling star," she whispered, a shudder enveloping her. She had always been told by her grandmother that a falling star represented someone's dying. She was quickly reminded of her grandparents' deaths, and sadness swept through her. But a falling star now had to mean a future death and she had to wonder whose.

# Chapter Twenty-Four

Samantha was burdened with sadness as she stood out away from Johnston Oaks, surveying everything, knowing that even by nightfall it would all be but a memory to her. Everything was eerily quiet. She looked toward the slaves' quarters. Even the slaves were gone, being led this very moment to Franklin's ship at the dock where preparations were being made to leave for Brazil.

Under the cover of dark, Samantha would once more be on board a ship that would be eluding the northern warships. If they succeeded, it would be the last, for a new home was to be established in Brazil, leaving Johnston Oaks to gather cobwebs of time.

Dusk was approaching, the sun dipping low in the sky. A soft breeze fluttered the silk skirt of Samantha's dress up and around her ankles. Her hair lay loose and long in its fiery reds across her bare shoulders where the bodice was swept low, yet not too revealing.

Her chest rose and fell with her easy, quiet breathing as she toyed with the trimming of lace at the edge of her long sleeves. She hated good-byes even if they were directed toward an inanimate object like her house. A part of her would always remain there, as though she were only leaving for a summer jaunt to her grandparents' farm, to return to the Carolinas again in late summer.

A choked sob rose from her throat. She covered her mouth with a hand, still having not fully accepted the fate of her grandparents. As each morning blossomed into a full day, hate grew stronger inside her against Marion Yarborough. Somehow she would avenge her grandparents' deaths. He was the only man who could have the smiling scar of which Julia had made mention.

"But I must forget for now," she determinedly whispered. "I've some minor details to see to in the house. What furniture hasn't been loaded on board the ship must be covered. One day I will return. I must."

Lifting the skirt of her dress up into her arms, she swung around and began walking toward the house, inhaling the jasmined fragrance of the flowers in the garden and already missing the avenue of oaks with its moss-hung trees. What could she expect to find in Brazil but hotter temperatures and natives who spoke not one word of English?

Samantha already felt isolated just thinking about it, with the wide span of ocean to be at her front door, closing her off from life as she had always known it.

"And Troy," she whispered, her heart carrying a heavy ache inside it, growing heavier as the hour grew closer to sailing time. "My love, oh, my love."

Samantha stopped with a start when she saw a figure of a man off to the right of her, in the growth of stately live oaks. She tensed and began edging in the direction of the house, fearing that this man might be a Union soldier or even perhaps an escaped convict from the shackles in Charleston.

Whoever he was, the man was not one with whom she would wish to make an acquaintance, for he was obviously trying to keep his presence a secret by the way in which he was approaching Johnston Oaks.

The man darted from behind another tree, to another. Samantha felt frozen to the ground. "Lord, what am I to do?" Samantha whispered. The man had moved so quickly, he had only been a blur to her. And now, she expected him to fully reveal himself and make a mad dash toward her and use her to gain entrance into the house, with possible thoughts to rob—or—rape.

"I must get to the house," she murmured. "My pistol!"

She broke into a run, her breath catching in her throat as she tripped on a loose stone in the front walk and toppled to the ground in a heap of skirt and petticoats. She cringed when she heard the haste of footsteps approaching behind her. Pushing herself up she once more began to run, panting hard. And when she finally reached the lower step and lifted a foot toward it, the familiar voice made her stop and become swallowed up by heartbeats.

"Sam, stop," Troy said, running hard, yet guardedly watching on all sides of him. He had seen the ship at the dock. He was glad that he had chosen to drop the anchor of his ship further up the river, in a hidden cove. It had been hard waiting since sunup for daylight to begin to fade again, to feel safe to leave his ship on foot.

It had been pure torture to be so close to Samantha and to control his need to see her. But in these troubled times the black screen of night had become the time to transact business instead of the light of day.

"Troy! Lord, Troy!" Samantha softly cried, now running to meet him. She fell into his arms, and he lowered his lips to hers and kissed her. His fingers twined through her hair. Samantha's hands glided across his shoulders, and she clung to him as never before. He was a dream materializing. His kiss was sweet, his body firm against her as she wriggled more into its curve.

Then he released her and looked with heavy lashes down at her. "Sam, I had to come. Damn if I know how I waited this long," he said huskily. "But I just couldn't come. Things are a hell of a mess out there—so harried. But I should have come anyway. Darling, I've missed you. Tell me that you've missed me as much."

"I've missed you. I've *missed* you," Samantha softly cried. "And, Troy, I'm so sorry for having doubted you even for that one moment. I should have known that you wanted to come to me. Thank God you're even alive."

"The ship at the dock," he said, nodding in that direction. "Whose? And are we safe to be together for a little while? When night falls I must return to my ship so it can sail safely from the harbor."

"Troy, you've come just in time," Samantha said, taking his hands, squeezing them. "It's as though God sent you, knowing that I would be gone after tonight."

"Gone? Where? Who with?"

"The ship that you are seeing is Franklin LaFontaine's. I believe you remember my mention of him?"

"How could I forget? Sam, don't tell me that you're giving in to his demands of marriage because you couldn't make it here at Johnston Oaks, without your father."

"Troy, no, it's not what you think," she murmured. "Father is even alive."

"What?" he gasped.

Samantha peered toward the river and then up at the windows of the house. She felt as though she had time to spare before her father's return since he had just left and much had to be loaded onto the ship.

"Come in the house with me," she urged, already half dragging him by a hand up the steps. "We'll go to the privacy of my room. I've much to tell you."

"Sam, I don't have long."

"Neither do I, Troy. Please just come on. Time is wasting." She had plans to give him the map, though he seemed to have lost interest in it. Yes, she would give it to him after they talked. Talk was more important, and if time did not allow anything else, she would give him the map sometime in the future. Something told her that they would have a future now that he returned to her. It gave her the chance to tell him where she was being forced to travel with her father and Franklin. Thank God she was even given the opportunity to tell him!

They sneaked through the quiet house and on up the beautiful sweep of stairs until they were inside Samantha's bedroom.

The bed was stripped of sheets and blankets but that did not keep Troy from guiding Samantha down upon it. He stretched out atop her, his lips now at the hollow of her satin throat, his hands possessing her breasts through her dress.

Samantha's cheeks flamed. Her breath was being swept clean away from her by the hunger in his lips and hands. She ached with desire of him. Her pulse raced, and the pain between her thighs rose higher, searing her insides.

Yet she knew that time did not allow the total embrace that was required to feed these desires.

352

"Troy," Samantha said, breathless. "We can't. We musn't."

"We must. My nights have been hell with want of you."

"Troy, please."

He lifted the skirt of her dress and slipped her petticoats down and away from her, then her delicate underpanties. He placed his hands over the patch of hair that guarded her womanhood. A tremor coursed through him when he felt its utter softness. Skillfully, he slipped a single finger up inside her, the soft wetness there making him become almost wild with this passion that plagued him.

Perspiration beaded Samantha's brow. She licked her dry lips seductively then lowered her hand to his man's hardness. She knew she could not be denied what she hungered for, merely because a ship awaited them both. The thought that these were two separate ships, carrying them in two separate directions, made her even more determined to be wholly with him. If not now, perhaps never.

Brazenly, she unfastened his breeches and slipped a hand inside. Her breath was stolen from her when she touched his swollen need of her.

"Sam," Troy said, a guttural moan surfacing from deep inside him. "God."

"Troy, love me. Make it so I can feel it, forever."

Troy lowered his breeches, slipping them and his shoes off while Samantha eased off her shoes and then her dress. But he left his frock coat and shirt on, fearing time was against them. He reached his hands to her breasts and ran his fingers around them in soft circles. Lowering his mouth to a breast, he licked its taut tip, making it

353

harden against his tongue. And then he spread himself completely over her and gently eased himself inside her.

Samantha sighed. She closed her eyes and let ecstasy fill her brain as he stroked her gently, then harder. She wrapped her legs about his hips, drawing him more fully inside her.

His lips now searched hers out. She could feel them trembling. She placed her hands to his cheeks and caressed him as she let her tongue meet his entrance into her mouth.

They rose. They fell. Their breaths mingled. And as their pleasure peaked in soft quiverings of their body, they still clung, their lips once more tasting bliss in their height of rapture.

Samantha was the first to break this sensuous, almost magic moment. She leaned her lips away from his. "Darling, we must get dressed," she whispered. "Seems we've done more than talk." She looked toward the window, seeing pale orange streaks in the sky as the sun cast its last rays across it.

"Yes. I believe so," Troy said. He brushed a kiss across her lips and her breasts, then rose from the bed, followed by her. Quickly, they once more dressed while Samantha told about her father's return, Julia's misfortune, and even more sadly, about her grandparents' deaths. Then she spoke of Brazil and the plans to travel there.

"Brazil?" Troy gasped. "Sam—"

The bedroom door opened abruptly. Craig stood in the doorway, staring from Samantha to Troy. His hand went swiftly to the pistol belted at his waist and soon had it aimed at Troy.

"Step aside," Craig growled, nodding toward Troy. "Get away from my daughter. Sam, come here. Quickly."

"Father, don't," Samantha said, rushing to his side.

"Who is this intruder?" Craig growled. "What the hell is he doing here, in your bedroom, with you?"

"Father, he's not an enemy. He's—"

"At this moment in time, everyone is considered an enemy," Craig shouted. "Sam, how did he get up here?"

"I invited him," she said stubbornly. "Father, this is Troy Gilbert. He's the one who rescued me from the sinking *Magnolia*. He rescued your crew. Put your pistol away. He can be trusted."

Franklin appeared at the door. He slipped into the room, past Craig and Samantha. "Damn. What have we here?" he gasped, looking Troy up and down.

Troy glared at Franklin, realizing that he had just come face-to-face with the man who might be a threat to Samantha on the voyage to Brazil. He doubled his fists at his side and kept them there by the barrel of Samantha's father's pistol.

"Get a length of cloth from the curtain, Franklin," Craig ordered. "And tie this gent to the post of Sam's bed."

Samantha clasped her hands together before her, frantic. She pleaded with her eyes. "Father, Troy is no threat!" she screamed. "Why are you doing this insane thing?"

"Sam, we must be allowed to make the journey to Brazil without any interference from anyone."

"Troy won't interfere!" she pleaded. She swung around and anxiously faced Troy. "Tell him that you won't, Troy! Tell him that he's wrong!"

"Seems anything I say will be ignored," Troy grumbled. "Your father appears to be a desperate man. Desperate men do desperate things."

355

Samantha swung around and looked up at her father. "Please, Father."

"I don't know what the hell he was doing up here in your room, and I don't have time to find out," Craig said thickly. "All I know is that if he knows our destination, then he is a threat."

Troy growled beneath his breath as Franklin shoved him toward the bed and forced him to stand against a poster of the canopied bed. He flinched as the strips of cloth cut into the flesh of his wrists as Franklin tied him securely to the bed.

"No," Samantha sobbed.

Seeing that Troy was secured, Craig motioned with the pistol toward Samantha. "Hurry to the ship, Sam," he said flatly.

"No! I can't!"

Craig pointed the pistol in her direction. "I don't know what this man is to you, but, by damn, Sam, you'll do as I say," he snarled. "Even if I have to make you do it by gunpoint."

"You wouldn't."

"Wouldn't I?"

"Father!"

"My life is at stake here, Sam."

"Sam, he's desperate! Do as he says!" Troy yelled.

"But, Troy," Samantha said, stifling a sob behind her hand.

"Go, Sam!" Troy shouted.

"Yes. Move," Craig snapped, taking Samantha by an arm, leading her from the room.

"Father, I don't even know you anymore," Samantha cried. "How could you do this?"

"Sam, just get to the boat. We'll discuss this later."

Samantha laughed hysterically. "Later?" she said. "And Troy? What will become of him?"

"I do what I must," Craig grumbled. "Please understand, Sam."

"Never!" she cried. "Never!"

When she was led outside, with Franklin now following close behind them, Samantha took one last look up at her bedroom window, wondering about Troy's fate, somehow not even caring about her own.

Then she looked wildly about her. "Checkers!" she said. "Where's Checkers? We can't leave him behind!"

"We can't worry about him," Craig said. "We tried to find him when Jewel was leading Julia to the ship. Checkers has chosen a wrong time to be sniffing out a female companion."

Samantha struggled against his firm grip but knew that it was useless. She was rushed across the gangplank and soon saw the sails bellying against the wind and out to sea, Franklin's ship having successfully eluded the warships.

"Troy," she whispered, her hair whipping in the sea breeze, the sky a dark velvet overhead. "Good-bye, my love. I'm so very, very sorry."

# Chapter Twenty-Five

There were white puffs of clouds skipping along the far horizon, the sun outlining them in orange as it crept low behind them.

Samantha stood at the ship's rail, absorbing the warm sea breeze before going below deck to her cabin for another full, lonely night with only her memories as her companion. She had left instructions for a tub to be taken to her private quarters, and for it to be readied with water for her one pleasure that she looked forward to each night. She was glad that she had thought to place her bottle of bubble bath in her valise. She could crawl into her bath and get lost beneath the umbrella of floating suds.

Dressed in a high-necked shirt and gathered, dark cotton skirt, she felt she looked like the picture of spinsterhood, hoping this would discourage the ship's crew from lusting after her. Even her hair had been drawn up into a tight bun atop her head. She didn't want to think of men—any men.

Yet she was puzzled by Franklin's attitude toward her

since beginning the journey to Brazil. He hadn't yet approached her in any way except with his eyes. He seemed to be watching her every move, yet he never so much as even smiled at her. It was as if he were studying her, looking at her like he hadn't ever really known her.

This gave Samantha a sense of foreboding, never knowing quite what to expect next from the man who had made chase of her since she had blossomed into full womanhood. "Perhaps it's because Father is so close on this ship," she whispered. "Franklin is afraid to make a move toward me in the way he most prefers."

Shrugging, she decided to take one last, lingering look at the beauty of the vastness of blue which stretched out before her. Nary a whitecap disturbed the serene setting, though the sails whipped above her in the breeze and the mast groaned and creaked almost ominously.

She licked the saltiness of the sea water from her lips and wiped a desultory spray of water from her face. Then she blinked her eyes and peered more intensely toward the horizon when she saw a movement of white. "Is that another ship's sail?" she whispered.

And then it was gone, almost as quickly as it had materialized. All that Samantha could see again were the clouds and the sky painted with pale orange streaks, with the sun sinking lower in the sky.

Samantha sighed heavily. "It was only my eyes playing tricks on me," she murmured. "Clouds can take on the shapes of many things in one's mind, especially when one is lonely."

Swinging around and away from the rail, Samantha went below deck, into a dimly lighted corridor which led to all the ship's various cabins. She went past several, eyeing one lingeringly in particular, knowing that behind its closed door was Julia and her father.

Samantha couldn't help but feel the same old pangs of jealousy toward her cousin. Julia had managed to draw Craig Johnston fully into her web of passion by tricking him into marrying her. Day in and day out Julia and Craig had spent time alone in the master cabin. Never had Samantha thought her father could have such feelings for a woman. With Julia he had forgotten anyone else even existed. It was hard for Samantha to accept; this different side to her father. But he did appear happier than ever before in his life and this, at least, made Samantha glad for him.

Hopefully Julia wasn't performing another masterful act. Perhaps this time it was for real. Perhaps Julia truly loved her father. She did appear to be sincere when she was with him.

"God, for Father's sake, let it be so," she softly prayed. "And even for Julia's sake." Samantha remembered how Craig Johnston had turned his back on his first wife. "Yes, it could happen to Julia," she surmised. "If it could happen to my sweet mother, it could happen to my spoiled cousin!" Trying to not care or think further on it, she moved on toward her own cabin.

Craig studied Julia as she lay so peacefully asleep at his side, curled up like a kitten, purring. His gaze followed her delicate satin thighs, to her small swells of breasts with their dark, taut nipples, and the soft down of hair the color of the sun which covered the core of her womanhood.

Gently he placed a hand over that golden patch of hair between her thighs, his heart erratic, his stomach a mass of spreading warmth, a desire again kindling inside him.

Caressing her bud of pleasure he watched her face as even in her sleep she was responding to his touch. It was as if she had been poured from a mold of fine perfection: Her jawline curved gently; her lips were seductively full, the straight, white line of her teeth barely exposed now as her lips softly parted in a moan. Thick lashes hid beneath them eyes of the sheerest blues. Her hair was like golden spun silk spread out beneath her head on the white satin, lace-trimmed pillow.

"Craig?" Julia whispered, her lashes now fluttering open. She giggled. "What a way to awaken. Darling, we've made love most of the day. Shall we even again? You know that I'm being driven wild again with your caress."

Craig ran his hands up and down the slender length of her body, his fingers trembling when he felt the utter softness. "I can never get enough of you," he said huskily. Her breasts swelled beneath his hands, the nipples becoming ripening blossoms, nectar to be tasted and savored.

"My poor baby," Julia sighed, twining her fingers through his hair. "You were without a woman for too long. Let me make up for your lost years."

"In one day?" he chuckled. Then a drunken expression fell upon his face as she guided his lips to a breast.

"I'm yours," she said throatily. "Enjoy me, my love. Fully enjoy me."

Craig felt the tension mount in his loins, a tightness that pained him, almost excruciating in its unmerciful grip. But he had to go slow, make his young wife see that he was as skilled a lover as a younger husband would be. He had to be virile, patient; not want the flames to burn out inside him without first giving her full pleasure.

Julia licked her lips and closed her eyes luxuriously when she felt his mouth close over a breast. He spiraled his tongue hotly around the throbbing nipple. He gently held her against him. She had never known that love could be this way. Always before it had been wild and demanding, almost as though she and her lovers had been searching for something unattainable.

But now? She felt as though she were spread out on soft sand with the effervescent foam of the surf washing gently over her, the sun warm and soft on her bare flesh.

"Darling Julia," Craig said, looking down at her as he rose to place his body along hers, feeling the sweet softness of her almost reaching up to meet his approach.

Before Julia had always enjoyed controlling a man. But with Craig it was different. She wanted to share, to give, more than take. Why, she didn't know. But she would relish these moments with her husband and hope they would never end. Thus far Samantha hadn't ruined anything by telling the sordid truth of Julia's past. But Julia lived with this dread. Samantha could, if she wanted, destroy all of Julia and Craig's future happiness. Julia had to hope that Samantha's love for her father would cause Samantha to think twice before telling him anything. Even Samantha had been able to see that Craig Johnston was happy in his newfound way of life which included a wife.

But once in Brazil would things change? Would Craig be too occupied, then, by needs other than that of a woman? Julia knew that Craig felt that owning land was as important as romance.

"Always love me," Julia said, a soft pleading edging her voice. "Always need me, Craig. I would surely die without you."

His eyes were dark with shadowed passion, and his face was blotched with color where his whiskers grew red beneath the coarseness of his skin. He touched her lips wonderingly with a forefinger, tracing the ruby red line.

"Darling, don't ever say that you'd die without me," he softly scolded. "No one should be that important to you, ever."

"I want to be that important to you," she said, openly pouting.

"You are," he chuckled. He brushed a gentle kiss across her lips. "See how I don't practice what I preach? I'd also die without you."

She drew a ragged breath as his lips once more found her breast, and his teeth teasingly nipped it. "You have me," she whispered. "Forever and ever."

He looked into her eyes, his fingers enjoying the softness of her breast. "Darling, we must face reality," he said thickly.

"What reality is that?" she said, locking a leg up and over him to draw his swollen man's strength more firmly against her abdomen.

"That you will outlive me for probably twenty, or even thirty years," he answered.

"Oh, pooh," she said with a toss of her head. "You will outlive me. You'll see, my love."

She framed his face between her hands, raking her eyes favorably over him, seeing his ruddy complexion, green eyes, and red hair, and loving it all. She loved even the rudimentary lines which were at the corners of his eyes and around his mouth.

Strange that she could never really love a man before. But he was different. He elicited the sincere side to her nature which had never before been explored and developed.

"Darling Craig, surely we've more to talk about than who will outlive whom," she softly teased. She guided his lips down to hers and kissed him, then spiraled her tongue between his lips, curling the sensual curves of her body against him.

He entered her easily, then thrust deeply, this raging hunger making him mindless. She answered him by lifting her hips, no longer the frail, porcelainlike doll that should be carefully treated. She was now an inferno, flaming hotly against him.

Craig moaned. His hands went feverishly over her, unable to get enough of her, consumed by needs before unknown to him. Suddenly she had become an unleashed tigress, her fingernails scratching his back, her body writhing and arching, draining him, almost seeming to draw him right into her.

"God," Craig groaned, feeling the web of rapture ensnaring him as Julia now sank her fingernails into his sleek buttocks, forcing him to stay locked inside her.

"I can hardly bear it, it's so beautiful," Julia purred, her eyes hazy with building passion. "Darling, darling."

Craig looked down at her, seeing her differently than before. She was no longer the gentle, sweet thing which needed to be protected. She was a vixen for sure, quite skilled in ways of making love. It wasn't skills taught her by him, and knowing this gnawed at his insides.

But the building sexual tension caused by her skills could not be denied, and he knew that this was more important now than any doubts he had that plagued him of her. And she was his wife! He had needed a wife for so long. He wouldn't let doubts come between them. What she offered him was too good to let slip away.

He kissed her with a fierce, possessive heat, hoping to make her only want him. He cupped her soft swells of breasts and harshly kneaded them, sensing that she desired this more than the gentle ways of loving. He thrust eagerly inside her, feeling the spiraling of warmth spreading in his loins, then groaned loudly as the release came in an explosive shudder.

He felt her arms clasp him tightly about the neck. Her breasts were now crushed into his chest, her love bud reaching upward to graze erotically against him, back and forth, until she arched harder into him, moaning, her eyes a haze of lustful wonder.

When the shudders ceased and Julia blinked her eyes and found Craig's crisp green eyes looking incredulously down at her, she was suddenly afraid.

"What's wrong?" she asked, gingerly placing a hand to his cheek. "Why are you looking at me in such a way, darling?"

"I'm not sure if I know," he said thickly.

"Well, you must," she said, leaning up on an elbow. She studied his expression. She felt an icy coldness splash through her. "Craig!" she demanded, rising to a sitting position as his eyes were still on her. He rose from the bed and drew his breeches on. "What is it? Did I do something wrong?"

"No," he said hoarsely, buttoning his breeches, smoothing his hands down the fly, as though subconsciously aware of himself there. "You did everything right."

"Then why do you continue to stare at me so?" she asked shakily. "It's as though you're seeing right through me." She crept from the bed and wriggled her naked curves against him. "Darling, what do you see?" she asked again.

"I'm not quite sure."

She spun away from him, pale and breathing hard. "You're frightening me, Craig," she said dryly. "Tell me what I've done. I can't bear this. You must tell me."

"If I tell you, it will hurt you."

"It hurts not knowing."

"When we made love this time?" he said, slipping into his shirt.

"Yes? What—about—it?" she barely asked.

"It wasn't *you*, Julia."

"What?" she gasped.

"It was a whore."

He slipped into his shoes and hurriedly left the cabin, leaving Julia standing, stunned, speechless.

Julia placed her fingers to her temples, slowly shaking her head back and forth, trying to clear her thoughts. Tears swam in her eyes, blurring her vision. His words echoed loudly inside her head. "Surely this is a nightmare I will soon awaken from," she sobbed. She looked down at her nudity, suddenly ashamed of her body and how it had obviously betrayed her.

Yet, how she had loved Craig—it wasn't that wantonly. There were many other ways a woman pleasured a man that could be considered whorish. What she had done had been normal, as far as she could see.

"Oh!" she stormed, stomping a bare foot on the floor. "What am I to do? I've surely lost him." Her eyes shot around her, looking for her clothes. "I must go to him," she whispered. "We must settle this now. He can't do me this way. I've done nothing wrong."

She hurried into a dress and shoes, faintly touching

366

her hair with a brush. Her thoughts went to her Aunt Grace, Craig's first wife. Flashes of remembrances were now haunting Julia. She remembered how Grace seemed so unfulfilled as a woman and how Craig had treated her so coldly. Never once had Julia seen them embrace! Even then, Julia had wondered about it. Even then she had fantasies of the handsome man with the green, brooding, moody eyes.

But Julia had only been twelve at the time, just stepping into the realms of blossoming womanhood. Only dreams were afforded a girl that age, though the girl knew to look and wonder at the crotch of a man's pants.

"What does Craig expect of a wife?" she softly argued to herself, grabbing a shawl. She placed the shawl about her shoulders, then left the cabin in a huff. She glanced momentarily at the closed door that led inside Samantha's cabin, knowing that she would be thrilled to know of the sudden rift between her father and new wife. It was as though Samantha had even, personally, planned it, every step of the way.

Glowering, Julia stormed on down the narrow, low-ceilinged hallway, then up the steps and on out to top deck. She felt the sudden rush of wind and sea spray and saw the orange-streaked sky and then the orange disc of the sun as it dipped down into the ocean, taking its last look, it seemed, as another day became history.

Then Julia saw the tall frame of her husband leaning his full weight against the ship's rail, and an ache churned through her as she felt that she had lost his respect as well as his love. Why?

Trembling, she moved to his side, holding her shawl in place as the sea breeze whipped at its fringed edges. "Craig, we must have a talk," she said, looking up at him with wavering eyes. "I just don't understand your attitude." She swallowed hard. "Lord, Craig. You even— even as much called me a whore. Why? Please tell me."

"Return to the cabin," he growled, his arms stiffening with her presence. Then his eyes softened as he met her steady gaze. "You'll take a chill, Julia. The air is quite damp and cold."

"Please don't send me away," she softly cried.

"You'll catch pneumonia," he insisted. "Now do as you're told. Return to the cabin."

"I shall not," Julia said stubbornly, defiantly lifting her chin. "I am not a child to be ordered about. I am your wife."

Craig was torn with battling emotions. A part of him wanted to love her, to understand how she loved so boldly, so wildly. Yet he knew such loving came from experience. And a part of him already hated her.

"Yes. You are my wife," he said hoarsely. Seeing her frailness and innocent wide eyes compelled him to make a sudden movement, and he soon had her imprisoned in his arms. "Damn it, Julia, I do love you. I'm sorry if I behaved like a cad. Forgive me?"

She sobbed against his chest, hugging his words to her. "You gave me such a fright," she murmured. "I've never loved before you. I didn't know how to love, until you."

Craig's face shadowed in doubt yet with her pressed against him, he could not think any further than his own desire for her.

A cold spray of sea water reached his face, sending a chill through him. He leaned away from Julia and gave her a stern look of command. "Darling, you go on to the cabin and warm yourself," he encouraged. "I'll be there shortly."

"Why not return with me now?" she brooded. "You can catch cold as easily as me."

"I've something to do and then I'll return to the cabin."

"May I ask what?"

"Yes, you may," he chuckled.

"Then, what is going to delay your return?"

"I must look in on Samantha. She's been avoiding me. I must ask her why."

Julia's heart skipped a beat, her breath becoming short. "Must you?" she shallowly questioned. "Surely she is resting."

"This time of night?" Craig laughed. "Not Sam. She's too full of life to turn in this early."

"But, Craig—"

He gave her a brief kiss, then again gave her a stern look. "No buts," he grumbled. "Do as I say. I'll be there shortly."

A movement on the horizon gave him a sudden start. He stepped away from Julia and again leaned on the ship's rail, peering intensely into the distance.

"What is it?" Julia asked, cupping a hand over her eyes to look where his eyes were directed.

Craig laughed nervously. "I thought I saw a ship's sail," he said.

Fear grabbed at Julia's insides. Any ship in these waters could cause trouble. Craig and Franklin were both wanted men. She had to wonder what would happen to a wife under such circumstances should a husband be caught and jailed.

"Well? Did you?" she dared to ask.

Craig shrugged. "It's only the evening light," he scoffed. "It plays tricks on one's eyes." Then he led Julia toward the steps. "Now do as I said. Go to the cabin. Wait for me there."

"Yes. I hear you," she sighed. "While waiting I shall busy myself washing my hair."

"It already smells of flowers," Craig said, placing his nose down into it.

"It smells of saltwater," Julia argued. "As even I do. I plan to soak quite luxuriously in a bath of sudsy water. I shan't hear anything or see anything, my love. I shall be in another world."

"Don't travel too far," Craig chuckled. "I just might want to accompany you there."

Julia was thrilled to hear his teasings, feeling as though everything just might work out between them, after all. She had learned one thing, though: to not show such heated passion while making love with her husband. While with him, she had to share only a gentle passion.

# Chapter Twenty-Six

Samantha hurried on into her cabin. She smiled when she saw the lovely copper tub and its inviting scented water. The water had even been warmed for her, evidenced by the slight haze of steam rising from it.

"Yes. A nice bubble bath is what I need to rid me of my selfish thoughts and torments," she whispered, already dropping her skirt to the floor. She shed herself quickly of her remaining garments, removed the pins from her hair and let it tumble loosely around her shoulders.

Then after sprinkling several droplets of pink liquid from her bubble bath bottle, she climbed into the tub, relishing the warmth that was now caressing her flesh as she sank down into the water's velvety depths.

"Ah," Samantha sighed, relaxing her head against the end of the tub. She lifted her hair up to hang over the edge of the tub. Her fingers splashed the water around, mixing the bubble bath mixture until the surface of the water was hidden beneath a sparkling, crystallike layer of tiny bubbles. She then crept down lower in the water, so that only the upper lobes of her breasts could be seen, where bubbles clung in their perfumed swirls.

Letting her body soak in the water, she looked lazily around her. Franklin had acquired himself a masterful, luxurious ship for his sea ventures. He had given her quite a comfortable cabin, lavishly furnished.

The usual ship's bunk had been replaced by a bed, small, yet beautiful with its solid oak headboard carved with an intricate design. A velveteen overstuffed chair in a pale orchid color matched the velveteen bedspread and miniature drape which hid the ugly porthole behind it. A fancy dressing table had a matching, velvet gathered skirt around its base, and a mirror flanked on each side by fancy kerosene wall sconces reflected the cabin's paneled walls.

"Yes, quite lovely," she sighed.

She closed her eyes and tried to keep troubled thoughts from drifting back into her brain, wanting to savor this moment of pleasure. But nothing could keep her mind still. She was constantly plagued with worry about Troy. And then there was Checkers! What had been his fate?

Footsteps out in the corridor swept Samantha's mind clean. She tensed and looked toward the door. In her haste to take her bath she had forgotten to secure the lock at the door. Her gaze went to the bed, where beneath the mattress she kept her pistol hidden. There was too much distance between her and the bed, and being in the tub put her at even more of a disadvantage should a man decide to enter her cabin to accost her.

The footsteps faded away. Samantha sighed with relief. She eyed the lock. Should she climb from the water to secure it?

Knowing the inconvenience of doing so, she scoffed to

herself and sank even more deeply into the water and once again closed her eyes. When the door slowly opened, she didn't even hear it. She was drifting off into a much-needed doze, sleep having mostly eluded her since leaving Charleston Harbor.

When a hand slipped over her mouth and she felt the most identifiable touch of steel of a pistol's barrel pressed against the bare flesh of her left shoulder, she jumped with a start, her eyes flying widely open.

"Not a peep, Samantha," Franklin whispered. "If I have to, I'll shoot you and blame it on one of my crew. I've waited long enough to get a taste of you, Samantha. If you refuse to be my wife, I'll just have to take what I want by force."

Samantha mumbled against the tight fingers clasped over her lips. Her arms flailed, her legs kicked. Water splashed crazily in every direction.

"Samantha, stop fighting back," Franklin growled. "Did you fight off Troy Gilbert? I doubt that since you so brazenly took him up into the privacy of your bedroom. All along you've been whorin' around, and I thought you were an innocent virgin. I've been played for a fool, Samantha. Now I'll get what's been denied me."

He nudged the gun deeper into Samantha's shoulder, hurting her. "Now get out of the water and go to the bed," Franklin grumbled. "To think that I furnished this cabin with you in mind, thinking you were an angel of innocence! I shouldn't have wasted my money." He laughed huskily. "I had hoped to share the bed with you, but in a much different way. I had hoped the ship's captain could speak the necessary words over us that would make us as one. But now I wouldn't have you under these circumstances. I'll take what

I want, anyhow."

Samantha's insides were cold, her thoughts muddled as to how she could squirm out of this predicament that she had found herself in. One bolt at the door and she would have been spared this. She should have been more careful, expecting as much from Franklin for so long now. It seemed that his fear of being caught had been outweighed by his carnal needs.

"Get out of the tub," Franklin snarled. "I'm going to move my hand from your mouth, but let me remind you that should you scream, I'll have no recourse but to shoot you. It would be easy enough to point an accusing finger at one of my crew. Craig would never think me capable of killing you. He still thinks that I respect and plan to marry you."

When his fingers left Samantha's mouth, she turned and boldly faced him, glaring up at him. She wiped her mouth with her wet hands, freeing herself of the vile taste of him.

"You beast," she quietly hissed. "You'll be sorry. Father will kill you when he finds out."

"He won't believe you," Franklin argued. "He saw the slut in you that day he found that man in your bedroom."

"You're—you're despicable," Samantha said, stepping out of the tub, trying to hide herself behind her hands, shivering from both fear and anger. "If you think Father would believe you over me, you're daft."

Franklin unbuttoned the top button of his shirt with his left hand while still holding her at bay with the pistol in his right. He motioned with the gun toward the bed. "Get over there!" he flatly ordered. "I've wasted enough time talking."

Samantha edged toward the bed, glancing down at the

374

mattress, where beneath it lay her pistol. If she could just get him to lose his concentration!

Smiling wickedly but invitingly toward him, she went to the bed. She jerked the bedspread off and wrapped it around her, watching his eager, trembling fingers working at undressing himself.

"*On* the bed," he grumbled, tossing his shirt aside. "And remove that damn thing from around you. I've waited long enough for this. I want to see you before I take you."

"Franklin, I'm beginning to think that you don't have the nerve to see this thing through," she purposely taunted, pulling the bedspread even more tightly about her. "And now that I think about it with a more clear head, I don't think you have the guts to make me do anything."

She shook her hair back and across her shoulders as she lifted her chin haughtily.

"You'll soon see," he said, laughing throatily. He was clumsy with his shoes. But finally he had them both off and was struggling with his pants, his eyes narrow as he glared at her.

An involuntary shudder coursed through Samantha when she saw his bared manhood as he scooted his breeches down. How could she stand to let that man near her? He was even more disgusting looking unclothed than clothed. If he had been the first man whom she had seen naked, she would never have wished to see another!

She crept away from the bed to stand solidly against the wall as he stepped completely out of his breeches.

"Now, my love, let me show you how a real man makes love," Franklin said, leering. He began to inch toward her, but a light tap on the door made him stop, frozen in place when Craig's voice spoke out loud and clear.

"Sam? Are you decent?" Craig asked. "I'd like to have a talk with you if you're up to company."

Samantha's pulse began to race. She felt trapped, for if she were to yell out to him, wouldn't Franklin, in his crazed state, possibly even kill her father if he burst into the room?

"Shh," Franklin warned, his eyes wild. "Act like you're asleep." He kept his pistol aimed toward Samantha while he desperately scooped his clothes up into his arms. Kicking his shoes along, he went to hunker behind where the door would open, waiting, should Craig decide to check on Samantha.

"Sam?" Craig persisted. "Hon, we need to talk. So much has been left unsaid."

"He's not going to give up. He thinks you're just being stubborn. Not asleep," Franklin harshly whispered to Samantha. "Tell him you're too tired to talk. Send him away. Tell him you'll talk to him tomorrow."

Samantha placed a hand to her throat. She was so terrified for her father's safety, she found it hard to speak.

"Tell him," Franklin growled beneath his breath.

"Sam? I know you're in there," Craig said more determinedly. He opened the door suddenly and his jaw dropped when he saw Samantha standing against the far wall, trembling, and with the bedspread wrapped around her.

"What the—" he gasped, then fell awkwardly sideways when the door was slammed hard against him.

"Father! Watch out!" Samantha screamed, seeing Franklin raise the butt of the pistol over Craig's head.

Craig looked up just in time to see the pistol, and out of

the corner of his eyes, he saw Franklin's face and then lower, his nudity. "My God!" he shouted. He swung an arm up and knocked Franklin to the floor. In one fast move he was straddling Franklin and struggling to get the gun away from him.

Samantha watched, horrified, biting her lower lip and shivering beneath her bedspread cloak. "Father, be—careful—"

The loud blast of the gun filled the small spaces of the cabin. Samantha screamed, her insides knotted. To her horror, she saw her father's body jerk with the blast and crumple to his side, away from Franklin.

"No!" Samantha cried. She clutched the bedspread as she ran toward her father, but another loud blast erupted from somewhere outside the ship, causing her to stop in mid-step.

The ship tossed right and left, and the floor trembled beneath Samantha's feet. She was pitched one way and then another and fell to her knees as another cannon fire was heard. Again the ship emitted a soft groan and swayed.

Franklin scurried to his feet and stepped into his breeches, in a state of shock upon seeing the lifeless body at his feet. But the shouts, rush of feet and more gunfire above him, on top deck, caused him to come to his senses. He fastened his breeches, ignoring Samantha who now wept over her father, then rushed from the cabin in a panic.

Samantha clutched at her father. "No," she softly cried. "Not you, too. I've nothing left! Oh, Father! I'm so sorry. I should—have—shot Franklin before you even entered the room."

Though filled with remorseful shock, Samantha was

suddenly aware of the total silence outside the cabin. The cannon fire and shouts had ceased. The ship was once more steady in the water. She couldn't help but wonder what had happened. Had a northern warship followed and overtaken Franklin's ship? She hoped so! She wanted the worst to happen to him! She would even willingly go to prison herself to insure that Franklin would go. She hoped that he would even rot there! How could he have shot and killed his very own best friend?

"Father," she cried, rocking his head back and forth on her lap. "All is lost to you now. Your hopes, your dreams. And you won't even—even be buried beside Mother at Johnston Oaks. It's unfair. Terribly unfair!"

"Everyone on top deck!" a gruff voice rang out from the corridor. "No one must stay below. All hands and passengers on top deck and be quick about it!"

Samantha sobbed into her hand, ignoring the order, not caring for anything or anyone, now that her father was dead. It seemed that in only a matter of a few weeks she had lost everything near and dear to her. What in life was fair? For her, nothing had been.

It seemed an eternity since she had heard the man's gruff warning in the corridor. Samantha sat in a stunned haze, still cradling her father's head. With her eyes, she absorbed the red of his hair, his bushy cheek-whiskers, the peaceful slope of his jaw. He seemed only asleep, as though a soft whisper speaking his name would arouse him.

"Father, I let you down," Samantha murmured. "If I had been the son that you had wanted, surely things would have been different. As it was, I was a mere daughter, one who couldn't even defend you against the likes of Franklin LaFontaine."

Anger flashed suddenly in her crisp, green eyes. "It's too late for you," she hissed. "But not for me. I shall kill him *yet*, Father."

She placed his head gently on the floor, then drew the bedspread from around her shoulders and draped it gently over him, completely covering his body. Lowering her eyes, she said a silent, remorseful prayer, then determinedly rose to her feet.

"No matter who has overtaken this ship, I will end Franklin LaFontaine's life," she murmured to herself.

Gathering her discarded clothes up from the floor, she hurried into them. With trembling fingers, she lifted the corner of the mattress and withdrew her pistol from beneath it.

"I've already shot one man with this pistol. The second should be easier," she said coldly. "But this time I shall aim for the heart. I cannot miss. Father gave me the pistol to use against vermin. On Franklin, it will rightfully be used."

With her hair half fallen from her bun, she took one last look at her father. Tears once more stung her eyes, but she knew that time for tears was past. She had to have backbone. She had to be strong to win in this crazed world which had only men as its leaders, men who controlled women's destinies.

"No longer will I be swayed by any man," she hissed. Visions of Troy materialized in her mind's eye, weakening her set jaw and melting her heart. She knew that he would always be an exception.

Jerking her head around and firming her jaw, her lips pressed hard with determination, she went to the door with pistol in hand. But before she had the chance to open the door, it swung suddenly open and Troy stood before her, a pistol in his right hand. He lowered it to his side when he saw her.

"Sam?" he whispered throatily.

Samantha took a step backward, stunned. "Troy?" she gasped. "How?" But she didn't wait to hear his reply. She dropped her own pistol and rushed into his arms, sobbing. "Troy, darling," she said between sobs. "I've never—been—so glad—to see anyone."

"Sam, are you all right?" he asked, replacing his pistol in the belt at his waist, freeing his hand to fully embrace her. His gaze fell upon the covered body. He already knew that it was Samantha's father. When he forcefully questioned Franklin LaFontaine about Craig Johnston, Franklin had confessed to shooting him, but swore that it had been an accident.

Troy could only surmise how such an accident could have taken place in Samantha's cabin. Franklin LaFontaine had more than likely chosen this day to make his improper advances to Samantha. Thinking this made Troy want to kill him slowly and painfully.

Samantha laughed nervously. "Am I all right?" she said, drawing away from him. She brushed a loose strand of hair back from her eyes. "Troy, I don't think I'll ever be the same again." She shuddered violently as she glanced down at her father.

Troy followed her eyes. "Yes. I can understand. I see why," he murmured. "I'm sorry, Sam."

Samantha's eyes jerked upward, looking into Troy's. "How do you know who is beneath that bedspread?" she asked cautiously. "Troy, how is it that you are even on board this ship? Lord, for a moment there my happiness in seeing you clouded my reason. It was as though we had run into each other by accident on land. But we're at sea." She paled in color. "The cannon fire?" she whispered. "You? It was from the guns on your ship?"

"Yes," he said hoarsely. "They were mine."

"And you have boarded Franklin's ship?"

"As you can see, I did."

"And the orders awhile ago from a man for everyone aboard this ship is—your—enemy?"

"Not exactly, Sam."

"Then why?" Samantha demanded, yet almost afraid to hear his reply.

Troy looked quickly about the cabin. He nodded toward a chair. "Sam, maybe you'd best sit down," he said thickly. "I've much to explain."

"You bet your life you do," she said, now mistrusting him again, wondering if she could ever fully trust him. It was obvious that he had boarded Franklin's ship for all the wrong reasons.

"And I prefer to stand while you explain, thank you," she said icily, folding her arms stubbornly across her chest.

"Sam, you never even asked how I escaped from Johnston Oaks," Troy said. "Aren't you even a bit curious?"

"Ha! Does it do me any good anymore to wonder about anything? Seems I keep getting surprises tossed my way."

"Sam, I can understand why you've suddenly changed your mood," Troy said, reaching a hand toward her, drawing it quickly back, startled at how she openly flinched. He cleared his throat nervously and clasped his hands together behind him.

"As I was saying," he continued. "I can understand why you are suddenly so mistrustful of me. You have to know that I and my crew have overtaken Franklin's ship."

"Oh? Really?" she said sarcastically, her eyes snapping. "Now how could I ever assume that?"

"I plan to start from the beginning, whether you want to hear or not," he growled, now grabbing her by her shoulders, giving her a gentle shake.

He left his hands there, though she was struggling to be set free. "As you know, Sam, I was left tied to your bed," he said. "I was there until morning. My crew thought that I was spending the night with you because I didn't return to the ship as I had been expected to do. When mid-morning came the next day and I hadn't yet returned to my ship, a few of my men came searching and found me. But it was somewhat too late, Sam. Upon our arrival back to the ship, we were soon discovered by a northern warship."

Samantha's insides rolled. Even if she was angry at Troy, she knew the dangers of a northern warship discovering anyone other than their own ships in Charleston Harbor.

"Troy, no!" she said in a strain. "What—happened—then?"

"You really want to know?" he said blandly.

"Yes."

"We had no chance to fight back and escape," Troy grumbled. "You see another warship and then another was soon upon us. My ship was boarded. Answers were demanded of me, yet they quickly recognized me and my name. Some of the gents were even earlier acquaintances whom I had dealt with in business transactions."

He paused and dropped his hands to his side. "I'm sure that's why they went easy on me and made such a deal as they did with me," he said thickly. "Though they knew I had been aiding the South's blockade-runners, they gave me an out."

"An—out?" Samantha questioned, an eyebrow arching. "What sort?"

Troy momentarily lowered his gaze, wordless. Then he looked up and met her steady gaze. "Sam, one of my crew became frightened and said a mite too much to the captain of the warship, hoping to save his own neck in doing so."

"What did he tell the captain?" she dared to ask.

"He said that the warships shouldn't be bothering with us and our ship when they had such men as Craig Johnston and Franklin LaFontaine running loose."

"Lord," Samantha gasped, placing a hand to her throat.

"He proceeded to even explain just who these two men were, their part in the formation of the Confederate States of America, and that they were now on their way to Brazil, carrying many Southerners with them."

"I'm beginning to see," Samantha said thoughtfully.

"Of course the captain of the warship already knew of your father and Franklin. They are being sought," Troy continued. "And this is why I was set free."

"*Why*, Troy?"

"I was given an ultimatum. If I used my seafaring skills to go in pursuit of Franklin's ship and capture and return it and everyone on board to Charleston Harbor, then my crew and I would go free."

"Troy, no. You—agreed?"

"I had no choice."

Samantha hung her head and swallowed back a hard lump growing in her throat. "You became—a—traitor," she said. Her eyes raised angrily to his. "Even to me," she spat. "How could you agree to go after my father? You knew that even I—"

"Yes, I knew," Troy growled, once more holding her by her shoulders. "Sam, I also remember how crazed your father was behaving. He was a desperate man! He even led you from your house at gunpoint. I could no longer trust that he had your best interest at heart. I had to come after you!"

"At the sacrifice of my father?" she cried. "Troy, you knew his fate if you returned him."

"Sam, I could only think of you."

"That's not true! You thought of self! You're a coward, Troy Gilbert! A damn coward!"

She jerked free of him and walked to the far side of the room from him, softly weeping. Her whole world had now tumbled around her.

Troy went to her and jerked her around to face him. "Sam, do you forget so easily that your father left me, to possibly even die?" he snarled. "And he had to know the danger of my getting caught by leaving my ship so vulnerable without me in the cove."

"So you had a debt to pay," she hissed. "You decided to agree to capture Father to settle this debt with him."

"Sam, will you listen?" Troy demanded. "I had no choice. I was being forced by gunpoint every mile I've traveled from Charleston Harbor. Sam, some of the crew from the warships boarded mine to accompany me on the search for Franklin's ship. Every minute of the day and night I was looking down the barrel of a gun."

Samantha paled. "Troy, truly?" she murmured, seeing him through a stubborn haze of tears. "You were forced in that way? I thought that perhaps you had been left to follow on your own volition."

"Now wouldn't that be a bad way to handle things for the Northerners?" he said, frowning. "They know that I would never return to the harbor if I were set free for any reasons without being bodily forced."

"Troy, I'm sorry—for—having doubted you," Samantha softly said, blinking tears from her long, feathery lashes.

"It's understandable, darling," he said, gently flicking the tears away from the delicate lines of her cheeks.

"But, Troy, can you trust them? When you do return Franklin and his ship to Charleston Harbor, will the Northerners keep their word? Will you be free to go?"

"The man I dealt with was a man of his word," Troy said. "I don't doubt it for a minute that once I return Franklin and his ship to Charleston Harbor, I will be free to leave, except that—"

"Except what?" Samantha dared to ask.

"Except that I have to give my word to return to New York to tend to business other than that which involves the war."

"And you agreed?"

"Again I had no other choice but to do as I was asked, or shall I say, ordered."

"So you will?"

"I gave my word."

"And being the gentleman that you are, you will do as you promised."

"Exactly."

Troy turned around and looked down at the covered body. "Damn sorry about your father, Sam," he said thickly. "I truly didn't wish him harm."

"I believe you," she murmured, easing into his arms.

"Troy, darling, hold me. Just hold me for a while."

Troy held her closely to him, savoring her closeness. "I have to ask, Sam," he said hoarsely. "Did Franklin—"

"He tried."

"Your father?"

"Yes. He intervened. There was a struggle."

"Shh," Troy softly encouraged. "Don't say anymore. We're together now. I won't let anything happen to you. You're going to New York with me. We'll become man and wife and place all of this behind us."

"Troy, I want that. Oh, how I want that."

"Soon, darling. But we must first see to getting that damn Franklin LaFontaine to Charleston Harbor. It's going to be a pleasure to hand him over to the authorities."

Samantha saw her pistol which she had dropped to the floor. A tremor coursed through her with the memory of what she had planned to do with it. "Troy, I would have shot Franklin had you not arrived when you did," she said, clinging harder to his muscled body.

"Just place all thoughts of that man from your mind," Troy encouraged. "Think only of our future."

Samantha looked toward her jewelry case on the dressing table with a sudden thought of what lay inside. She eased out of Troy's embrace and walked determinedly to the case and lifted its lid, staring down at the locket that Franklin had given her.

"What are you doing, Sam?" Troy asked, going to her. He stiffened when he saw the necklace, having always associated Samantha with Franklin.

Samantha grabbed the necklace and circled her fingers tightly about it. "I've plans for this," she hissed. "Troy, I'm ready to go top deck, if you are."

"Yes. We must. I've already been gone too long."

Samantha looked sadly down at her father's covered body, then fell into step beside Troy as they left the cabin. When they reached top deck, Samantha's eyes searched Franklin out and when she found him, she went to glare up into his face. She held the locket up for him to see.

"Franklin, do you see this?" she hissed.

"Yes," he said, his eyes wavering, his hands tied behind him, now for sure a prisoner of war.

"Well, just watch this," Samantha said, walking to the ship's rail. She held the locket out over the water. "First you see it and then you don't," she said, laughing throatily.

She let the locket drop from her hand, watching the wounded look in Franklin's eyes as he watched. Then she went to Troy. "Darling, I hope that on our return voyage to Charleston Harbor, I can travel aboard your ship and not this wretched one," she said softly, letting Franklin watch as she gave Troy a kiss.

"Your wish is my command," Troy chuckled, still amused at how she had chosen to dispose of the locket. She was her old self now, with a revived spirit.

"My father?" she said, sadness tugging at her heart.

"His body will be transferred, also, to my ship," Troy said thickly. "We will return him to Johnston Oaks Plantation for proper burial."

Then the slight figure of Julia rushed forth. "Samantha, where's Craig?" she asked, desperately clutching onto Samantha's arm. "I became frightened by the gunfire and then the commotion. I stayed inside my cabin. I was only—now forced—to come topside. Where's Craig? I don't see him anywhere? What's happening here?"

Samantha paled. She had completely forgotten about Julia! She took Julia's trembling hands in hers, then explained what had happened. Julia's face turned white and then she fainted. She felt pangs of guilt as she watched Julia being carried to Troy's ship. She followed along quietly and let Troy guide her from Franklin's ship to his after he had given instructions as to how this return was to be handled.

Upon entering Troy's private master cabin, Samantha was taken aback when she saw a dog asleep beside Troy's bunk. When Troy screwed the wick of a lamp higher, brightening the room, Samantha's eyes grew wide with disbelief.

"Checkers!" she whispered. She recognized her collie's brown and white spotted fur as he slept with his head tucked between his paws. Samantha rushed to Checkers and dropped to her knees before him. "Troy, you found Checkers and rescued him," she cried.

Checkers turned his head with a start when he recognized her voice. He scrambled to his feet and began barking, his tail wagging frantically. He then lifted a paw toward Samantha and whined, his dark eyes imploring her.

Samantha gathered Checkers into her arms and anxiously hugged him. "Where did you find him, Troy?" she murmured, her heart warm.

"On my way back to the ship after leaving your house," Troy said softly, hunkering down beside Samantha. "He looked so forlorn, I couldn't leave him behind."

Samantha reached a hand to Troy's cheek. "Darling, oh, how I love you," she whispered.

# Chapter Twenty-Seven

Sleep eluded Samantha. Thoughts of her father lay heavily on her mind. She could still hear the gun's blast. She could still see her father lying in death's pallor. She was even haunted by the look on Julia's face when she had heard the news of her husband's death. Samantha had been wrong about Julia. Julia had truly loved her husband and mourned even now for him in the privacy of her cabin.

Samantha stood on the quarterdeck watching the dancing of lightning in the dark heavens and how it would occasionally light Franklin's ship which traveled a short distance from Troy's. It was now the same as a ghost ship with a scanty crew, only enough to keep the ship alive to get it back to Charleston Harbor. Everyone of importance, and even the murdering scoundrel Franklin, were now passengers of Troy's ship.

"I don't like the looks of that sky," Troy grumbled as he came to stand beside Samantha. His shirt flapped in the wind, and his hair whipped around his head.

Samantha wrapped her cape more closely around her,

its hood threatening to sweep away from her head. She jumped as a loud crash of thunder echoed across the black, pitching water.

"I've experienced one storm at sea," she said shallowly. "I'd not welcome another."

"I'd feel better about things if we were closer to Charleston Harbor," Troy worried. "As it is, Brazil is the closest of the two destinations. Franklin's ship had almost made it when mine overtook it."

Samantha let an arm snake out from beneath her cape and work its way around Troy's waist. She fit herself up close to him. "I'm so glad you did," she murmured. "Had you not come when you did, who's to say what Franklin would have done to me!"

"I'm damn sorry about your father, Sam," Troy said solemnly. "Had I just arrived sooner—"

"There's no sense in worrying over what could have been," Samantha said. "What happened—well, it was just meant to be, that's all."

She paused, then added, "But strange that it was my father's best friend who killed him. Father trusted Franklin so. But I knew Franklin better than Father ever did. I just knew that he would eventually try—try to—seduce me—if I kept refusing to marry him."

"The damn bastard," Troy growled. "I should just go down in the hold and strangle him. He doesn't deserve to see the light of another day."

Samantha placed a hand on his tight arm. "No. Please don't think that way," she said. "Leave the fate of Franklin up to the authorities. I'm sure they have their own ideas on how to handle him."

"Yes, I guess you're right," Troy said, raking his fingers nervously through his hair. "But I just don't like the idea that he's on board this ship with you."

"He's being guarded," Samantha murmured. "Aboard his ship, you'd feel as though he wouldn't be guarded as well with you unable to check on him from time to time. Now aren't I right, Troy?"

"Aren't you always?" he said, drawing her completely around to face him. He slipped his arms beneath the sides of her cape and momentarily cupped her breasts through her dress, then leaned himself into her as his lips met hers in an utter softness.

Samantha's heart fluttered, but the intimacy between them was interrupted by a more fierce flash of lightning and an ensuing clap of thunder.

"God!" Troy gasped, looking skyward. "We really are in for it." He gave Samantha a stern look. "Get below deck, darling. Though the waters are calm now, I don't expect them to be for long. Once the storm hits—"

Troy didn't get all of his words out before howling winds began, and water swelled around the ship. The forecastle groaned, the masts nodded, swayed and bent, and the sails were large and spread out.

More lurid lightning flashes lit up the sky and sea, a vivid sheen flashing back the ocean's anger.

Wild shouts from the crew sounded from the deck as the ship began to plunge and roll. Samantha felt the intensity of the wind against her as though she were being sucked into a tight tunnel. The hood of her cape whipped from her head. She clung to the ship's rail, barely hearing Troy's shouts of warning to her. When his muscled arm anchored about her waist and he began walking her toward the companionway steps, she clung to him with all her might, but that wasn't enough. Large sheets of water were washing up and over the deck, making it dangerously slick.

Samantha and Troy fell, shaking them apart. They began sliding away from each other, Troy shouting her name, while Samantha screamed. Her heart thundered against her ribs, and her face was burning from the harsh sting of the saltwater. Her clothes were clinging and wrapping about her, imprisoning her.

With great effort, she grabbed for a rope that was dangling from a mast. Her fingers burned as the rope threatened to slip from between them. But finally she had full hold of the rope and pulled herself up to cling to the mast, though it was swaying unmercifully, threatening to snap under the pressure of the gale force of the wind.

Frantically, Samantha began searching with her eyes for Troy. When she saw him she reached for him and cried out, almost choking with the effort. She could see him hanging on to the side of the ship as it tipped and spilled him into the ocean. But just as quickly the waves plunged against the bulwark and set the ship to sway sideways in the opposite direction, tossing Troy up and now sliding in Samantha's direction.

Anchoring herself against the ship's mast she reached a hand to Troy. "Darling, my hand!" she screamed, rain almost drowning her as it fell in torrents from the heavens. "Grab it, Troy. You'll be gone! Darling, grab it!"

She felt a fierce jerk to her body as he grabbed her hand, his fingers now tightly clasped onto hers. Finding strength she never knew she had, Samantha held onto Troy, his eyes wild as he looked up at her.

The wind whooped. The lightning flashed. Everywhere

about Samantha were the loud crashes, creaks, and bangs and slaps of high winds and seas. In huge right and left blows the waves tormented the ship.

To her amazement Samantha watched incredulously as flowers and leaves from somewhere off shore came strangely along with the gusts, a warning that land was somewhere close.

Brazil? she wondered. Are we there? Will the ship even capsize there?

And then the storm abated almost as quickly as it had begun, and the ship mercifully began to settle calmly in the waves.

"Thank the Lord," Samantha whispered.

Troy released her hand and rose to his feet, straightening his hair back from his eyes. He looked about him at the damage. Sails were torn and flapping loose from the masts. Yet, thankfully, the masts had withstood the strain, though the clumsy rope cordage of the shrouds had threatened to snap beneath the powerful gusts of wind.

The crew was now busy hustling and bustling about, working the pumps. The deck was being cleared of broken debris.

Troy turned with a start and looked toward Samantha, seeing her drenched cape clinging to her like a glove and the tangle of her hair.

"Are you all right?" he asked hoarsely, still breathless from his labors to keep alive.

Samantha's eyes went over him, seeing his ripped frock coat, the dangling cravat at his throat, and his fawn-colored breeches which were now drawn tight from wetness along his powerful, muscled legs, leaving not one thing about this part of his anatomy to the imagination.

Rushing into his arms, Samantha sobbed against his chest, so afraid had she been of losing him to the dark waters of the sea. "Darling, are you all right?" she asked, hugging him to her. "I was—so—so afraid for your life."

Troy leaned away from her, looking down at her. He brushed some wet strands of hair back from her face. "You saved my life," he said thickly. "If you hadn't grabbed my hand—"

She placed a finger to his lips. "Hush," she murmured. "Let's not even think about it."

Her gaze captured a clinging leaf on the deck. She remembered having seen flowers and leaves blowing in the rush of the wind. "Troy," she said, stooping to pick up the leaf, letting it lay limply in the palm of her hand. "We must be close to land. Do you think it's Brazil?"

A flower, purplish in color, floated by as water still washed across the top deck. Troy stooped and plucked it up into his hand. He studied it closely. "It looks like a wild orchid," he pondered aloud. "Perhaps from an island. Surely Brazil isn't this close."

"But the winds sent the ship along at quite a clip," Samantha softly argued, blowing the leaf from her hand.

"Yes. Perhaps," Troy said, then turned quickly around when he heard a commotion leeward side. "What the hell—"

Following alongside him, Samantha went with Troy to stand with him just a few feet from the ship's rail. She grew cold inside when she saw the cause of the excitement of the crew. Franklin's ship had not fared the storm as well as Troy's. Its loud groan sounded through the dark night. Boats were being hoisted out from it, and scarcely had the crew left the ship when the vessel sank before everyone's eyes.

"I wish he were on board his ship," Troy growled, clenching his fists to his side. "They deserve the same fate—the ship and its owner."

"That could be us," Samantha said, shivering. "It's a miracle it's not. How did your ship survive the gale, Troy?"

"It's got spirit," he laughed. "It's withstood worse."

Again he surveyed Samantha and the condition that the storm had left her in. "It's best you go and get out of those wet things," he said. "I'll come and see to you later after I've checked things out up here."

"How do you think things are below deck, in the hold?" she said as he guided her toward the companion-way ladder. "The slaves. Do you think they are all right?" She was mainly worrying about Joshua and Jewel. They had chosen to travel alongside their friends instead of topside as they had been generously offered.

"I'm sure they were tossed about a mite and that water managed to get in there, but I'm sure most fared well enough."

A rush of footsteps drew Troy and Samantha around to look at the anxious face of a wet, bedraggled sailor. "What is it, Lloyd?" Troy growled. "What's happened?"

Lloyd went nervously from one foot to the other, wringing water from his knit hat. "It's the prisoner, sir," he said, breathing hard. "Damn if he ain't escaped us."

"What?" Troy gasped, paling. "You personally were left in charge of the prisoner."

"I came topside to assist in keeping the ship from being swallowed whole by the waves," Lloyd said nervously. "I thought that was what was needed most, sir. I thought the prisoner was secured well enough to leave him for at least that length of time."

"Well then? How did the bastard escape?" Troy growled.

"Seems the force of the ship's rocking during the storm jerked the ropes free from his wrists and ankles," Lloyd said, his whiskered face distorted with worry.

"Well? Have you searched the ship for him?" Troy shouted, flailing his arms.

"There's one johnboat missin'," Lloyd explained. "It appears that Franklin LaFontaine must've escaped in it. There's also a few slaves missin'. The prisoner must've taken 'em with him to help with the oars, to get him safely to shore."

"Damn him," Troy grumbled, kneading his brow. He looked toward the dark waters of the Atlantic, then back at Lloyd. "Go talk among the crew that worked Franklin's ship. See if they have their bearings as to where we might be. Seems the wind has thrown us quite off our course."

"Aye, sir," Lloyd said, rushing on away and toward the hold hatch.

"Troy, Franklin surely will be lost at sea," Samantha murmured. "He wasn't wise to escape."

"He knows these waters better than I," Troy argued. "He's made this voyage enough times to know exactly where he's at. If land is near, he'll find it. It's not that easy to kill vermin such as he."

"He is no threat as far as I see it," Samantha said icily. "He may have been secure in a ship run by a skilled crew, but in a longboat with slaves? Troy, I doubt if he'll make it to shore. I doubt if anyone could in water like this, while only in a longboat."

"I've got to check the compass," Troy said, walking away in a huff. "I've got to see where the hell we are."

He went to the compass binnacle and cleared brine

from it. Then, as a crewman held a lighted lamp over the compass, Troy carefully studied it. His shoulders tensed, his brow furrowed as he realized just how far off course the wind had blown them. Brazil. It was only a few breaths of wind away. He peered through the dark in all directions, then stopped and looked somberly toward Samantha.

"Brazil. We must make our way toward it," he grumbled.

"Why, Troy?" Samantha dared to ask.

"It's the closest, Sam," he said.

"But even so, why must we land there?" Samantha persisted.

"I know ships well," Troy grumbled. "And this ship has waged quite a battle this night. It must be taken to land for necessary repairs. Only then can we again begin our voyage to Charleston Harbor."

A feeling of foreboding grabbed at Samantha's insides. From the very beginning, when her father had mentioned Brazil and making a residence there, Samantha had felt a silent dread. And now it was becoming a reality. With her father arriving there dead, it even increased the feelings of dread inside Samantha.

Suddenly her eyes grew wide. She swung around and clasped her fingers onto Troy's arm.

"Father!" she softly cried. "We were going to return him to Charleston for proper burial. Now we can't. Time will not be kind to his—his—body."

Troy wrapped his arms about her and drew her into his embrace. "Darling, surely you knew all along that we couldn't have taken him home," he said thickly. "I only agreed at first because you were too distraught to hear the truth. I was waiting for the right moment to tell you that we must have a burial at sea."

Samantha closed her eyes. "No," she whimpered. "I couldn't bear it."

"A burial at sea won't be necessary now," he then said. "We shall bury him as soon as we reach Brazil."

"That even sounds dreadful," Samantha shuddered. "On strange land? Forever? Away from Johnston Oaks? Oh, Troy."

She sobbed hard. He held her tightly. "Where he is buried should make no difference," he said, trying to reassure her. "It is only the shell of the man that will be placed in soil. The most important part has already separated from him. His soul has gone to bigger and better things. Try to look at it in that way, Sam."

"Yes. I shall," she said, wiping tears from her eyes as she stepped back away from Troy.

"And I see that I must take you bodily to our cabin and take those wet clothes off you myself, since you haven't yet done it yourself," he grumbled.

He looked about him and saw that his crew was laboring and setting things right without him, the orders already given to make way on toward Brazil.

Then he placed an arm about Samantha's waist and led her from top deck and on to their cabin, where even it had already been straightened and a lamp lighted.

Only traces of water were visible on the floor, where it had splashed beneath the closed door during the storm. It smelled of a musty dampness, causing Samantha's nose to unpleasantly curl.

"Here. Let me help you," Troy said as he closed and bolted the door behind him.

He worked with the bow at her neck where the cape was secured. The water had tightened the knot in the bow and even Troy's muscular, deft fingers could not loosen it.

Samantha couldn't help but giggle when she saw his frustration set in, his face reddening, his teeth clenched in anger.

"Troy," she teased. "I thought by now I'd be undressed and thrown across the bed."

"Damn this bow," he growled, then breathed a sigh of relief as the bow finally came unfastened. Gently, he lifted the cape from around her shoulders and let it drop in a wet heap to the floor.

His pulse raced when he saw the bold outline of her nipples protruding through the clinging cotton of her white blouse, the dark tips quite definable.

"You're a picture of seduction," he said huskily, placing his hands to her breasts, letting his thumbs press in on the taut tips.

Samantha laughed throatily as she held her drenched skirt out away from her. "How can you say that?" she said. "Lord, Troy, I'm a mess."

Her laughter died on her lips when he kissed her. Her insides began to flame with desire as Troy withdrew the tail of her blouse from the waist of her skirt and slid his hands up inside to sensually knead each breast.

"Troy, this surely isn't the time," Samantha said raspily, her eyes becoming glazed with a sudden onslaught of passion.

The creaking of the ship and the slap of water at the ship's side caused Troy to come back to his senses. "Yes. I do have to see to things," he said thickly. He spun away from Samantha and flicked his fingers through his hair, straightening it.

"You should at least take time to change into

something dry," Samantha said, going to him to run a hand over his wet frock coat. "You'll catch a death of cold, Troy."

"I can't worry about that. I've got to see to things and see that they are all right topside," he said, taking wide steps toward the door.

He gave her a look of longing over his shoulder. "I'll be back real soon. I believe we're close to land."

Samantha involuntarily shuddered. She hugged herself as she nodded a silent yes to him, then as he left, she went to a porthole to take a searching look from it. The dark screen of night was fading to morning. Shades of purplish hues were dancing along the horizon. And then Samantha saw it. A spread of green where land rose almost magically from the magnificent blues of the Atlantic.

"Brazil!" Samantha whispered, placing her hands to her cheeks. "That has to be—Brazil."

Almost breathless she hurried out of her wet things and into a dry cotton dress that displayed pleats at the waist and also at the bodice where the white of her bosom was revealed, as well as her long, slender neck.

Long sleeved and fully gathered, the dress the color of a field of summer wheat, Samantha was a vision of loveliness. Something deep inside told her that she must look her best at all times, for Julia was free again to search for a man to entertain her.

Though Julia's husband was yet to be buried and she had shown that she had truly loved him, Samantha didn't trust that Julia would be in mourning long. Samantha had known her cousin too long to expect anything from her.

"I must keep watch on her every minute," Samantha

whispered, giving her hair gentle strokes with a brush. Its dampness waned with each stroke, and the light from the lamp picked up the red sheen of it, causing it to shine like a morning sunrise in its utter brilliance.

Choosing it to hang loose and lustrous around her shoulders, Samantha slipped into dry slippers and hurried from the cabin, too anxious to wait for Troy's return. Then her insides froze when she heard Troy's voice coming from somewhere close by.

Samantha inched her way toward a door where his voice was coming from. Tensing, and with a jealous anger welling up inside her, she placed her ear to the door—Julia's door—and listened.

"I'm sure the storm frightened you, Julia," Troy said in a soft, soothing tone. "But as you see, we made it fine. After a short stop at Brazil, we'll be able to return to Charleston Harbor."

"I feel so alone, so isolated," Julia softly cried. "Samantha has you. I have no one. Whatever am I to do while I'm stranded in Brazil?"

"I will see to your comforts," Troy murmured.

There was a pause.

"Don't cry, Julia," Troy said. "Things will be all right. You'll see."

"I wish I'd never left New York," she cried. "Nothing has been right since. I wish I was in New York right now. I would find ways to forget all these morbid things that have happened to me."

"New York isn't all that far away," Troy encouraged.

"Oh, Troy," Julia sighed. "It's a whole world away."

"What I meant to say is that we will be there as soon as possible," he said. "But first, Brazil, and then Charleston Harbor."

"If not for the storm everything would be so different," Julia moaned. "Now what shall we even do for my dear Craig? He would want to be buried at Johnston Oaks."

Samantha's insides softened, finally hearing Julia worrying about something other than herself. She was worrying about her dead husband! And she had called him *dear*. Perhaps, just perhaps, Julia wasn't purposely playing on Troy's sympathies for her own selfish purpose after all. She seemed honestly distraught about everything!

Feeling guilty for having eavesdropped and for once more letting herself become jealous of her cousin, Samantha swung away from the door and hurried topside where perfumed breezes now filled the ship's sails. She went to the rail, enjoying the warm wind caressing her face and lifting her hair in fiery reds from her shoulders. She leaned her full weight against the rail, watching sunbeams dancing upon the waves and playing along the ship's side. It was hard to imagine that only a short few hours ago this water was the devil itself, black and menacing. Now it caused a peacefulness to settle over Samantha.

As land became closer she became breathless when she saw the exotic beauty that stretched out before her eyes. The jungle was a lush blue-green. Macaws moving in flocks splashed the sky with small explosions of color and boisterous squawking.

"Well? What do you think?" Troy said, suddenly from behind Samantha.

Samantha turned with a start, forcing herself to forget his soft words to Julia of only a moment ago. Jealousy was an ugly trait, an emotion that could fester in one's insides. She couldn't allow this to happen to her. Life was too short. Life was too precious to be spoiled by jealousy!

Welcoming Troy's arms about her waist, Samantha leaned leisurely against him when he stepped to her side. "It's lovely," she sighed. "It's so primitive. It could be so romantic."

He snuggled his nose momentarily into her hair. "Exactly my thoughts," he quietly teased. "I'm glad to see your change in attitude. We must make the best of the situation, right?"

"Right," Samantha softly laughed. Then a shadow crossed her face. "But, Troy, it is primitive," she said, worried. "What about the Indians who live here? Surely they won't appreciate the white man's arrival. Could our lives be in danger?"

Troy moved away from her and circled his fingers about the rail, closely scrutinizing the approaching land. "You must remember that there's been many more white men arriving before us," he explained. "Emperor Don Pedro the second has openly encouraged settlers in Brazil for many years. A prosperous plantation society has already been developed. Thousands of Negroes have been brought from Africa as slaves."

"Yes. I do see why Father and Franklin were so eager to come to Brazil," Samantha sighed. "They couldn't have ever tolerated or understood a free Negro population. Leaving Charleston seemed to be the only answer."

"But I must warn you, Sam," Troy said dryly. "Though plantations have been established here, they are nothing like you are used to in Charleston."

"Oh? What do you mean?"

"The houses are not as grand, and there are some Indian uprisings."

"But you said—"

"Yes. But I didn't say that the Indians agreed to all this that the white man or Negro have done in what originally was the Indian's land."

"Then there could be trouble?"

"Some of Franklin's crew who have already been in Brazil speak of even some headhunters among the Guarani Indians who live in villages not far from where Franklin has built his and your father's plantation houses."

Samantha blanched. "I wonder if father knew," she murmured. "He always made sure to not antagonize the Kiawah Indian."

Troy glowered. "From what I now know of Franklin he probably didn't inform your father of this because he wanted his old friend with him in Brazil," he said. "He wanted his old friend's daughter in Brazil, I should say."

"Friend? Ha!" Samantha scoffed. "A friend who kills?"

"From what I gathered it was an accident, Sam."

"It was no accident that he tried to forcefully rape me," she argued.

"I wasn't trying to defend the man, Sam. And we'll find the damn bastard," Troy grumbled. "He won't get the chance to even touch you again."

As the ship limped in closer to shore, Troy caught sight of a reflection of something beached along its edges. Then recognizing it, he smiled ruefully. "And speaking of Franklin," he chuckled. "He can't be too far away. There's the longboat that he stole from my ship. Seems he's made it quite safely to land."

"He could be far inland by now," Samantha sighed. "He won't allow himself to get caught. He's too clever."

"With you at my side?" Troy laughed. "Darling, that is reason alone for him to become careless. In wanting you, he will fall right into a trap."

"If he doesn't decide to go on inland, I'm sure I am not the reason," Samantha scoffed. "And come to think of it, Franklin won't give up his plantation and slaves all that easily. He'll fight to keep what's his. You'll see."

"Yes. He'll fight all right," Troy said, scowling. "He'll fight to get you back in his clutches."

A shiver surged through Samantha. "Let's please quit talking about that poor excuse of a man," she said. "We've more important things to worry about—like where is Father's plantation? How far inland is it?"

"Now don't you fret one more minute over that," Troy said. "Franklin's crew will lead us there, and I've been assured that it is not even a blink of an eye away through the jungle that you see edging the land. Beyond that is fertile land."

"Are there mountains, Troy?"

"I've been told that there are very few high mountains. But there are many large, treeless plains as well as continuous forests where many rivers can be found dissecting the land."

"It could be exciting if the circumstances were different," she sighed. "As it is, we have a burial to attend to upon our very first arriving."

"We do what we must," Troy said thickly. He shielded his eyes as he turned to look up at the sails that were losing the wind due to the crew's acting quickly to draw them in.

Then he took Samantha's hands and squeezed them affectionately. "And I must now see to the crew," he said. "The ship is creaking too much as far as I'm concerned. I'm praying that it can even be properly repaired to get us away from here."

"Do you have your doubts?" Samantha asked, swallowing hard.

"One never knows. Ships are unpredictable as are storms. When you put the two together, you can only hope for the best."

The air was damp with moisture, and the sun had become fiercely hot. Samantha watched the ship inch closer to shore. It was close enough now for her to hear the screaming and screeching of monkeys and for her to see the tangled undergrowth and dense thickets that reached into the jungle.

She turned to take a look at the wide expanse of the ocean behind her. Clouds dragged along the horizon, tattered by the wind, separating the blue of the sky from the turqoise of the Atlantic.

Samantha felt as though a great wall was isolating her from the rest of the world she had always known. It was strange, this feeling of isolation.

# *Chapter Twenty-Eight*

Only a few left the ship. Most of the crew and all but two of the slaves remained on board until after the private burial of Craig Johnston. Samantha and Julia had agreed on a spot for the burial: in the soft deep of the jungle where butterflies fluttered in blue splashes, and where hummingbirds scarcely larger than a man's thumb darted from flower to flower.

Thick, lush creepers climbed the trees. Ferns grew upon ferns along the ground. Samantha now stood back away from the grave with Troy, Jewel, and Joshua, as Julia placed fragile orchids on the mound of earth covered by plaited coconut fronds.

Then with square shoulders and tear-streaked eyes Julia left the grave behind and went to the somber viewers.

"I'm ready," she said, flicking a tear from her cheek. "I've said my last good-byes. There's nothing more to be done here."

Samantha looked on past Julia at the grave. A knot formed in her throat, and her heart sorely ached. She wiped a tear from a thick lash, and then her attention was suddenly drawn elsewhere. Her eyes darted upward. Through the treetops she caught sight of smoke.

"Troy!" she gasped, grabbing his arm.

Troy had already seen and smelled it. "Something is burning," he said shallowly. His gaze turned in the direction from where the smoke was coming. Thankfully, it was opposite from where the Atlantic and his ship lay.

"What could it be?" Samantha asked, her heart pounding wildly.

"There's only one way to find out," Troy grumbled.

He thrust his rifle in the air and began handing out orders. "Joshua, you come with me," he shouted. "You women get back to the ship and fast. When you get there send some of the crew. We may run into some trouble. I need all the guns possible."

"I'm going with you," Samantha argued. "I'll not go back to that ship. I've just left it. And I won't be separated from you, Troy. I couldn't bear not knowing what's happening to you."

Troy glowered down at her. His cotton shirt was half unbuttoned to the waist, revealing his powerful chest and curls of chest hair. "Damn it, Sam, this is no time to get stubborn," he growled. "This isn't America. This is Brazil. Who knows what awaits us beyond these trees? Now do as I say. Go with Jewel and Julia back to the ship."

In her white blouse and with her hair of flame lifting from her shoulders in the steady breeze, and with the toe of her boots peeking from beneath her dark skirt, Samantha took a stubborn step forward.

She lifted her skirt and removed her pistol that she had thrust inside the top of her boot. "You say you need guns?" she dared. "Then you have one. Mine. But only if I am the one carrying it."

Troy laughed throatily. "Sam, you're not serious," he said. He gestured toward the pistol. "You call that tiny thing a gun? Surely you're jesting."

"Do I have to prove my skills by shooting it now, all the while wasting time, Troy?"

Troy looked anxiously up at the sky. Smoke was now billowing higher and darker than before. Then he once more nervously eyed Samantha. Maybe it was best to take her with him. Perhaps she would be safer. At least it would be his decision as to what to do to protect her.

He nodded his head. "All right," he said. "Come on. But mind you, you leave your stubborn streak here on this very spot! You must do everything I say every step of the way. Do you hear me, Sam?"

"Yes," she said anxiously. "I will. I promise."

With a weary eye, Troy looked from Jewel to Julia, then back to Jewel. "Can you get Julia back to the ship, Jewel?" he asked hoarsely. "Or should I send Joshua on along with you?"

Jewel took Julia firmly by a hand and began walking away with her. "Julia is safe with me," she said from across her shoulder. "Jus' you go on and sees to the seein'."

Joshua smiled smugly. "They both will be all right," he said. "My woman is strong willed and muscled. She'll see to Julia. Don' fret none, Massa Troy."

"Then let's get a move on," Troy said, looking again at the smoke overhead. "This whole damn jungle may go up in flames."

Samantha fell into step between Troy and Joshua, becoming quickly breathless. The humidity was closing in on her, and her brow was laced with perspiration. The chatter of the monkeys and the calls from the birds seemed to be mocking her as she stumbled over tangled underbrush and swung at low-hanging limbs which scraped against her head and face.

But soon all of this was left behind as she saw an open plain which displayed row after row of cotton plants and at the far stretch of this land, the fiery inferno of two large houses in flame.

"My Lord," Samantha gasped, her eyes wide.

"I think we've just found your father's and Franklin's plantations," Troy grumbled. "Seems someone else found them before us, though."

"Who?" Samantha murmured.

Troy let his gaze move cautiously about. Then he became aware of the total silence. All that could be heard was the crackling of the flames that reached to the sky. There wasn't a soul in sight. Not one slave. Not one American. The two plantations were deserted.

"Indians," Troy suddenly said. "I bet it was the Guarani Indians."

"Franklin," Samantha said in a trembling tone. "Do you think he was killed by the—"

"Yes. I imagine so," Troy answered. "Seems he returned to Brazil just to be slain."

Samantha's insides splashed cold. "How horrible," she said. She had hated Franklin, but the thought of being slain by Indians was something not to be wished on anyone.

"We'd bes' get back to the ship, Massa Troy," Joshua said, his dark eyes wild with fear, his shoulders hunched, as though he were ready to pounce at any sudden movement.

"We can't just yet," Troy said, again scanning the horizon with a quick sweep of his eyes. "We must see if there are any survivors. We can't ignore what's happened here."

"I ain't ignorin' nothin'," Joshua said hoarsely. "I understands too well the dangers of lingerin' where we ain't wanted. Bes' we get back to the ship, Massa Troy. Bes' we get back now."

Troy glared at Joshua. "Joshua, I certainly don't own you," he spat. "But you had better do as I say. Do you understand?"

Recoiling as though he had been hit, Joshua bobbed his head up and down. "Anything you say, Massa Troy," he mumbled.

"Then let's hurry on," Troy said, clasping his hand more tightly about his rifle.

Then his eyes wavered as he looked down at Samantha who had become much too quiet. "Are you all right, hon?" he softly asked. "Are you sorry you didn't go back to the ship?"

"Yes I'm fine, and no, I'm not sorry I didn't return to your ship," she said dryly. "Go on, Troy. I'll be right beside you." She laughed, almost too softly to be heard. "I won't let you get one inch away from me," she said. "I must admit, I've never been as frightened any time in my life as now."

"I must confess, I'm damn scared myself," Troy chuckled.

Samantha's insides warmed as he smiled almost boyishly down at her. Then she again fell in step between him and Joshua as they began making their way between cotton plants toward the burning houses.

The sun beat down unmercifully upon Samantha's

411

bare head. Her temples pounded, her fingers trembled, and she found it hard to keep her pistol steady.

The heat of the sun fused with that of the flames as Samantha now stood before the houses, in awe at how large they were. Troy had been wrong when he said that she wouldn't find a house in Brazil as grand as in Charleston. Though completely engulfed in flames and rolling black smoke, she could see the great pillars that graced the front of each house. The shutters at the windows were now smoking as the fire reached from inside the houses to the outside.

"They were magnificent houses," she whispered. "Father could have felt at home here. I'm sure of it."

"Let's look around and see if anyone is here," Troy said.

Samantha tore her eyes away from the houses and ran alongside Troy. She looked wildly about her. No one was in sight. There were no traces of violence, no massacres of slaves, nor the slain body of Franklin anywhere to be found.

"Damn peculiar," Troy said. "Where is everyone?"

"Perhaps trapped—in—the house?" Samantha said, cringing with the thought.

"I doubt that," Troy said, then he stopped suddenly and spun around on a heel. He grabbed Samantha when she ran into him.

She laughed nervously, feeling awkward in her clumsiness. "Why did you stop like that?" she asked, easing away from him.

"I just happened to remember something," he said thickly.

"Something pleasant, I hope," Samantha said, breathing hard, straightening the folds of her skirt.

"Not quite."

"Then I'm not sure if I care to hear, Troy."

"I think you'd better."

"Then what?"

"Headhunters," he said, his eyes once more darting about him. "I'm remembering what I was told—about—the Guarani Indian headhunters."

Samantha paled. "No," she gasped. "You don't think—"

"It could account for a lot of things," he said. "The houses burning, the fact that no one is here. Perhaps—"

Samantha covered her mouth with a hand, suddenly feeling ill. "Troy, please say no more," she said in a rush of words. "The thought of—" She turned her head and closed her eyes.

"Franklin," Troy mumbled. "What a way to die."

With a jerk, Samantha looked quickly back toward Troy. "Troy, please," she begged. "I don't want to hear anymore. I want to return to the ship. We're sitting ducks here. We could—be—next."

A loud splintering of wood and an ensuing crash caused Samantha to lunge for Troy with fright. She hugged him tightly to her.

"It's one of the houses," he said thickly. "It's collapsed."

Another loud crash echoed ominously around them.

"The second house gave way," Troy said, almost hypnotized by the dancing flames and spiraling smoke.

"Let's go," Samantha cried, looking up at Troy, seeing his dazed expression. "Troy! We must return to the ship!"

"Yes. I'm sure you're right," Troy said, blinking his eyes nervously as he refocused them and looked on past the fire, seeing the rush of his ship's crew as they came bearing arms toward him. A quiet panic seized Troy. It appeared that all the sailors had left the ship. Perhaps no one was left in charge.

Samantha heard the sailors' approach. She took a quick step away from Troy to stand beside Joshua as she heard Troy shout to his men to return to the ship. She saw the looks of bewilderment in most of their eyes before they turned and fled in the direction from whence they had come.

"You're so angry," Samantha murmured, as Troy came back to her. "Why, Troy? What have those men done to anger you so?"

"Too many left the ship," he growled. "Anything could happen. God, Sam, what if it was the ship burning instead of the houses?"

"Are you saying—"

"Yes. That whoever is responsible for these fires could very easily start another."

Their eyes locked in fear, then Troy grabbed Samantha's hand and began to run with her. He looked over his shoulder at Joshua. "Let's get back to the ship!" he yelled. "Quickly, Joshua!"

As the houses had fallen, sparks had shot forth and had fallen onto cotton plants. There was now row after row of spreading flames. Samantha coughed, her eyes and throat burning as she ran between two of these rows. She began screaming when the edge of skirt caught fire. Troy unbuttoned her skirt. He jerked it from her and tossed it aside.

"Draw the petticoat tightly up in your arms," he shouted. "Come on. Let's get the hell out of here."

Involuntary tears caused by the smoke made paths

414

down Samantha's face. She held her petticoat up and close to her as she ran, panting, as fast as her feet would carry her.

Then the protective cover of the jungle was finally reached. The shine of water lured Samantha to a meandering stream that dissected the jungle floor in half.

Dropping to her knees beside the water, struggling for breath, Samantha placed her pistol on the ground beside her. Leaning her hands into the water, she welcomed its coolness. She cupped her hands full of water and lifted them to her lips, eagerly drinking the refreshing liquid.

Troy's reflection looked at Samantha from the one side. He also drank thirstily while Joshua stood watch. And then Troy's arm slinked about Samantha's heaving shoulders.

"I'm proud of you," he said.

Samantha wiped wetness from her lips and looked at him, wondering if she had as many black smoke smudges on her face and clothes as he did. She knew that she reeked of smoke.

"Proud?" she murmured. "Why are you proud of me, Troy?"

"You're such a fighter," he said, tracing her facial features with a forefinger. "You've got spunk, hon. I admire that in a woman."

"Oh, you do, do you?" she giggled. "If I recall I almost begged you to return to the ship. I would say that bespeaks of cowardice, though I hate to admit it."

"Never a coward," he said, weaving his fingers through the hair at her neck. He drew her lips to his and kissed her gently, but for only a moment.

Samantha's head was swimming from the kiss, then she realized just how misplaced such feelings were in the wake of danger.

Troy's lips parted from hers. "I guess we'd best not start something we can't finish," he chuckled. His blue eyes studied her upturned face. "Are you rested, darling? Can you go on?"

"Yes, I'm fine," she murmured. "And remember? I'm spunky—a fighter."

She laughed softly as he helped her up from the ground. She looked at his rifle and then at her pistol. Strange where life had led them. Somehow it seemed hundreds of years ago since she had first laid eyes on him. So much had happened since then, and most of it quite unsettling in one way or the other.

Would life ever be simple again? Would she and Troy ever have the opportunity to share a leisurely, undisturbed gentle passion? As it was, they had to grab every moment possible for even a brief kiss!

"Then let's make tracks," Troy said, again taking her by the hand. "I won't feel safe until we're back aboard the ship."

"Will you even then?" Samantha questioned, again growing breathless as they ran across lush creepers and beneath hanging vines.

"No. I guess not," Troy answered. "But we don't have much choice, do we?"

"The ship. It has to be repaired. How long do you think it will take, Troy?"

"Since I've had the chance to see the damage, I can at least assure you that the ship's fixable," he said. "But how long? That's a question I just can't answer."

"We could be attacked at any time if the ship stays where it is now moored," Samantha worried aloud.

"I intend to try and do something about that," Troy said. "The ship has to be moved to where we will have a better view of what's happening on land."

"There's such a place?"

"We'll find it. There has to be a place somewhere along shore where the beach leads into barren land instead of jungle."

"I hope you're right," Samantha said, catching her breath when she finally saw the ship through the trees.

Troy slowed his pace, sensing that Samantha had run her limit. He placed his free arm about her waist and led her onto the longboat. Joshua helped get the boat out in the water along with Troy, and then they both climbed into it and began paddling to the moored ship.

"Perhaps we can find a place where we can get the ship closer to land," Troy said, giving Samantha a look from over his shoulder, seeing her weariness as she clutched to the seat. "It would make it easier for repairs."

"I'll be so glad to get back to America," Samantha grumbled. "I'm so tired of this way of life. When will it end, Troy?"

"Soon, I hope," Troy answered. "But once we do get back to Charleston Harbor, I've got to report to the authorities. It could be awkward, Sam, without your father or Franklin at my side."

"You've got the Union soldiers still on board who were sent to keep an eye on you," Samantha reassured, frowning at Troy's reference at not having her father to hand over to the authorities. But she knew that he hadn't meant anything by it. "They'll be your witnesses, Troy. Surely you'll get to go on your way."

"I only have their word that this would happen," he grumbled. "Nothing was placed on paper to assure me my freedom."

"A man is only as good as his word," Samantha said stiffly. "Surely you will be done right."

"We'll see. But for now we must solve the problems that are facing us today. Tomorrow will take care of itself."

The longboat came alongside Troy's powerful ship, and soon Samantha found herself back on board, growing numb with new discoveries. Everything was too quiet. Upon closer observation she saw that some of Troy's crew lay unconscious along the deck. And then it was discovered that the rest of the crew had been locked into the hold of the ship and the slaves were gone.

Lloyd was the first to come up from the hold, his eyes raging war in them. "They overpowered us and escaped," he growled. "The slaves heard talk of the smoke in the jungle and headhunters and got scared and fled. Damn it all to hell, the only one left is that fat one—the one named Jewel. She's protectin' Julia with a shotgun, she is."

Troy didn't want to hear anymore. He stepped up to the ship's rail and looked toward the jungle.

"Troy, what do we do now?" Samantha asked, edging up next to him.

Troy turned on a heel and gave her a silent, haunting stare, then walked on past her and began giving orders to find a more barren shore for mooring the ship. The anchor chain creaked as it was drawn up, and the winds began filling the sails as the ship again began limping along in the water.

Samantha clung to the ship's rail, tears thick in her eyes, saying her last silent good-byes to her father. He had been a good man. He had always fought hard for what he thought was right. Strange that now the slaves he had always considered vital to his existence had chosen to stay where he now lay at rest.

# Chapter Twenty=Nine

The ship had now been moored for two days. From the golden beach one could see flat plains for miles, yet to the right and left of this straight stretch of land lay the soft edges of the jungle.

Sails were being repaired aboard ship, masts strengthened, and carpenters and mates were busy stuffing caulking into the ship's opened seams.

Franklin had almost been forgotten, yet worry of the slaves came out daily in conversation. They had become too dependent on their masters for survival. In the jungle, how could they exist?

Troy had surmised that those who survived just might become slaves for other plantation owners who were known to be a part of the new Brazil. Franklin had earlier brought many families over on his ship from the Carolinas and neighboring states. Surely these plantations weren't too far from Franklin's and Craig's, yet Troy hadn't wanted to venture out to see if his assumption was correct. He was eager to get his ship back out to sea. Too much time had already gone by.

Troy and Samantha were strolling barefoot along the beach, feeling safe enough as men stood guard on the deck of the ship. Checkers romped along ahead of them, seeming to enjoy his moments away from the confines of the ship.

"The sand is so deliciously warm between my toes," Samantha said smiling. She reached her arm lazily over her head, the tail of her shirt hiking up out of her jeans, revealing the flat satin of her stomach. "I almost wish we could stay here forever now that I've grown used to it. I love the surf, the lushness of the jungle." She swung around and grabbed Troy's hands. "Don't you think it's exotic, darling?" she purred.

"Exotic, yes, safe, no," Troy grumbled. "The longer we stay here the more dangerous it becomes for us. We've already been discovered, you know." His eyes squinted as he looked toward the jungle. "Have you seen her today, Sam?" he asked matter-of-factly.

"The Indian maiden?" she asked, her gaze following his. "No. But you know how quickly she materializes and disappears. It's almost like the hummingbirds we see. First they are here and then they are gone."

"The next time I see her I'm going to follow her," Troy said, easing his hands from Samantha's. He stooped and bent a knee to rest on the sand, and began letting the sand sift like flour through his outstretched fingers.

"You're not serious," Samantha said, moving to her knees beside him. "Why would you do that?" She was glad that she had thought to pack her jeans into her travel trunks, for to her they were an important part of her wardrobe. She enjoyed the freedom they afforded her, especially now, while on the beach.

"The Indian maiden is intriguing, to say the least,"

Troy said chuckling.

Samantha's eyes blazed. She gave Troy a shove, causing him to topple sideways onto the sand. "You beast," she laughed. "If you think I'd let you go after that beautiful creature, you're daft."

Troy reached up and laced his fingers through her hair and drew her down on the sand beside him. "Aw, do I hear a hint of jealousy in your voice?" he teased. "Now you couldn't be jealous of some wild little thing who probably doesn't even know the first word of English, could you?"

"That would make her even more intriguing, wouldn't it, darling?" Samantha purred, slinking closer to him, drawn into passion's web as his hand slipped inside her shirt and softly cupped a breast.

"That and her dark, innocent eyes," Troy further teased. "Ah, what secrets must lie in their depths."

"Troy, please quit talking about her as though you're fantasizing about seducing her," Samantha said, her pulse racing as Troy now imprisoned her beneath him, ignoring the fact that they were in full view of those who cared to look from the ship.

Samantha knew the dangers of Troy's kisses and caresses and knew how hard it was to back away from him once he had fully ignited the flame inside her. Splaying her hands against his chest, she pushed him away from her. She caught the desire's glimmer in his ocean blue eyes and fought the urge that such a look dared her to do.

"Darling," she softly laughed. "Quit looking at me like that. You surely know that I'm melting with need of you right here on the spot."

"You mentioned seduction," he said huskily. "My dear, you were right. But you had the wrong female

421

in mind."

Feeling a flush suffuse her cheeks, Samantha smiled coyly back at him. "Pray tell, my sweet, who it is you wish to live out your fantasies with," she said in a throaty whisper.

"My darling, you have to know that there is only you," he murmured, taking her hands from his chest, pulling her up against him. "But for now, just a kiss?"

"Yes," Samantha whispered. "Just—a—kiss."

Their lips met, gentle and sweet. Samantha felt the grip of ecstasy coil inside her. She moaned as he ground his body hard into hers, letting her feel the hard outline of his risen sex against her thigh.

She wriggled until again she was free. "Darling," she said, frustration causing her heart to pound against her ribs. "I'm sure we've created an audience. You're going to cause those women-hungry men who make up your crew to go mad with need."

Troy rose to his feet and helped her up beside him. "They had all better be attending to their duties," he grumbled. "I've paid them well. Even my best friends who still are a part of the crew."

He glanced up at the ship. "Do you know—this is one of the hardest things about this voyage," he said softly. "Knowing how I've inconvenienced those men to leave their families and travel with me. As you've noticed, most are avoiding me now. I'm sure they're sore as hell at me for causing the ship to be sidetracked to Brazil. If I hadn't come to see you that last time—"

"Those men knew the risks and they agreed whole-heartedly to your plans," Samantha argued.

"The plans I told them about did not include a red-haired, green-eyed lady," he said dryly. "You've got to know, Sam, that they do resent your being on board."

"All the more for you not to manhandle me for all to see," she fumed, storming away from him, more hurt than angry by his words. He seemed to be blaming her. She wondered if he had forgotten how much she had lost on this ill-fated voyage to Brazil. When one lost a father, it was like losing a part of one's self.

"Samantha, wait up," Troy said from behind her.

Samantha stopped and turned to face him. He went to her and framed her face between his hands.

"I'm not sure what I said to get your dander up but I'm sorry," he murmured. "Now where do you think you're going in such a huff?"

"Back to the ship," she said stiffly.

"But I thought you were enjoying the sand between your toes," he teased. "Let's walk just a bit further down the beach. What do you say?"

Footsteps approaching was cause for Samantha's delay in response. She turned her head just in time to see Joshua rushing toward her, worry lines wrinkling his dark face.

Samantha broke away from Troy and met Joshua's approach. "Joshua, what is it?" she asked. "You look so—so—worried."

Joshua took a handkerchief from his pocket and dabbed at beaded perspiration on his brow. "Miss Samantha, Jewel sent me to fetch you," he said hoarsely. "It's Miss Julia. She's ailin'."

Samantha quickly remembered how withdrawn and pale Julia had been since the burial of her husband. She had not at all been her high-spirited self. Samantha had even found herself worrying about her cousin. She gave Troy a questioning glance, then brushed on past Joshua and headed toward the ship. Troy fell in step beside her.

"What do you think is wrong with Julia?" he asked, scraping sand from the back of his breeches. "I've noticed her hanging her head over the rail of the ship the past two mornings. She appeared to be quite ill."

Samantha gave him an incredulous look. She stopped and grabbed him by the arm. "Why didn't you tell me?" she asked, eyes wide.

"Why should I?" he said, forking an eyebrow. "She is not the favored topic between us."

"But if she's ill—"

"You really care, Sam?"

Samantha gasped. "You'd think I wouldn't?"

Troy lowered his eyes. "That was crude of me, wasn't it?" he murmured.

"It wasn't like you," she said, placing a hand gently to his cheek.

"Let's go together and see how she is," he encouraged.

"Do you really want to?"

"Yes. She is my responsibility, you know, since she's a passenger on my ship."

"That's the only reason, Troy?" Samantha asked, her old jealousies awakening inside her.

"No. I want to, because of you. She is your cousin. Remember? One day she'll be my cousin."

Samantha laughed softly, then her smile faded when she saw a movement in the jungle, over Troy's shoulder. "Troy, she's there," she said in a low rush of words.

Troy's eyebrows forked. "Who's where?" he said, turning on a heel, following Samantha's steady stare.

"It was the Indian maiden," Samantha said, clutching onto Troy's arm. "She was dressed in white—a long tunic—gathered at the waist by a wide purple sash."

Troy's eyes slowly scanned the jungle but saw nothing. He laughed absently. "The tropical sun is causing you to imagine things," he said.

"She was there. I saw her," Samantha argued. "You know how quickly she can disappear."

Troy kneaded his brow. "Well, she isn't there now," he grumbled. "Damn. I'd sure like to know what she finds so interesting about us."

"You're just as curious about her, Troy."

"Yes, that I am."

"Not that I'm happy about your curiosity in another woman, be she of white or dark skin," Samantha said, giving him a challenging, sour glance.

"I think I've already heard that particular lecture," Troy chuckled, guiding her by the elbow on up the gangplank as Joshua and Checkers lagged along behind them.

"Sorry,"Samantha laughed.

Together they went below deck to Julia's cabin. Samantha inched the door open and caught sight of Julia stretched out atop her bunk, groaning as she clutched a blanket up just beneath her chin.

Troy blanched when he saw Julia. He leaned down in Samantha's face. "You go on in," he softly encouraged. "I'll wait here. But let me know real soon what you find is the cause for Julia's discomfort."

Samantha nodded, then stepped gingerly on inside the cabin. A kerosene lamp was lighted on a table beside the bunk, casting a soft glow on Julia's ashen face. Jewel was there on her knees, bathing Julia's brow with a damp cloth.

When Julia let out another pitiful moan, Samantha's insides tightened, yet she crept onward until she was standing over Julia, looking down at her.

"Jewel, what seems to be the cause?" Samantha softly asked.

Jewel's dark eyes turned up to Samantha. "She's fightin' agains' losin' her chil'," she said somberly. "Po' thing, she be only a few weeks along and ain't strong enough to carry a baby full term."

Samantha's breath caught in her throat. "She's— with—child?" she gasped.

Julia looked up at Samantha through tears, her eyes drawn with pain. "Your father's," she said raspily. "Samantha, perhaps a son your father—always—hoped for."

The word *son* seemed to stab Samantha in the heart. She had always felt her father's resentment for her having been a daughter. "Did Father know before he died?" she asked shallowly, again hating herself for feeling jealous, this time for a child who might never even take its first breath of life.

"I—I told him of the possibility the very day—that he—died," Julia sobbed, turning her eyes toward the wall. Her fingers tightened on the blanket as she let out another loud wail of pain.

Samantha felt desperate, suddenly wanting the child to be born. If it was a son, he could carry on the Johnston name. If it was a daughter, Samantha would welcome her as her sister. She had always secretly yearned for a sister.

"Jewel," she said, her back straightening. "What can I do to help?"

"It's up to de Lord," Jewel answered. "Just stay close by. Should she begin true labor, then is when ol' Jewel'd need he'p."

Samantha heard Troy clear his throat nervously. She

swung around and went to him and explained the unhappy situation. Together they paced, waiting word.

Then Jewel came to them, her face shining in a broad smile. "The crisis is past," she said, patting Samantha on the arm. "Seems Julia has won de' battle. De' pains have stopped. Thank de Lord! De' Lord heard my prayers."

"Can we go and see her now?" Samantha asked anxiously.

"Bes' only you go, Samantha honey," Jewel said, smiling sheepishly up at Troy. "She's sleepin' like a baby. Too many footsteps might disturb her rest."

Samantha looked up at Troy and received his silent nod of okay, then went to stand over Julia and studied the face no longer distorted in pain. Something grabbed at Samantha's heart. It skipped a beat as the other time when she saw the resemblance of her mother in Julia as she lay so peacefully sleeping. Was it the frailness? Was it the soft curve of her jawline, the tiny nose? Or was it her mouth—a mouth of sensuous beauty?

"How? Why?" Samantha uttered, not understanding.

When Julia smacked her lips and rolled over onto her side, breathing softly, Samantha turned and tiptoed from the room, stunned by her strange discovery.

Jewel stood outside the door waiting for Samantha. One glance was all it took for Jewel to know that something peculiar had happened in the cabin, and she couldn't understand what happened, since Julia was surely still sound asleep. But it was there in Samantha's eyes and on her face. It was as though she had seen a ghost.

"Samantha, honey?" Jewel asked, glancing at Samantha and then into the dim shadows of Julia's cabin.

"It's nothing, Jewel," Samantha said, laughing awkwardly. "Seems being on this ship and away from Johnston Oaks causes my imagination to play tricks on me."

"Did Julia wake up and say somethin' to you?"

"No. Truly, Jewel. I'm fine."

Samantha looked around for Troy. "Where's Troy?" she asked.

"He said somethin' 'bout checkin' on somethin' he saw in the jungle," Jewel said, patting Samantha gently on the arm. "Bes' you go to yo' cabin. Ol' Jewel see to it that you gets a nice, hot bath and then a nap."

Samantha's pulse raced. "Troy said that he was going to check on something in the jungle?" she said anxiously, watching Jewel as she awaited an answer.

"Yes'm. Tha's what he done said."

Flinging her hair back from her shoulders, Samantha began hurrying away from Jewel. "Then I must go with him," she said from across her shoulder. "A bath and nap will come later, Jewel."

Jewel began wringing her hands nervously. "Samantha, Massa Troy didn't say nothin' 'bout you goin', too. Come back. Min' yo' own business."

"This is my business, Jewel," Samantha shouted back. "Believe me it is."

Samantha went to her cabin and slipped into some boots and tied a ribbon about her hair to keep it back from her eyes. She grabbed her pistol and thrust it down into the waist of her jeans, then determinedly left her cabin.

Rushing to top deck and then down the gangplank, Samantha began searching for Troy, looking in the direction where they had seen the Indian maiden. She stopped long enough to shield her eyes from the pounding rays of the sun with a hand, looking more intensely through the soft greens of the jungle.

When she caught a glimpse of Troy's white shirt, she broke into a run. As before when in the jungle, the humid dampness closed in on her, making it hard for her to breathe. She panted, and her face felt hot, perspiration running from her brow in streams.

But finally she found herself only a few footsteps away from Troy. When he heard her fast approach, he swung around and glared angrily at her.

"Sam, what the devil do you think you're doing?" he growled, placing his hands on his hips. "Where do you think you're going?"

Struggling for breath and wiping perspiration from her hot cheeks, she stopped before him and looked up at him. When she caught her breath she smiled coyly.

"I'm going with you," she said matter-of-factly.

"The hell you are," Troy spat, his blue eyes flashing angrily back at her. He pointed toward the ship. "Now get back to the ship, Sam. It's too dangerous for you to be here."

"Since when do I have to obey your commands?" she snapped back, lifting her chin defiantly. "Don't treat me as one of your crew, Troy. I refuse to even let you try."

Troy's eyes rolled upward. "Sam, your stubborn streak is showing again," he groaned. "I thought you agreed to behave yourself."

Sam's eyes grew wide. "Behave myself?" she said incredulously. "Now you're treating me like a child!"

Troy clasped his fingers angrily to her shoulders. "This isn't the time to be arguing over anything," he growled. "You must get back to the ship."

"So you can follow a beautiful, primitive lady?" she hissed. "Never, Troy."

"Your damn jealousy is sometimes more annoying than your stubbornness," he sighed.

Samantha's eyes caught movement over Troy's shoulder, ahead in the brush. Again she saw the white tunic and purple sash. "Troy, while you're standing here being bossy, she's getting away," she teased.

"I'm sure she's already too far in the jungle for me ever to catch up with her now," he grumbled, dropping his hands, resting one on a holstered gun at his waist. "Thanks to you, my sweet."

Samantha nodded toward where she had just seen the maiden. "Take a look, Troy," she said softly. "I do believe you're wrong. She's there. Just up ahead. I just saw her."

Troy turned on a heel and caught a glimpse of the white tunic just as the maiden again slipped out of sight. "Damn it," he grumbled. "I saw her but she's gone again."

"But she's not so far away we can't catch up with her," Samantha encouraged.

"*We?*" Troy said, again incredulously eyeing Samantha.

"Yes, *we*. I am going, Troy," Samantha said flatly. "And if we don't go ahead now, we're sure to miss her altogether."

"You're impossible," Troy sighed.

Then, surprising Samantha, he swept an arm around her waist and drew her next to him as he began moving on through the jungle.

"But come on," he grumbled. "Time's wasting."

Samantha smiled smugly at her victory, but she didn't say anything for fear he would just as quickly change his mind. Instead, she talked of other things.

430

"Why are you so determined to follow this Indian?" she asked. "What if she belongs to a group of headhunters? What if she's luring us into a trap?"

"There's something about her that makes me believe she's not a part of any devious plot against us," Troy said, kicking at a tangle of underbrush and removing it.

"How could you possibly think that?" Samantha scoffed. "Surely there's more to this than meets the eye, Troy. What are your reasons for following her?"

"Curiosity. Unadulterated curiosity, I suppose," he chuckled. "Anything wrong with that?"

"Perhaps," she said. "But haven't you heard the old saying that curiosity kills the cat?"

"Scares me to death," he chuckled, teasingly drawing her even more tightly to his side.

Samantha grew solemn. "Troy, what if we *are* walking into a trap?" she said dryly. "Perhaps we should have been escorted by some of your armed crew. You do remember the burning houses and the disappearance of the slaves and Franklin, don't you?"

"I must confess that thinking about that curls my toes," he grumbled. "But I feel that if we came storming into the jungle with several armed men, we'd for sure be asking for trouble. As it is, we may be treated fairly." His brow furrowed. He gave Samantha a bitter stare. "Damn it, Sam," he growled. "I won't rest nights until I know Franklin's fate."

Samantha broke away from him. She stopped and placed a hand on his arm. "Is that what this is really all about?" she asked. "Franklin? You've no interest whatever in that Indian maiden?"

"Well, now, I didn't say that," he teased.

"Oh, Troy," Samantha argued. "Get serious. You've

come into the jungle, following the Indian, hoping to find clues into Franklin's whereabouts, haven't you?"

"Something like that," he said, his eyes moody. "I'd feel much better about my future—our future—if I could hand Franklin over to the authorities once we enter Charleston Harbor."

"We've talked about that before," Samantha sighed. "We had agreed that the Union officers on board your ship would be witness to what happened."

"That's not enough," Troy said dryly. "Not if I can help it."

"What then?"

"There's you, Sam."

"Me?"

"As long as there's a possibility of Franklin's being alive, he's a threat to you."

Samantha paled. She hadn't considered this possibility.

"So? Shall we go and see if we can find news of the bastard, Sam?"

"Whatever you say, Troy."

He chuckled. "Now you agree with my suggestion," he said. "But only after you knew we'd gone too far for you to turn back and return safely to the ship alone."

"Clever, aren't I?" Samantha giggled. She felt all warm inside as he lowered a brief kiss to her lips, and then they walked on together, their eyes again searching for the white tunic and the purple sash.

# *Chapter Thirty*

A small waterfall catching the shafts of sunlight drew Samantha and Troy toward it, taking them to the very edges of the jungle.

Troy quickly held his arm in front of Samantha, blocking her further approach. Samantha saw the reason why. Their search had led them to a small village that had been built along the shore of a narrow, unruffled river that slowly meandered toward the blue waters of the Atlantic.

Colorful macaws were flying about, in and out of the spray of the waterfall that tumbled smoothly over a small rise of rock. Indian maidens, dressed in long, white tunics with assorted, colorful sashes about their waists and wearing mantas, arranged to form both a headdress and a wrapping for the shoulders, were at the river, filling large earthen jars with water and carrying them on their shoulders back toward the village.

The village included several *ajoupas* which were palm thatch huts made from clay with palm leaf roofs. The houses faced a square in which stone images in the shape of animals and birds stood. There weren't many warriors in the village readily seen, only a few at the river, building canoes. They wore brief loincloths, and their dark hair had been strangely shaved in various fashions, each one much different from the next.

Suddenly the Indian maiden in pursuit stepped from behind a tree and boldly faced Samantha and Troy. Her face was almost miniature, and her features were so tiny, yet she was beautiful in her copper sheen. Her shining black braids were entwined with flowers. She wore large loops of golden earrings in each earlobe. Her expressive, large dark eyes, warm and friendly, sparkled like the sunbeams in the water. She appeared to be the only maiden who wore no mantas to hide her hair. Troy had to wonder if that meant that she was special in this particular tribe of Indians.

*"Cómo se llama usted?"* the maiden asked in a low, sultry voice, directing her question to Troy.

Having learned the skills of speaking Spanish in his childhood, Troy quickly recognized the question being asked. She wanted to know his name. He was surprised that she spoke Spanish. Yet, if she spoke Spanish, could she also know the English language?

*"Habla usted Ingles?"* he tested.

*"Si,"* she said, a smile lighting her face. "Coiiyur speaks some English."

Troy's shoulders relaxed. He gave Samantha a triumphant smile, then looked back at the lovely temptress standing before him.

"Coiiyur?" he said, obviously struggling with the pronunciation. "That is your name?"

"It means Morning Star in the language of the Guarani Indian," Morning Star laughed softly. "Morning Star is easier to say, *si*?''

Troy returned her laugh. ''*Si*. Yes. Much easier,'' he said. ''You are fluent in three languages?''

''My father, Strong Eagle, taught me well,'' she said. Her eyes shifted to Samantha. She took a step forward and inched her hand upward, daring a touch to Samantha's red, satiny hair. ''Lovely. It is the color of the setting sun.''

Samantha smiled. ''*Muchas Gracias*,'' she murmured, showing Troy that she also knew a thing or two about different languages. She didn't like what she saw in his eyes. He seemed completely captivated by the Indian. But how could he not be? She was enchantingly beautiful.

''Are you called by a name which matches your hair?'' Morning Star asked, still looking admiringly at Samantha's hair.

''No. My name is Samantha Johnston,'' Samantha said.

''And yours?'' Morning Star said, looking up at Troy. ''What is your name, and why did you choose to follow me?''

''Troy. Troy Gilbert,'' Troy mumbled, somehow uneasy under her steady stare. ''Sam and I saw you watching us. We thought we'd see why you were, and—''

''Sam?'' Morning Star asked, interrupting him, looking on past Troy, as though expecting someone else to appear from the shadows of the jungle. ''Who is this Sam you speak of?''

Troy chuckled. He placed an arm about Samantha's waist and drew her against his side. ''Samantha is Sam,'' he said. ''It is her nickname.''

Morning Star frowned. ''Nickname?'' she questioned.

"I do not know such a word."

"It is a descriptive name given instead of or in addition to a person's given name," he carefully explained. "In a sense Morning Star is a nickname. Do you understand?"

Morning Star placed a forefinger contemplatively to her chin. "I think so," she murmured. Then she folded her arms across her chest. "You say you come because you saw me watching you. Is that the only reason? Other white men have come for ugly reasons. The Guarani lose trust in the white man."

Samantha tensed, and feeling Troy's arm tightening about her waist didn't make her feel better about things. She gave him a wary look. She could see his uneasiness by the way his cheek twitched nervously.

"Why were you watching us?" Troy asked.

Morning Star lowered her eyes and then rose them slowly upward and again looked at Samantha's hair. "It is the color of her hair," she murmured. "It is—it is—what I would think would be found on the sun goddess."

Samantha gasped softly. "My hair is what you are so fascinated with?" she said, running her fingers over the sides of her hair, where it was drawn back and tied by a ribbon.

"*Si,*" Morning Star said, her dark eyes smiling. Then her gaze moved back to Troy and her smile faded. "You no tell me why you're here."

"There is a white man—a man who is not very nice, who we are in search of," Troy said thickly. "We thought you seemed friendly enough—one who might tell us if you knew of such a man."

"His name?" Morning Star asked, her radiance fading into doubtful shadows crossing her face.

"Franklin LaFontaine," Troy said, hope rising inside

436

him when he saw a flash of recognition lighting her eyes.

"Is he not your friend?" she cautiously asked.

"Like I said—he is not a nice man," Troy said. "Such a man is not my friend nor Samantha's."

Morning Star nodded her head. "*Sí*. I know such a man," she said, matter-of-factly, then a look of wonder showed in her expressive eyes. "Why would this man burn his house and then the other one?" she blurted.

Troy was taken aback by this sudden question. Samantha's breath caught in her throat. She gazed up at Troy, stunned. Troy looked back at her, his lips set in a narrow line. Then, once again, he focused his full attention back on Morning Star.

"What do you mean?" he asked hoarsely.

"Morning Star is always restless," she said. "I wander. I see many things. I was watching the black-skinned people working in the cotton fields, then suddenly I see this man by the name of Franklin begin setting fire to his house and then—then the other. Why would a man do this? In Morning Star's eyes the houses were great castles."

Again Samantha and Troy exchanged quick glances.

"Franklin—did—that?" Samantha gasped. "Troy, why would he?"

Troy took a step toward Morning Star. "How do you know it was that particular man?" he asked dryly.

"He has had past differences with my father," she said softly. Then she proudly lifted her chin. "My father is the chieftain of this tribe of Guarani Indians. I am the people's princess. I am Princess Coiiyur. Anyone who takes land in this area has to answer to my father."

"I thought the land was owned by Emperor Don Pedro the second," Troy said thickly, nervously shifting his feet, feeling uncomfortable about getting into politics with the Indian, especially now that he knew her status as princess. She surely had much to say about how things were run in this region.

"The Guarani are the sole owners," Morning Star said coolly. "If the white man is tricked into paying Don Pedro money, so be it, but he is paying twice because he also pays my father."

"I see," Troy said, kneading his brow. He cleared his throat nervously. "Franklin LaFontaine. Did you see what happened to him and his slaves after he set fire to his house?"

"He was a crazy man," Morning Star said, shrugging. "He chased the black people off, then fled into the jungle himself. Morning Star has not seen him since."

Samantha shook her head slowly back and forth. "Why would Franklin do this?" she murmured.

"There is only one answer that makes any sense," Troy grumbled. "He knew that we would catch up with him sooner or later. He knew that he would lose everything in the end: his house, his slaves, his plantation. He made sure nobody else would have them."

"Even the house built for father?"

"Even that. Franklin considered that house his since he most surely supervised its being built."

"He was even stranger than I had ever imagined," Samantha whispered. "He was a man unlike any I—I ever knew before."

Then she remembered another man: Marion Yarborough. Though he was another world away, he was always there haunting her consciousness. He and Franklin surely had been poured from the same ugly mold.

"No. I forgot another man," she quickly interjected. "Marion Yarborough. He's also as despicable." She had almost forgotten that she had this particular man to deal with once she was back in America. How could she have forgotten that he had murdered and raped? She still had to find a way to seek revenge.

"And Franklin's a man very much alive," Troy growled.

Samantha's hand went to her throat. "I didn't even think about that," she said dryly. Her gaze moved slowly around Troy and into the soft greens of the jungle. "He could even be there now, watching us."

"Morning Star can tell that you say the truth when you say that this white man named Franklin not your friend," Morning Star said. "There is much fear in your eyes, Samantha. Do not be afraid. The Guarani warriors will protect you while you here." She looked toward the village. "Come. Meet my father. He is in his council house with most of his warriors. It is their time to meet and talk."

Troy's eyes wavered. "If it is their time to have council then we will be interfering," he said hoarsely. "Samantha and I don't want to do anything to anger your chieftain father."

"Do not forget who I am," Morning Star said softly, her eyes once again sparkling, warm and friendly. "I am the princess. Everything stops—even talk—when I enter a room."

Samantha gave Troy a sour look when she saw his mood lightening as a smile lifted his lips.

"I'm sure it does," he chuckled.

"Then you will be my guests?" Morning Star said excitedly, placing a delicate hand on Troy's and

Samantha's arms. "It is good to find special friends among the white man."

"We'd be delighted to be your guests," Troy said, laughing softly at her exuberance. "Won't we, Sam?"

Samantha's eyes blazed back at him. They had found out what they had come for; they knew that Franklin wasn't dead; so why didn't they return to the safety of the ship? As far as she could tell, there was no reason whatsoever to carry this thing any further with the Indian maiden. It seemed to her that the only reason possible was Troy's infatuation with the beautiful Indian maiden, a princess even.

Morning Star didn't wait for Samantha's answer. "Just please follow me," she said, already walking alongside the banks of the river in the direction of the village.

Samantha fell into step beside Troy, still glowering up at him.

"You don't seem too anxious to be a special guest, hon," he whispered down at her.

"There surely is a reason why she wants us to be," she whispered back.

"Why would you think?"

"Our heads."

"What?"

"Some of the Guarani Indians are headhunters. Who's to say even Princess Morning Star isn't? You know her interest in my hair."

"Perhaps she just wants your scalp," Troy teased.

Samantha blanched. "Good Lord, Troy," she gasped. "Do you think she really might?"

"It would make a lovely wig," he continued to tease.

Samantha stumbled over a rock. Troy caught her. She implored him with the crisp green of her eyes. "Troy, you *are* teasing, aren't you?" she softly asked, as he helped to steady her back on her feet.

"Darling, surely you can tell when I am."

"But this is different."

"How?"

"We're about to meet with primitive people. Who knows what they'll do with us?"

"Trust me, darling," Troy said, brushing a kiss across her lips. "We're safe. Just trust me?"

"Well, I guess I have no other choice," Samantha said, again walking alongside him, hearing the silent hush as Morning Star led them into the village square.

Dark, brooding eyes peeked out from all the village hut doors and windows. Everyone who had been outside only moments ago had disappeared. The world stood still, except for Samantha, Troy, and Morning Star.

Morning Star gestured with a hand toward a larger hut which had been built in the center of the square. Smoke spiraled from a smoke hole at the top, and sheets of grass mats hung over the doors and windows.

Morning Star lifted the mat at the door. "I shall first alert my father," she said, then disappeared inside.

Troy shifted on his feet nervously, raking his fingers through his hair. Samantha silently observed his nervousness, anxiety building up in her when Morning Star didn't come from the hut as quickly as expected.

"What's taking so long?" Samantha whispered, moving closer to Troy.

"Perhaps she's being scolded by her father," Troy said teasingly, trying to lighten the mood between them.

"You're the one badly in need of a scolding," Samantha snapped. "Troy, what have you gotten us into?"

"No one twisted your arm to force you to come with me," he snapped back.

Morning Star finally returned. She smiled sheepishly from Troy to Samantha. "My father and his warriors do not wish to see you at this time," she said. "They are deep in council. Let me direct you to my hut where I will serve you well and then leave you to rest until the counciling ends in my father's council house."

Samantha gave Troy a sour glance, wanting to torment him about this princess who had bragged of being so important. Samantha had to wonder just how safe Troy thought them to be now. They most certainly hadn't been welcomed into the village with open arms!

When a grass mat rose from behind a window and a large man with dark, daring eyes looked directly at Samantha, her knees grew weak and her pulse began to race. The man wore a fancy headdress which had large, colorful plumes and many shades of feathers woven into it. Loops of gold earrings were at each earlobe, and about his neck, lying against a massive, bare copper-colored chest, were necklaces made of rare metals, encrusted with precious stones. His nose was broad and flat, his lips full and his cheeks round. But it was his eyes that unnerved Samantha as she felt they were boring holes through her.

"Come. My hut is a special one, away from the others," Morning Star said, lifting the skirt of her tunic as she padded barefoot across the beaten-down earth which spread out grassless around all the huts.

Samantha inched even closer to Troy. "We'd best leave, don't you think?" she murmured. "Troy, didn't you see that large Indian staring out at me from the council house?"

"Darling, I'm beginning to worry about you and your imagination," he said, giving her a wry smile.

"What?" she gasped.

"I didn't see any such man," Troy said, shrugging.

Anger rose color into Samantha's cheeks. "That's because you are blinded by this Indian maiden's loveliness," she hissed, then closed her lips in a straight line, determined to say no more. If their fate was to die together, so be it. There was nothing more that she could do about it. It was for sure that her one small pistol couldn't assure her freedom!

Morning Star led them away from the square of huts to one whose walls were vine-covered, where a courtyard garden displayed colorful flocks of flowers and even orange trees with bright circles of oranges hanging bountifully from the limbs.

Raising the grass mat at the door, Morning Star welcomed her guests inside her dwelling.

Samantha's eyes widened as her gaze moved about the room. There was a soft fire burning in the firespace built low into the ground, circled by gray stones, yet this was emitting enough light to make everything in the dwelling quite visible in its uniqueness.

Skins of animals fashioned into rugs and small hangings were everywhere. Unusual songbirds were in three gilded cages, adding a touch of beauty with their colorful plumages. The shine from precious jewels encrusted into metal lay on a table fashioned from coils of strong rope made of the *cortadera* plant.

"Sit by the fire," Morning Star said. "I will leave you to go instruct Tukira to bring refreshment."

Holding onto her elbow, Troy helped Samantha down onto a fur rug. "And who is this Tukira?" he asked cautiously, easing down beside Samantha to also sit.

"My maiden who sees to my personal comforts," Morning Star said, smiling sweetly down at Troy. "Morning Star will return. Soon."

Samantha drew her legs up to her chest and hugged them, looking into the dancing flames of the fire. All argument had left her.

"You're so quiet, Sam," Troy said, snaking an arm about her waist. "Are you afraid?"

She let her eyes move to him, seeing how his thick lashes shadowed his eyes in the soft glow of the fire. "If I were, I wouldn't admit to it," she said stubbornly.

"No, I guess not," Troy chuckled. He nuzzled her neck. "Darling, I find this stimulating."

"Lord, Troy," Samantha gasped, shoving him away from her. "How can you even think about such a thing, now?"

He nodded his head. "Take a look around you," he said. "Now is this exotic or isn't it?"

She laughed scornfully. "If you mean dead animals' skins, no, I'd say not."

A bird began to warble throatily from one of the cages. Another began to answer back.

"*That* is what I'm speaking of," Troy said. "Those birds evoke a feeling of being alone on a tropical island, wouldn't you say? And then there's this fire—"

"Oh, hush!" Samantha fumed. "Whose imagination is growing wild now?"

She gave him another sour glance when she heard his continued, annoying chuckles of amusement. Then her eyes turned quickly to the door as Morning Star returned, and another beautiful maiden followed silently behind her, bearing a wicker basket which was then

444

placed on the earthen floor at Troy's feet.

Morning Star slapped her hands together, ordering Tukira from the hut by doing so. Then, smiling, she settled down beside Troy and began removing ceramic bowls filled with assorted foods from the basket.

"We shall share food, talk, and then I shall leave you to rest," Morning Star murmured.

Samantha's eyebrows raised suspiciously, wondering why Morning Star had mentioned leaving them to rest alone not once, but twice. What was the plan? To stuff the white intruders with food, then behead them? A shiver ran up and down her spine with the thought.

Platters carved from wood were placed before Samantha and Troy. They each watched as Morning Star plied them with exotic food, the aromas making it hard to resist.

"First there is *cancha* which is toasted corn. Then I give you *cau cau* which is made of white potatoes, beef tripe, hot peppers, and *herba buena*, a type of wild spearmint," Morning Star murmured. "Also I shall offer you *rocotos rellenos*, stuffed peppers and *anticuchos*, marinated beef heart, and *ceviche* which is fish and shellfish that has been prepared in lemon juice."

Tukira came back into the hut carrying a large earthen jar on her shoulder and two cups on a flat, wooden tray. She placed these on the floor and again hurried from the hut.

"And for your drinks, I offer you *chicha*, a beverage made from fermented, crushed corn," she said, giving Troy and Samantha a small smile, which to Troy harbored on suspicious. The word *fermented* could be the key to her coy smile. He looked at the liquid as she poured it in the cups. It was yellow and cloudy, but it didn't have

445

the smell of fermented wine or of whiskey, so he shrugged off his suspicions and took a slow sip.

The bitterness nipped at his tongue, making him again wonder, but the platter of food being pushed up at him made him dismiss any thoughts of worry, and he heartily ate.

Samantha fingered quietly with the food. She was more thirsty than hungry, so she accepted the delicious, yet strange liquid, continually being added to her cup as she emptied it. She didn't notice that Morning Star wasn't eating or drinking and that drums had begun to sound outside the hut, combined with the chanting of many warriors.

Morning Star chattered incessantly, watching the glassiness in Samantha's and Troy's eyes become more vivid as each sip of *chica* was taken.

"When I first saw your hair, Samantha, I truly thought you were the sun goddess come to bless our people," Morning Star said, again hungrily eyeing the red shine to Samantha's hair. Morning Star boldly reached her tiny fingers to the length of ribbon tied about Samantha's long coil of hair and released it. Her eyes beamed as Samantha's hair tumbled loose to fall across her shoulders in a satin, red sheen.

Samantha giggled lazily and wove her fingers through her loosened hair. "You like it so well?" she purred. "I am honored, Morning Star." She reached her fingers to Morning Star's braid of hair and its display of flowers. "I like yours too, Morning Star," she giggled. "I'll trade you."

Troy's eyebrows forked as he stared incredulously at Samantha. It was obvious that she was in a drunken state. Even his head was swimming crazily. He looked down into the cup which he held. Strange how the yellow liquid seemed to be spinning!

Shaking his head in an attempt to clear it of its fuzziness he set the cup down on the floor and attempted to rise. But his skin flamed where Morning Star softly touched his hand, urging him to remain sitting next to her. He gave her a lazy smile, then resumed eating while she again rattled on.

"Our village had a heavenly visitor one other time," Morning Star said dreamily. "It was the moon goddess. She loved to pick flowers in the land of the Guaranis. She came only during the day. At night she had to be in the sky, ready to cast her silver light over the land."

She refilled Samantha's cup, then continued her throaty-toned tale. "The moon goddess's companion was the cloud goddess," she purred. "Each took the form and manner of dress of a Guarani maiden so they could wander through the fields and jungles and no one would know they were goddesses." Her eyes grew sad. "Suddenly the moon goddess and her beautiful golden hair came no more to our village," she sighed. "Her lovely hair, it—"

She said no more about it and again stroked her fingers along Samantha's lovely hair. "*Sí*, so lovely," she whispered. Then she rose quickly to her feet, slapping her hands together in a command for Tukira to come and gather up the uneaten food and platters, leaving the earthen jar and cups behind.

"Now I will leave you to your rest," Morning Star said, smiling at Samantha and Troy. "I will come to you when my father is ready to accept you into the council house."

With a silent sweep of the skirt of her tunic she took her leave. Troy rose to his feet and went to look from the door, now in wonder of the pounding drums and the low chants. But Samantha's fingers suddenly walking up his breeches' legs was cause for him to forget everything but her. He had a demanding need of her, a hunger never known to him before, and from the way she was groping for him, he knew that her need matched his. Strange that it was here, in such a place, at such a time.

He fell to his knees, unbuttoned her shirt and kissed her breast, consuming its taut tip with the liquid fire of his tongue. Her sensuous moan drove him maddeningly onward. He bent her back onto the skins and possessed her with his hands, wildly kneading her breast with one while lowering her jeans with the other.

When her boots stopped the jeans at her ankles, he went with a low snarl to them and jerked the boots and then the jeans away from her.

Consumed by this delicious languor that had him in its spell, Troy lifted one of Samantha's feet to his lips. Toe by toe he kissed her, then left a trail of fire as his eager lips tasted her sweetness along the inner silkiness of her legs until the insides of her thighs were reached. He felt her tremor against his mouth as he drank from her sweetness where her legs willingly parted, and then he moved his lips higher until he coaxed her lips apart and let his tongue seductively take charge of her mouth.

Samantha's arms went about him in a torrid embrace. She knew not when he had lowered his breeches, but she was well aware of his hardness as it entered her and began weaving its spell of bliss as he stroked her—stroked her—stroked her.

Moaning, she clasped her legs tightly about his rock-hard hips and rode with him. His lips were hot and hungry. His tongue was a leadened spear inside her mouth.

She clung. She sighed. Her desire swelled. Her passion peaked. And suddenly utter joy was reached as they shuddered excitingly against the other.

Smiling contentedly, Samantha sank back onto the softness of the fur stretched out beneath her. Never before had she experienced such unleashed pleasure. She licked her lips hungrily when she felt Troy's hands once more branding her with hot touches. And then she felt herself softly drifting off into a sleepy haze, only slightly awakening when she saw the small, diminutive figure of Morning Star creep into the hut and begin undressing before Troy's glazed eyes.

Something deep inside Samantha's consciousness wanted to rebel, but something held her back. It was this drugged feeling. Yes! She and Troy had been purposely drugged! She fluttered her lashes, willing herself to stay awake.

"No," Samantha cried as Morning Star smiled wickedly down at Troy, her intentions clear in the sparkling passion of her eyes.

Troy barely heard Samantha's protest. She seemed to be speaking from far away, inside a deep tunnel. Morning Star's smile teased his senses. Her hands on his arms, drawing him closer to her, dangerously firing his insides.

Samantha pushed her heady limbs up from the floor and crawled toward Troy and Morning Star. Cold sweat rose on her brow with the effort, and her lungs heaved. But then she was finally there. With a lunge she pulled Morning Star away from Troy.

Troy blinked his eyes when he saw Samantha jump on

top of Morning Star and attack her.

"You heathen witch!" Samantha cried, now pulling Morning Star's hair. "You can't get—away—with this!"

Morning Star let out a yelp, then she reached up and grabbed Samantha's breasts, giving them a yank.

"No!" Samantha sobbed, flinching with pain. She worked Morning Star's fingers away, then doubled up a fist and hit her in the chin, causing a cool crack to reverberate from wall to wall of the hut.

Reeling from the pain inflicted to her knuckles, Samantha placed them to her lips. Then she became aware that Morning Star no longer fought back. She was now stretched out, lifeless, beneath Samantha, blood trickling from the corner of her mouth. Samantha had rendered her unconscious! She smiled proudly, then heard Troy's voice reaching out for her, slurred and hardly audible.

"Sam?" Troy said drunkenly. "Darling." He rose to his knees and crawled toward her.

Samantha was glad that her faculties and strength had returned fully. It was apparent that Troy's eyes were still glassy. Yet she couldn't help but glare at him.

"Don't Sam darling me," she hissed, gathering her clothes in her arms. "You were enjoying her touch too much. Surely you had at least an inkling of what you were doing."

Troy let his tongue rake across his lips, feeling their complete dryness. He shook his head and blinked his eyes, finally becoming fully aware of everything. He stared blankly down at the nude, lifeless form of Morning Star and then up at Samantha who was fuming as she was now fully dressed and slipping her boots on.

450

"Sam, I honestly don't know what happened," he grumbled.

She threw his clothes at him. "Get into these. We've got to get out of here," she said icily. "I'm afraid there are more plans for us that we won't like."

Troy was still a bit dizzy when he rose to dress. Samantha placed her pistol in the waist of her jeans, then handed Troy's pistol to him. "Are you ready, Troy?" she asked, looking nervously toward the door, and then at Troy as he slipped into his last article of clothing. "Either we sneak out or we make a run for it."

"Run?" Troy chuckled. "God, Sam. My legs are hardly holding me up. They're like rubber."

A low rumbling sound and the earthen floor of the hut shifting strangely beneath their feet made Samantha and Troy exchange looks of wonder. They became aware of the sudden silence of the drums, and even the warriors had ceased their monotonous chants.

Another rumble was followed by the ground shaking, shifting the animal skins from side to side. Even Morning Star's body quivered with the strange movement.

"Sam, it could only be—"

Samantha completed his sentence. "An— earthquake?" she gasped.

"An earthquake!" Troy shouted, grabbing for Samantha as another shifting of earth tossed her sideways. The hut leaned and swayed, and the poles holding it up squeaked ominously.

"Troy!" Samantha cried, clinging to his arm.

"Rubbery legs or not, we've got to get the hell out of here!" Troy shouted. "We've got to get to the ship!"

He tensed when he heard loud shrieks of horror

451

surfacing from outside as another rumble was followed by the loud sound of splintering wood. He grabbed Samantha's hand and together they ran from the hut, mortified to find that half the huts in the village were collapsed and burning, and the Indians were running and screaming for their lives in all directions.

Wide zigzags of cracks could be seen in the ground where the earth had opened up and was still becoming wider. The sky was a peculiar yellow color, the piled density of altocumulus clouds becoming monstrous and black, howling down over the village.

And then the rain began to fall in wild torrents, almost blinding Samantha and Troy as they struggled to avoid the largest cracks in the earth. They jumped over one and then another. Gasping when they landed at the very edge of one which threatened to swallow them whole, they continued to run, knowing that their lives depended on each and every step that they took.

The village was left behind. Samantha labored for breath as she continued to run. She wiped her whipping hair and the rush of rain from her eyes and, while doing so, she ran into something that was suddenly in her path, knocking her from her feet.

Troy jerked around when he heard her scream, and when he saw what he had somehow missed in his eagerness to get through the jungle, he was jolted with alarm and quickly sick to his stomach.

Samantha pushed her way up from the ground, reaching for a thin pole that was thrust into the ground to support her weight against. When she looked up and saw what was lodged at the top of the pole, she became ghostly white and fell clumsily back to the ground.

She hid her head behind her hands and began

screaming. No matter how hard she tried, she couldn't block the empty sockets of Franklin's head from her consciousness. Nor could she forget the drawn, pained expression of his mouth. Franklin must have been screaming when he took his last breath of life. Even now Samantha could hear him, yet strangely it sounded more like herself!

Troy dropped to his knees and began shaking Samantha. "Sam! Get hold of yourself," he shouted. "Quit that damn screaming! We must get to the ship! Now!"

He couldn't help but glance at another pole only a few feet away. It displayed yet another head: that of what once had surely been a beautiful woman. Her golden hair fought back at the breeze tangling it in wet shreds, as though it had life in it.

"The moon goddess Morning Star spoke about," Troy shallowly whispered. "She was just another innocent woman, probably from a plantation. Probably American."

Samantha now only sobbed. She shook her head slowly back and forth. "It's so horrible," she cried. "Franklin must have—have—died in a most terribly way. Morning Star lied about him. She lied. She probably even killed him herself."

Wiping tears from her eyes she suddenly saw the second pole and the second head. Her eyes froze in terror. She stifled another scream with pressed hands against her lips.

"I'm sure she's Morning Star's moon goddess," Troy said bitterly.

"We would've—would've been next," Samantha cried. She was now seeing two other poles that bore no

453

heads. "Surely those poles were—were being prepared for us."

"Let's not hang around to find out," Troy grumbled. He placed his hands to her waist and helped her up. "Seems Mother Nature saved us, darling. If not for the earthquake, who knows what our fate would've been?"

"The ship!" Samantha gasped. "Do you think it was harmed by the earthquake?"

"Tidal waves are known to accompany an earthquake," Troy said dryly as he led her on through the jungle. "But as you see there are no signs of that here. It seems the moisture is just from the rain, from a rising ocean."

The center of the storm whirled on off to the north. The sky became a friendly blue, but the humidity was intense. When the ship came into full view Samantha let out a soft squeal of delight. It seemed all right. Then she questioned Troy with her eyes.

"Is your ship repaired enough? Can it carry us away from here?" she murmured. "This is a horrible place, one that will cause nightmares for years, I am sure."

"It must be ready for traveling," he growled. "As I see it, we have no choice but to get far out to sea. Though the earthquake wreaked havoc in the Indians' village, they will remember that we escaped."

Visions of Franklin's fate plagued Samantha's consciousness. She emitted a soft moan, shuddering involuntarily.

"What's the matter, Sam?" Troy asked, giving her a troubled glance.

"I'm remembering Franklin," she said shallowly. "I'm also remembering the tale that Morning Star told us—about how Franklin burned his house, and then Father's?

How did it happen, Troy? Do you think Franklin did that? Or was it just a story invented by Morning Star?"

"I believe that part of her tale was true," he said. "I think it was after that that the Guarani captured Franklin and—and—well, you know what else."

"Know? I shall never forget," Samantha said, shaking her head wearily.

Running breathlessly on up the gangplank, Troy began shouting out orders. Soon the anchor was hoisted up and the sails filled. Samantha stood beside Troy at the rail, wet and trembling, as the Brazil skyline was slowly receding in the distance.

Samantha tensed when she saw the slight figure of Morning Star at the soft edges of the jungle. She was like a beautiful apparition in her white tunic, and when Morning Star raised a hand in farewell, Samantha cringed when she saw Troy return the wave.

"Troy!" Samantha scolded. "How could you? She is most surely a witch in angel's disguise."

"Aw, what can an innocent wave hurt?" he said with a shrug. "She did give us a few exciting moments in our life, didn't she?" He kneaded his chin. "Hmm. I'd sure like to know the recipe for that *chicha,*" he chuckled. "I'd like to serve you some of that potent liquid on our wedding night."

Samantha couldn't help but lose her anger as he cast her a most devilish, appealing smile. She melted inside beneath the heated blue of his eyes.

## Chapter Thirty-One

The foggy mist was spangled with the rising sun, tinting the eastern sky a mellow pink. Samantha awakened as shafts of this early light crept through the porthole beside the bed where she lay next to Troy, who still peacefully dozed.

Stretching her arms above her head and yawning she was still aglow from the lovemaking of the previous night. The voyage thus far from Brazil's shores had been peaceful, the ship performing as masterfully as its master.

Samantha turned on her side and fit herself into the curve of Troy's body as he faced away from her, on his side. She pressed her breasts hard into his back and fit her soft curves against the hardness of his buttocks. She closed her eyes, perfectly content, draping her right arm over his chest. Her fingers sought out one of his nipples encircled by a curly fuzz of chest hair. She playfully circled the nipple with a finger, then squeezed it between her thumb and forefinger.

She smiled devilishly when she heard his low moan of

pleasure, then jumped with a start and opened her eyes when he flipped over to face her, chuckling, his blue eyes gleaming.

"Vixen," he said huskily, drawing her fully against him. His handsomeness and the hardness of his powerful body holding her prisoner momentarily stole her breath from her.

"The morning is not yet ripe, but you are, eh?" he chuckled.

He began to stroke the tender flesh of her back that curved down to her soft, round buttocks, causing a warm pleasure to spread through Samantha's body. "My darling, my day isn't complete without first being with you," she whispered, wriggling to capture his hand more fully against her. "Charleston Harbor is near. We will be separated momentarily while there."

"Only because you wish it to be that way," he grumbled.

"I do so want to see Johnston Oaks once more before we travel on to New York," she begged. "You do understand why, don't you, since you have convinced me that I will be safer in New York until the war is over?"

"Yes. I understand," he said thickly.

"Then do not make me feel as though you are scolding me because I want to do this thing," she whispered.

"It must be done while I am being questioned by the authorities," he said, slipping a finger between her thighs and caressing her sweet bud of desire. "It could even be dangerous for you to travel by buggy to your plantation."

"Joshua will be with me," she murmured. "He will see to my safety."

Her eyes hazed over with passion as he continued to caress her. "But, Troy, let's—let's not talk anymore,"

457

she softly cried. "Let's just enjoy these last moments alone. Lord, how you enflame my insides."

As he turned her so that he could mount her, her eyes swept over the full length of him, seeing his wide shoulders tapered to his narrow hips, the slight fuzz of hair that grew from his chest, the flatness of his belly, and his swollen manhood blossoming out to show his need of her. The muscles in his long, firm legs tightened as he lifted himself up and then made his plunge deeply inside her.

His body then met hers in an utter sweetness. His mouth gently went to hers and gave her a trembling, lengthy kiss. With skill his left hand circled a breast, relishing the touch of how it seemed to swell right in his fingers. His other hand reached beneath her, tracing the outline of the soft flesh of her buttocks. He then slipped his hand around and let a finger softly probe her other sensitive pleasure point.

Seductively moaning, Samantha lifted her legs around him, flowering herself more open to the demands of his finger and manhood. She closed her eyes, filled with a sweet languor as his lips were now at the silken curve of her throat and then at the nipple of a breast.

"My love," Samantha sighed, soaring, wishing never to return to earth.

Troy again kissed her, his hands gently caressing her cheeks, his strokes inside her gentle, sweet. He groaned longingly as she eased her tongue between his lips and teased him with soft swirls inside his mouth. And when he drew his lips away and looked down at her face that was flushed with the radiance of rapture, she could tell by the heaviness of his lashes and heat of his eyes that he was in the same grip of passion as she.

"Darling, now," he said huskily.

"Yes," she whispered. "Now."

He buried his face into the red flame of her outspread hair, his eager hands filled with the creamy, magnificence of her breasts. He drove himself farther and harder inside her, filling her over and over again with his skilled strokes.

Then he kissed her—a kiss of fire—a kiss of total demand as their bodies spoke to each other in a message that bespoke fulfillment, laced with a wild, fiery passion.

Afterward, they still clung together in a blissful afterglow. Troy nibbled at Samantha's neck, tasting the honey nectar of her flesh.

"Always love me," she sighed, placing a gentle kiss to the taut muscle at his shoulder.

"Always," he murmured, tracing the outline of her thighs with the palms of his hands. "We shall make it legal as soon as we arrive safely to New York."

"In my heart it has always been right with or without a preacher's words making it so," she said, now combing her fingers through the midnight black of his hair. "Nothing so beautiful could be wrong."

"Perfect," he sighed. "You are a perfect lover, my sweet."

His lips captured hers beneath them. His fingers circled a breast and softly squeezed it, drawing an erotic groan of pleasure from the depth of Samantha's being. Her fingers searched his body until they found his velvet-tipped shaft of love. She circled its pulsing strength with the possessive grip of her hand and began skillfully stirring renewed ardor inside him. His lips parted hers, his tongue darting between her teeth.

Troy parted her thighs with a knee and found she was

willing to be thrilled again by his fullness. His lips parted slightly from hers. His breath was hot on her cheek. "You're insatiable," he chuckled huskily. "And you're mine."

"Yes. All of me," she purred.

Again they climbed a tall peak of passion until they reached the summit which then led them into a quiet explosion of complete rapture.

Troy then laughed softly, rising away from her, yet still smelling her and tasting her on his lips. "This has got to end," he said, climbing from the bed. He went to a basin and lowered his hands into the cool pool of water, cupped them full, then lowered his head over the basin and splashed water up onto his face.

Samantha sneaked from the bed and crept up behind him, fitting herself into him. She wrapped her arms about his waist and imprisoned him there. "I don't want to do anything today but enjoy you," she teased. "Darling, my insides are like vintage champagne—so sparkling and bubbly. Why must we stop now? Please let's go back to bed."

Again filling his hands with water, Troy gave her a sly look over his shoulder. "Unhand me, wench," he ordered teasingly.

"Never!" she laughed, locking her fingers together across his flat stomach.

"My pleas fall upon deaf ears, do they?" he asked, forking his eyebrows.

"I shall never let you go," she said giggling. "Never!"

Troy reached around with his hands filled with water and threw it onto the creamy swells of her breasts. When the iciness made contact with her flesh, Samantha let out a loud squeal and broke quickly away from Troy.

"How could you?" she scolded, wiping the water from her breasts.

Troy chuckled amusedly, then his eyes grew hot with desire as he saw droplets of water shining in her navel. He lifted her up and spread her across the bed, then lowered his tongue and licked the water droplets away.

His hands went to her hips. His fingers dug into her flesh, lifting the delicate, jasmined core of her desire closer to his lips. With a husky growl he kissed her there, feeling her writhing to draw him even further into her.

Twining her fingers through his hair, Samantha flowered herself fully open to him and draped her legs leisurely over his shoulders. His tongue felt like wettened satin as it glided over her. She moaned languidly and tossed her head feverishly, again feeling the pleasurable feelings building inside her. And then it crashed violently through her, like a volcano erupting, and hot lava licked through her, leaving her limp.

"There. That's all my treats offered to my lady this morning," Troy said huskily, rising away from her.

She looked dazedly at him through thick, heavy lashes. She smiled up at him as he began dressing. "I'll miss you," she murmured.

"God, Sam, you talk as though we're parting for good," he grumbled, buttoning his shirt.

"Each day away from you seems like forever," she sighed.

"One full day won't even pass while we each take care of our duties in Charleston," he said, nodding toward the porthole. "As you see it is early morning. Before the sun rises straight up in the heavens we shall be entering the harbor."

"I'm afraid," Samantha said, shivering. She rose from

461

the bed and put on a pale green velvet robe, tying it at her waist.

"There's nothing to fear," Troy said, brushing his hair, shaping it perfectly against his scalp. "I've met my end of the bargain—so shall the ones commanding the northern warships which line Charleston Harbor. It will be over quite quickly. It will be I waiting for you to return to the ship."

"You'll be able to drop anchor at Johnston Oaks, do you think, after the authorities pardon you?"

"Almost certainly, darling."

"Almost?"

"All right, I shall change my choice of words. My ship will be at Johnston Oaks dock just as you are ready to board it."

"Now that's what I wanted to hear," Samantha said. Then her thoughts wandered to someone else. A shadow crossed her face as she frowned.

"Julia plans to stay on board your ship, as does Jewel," she said dryly. "I guess that shouldn't matter, should it?"

"Naw," he said, tossing his hairbrush onto a table. "Not at all."

The same old jealousies of her cousin gnawed at Samantha's insides, though Julia was now content in her blossoming pregnancy and had not flirted with Troy on the lengthy voyage from Brazil.

"But since Johnston Oaks is now legally hers," she quickly interjected, "perhaps she should travel with me, to see how the plantation fares."

"No," Troy said nonchalantly. "In her condition she shouldn't be subjected to any emotional trauma. It wouldn't be wise for her to go to Johnston Oaks to be reminded of her husband's death all over again."

He shook his head. "No. It's best we do as originally planned. She will go to New York and stay with us until her child is born. Then she can decide where to live. Should the war end, she would surely want to raise the child at Johnston Oaks. Until then, well, she'd best live somewhere else."

"Since when do you appoint yourself Julia's guardian, even her lord and master," Samantha suddenly stormed, no longer able to hold her feelings intact. "Troy, has she wrapped you around her little finger again? Has she done this when my back has been turned? I thought she had changed. I thought her whole world had become the child she is carrying. Why must everyone always coddle her so?"

Troy took a step backward, feeling as though he had been hit. He looked at her and saw the flashing in her eyes and the trembling of her lips. Would the rivalry between these two cousins ever stop?

With two wide and heavy steps he went to Samantha and clasped his hands onto her shoulders. He gave her a slight shake, glowering down at her. "Just listen to yourself," he growled. "You're talking like a jealous, spoiled brat. And there's nothing to be jealous of, Sam. Why don't you believe me when I tell you that?"

Coiling her arms about him she snuggled against his chest. "I'm sorry," she murmured. "I don't know why I go into such tirades. Forgiven?"

"This time, yes. The next time, I don't know, Sam," he whispered harshly. "I want a wife who believes in me, damn it. God, you even thought I was enjoying myself with that Indian witch who drugged me mindless."

"You can't deny the pleasure you were receiving by

being with her," Samantha softly argued, afraid to look up into his eyes when she felt his gasp of frustration.

"I don't even recall being with her," he said hoarsely. "How could I say now that I felt pleasure? I don't recall any such feelings."

Samantha eased out of his arms. "Yes, I do believe you," she said softly. "I was just as drugged as you—remember?"

Troy chucked. "How could I?" he said.

"Oh, yes," she laughed. "You can't remember anything that happened."

"Until the earthquake," he corrected.

An involuntary shiver coursed through Samantha. In her mind's eye she was seeing the two poles and the gruesome heads attached to each. She flung herself into Troy's arms and hugged him tightly to her.

"Sometimes I remember more than the earthquake," she softly cried. "I remember Franklin and how—he—died."

"It'll take awhile," he crooned, running his fingers through the fiery red lengths of her hair.

She sniffled. "Yes, I know," she said, looking up into his blue eyes.

"I really must go topside and check on things, darling," he said softly. "Will you be all right?"

"Yes. And I've plenty to do. I've my bath to take and my dress to choose for my short jaunt to Johnston Oaks."

"Either wear one which displays a high neckline or wear a shawl," he said hoarsely, frowning toward her.

"Why should I worry so about what I wear?"

"The city will be buzzing with soldiers. I want none to see more of you than they need to."

"Yes, sir," Samantha giggled. "Whatever you say, *sir.*"

"Well, I'll be damned," Troy chuckled, placing his hands on his hips, looking incredulously down at her. "You're actually going to agree without an argument. I think I've died and gone to heaven."

Samantha covered her mouth with her hands and again softly laughed.

Troy's ship sat in the water between two Union ships at Charleston Harbor. A longboat had taken Samantha and Joshua to shore where they had managed to find someone who had lent them a buggy for a good price, to travel to Johnston Oaks.

The day was gray with a soft, cool breeze blowing in from the harbor. Samantha clutched the shawl more closely about her shoulders, looking around wide-eyed and disbelieving as Joshua directed the horse through the city of Charleston. Soldiers were everywhere, their gray uniforms in rags, carrying bedrolls on their backs and canteens at their sides, or resting against a musket as the gun stood up from the road at a precarious angle.

Cotton lint lay in drifts against the curbs like snow. There was a mournful wail of a French harp drifting from an opened door of a house close by. The city appeared to be a wilderness of ruin, its heart a mass of blackened chimneys and crumbling walls.

The streets were weed-infested where carcasses of horses with bloated bellies lay, their stiffened legs sticking out.

In the uncleared areas, black-clad women wearing

bandanas over their mouths and noses went among bodies stretched out along the ground. They bent, crooning a steady low lament as a body was turned faceup, and they recognized it as their loved one.

White-clad stretcher bearers wearing white masks carried corpses to wagons which, when loaded, lumbered away, drawn by teams of six mules in tandem to be replaced by others returning for more.

Flies were thick, and here and there a chimney stood alone as though the chimney had been built without the house to go with it.

Samantha was deeply saddened and relieved when the city was left behind. The country road was void of passersby. Even the songbirds had seemed to have lost their beautiful warbles. Samantha looked at Joshua. As he flicked the reins and commanded the horse onward, he did so with half a heart, his shoulders heavily slumped. She understood. He had seen the poor freed slaves who were roaming the streets of Charleston. He was remembering the slaves who had fled into the Brazilian jungle. No matter where the Negro went he seemed no better off.

Finally the bends in the road grew familiar. Up ahead and to the left faint signs of the swamp which led into Ashley River shone dark through the trees. To the right ships could be seen guarding Charleston Harbor, and Samantha had to wonder if Troy was going to be free to come to her later at Johnston Oaks. The Union naval officer had been cordial enough to her, letting her leave Troy's ship to go ashore.

Yet she had given him her best smile and most hearty handshake. She seemed to have made a good impression on those gentlemen from the North. Now if only Troy had the same sort of persuasion as she.

Suddenly Samantha's throat became dry and her heart skipped a beat. Just ahead she caught sight of the gravel drive. What had at one time been an avenue of stately live oaks with their beautiful gray beards of Spanish moss hanging from them were now only a scarce few. Most had been cut down with unrespecting recklessness.

Samantha could only guess why. What would wood be used for if not for firewood? But who? When?

She shook her head pitifully. She dared not venture a look at Johnston Oaks just yet. Surely it had been used by soldiers for all the wrong reasons. Even if it were used by the Confederate soldiers, it would be wrong if the house had been damaged in any way!

Unable to hold back any longer, she let her gaze move slowly there. She saw the only thing that seemed to be neglected was the yard. Her heart pounded out her thanks.

Her eyes drank up the sight of the magnificent three-storied plantation house with its rectangular-pillared facade and wide porches, stained glass windows, and mansard roof. As it had for many years now, it was collecting a steady river breeze from its perch high on a hill where its terraced lawn spread out down to the blue waters of Ashley River.

From her upper bedroom she knew she had to keep an eye out for Troy's ship's approach since all upper rooms of Johnston Oaks had a commanding view of Charleston Harbor.

Coming home. A second time she had returned home alone, without her father. It caused a sad ache to circle around her heart, knowing that she was again returning home without her father. Yet, in the house, she would always feel his presence.

Samantha grew restless as the buggy ambled along. Yet she continued to study Johnston Oaks. She looked at the windows and wondered why some of the shutters were open. Upon leaving, she and her father checked that all shutters had been closed to the ravages of the weather.

Then her stomach lurched. There could only be one reason for the shutters to be open. The house had been occupied by someone other than the Johnston family. Who? And what damage had been inflicted?

Unable to bear the waiting any longer, she commanded Joshua to stop. She climbed from the buggy, lifted the tail of her skirt and petticoats up into her arms and ran toward the house, leaving Joshua's shouts of warning behind her.

Her shawl slipped from her shoulders and went flying away from her. Her hair whipped in the breeze, and her heart pounded hard. Then, when the granite steps were reached which led up to the porch and magnificent oak door, she became afraid. Anyone could still be inside.

Seeing no horses nor hearing any sounds other than that of the rustling of the dry cotton bolls hanging from wilted, parched plants in the fields not far from the house, she flew up the steps and into the house.

Once inside she peered through the darkness, the few opened shutters at the windows only emitting enough light to make slight splashes of daylight on the ceiling of the hallway.

Breathing hard, Samantha went on into the parlor and threw the shutters fully open at a window, then turned and absorbed the utter destruction of the room.

The crystal chandelier which had at one time hung so

elegantly from the ceiling now lay in hundreds of shining pieces along the oak floors, marred with mud designs in the shapes of footprints. The silk-covered sofas were ripped and soiled; the ancient Chinese, marble-topped tables and white damask-covered chairs were turned upside down.

The grand piano had been, thankfully, left unharmed, but the waterford hurricane lamp that had at one time sat upon it was no longer there.

Then her gaze went slowly to the marble fireplace at the far end of the room. Hope rose inside her. She knew of one thing that surely hadn't been disturbed by intruders.

With trembling fingers and weakened knees she walked determinedly to the fireplace and eased the loose brick out from the others. Smiling victoriously, she reached for the folded map that she had hidden there. Oh, how long ago had it been? It seemed forever.

She began to unfold the map, but Joshua's rushing footsteps into the room made her fingers once more close possessively about it.

"It's Massa Troy's ship," Joshua said, winded. "It's approachin'. Miss Samantha, don' waste no mo' time hea'. We must go to the ship. That's what he tol' us to do. He says when we sees his ship, to come runnin'."

Samantha's insides grew warm. She clasped the map to her heart. Troy had been pardoned of all crime accused him. He was free to go where he pleased.

Slowly looking about her, she realized that she would never be truly free. A part of her would always remain here at Johnston Oaks, imprisoned inside the walls with memories that could never fade.

"Miss Samantha," Joshua persisted, taking her by an

469

elbow. "We mus' leave. Now."

His gaze settled on the map as they moved together toward the door. "Wha's that?" he questioned, his dark eyes wide.

Samantha closed her fingers more tightly about the map. "Oh, nothing," she sighed. "Truly. It is just a piece of paper. Nothing at all of importance, Joshua."

One of Joshua's heavy, gray eyebrows lifted quizzically. He couldn't help but wonder about a piece of paper she called worthless yet held onto as though her life depended on it.

Samantha saw Joshua's questioning stare. She smiled to herself. One day she would give the map to Troy. But for now she would keep it to herself. It was a part of their beginnings—why they had even become lovers. She didn't want to part with something as valuable as that just yet.

## Chapter Thirty-Two

The tiny baby's lips were moving in his sleep as though a breast was there and he was feeding from it. Instead Geoffrey Craig Johnston was alone, quite asleep in his cradle which displayed a preponderance of lace, and blue, satin ribbons. Samantha stood over the cradle, her heart warm with pride. She had a brother. And wouldn't her father have been proud to have had a son who bore his name?

"Geoffrey Craig," Samantha whispered, testing the name on her lips. She smiled. "Yes. Father would have approved."

The sun was rising gently in the sky, casting velvet streamers of soft light into the nursery which was only one room of the many in Troy's grand townhouse in Manhattan. They had safely reached New York many weeks ago. A part of Samantha's past had been brought with her. Joshua, Jewel, and her cousin Julia and also Samantha's beloved dog Checkers.

"And now my darling brother," she sighed to herself.

Joshua had fit in well as a proper butler, and Jewel

continued her duties as maid, yet not solely to Samantha. There still were Julia's demands and now the baby's as well.

But Samantha was no longer jealous of Julia. The wedding band on Samantha's finger was her vote of confidence. And Julia had seemed to have changed with the birth of her son. Geoffrey Craig seemed to now occupy all corners of her heart.

The creaking of the door behind her caused Samantha to turn around. When she saw the doorway framing her handsome husband she smiled radiantly and reached her hands out to him.

"Come here," she whispered. "Geoffrey Craig seems to have grown overnight. He's such a dear!"

Her gaze traveled admiringly over her husband. He was the epitome of handsomeness in his businessman's attire. His brown frock coat and satin waistcoat matched his fawn-colored breeches well, and his white satin cravat and ruffled shirt accentuated the dark tan of his face and the midnight black of his hair. Even in the morning's pale golden light his blue eyes glowed like crystal.

"Did he finally sleep all night or was I dreaming?" Troy whispered, emitting a low chuckle. He placed his hands in Samantha's and drew her into his arms and kissed her.

Samantha melted into his embrace, tingling all over beneath the utter sweetness of his kiss. She dreaded the days that lay ahead of her without him, but she had delayed the trip to Illinois long enough. It had to be done. She had to go see Doc Raley in Springfield, to find out what sort of family secret had been kept from her. And there was also Marion Yarborough to be dealt with. Finally she would get to avenge her grandparents' death.

Troy placed his hand to her cheeks, framing her face, and looked down at her. "Samantha, I wish you'd reconsider," he said solemnly. His eyes traveled over her, seeing her brown wool travel suit with its stiff, high collar, long sleeves, and flared skirt worn over crinolines.

With her matching hat and its velvet trim and bow which tied beneath her chin, she looked quite sophisticated—like one who could take care of herself quite well on such a lengthy journey from New York to Illinois. Yet Troy knew that danger still lurked out there, though it was true that most of the Civil War battles were now being waged on Southern soil, far from the country through which Samantha would be traveling.

Samantha eased out of his arms. She brushed a stray curl back beneath her hat and looked stubbornly up at Troy. "Don't tell me you've had a change of heart," she softly argued. "You're not going to tell me that you don't approve of my going. Troy, we've already settled that argument. You know that I must."

"You could go later, Sam. When I, or perhaps Julia, could go with you. Or Joshua. Lord, Sam, at least agree to his traveling with you."

Her chin tilted. "What has to be done has to be done now, and I prefer to do it alone," she said, then her eyes softened. "No, darling. You know that I'd prefer your going with me. But you can't. You've your business affairs to tend to. And I just can't wait any longer. I've a need to get all of this behind me. And I can't until I go to Springfield and do it."

"My, but you are a stubborn wench," he chuckled. He placed an arm about her waist and pulled her into his side, and together they went to the cradle and looked down at the tiny, pink face.

"Look at Geoffrey Craig's hair," Samantha mused aloud. "It's going to be red. Just like Father's."

Troy chuckled. "Sam, all I see is some fuzz where hair should be," he said.

"But the fuzz is red," she said, her eyes innocently wide as she looked up at Troy. "Surely you see it."

Troy lowered his lips to hers and passed a quick kiss across them. "I think you're seeing what you want to see," he whispered.

"He's going to be Father all over again," Samantha said, reaching down to pull a soft blue blanket up to the baby's chin.

Troy placed both his hands at Samantha's waist and turned her to face him. "When will we have a playmate for Geoffrey Craig?" he said huskily.

A blush rose to Samantha's cheeks. "Are you saying what I think you're saying, darling?"

"Yes. I'd like to begin a family right away," he said thickly. "I've never had much of one."

"You've never spoken of family before," she murmured, her eyes studying his face as she saw it become shadowed in thought.

"There's not much to say," he said dryly. "I was an only son. My parents died many years ago. I inherited my parents' wealth. As simple as that, Sam."

"I'm sorry, Troy," Samantha said, placing a hand tenderly to his cheek. "In a sense we've a lot to make up to each other."

"What do you mean, darling?" he asked, an eyebrow arching.

"My childhood was lonely. Yours was lonely. We must fill our house now with many children and—much—love."

They embraced, sharing heaven in one another's arms.

The train ride had been a long and arduous one, but Samantha was finally in Springfield. She had just visited her grandparents' graves, the desolation of their farm and was now sitting in Doc Raley's outer office, awaiting their first meeting.

Her impatience showed by the drumming of her fingers on the arm of the leather chair in which she sat and the flashing of her green eyes, wanting to get on with this since she hadn't the opportunity as yet to seek out Marion Yarborough, to personally deal with him.

Inside her drawstring purse which lay on her lap was her lady's pistol. Her hand crept slowly to it and touched its hardness, a slow smile lifting her lips.

"Soon, Marion," she whispered. "I shall avenge my grandparents. Somehow."

Her gaze darted around the room, absorbing the framed, yellowed certificates which hung on the wall opposite her. The dates on these revealed just how old Doc Raley was and how long ago he had received his medical degrees.

This outer office was dark, with only one window, and was emanating light through it, casting shadows down upon filth-laden, ripped leather chairs and tables piled with crumpled magazines and newspapers.

Stale cigar smoke permeated the room, along with an aroma of medical supplies.

The door which led into an inner office opened abruptly, and Samantha rose quickly to her feet. She found herself looking down at a short, elderly man whose face was almost hidden beneath a thick growth of gray whiskers, and his hair was thick and the color of snow.

His eyes were bright in spite of his age, and his lips were full and rosy red. He was dressed in a loose, black suit, and his white shirt was yellow, seeming to match the certificates on the walls.

"Samantha? Samantha Gilbert?" Doc Raley said, one eyebrow raised as he looked her up and down.

"Yes. I'm Samantha," Samantha murmured, unable to stifle a blush as he looked at her.

"I received your wire. Easy to figure why you're here," Doc Raley said. "Come on into my office. Guess it needs told to you, young lady. I've kept the secret locked inside this hard head of mine for much too long as it is."

Samantha followed him into a room that she had expected to be an office with a desk. Instead, she found shelves filled with medical supplies and an examination table spread with a bleached-white, immaculate sheet. The room had an even stronger medicinal smell than the outer room and even burned her nostrils. She was pointed to a stool.

"Sit. This won't take long," Doc Raley said in a low growl.

Samantha eased down onto the stool, swallowing hard as he sat down on one directly in front of her. She felt as though she was going to be examined by this elderly doctor whose hands appeared swollen and not at all like they could perform skillfully on an ailing patient. But she had to believe that in his youth, he had probably been the best.

She cleared her throat nervously. "My grandmother told me to come to you—"

He interrupted. "Yes. I know. She informed me shortly before her untimely death that she had finally

476

told you at least *that* much about the family secret."

"Please tell me, sir," Samantha encouraged, squaring her shoulders. "I've other things to do before returning to New York."

He gave her a hard stare, then spoke. "Is—uh—Julia also in New York?" he quietly asked.

"Why, yes," Samantha said, eyes wide. "Why do you ask about Julia?"

"Julia is the one who's been protected from ugly gossip all these years," he said matter-of-factly. "And also your mother. She was also spared. Yet, in a way she wasn't. I heard that after her rape, something died inside her. She lost her will to live, it seems."

"Rape?" Samantha gasped, almost choking on the ugly word.

"The first time the sonofabitch touched your mother, she was willing, even maybe encouraged it. But after all she went through when Yarborough refused to marry her and then to be forcefully raped by the same man later after she was married, yes, something died inside her."

Samantha's head was spinning. She rose from the stool, her knees almost too rubbery to hold her up. "Please—slow—down," she choked. "What you are saying—is—"

"That Marion Yarborough and your mother were sexually active when your mother was young, vital, and foolishly in love with that man," Doc Raley said, shaking his head. "To this day I don't know what got into her. But he was a handsome man in those days, though cold and greedy already where money was concerned."

"Lord! My mother and Marion Yarborough!" Samantha softly cried, hanging her face in her hands. Then her eyes shot upward. "But what does this have to do with anything? Why are you telling me this? Why do I even have to be told?"

"It's for Julia's sake. Your grandparents never had the heart to tell her who her true parents were. But your grandmother didn't want to carry the truth to the grave with her. She felt someone in the family should know. You were chosen since you were the strongest between you and Julia."

"You're not saying that Marion Yarborough—is—is Julia's father? That my mother was her mother, are you? That Julia is—is—even my sister?"

"Half sister," he corrected.

"Half or whole!" she gasped. "That doesn't matter. What does is that my mother and Marion—"

"And, Samantha, when your mother was raped by Marion Yarborough, she had just only found out that she was pregnant with you. She almost miscarried you because of the trauma of it. I know this all as fact, because she was in Springfield at the time, and I was the one who told her that she was pregnant and nursed her back to health after the rape."

"No," Samantha softly cried. Then anger flamed her insides. "Why weren't the authorities notified? Why wasn't Marion Yarborough forced to pay for his crime?"

"The embarrassment, the humiliation, and the fear that your father would disown your mother. She feared that Marion Yarborough would reveal her past to your father—the fact that she had been loose, sexually, with him."

Then Samantha looked at him quizzically. "Julia! How was it that she was raised by . . ." Her words faded with remembrances. She knew that her mother had spent some time in New York with her uncle and aunt, Terence and Phoebe Ainsworth, and now she knew why. To have

478

an illegitimate daughter! Phoebe and Terence had been childless except for Julia. They had willingly accepted the child to raise as their own. And after Samantha's mother had given up her daughter, she had resumed life as though nothing had happened. She had gotten married to Craig Johnston sometime later, became pregnant again, then raped.

Now Samantha understood why Marion Yarborough had always looked at her so strangely and had made references about her mother to her. He had thought that possibly *she*, Samantha, was his daughter, since Samantha's mother had given birth within the time that he would have thought the child to be his. He had never suspected Julia as being his, for no one had ever known about Julia's having parents other than Phoebe and Terence. In truth, Marion Yarborough had not only raped Samantha's mother but also his own daughter!

The thought turned Samantha's stomach.

Also she knew now why she had never seen her mother and father share a bedroom. After the rape, her mother had never been the same, mentally, and had eventually died a broken woman.

"So there you've got it, all in a nutshell," Doc Raley said, scooting off his stool, to stand and look up into Samantha's face.

"But there's one more thing," he added. "The scar that Marion Yarborough carries? It was put there by your grandfather." He chuckled amusedly. "Yes, ol' Melvin himself slapped that scar on the sonofabitch's lip. He caught Marion sneaking about his land one night and slashed him with a knife. You should have heard that sonofabitch yowling when he came in here to be stitched up."

His eyes gleamed. He kneaded his whiskers. "I fixed

him up good, I did," he bragged. "I sewed his damn lip so's no woman would ever want to kiss him again."

Samantha's eyes brightened. She wouldn't have expected a gentle-appearing man like Doc Raley to have a devious side to him. But, oh, how glad she was that he did. In a way, Marion Yarborough had been paying for his sins against her mother for many years already.

Doc Raley placed a hand gently on Samantha's arm. "And, Samantha, legal papers were drawn up before your grandparents' death," he said.

He went to a drawer in his tall, glass-enclosed medicine cabinet and withdrew an envelope. He handed it to her. "In this you will read that you have inherited all of your grandparents' property. It's yours to do with it as you wish."

Samantha trembled as she took the envelope in her hand. She would read the instructions later. She already knew what was important. The land that Marion Yarborough had always wanted was now hers.

"Godspeed, Samantha," Doc Raley said as he led her from the office. "I'm sorry if my sad tidings have disturbed you in any way."

Samantha folded and tucked the envelope inside her purse. "What I've learned is disturbing, but much deals with my past life and can easily be forgotten," she murmured. "My husband is my new life. After I deal with one more item of my past here in Springfield, I plan to return to New York and to my husband and be happy."

"And Julia? What about her?" he queried.

"Julia?" she softly laughed. "For awhile I was concerned about her. But now she's fine. She is now a proud mother of a darling son."

"Oh?" he interjected. "A child? Who is the lucky man?"

Samantha's smile faded. She couldn't reveal who Julia's husband had been to this aging doctor who already knew too much about her family. She saw no need in adding fuel to the fire of the family secrets. What a scandal could be raised if everyone knew that Craig Johnston had actually married his stepdaughter!

No. Somehow this wouldn't seem proper to let this bit of gossip reach anyone's ears!

"There is no man now," she murmured. "She was married only a short while before her husband died. She is now—a—widow."

"What a shame," Doc Raley said, kneading his chin thoughtfully. He felt as though something wasn't being told him. But he was not one to pry.

"Yes. It's tragic, but Julia has accepted what life has handed her," Samantha said, clearing her throat nervously.

"And Marion Yarborough? What's to be done about him?" Doc Raley softly queried.

"I'm not quite sure just yet what I'll do about that vile man Marion Yarborough," Samantha said dryly.

Doc Raley patted her arm. "You'll figure it out," he said. He walked her to the door and opened it. "And what are your plans for your grandparents' property now that it's yours? You gonna sell it? Bein' in New York, you won't have a need for it, will you?"

Samantha's eyes brightened with a sudden thought which led to a quick decision. The land that Marion Yarborough had always wanted! He still wouldn't have it. She was the owner now and had all control of what was to be done with it.

Yes! She would use the same sort of punishment on Marion Yarborough that her grandparents had always used. She would also deny him the land. This would be enough for her. For now. She would carry on the legacy of her grandparents in the way they had chosen to repay Marion for all the heartache that he had caused the Ainsworth family. He would be denied access to land that lay between what he already owned.

Yes! His property would still be divided by Ainsworth property which seemed to eat more away at his gut with each day, week, and month.

Perhaps later I'll think of even a better way to settle my debt with him, Samantha thought smugly to herself. But for now, this is a much easier and quieter way.

She whirled around and faced Doc Raley. "The land which is now mine?" she finally answered. "For now, it will remain to be called Ainsworth land. I shall care for it as my grandparents did, but from afar. I shall find and appoint someone to keep an eye on it and keep it presentable in my absence. For now I will be content enough with this decision."

"Whatever you think best," Doc Raley said, shrugging. "Best to you, young lady."

"Thank you," Samantha said, moving out with him, onto the veranda of his office. She smiled warmly down at him, now anxious to board the train which would take her back to Troy and his talent for helping her to forget all of her heartaches of the past.

She was glad that she had decided against shooting Marion Yarborough. She didn't see the need to waste a bullet. Men like him were already dead inside. He had the chore of facing life each day, struggling to live with his conscience. And didn't he have a reminder of his evil past with him every day when he looked into a mirror to shave? Didn't he have the smiling scar?

# *Chapter Thirty-Three*

*April 15, 1865*

Candles burned softly on the nightstand beside the bed in Samantha and Troy's grand New York townhouse bedroom. A half-emptied bottle of champagne sat on the floor. Samantha stood before Troy, giddy and glowing from a gentle passion warming her insides, letting her silk chemise flutter from around her to the floor.

Troy's eyes were heating her flesh as he lay nude on the bed, watching her. Samantha's hands trembled with anxious need of him as her fingers ran through her hair that had been swept up atop her head in fiery red swirls of curls. This night's outing had included a slow, quite enjoyable dinner at one of New York's finest restaurants and the ballet.

"Do you enjoy teasing me?" Troy chuckled. "Come here, wench. Don't take so long to get in bed with me."

"I will. Soon," Samantha purred. She let one long curl unfold and drop to her shoulder as she flipped a hairpin aside, proceeding then with another until only one curl lay at the very crown of her head.

"Sam!" Troy groaned, gesturing with his hand to come to him.

"Darling, do you remember the night that you abducted me from the stagecoach?" she asked, her green eyes twinkling with mischief.

"How could I ever forget that night?" Troy laughed. "You were even more a wench that night than now."

"Oh, now, my dear, you just may change your mind," Samantha continued to tease. She paused, leaving her fingers at the last curl before unfolding it.

Then she said, "Do you also remember that you didn't find your map in my purse?" she asked, smiling devilishly down at him.

"Ah, yes. The map," Troy sighed. "Seems it lost its importance after my capture and eventual release by the North. The code, as you remember, represented the men on board my ship. Once they were cleared, along with me, it mattered not that the map fell into the wrong hands. That's why I've not pestered you anymore for it."

"I don't know how it slipped my mind 'til now that I took the map from its hiding place on the day I returned to Johnston Oaks while you were being detained in Charleston Harbor. I placed the map inside a purse that I only this day chose to carry. Strange how you and I both forgot about the map, don't you think?"

"As I said. It lost its importance. As even now, it doesn't interest me," Troy growled. His eyebrows arched. "Sam, what's this all about? Why are you bringing this up now?"

"Darling, would you like to take a guess as to where I did have it hidden that night?" she persisted.

"Sam, please," Troy moaned. "Come to bed and cut

this foolish nonsense."

"Troy, just make a guess," Samantha pouted.

"I don't give a damn."

"You did at one time. It was even the driving force behind all your actions. I even suspected that the map was your main interest in me, because it was I who had it."

"That was then. Now is now," Troy said, reaching for her, grabbing her leg. He playfully pulled her down on the bed beside him. "There. Isn't this more like it?" He leaned over her and let his tongue flick around the nipple of one of her breasts.

"Troy, you spoiled my surprise," Samantha said, quivering with ecstasy as his lips sought out a breast. Her mind began to slowly spin.

"Who needs surprises when I have you?" he said, rising up over her, now kissing the hollow of her throat. His loins ached, his swollen sex throbbed as he pressed it against her thigh.

"I love you so," Samantha whispered, throwing her arms about his neck.

Troy's fingers wove through her hair and led her lips to his. "Kiss me," he said huskily. Then his eyes caught sight of the one coil of curl left at her crown, and he rose away from her, chuckling.

"What's that?" he said, touching the curl. "A new hairstyle, Sam?"

He quickly removed the pin, and when the curl fell loosely free and something dropped from inside it, Troy jumped with alarm.

"What the—" he gasped, slowly recognizing the folded map.

Samantha grabbed the map as it settled to the mattress.

"Darling, my surprise," she laughed, now handing the map to him.

"In your hair?" he asked incredulously.

"That night when you stole me from the stagecoach it was a perfect hiding place." She giggled. "Now wouldn't you agree? And all through the ballet and dinner tonight it lay hidden there, and you never noticed."

"Damn!" Troy chuckled, amused at her cleverness.

Samantha leaned up on an elbow and handed the map to him. "Darling, finally it is once more yours," she murmured. "Now what are your plans for it?"

"Plans?" he asked, rising to a sitting position. He unfolded the map and gazed down upon it, full of memories of his adventures at sea. Then he scooted over close to a candle and placed a corner of the map into the candle's flame.

"Troy!" Samantha softly gasped. "You're burning it?"

He held it out away from him as he climbed from the bed. He strolled casually to the fireplace and let it flutter down, into the grate. "Ashes to ashes, dust to dust," he chuckled.

Then he went back to the bed, scooting to his knees to straddle himself over Samantha. "And now, on to more pleasant things," he said huskily.

He stretched out fully above her and drew her into his arms, relishing the feel of her breasts against his chest. His lips gently touched hers, and then more demandingly. She writhed beneath him as he filled her with his powerful man's strength. And then their bodies melted into the other, fusing as one, as they once more sought the bliss of ecstasy's escape.

"Darling," Troy said as he moved his lips to her ear to

nibble her earlobe.

"My love," Samantha said, letting herself become swallowed whole by the rapture that he had brought to her life.

They worked together slowly, enjoying every moment, knowing that they now had forever to share such a deserved gentle passion. And once they had reached the desired goal this one more time, they lay in one another's arms, wordless. The experience had been so sweet.

Troy ran his hands down the silken curve of her thigh, his lips pressed against the swell of a breast. Samantha's fingernails played along his handsome profile, then she went sent butterfly kisses across his chest. And when she moved her lips lower, he chuckled and urged her face back up so that he could give her a trembling, light kiss.

"It was all worth it," he whispered.

"What?" she asked, scooting into the curve of his body.

"The waiting."

"Waiting? For what?"

"For the map," he said, suppressing a laugh when seeing a surprised look flash in her eyes.

"Troy, what do you mean?" she gasped.

"It took marrying you to get the map," he said. "While waiting for you to relinquish it, I'd say we've shared some—uh—would you say, some fun times?"

Samantha's insides splashed cold. The old, gnawing feeling of mistrust was once more there. "What do you mean?" she said icily. "Are you saying that you married me to just get that damn map? Are you now going to leave me?"

Troy broke into a fit of raucous laughter, until tears streamed from his eyes. "God, you should see that

487

expression on your face," he said. "It's worth a million, darling."

Samantha rose from the bed in a huff and placed her hands on her hips as she glared down at him. "I don't see what's so damn funny," she hissed.

"No. I guess you wouldn't," Troy said, his eyes still dancing with amusement. "It's a cruel joke that I just played on you. I'm sorry, darling."

"Then you didn't mean it?"

"How could you ever think I did?"

Samantha jumped back on the bed and lunged at him. "Why you—" She laughed.

He drew her into his arms and kissed her, his hands moving gently over her.

A light tap at the door made them both freeze in their movements. They questioned each other with their eyes. "Who—?" Samantha whispered.

"One way to find out," Troy said with a shrug.

Samantha moved quickly from the bed and wrapped a robe snugly around her while Troy stepped into his breeches and then a shirt. He went to the door and opened it, finding Julia there, her face drawn and somber.

"Come on in, Julia," Troy encouraged, still handling her with gentle movements. To him, she would always be the type who needed pampering, though as of late, she had been keeping company with one gentleman caller after another.

Samantha went to Julia and saw her nervous expression. She placed a hand to her arm. "Julia, tell us," she urged. "What's happened? You look as though you've seen a ghost." Samantha had accepted Julia's renewed feisty ways. It had suddenly become good—to have—a—sister.

In her soft silk dress which was low cut at the bodice and fully gathered at the waist, emphasizing her tiny waist, she was the picture of loveliness. Her hair hung long and golden across her shoulders, and her blue eyes were wide with worry.

"News has just been brought to us of President Lincoln's death," she said quietly, looking from Samantha, to Troy.

"Lincoln? Dead?" Troy said, his head jerking with the shock of the news. "God. How?"

Samantha stepped back away from Julia and instead clung to Troy's arm. Only moments ago all seemed right with the world. Now, suddenly the world even seemed doomed!

"President Lincoln was shot. He was assassinated. He was attending the performance of *Our American Cousin* in Washington," Julia said softly. "He was shot last night, shortly after ten o'clock, by John Wilkes Booth. He shot the president in the head from the rear of the president's box. Our president died this very morning."

"How horrible," Samantha said, covering her mouth with a hand. She felt the loss as sadness wove its way into her heart. She had fought against Lincoln's wishes, only because of her father. All along, she had believed as he had—that everyone had the right to be free, no matter the color of the skin.

"John Wilkes Booth shot him?" Troy said thickly. "God. He's one of the best known actors of the day. What would prompt him to do such a terrible thing? He had everything going for him. And to shoot the president? How could anyone do that?"

"I'll return to my room now," Julia said, smiling weakly. "I feel that I interrupted something here. But I thought you would want to know."

Samantha walked Julia to the door. "Thank you, hon," she said, kissing her softly on the cheek. "I'll come to your room soon, for our nightly chat."

"Yes. Do," Julia said, then walked on away from her.

Troy went to Samantha and drew her into his arms, then laughed softly as Checkers came into the room and wriggled between them. "Okay, Checkers, go on," Troy said. "Your time will come later. Right now, I think my lady needs my kind of love."

Samantha watched Checkers meander away to settle down beside the bed, placing his head between his paws. Then she worked her way back into Troy's arms. "Darling, it seems that no matter how right things can appear to be, the next moment can always change," she whispered. "Hold me. Just hold me."

"You're safe with me," he said thickly. "Let's just remember this night the good things in life. Let's just think of the gentle passion we are now free to share. Tomorrow? We will let that take care of itself."

"So often others shape our futures for us," Samantha said sadly. "What happened last night to our president? John Wilkes Booth has changed history. Will it be for the worse, or better? I so sorely admired Lincoln. What can Johnson do to take his place?"

"Sam, please," Troy said, kissing her softly on the tip of the nose. "Remember? Tonight is ours. We won't worry about anything else. What good does it do?"

"Troy, that doesn't sound like you," Samantha said, looking up at him, wondering.

"Only because I want to put your mind to ease," he explained. "I know the turmoil that you must be feeling about this tragedy. You see? I feel it also."

"Yes. I'm quite upset by what's happened."

"Then, darling, let's make the best of the situation," he said. "Let's take comfort from each other."

"Yes. You, me, and this passion's fire that you and I have brought into each other's lives," she purred.

Troy framed her face between his hands and gently kissed her, expressing all the love he had to give.

Each month you'll receive 4 brand new Zebra Historical Romance novels as soon as they are published. Look them over *Free* for 10 days. If you're not delighted simply return them and owe nothing. But if you enjoy them as much as we think you will, you'll pay *only* $3.50 each and save 45¢ over the cover price. (You save a total of $1.80 each month.) *There is no shipping and handling charge or other hidden charges.*

## —————— *Fill Out the Coupon*——————

Start your subscription now and start saving. Fill out the coupon and mail it *today*. You'll get your FREE book along with your first month's books to preview.